The Burning Plain

The Burning Plain

MICHAEL NAVA

G. P. PUTNAM'S SONS / NEW YORK

G. P. PUTNAM'S SONS
Publishers Since 1838
a member of
Penguin Putnam Inc.
200 Madison Avenue
New York, NY 10016

Library of Congress Cataloging-in-Publication Data

Nava, Michael.
  The burning plain / by Michael Nava.
      p.   cm.
    ISBN 0-399-14310-6 (alk. paper)
    I. Title.
  PS3564.A8746B87   1997   97-18128 CIP
  813'.54—dc21

Printed in the United States of America

10   9   8   7   6   5   4   3   2   1

This book is printed on acid-free paper. ∞

Book design by Gretchen Achilles

ACKNOWLEDGMENTS

I want to thank the following people: Katherine V. Forrest, for her sage advice and valued friendship; Charlotte Sheedy, agent and advocate; Neil Nyren, conscientious editor; Paul Reidinger, for the free lunches and long conversation about this craft of writing; Rob Miller, Dan Edelman, the people at Paramount, for movie and legal lore (and if I got it wrong, my apologies); Phyllis Burke, for her book *Gender Shock* (a crucial work); and of course the Daughters of Darkness, who kept me company.

Enormous herds of naked souls I saw,
  lamenting till their eyes were burned of tears;
  they seemed condemned by an unequal law,
for some were stretched supine upon the ground,
  some squatted with their arms about themselves
  and others without pause roamed round and round.
  —*The Inferno*

Crime is terribly revealing.
  —*Agatha Christie*

The Burning Plain

chapter 1

I WAS SITTING by myself at a plastic table outside the coffee kiosk in the plaza between the county courthouse and the Hall of Records in downtown Los Angeles on a warm, polluted morning in late April. It was nine-forty-two. The office workers had reluctantly straggled off to their jobs, leaving empty cups, pastry crumbs, packets of sugar and lipstick-stained napkins on the surrounding tables. A homeless woman—a swirl of rags, a baked face—rooted through the litter. She carefully wrapped the remains of a bran muffin in a paper napkin, tucked it into a soiled pocket and approached me with an outstretched hand. Her eyes were like wounds. I gave her a dollar, to the frowning displeasure of the boy behind the counter at the kiosk. The sky was metallic, as if the city was enclosed by a dome, and nothing stirred among the dusty plants and trees in the plaza. The poisonous air made my eyes sting. I sipped lukewarm coffee and glanced at the paper. There was a picture of a heavyset man in a tuxedo, standing at a podium with an over-sized Oscar behind him. The caption identified him as Duke Asuras, head of Parnassus Pictures, and quoted him as having said at the recent Academy Awards ceremony, "Filmmaking isn't an industry, it's warfare and the whole world is our battleground." I glanced at my watch. It was time to go to court.

The county courthouse filled three blocks along First Street with concrete and polished granite, a severe and gargantuan building in a neighborhood of severe and gargantuan buildings: the Halls of Records and Administration, the Criminal Courts Building, the Chandler Pavilion, Times Mirror Square, City Hall. Civil matters were heard at the county courthouse, and as a criminal defense lawyer I hadn't spent much time there. Still, I never failed to be impressed by the frieze high above the Hill Street entrance that depicted Justice balancing the scales on her head while on either side of her knelt a heroically muscled male figure, each with a stone tablet he displayed to the passersby. *Lux et Veritas* was carved on one tablet, *Lex* on the other. Light and truth. Law. That was the promise, but as I stepped into the court-house on my way to the final hearing on the disposition of my lover's corpse, the phrase that passed through my mind was "Hell is other people."

Taped to the door of Department 22 was a schedule of the matters

pending that day before Judge Goodman. Heading the list was a will contest: *In re the Estate of Joshua Scott Mandel.* The parties were me, Henry
Rios as executor of the estate and the objectors, Josh's parents, Sam and
Selma Mandel. This wasn't the usual fight over competing claims to property or money; Josh's worldly possessions had filled a dozen paper sacks
and a U-Haul van. At issue were his written instructions that upon his
death his body be cremated and the ashes scattered by his friends and
family.

Josh had died of complications from AIDS at the age of twenty-nine.
For five years, we'd been lovers, until he left me for another man, who,
like Josh, had AIDS. After Steven had died and Josh's own health began to fail, I became his main caretaker. Even before the last series of
infections and illnesses that carried him off, Josh had insisted on cremation rather than burial. He'd advanced a number of reasons, everything
from the environmental ("There's already a big landfill problem, Henry")
to the mystical ("The Hindus believe that fire releases your soul"); but
reason aside, Josh was phobic about burial. Toward the end, he'd been
plagued by nightmares of being buried alive and he made me promise,
repeatedly, to honor the request for cremation he had included with
his will.

I'd assumed he had spoken to his parents about his wish, but when I
went about making the arrangements after he died, I learned I was wrong.
Not only had Josh not told his parents he wanted to be cremated, they were
horrified at the prospect.

"Jews," his father told me in our last phone conversation, "are not
cremated."

"It's what he wanted."

As if I hadn't spoken, Sam Mandel said, "My son will be buried beside
his grandparents."

"I'm sorry, Sam. I promised him."

I knew Sam had viewed his son's homosexuality as a calamity of Biblical
proportions, so I tried not to take personally his scarcely concealed loathing
for me; but when he dismissed me with a contemptuous, "You promised him?
Who are you? I'm his father," I blew up.

"Now," I said. "Now that he's dead and can't embarrass you anymore.
You weren't so anxious to be his father while he was dying."

"You evil man," he said. "You killed him."

"Josh is dead because you made him feel so ashamed of himself he
thought he deserved to contract AIDS."

"Liar! You gave it to him."

"You know that's not true."

He hung up on me.

The next day, the Mandels filed a lawsuit to remove me as executor on the grounds of undue influence. They sought a temporary injunction to prevent me from proceeding with the cremation. Included in their request was Sam's affidavit alleging that I had infected Josh with HIV, alienated him from his family and now proposed to dispose of his remains in a manner offensive to their religion. Selma Mandel, with whom I'd sat the last vigil at Josh's deathbed, now claimed that I had prevented her from seeing Josh after I brought him home from the hospital. Their attorney, Howard Lev, implied in not so subtle terms that a decision against the Mandels was tantamount to an act of anti-Semitism. The court granted the preliminary injunction while it determined the merits of their action, and ordered me to release Josh's body to the custody of the medical examiner, who removed it to the county morgue.

I think we had all expected the case to be determined swiftly, but this was the year of three strikes. Every criminal defendant in the county of Los Angeles faced with a possible third felony conviction and twenty-five to life was demanding a trial, and even probate judges had been pressed into service. Our case was tried in bits and pieces over a period of six months. My dreams were straight out of Edgar Allan Poe; worm-eaten flesh, ravenous ghosts. I only had to look at the Mandels to know they were having the same dreams.

"Counsel," Judge Goodman had said to Lev and me the last time we were before her, "surely, some compromise is possible."

"The Mandels cannot compromise their religious principles," Lev replied.

"Mr. Rios?"

"I'm sorry, Judge, but I'd be derelict in my duties as Josh's executor if I didn't follow through with his last request."

She sighed. "All right. Come back in April for final judgment. My clerk will give you a date."

Afterward, in the hallway outside of Judge Goodman's courtroom, Lev said, "What have you got against these people, Henry? All they want is their son back."

"Back from where?"

"They had relatives who died in the camps," he chided me. "Their bodies were burned in Hitler's crematoria. Doesn't that move you at all?"

"Of course," I said, "but I don't see that what their family suffered gives them the right to shove Josh back into the closet."

"They only want to bury him."

"What they want is to return him to the family fold and erase all evidence he was gay. I've seen it happen over and over, but Josh wouldn't have let it happen to him, and I won't, either."

"He belongs to them," Lev said angrily. "They're his family. You're the stranger here, trying to make some political statement out of their loss."

"The hard lesson of Josh's life was that he belonged to himself."

"Ah, well. Fine. I'll see you back in court."

"PLEASE RISE," the bailiff said. "Department 22 is now in session, the Honorable Judith Goodman presiding."

Judge Goodman took the bench and shuffled some papers in front of her. She was probably thirty-four, thirty-five, a decade younger than me, an attractive woman with cascading blond hair, who had presided over the case with a pained, trapped expression. Sometimes, while someone was testifying, I watched the furrows deepen in her brow and I could almost hear her thinking, *God, I hate this case.* Looking at her now, I watched the mask that descends over the features of judges about to render an unpopular decision descend over hers, and I knew I had won. I did not feel victorious. I was only aware of how cold it was in the courtroom, so cold that the reporter who sat beneath the bench with her fingers poised over her reporting machine was wearing thin leather gloves. As the judge began to speak, I glanced at the Mandels. Sam stared fixedly at the Great Seal of California on the wall above the judge's head. Selma stole a look at me; her heart-shaped face was tired, cried-out. When I caught her eye, she quickly turned away. I could tell by the slump in Howard Lev's shoulders that he had read in Judge Goodman's face the same result as me.

"We are here today in *In re Estate of Mandel,*" Judge Goodman was saying. "The objectors, the decedent's parents, are attempting to remove the executor of decedent's estate on grounds of undue influence. I have considered the following evidence," she continued, and listed it slowly for the benefit of the court reporter. "On a personal level, this is a troubling case, because it pits the decedent's family against his dearest friend and companion. As a legal question, however, the result is clear to me. For purposes of this proceeding, undue influence has been defined in *Estate of Dale* as conduct which subjugates the will of the testator to the will of another. To prevail in this action, the Mandels were required to prove that Mr. Rios overcame Joshua's free will with respect to the funerary arrangements specified by Josh in the codicil to his will dated last September sixteenth." She paused, took a breath and said, "I find that the Mandels have not satisfied their burden of showing undue influence . . ."

From the other side of the courtroom, I heard Selma gasp, "Oh, oh . . ."

When she finished reading her judgment, Judge Goodman said to Lev, "Mr. Lev, I'm prepared to issue an order to Mr. Rios today that would allow him to take possession of the body from the county medical examiner, but I'll refrain from making that order if the Mandels intend to appeal the judgment."

Lev shambled to his feet. "I've discussed it with my clients. They can't afford to pursue the case to the appellate level. The only appeal they can afford to make is to Mr. Rios's sense of decency."

"The time for argument is over," the judge murmured. "Mr. Rios, I'm signing the order."

"Thank you, Your Honor."

THE NEXT MORNING, armed with the order, I stood in a cold room in the county morgue while a deputy medical examiner wheeled in a gurney with a body on it, covered by a sheet. He pulled the sheet back.

"This him?"

Six months of refrigeration had so drained the last vestiges of life from the blue-skinned, emaciated body that for a long minute I wasn't sure it was Josh. His body looked like the kind of thing that was dropped from the rafters of the haunted house at an amusement park to make kids scream. There was no trace in those forlorn features of the cranky, funny intelligence that had been Josh Mandel. It was just a thing, a husk, from which Josh was long gone. And yet it was the body I had held next to mine, had reached for in lust, pushed aside in anger, comforted, loved, missed. All that struggle, all that feeling gone down the black hole, leaving nothing but this effigy.

"Excuse me," the M.E. said impatiently. "Is this him?"

"Yes, it is," I said. "It's him."

TWO DAYS LATER, his ashes were delivered to me in a bronze urn via UPS. Josh's will specified that his family participate in the scattering of the ashes. As unlikely as it was the Mandels would agree, I felt duty-bound to remind them of his request before disposing of the ashes, but I couldn't bring myself to do it just yet. I put the urn on the mantel above the fireplace, off to the side, and went back to work in the room I'd fitted out as my office.

I'd been a lawyer for twenty-one years, having graduated third in my class from Stanford in the mid-seventies. Back then, the words "idealist" and "lawyer" could still be spoken in the same sentence without a sneer, and no one questioned why I would take my prestigious degree and join the local public defender's office rather than hang my shingle with a big-city firm. Criminal defense was the only kind of law I had ever wanted to practice. I was inspired in equal parts by a childhood veneration of Abraham Lincoln, the TV series *Perry Mason*, my father's brutality and my awareness, from the time I was sixteen, that I was gay. The last two were related. My Mexican immigrant father was a hard man who had survived a hard life, and he despised the softness he detected in his only son and was determined to beat it out of me. All his beatings had accomplished was to incite in me a hatred of authority and injustice. Not until I fell in love with my best friend in high school did I begin to understand that what had driven my father's violence was every father's ultimate nightmare: a homosexual son. A *maricón*. Had I been able to change, I would have done it without hesitation, but in the deepest part of me I knew change was not possible, only deception, and that would have inevitably implicated other people in my lie. I was too much an altar boy for that. I compromised: if I could not not be gay, I would compensate for it with good works. My compromise led me, at twenty-four, into a courtroom to defend my first client, a man not unlike my father, accused of murdering another man in a brawl in a *cantina* in the San Jose barrio.

I hung the jury, eight to four for acquittal, with a mistaken identity defense, and the charges were dropped. It was the fast track after that, big cases, big wins, a reputation for thoroughness and eloquence I still lived off of; all those years of committing Lincoln's speeches to heart had paid off. I was too busy for a private life, too busy to be gay, so busy that I didn't notice the water closing over my head until I was drowning in loneliness and booze. I lost my job. I sobered up. I got drunk again. I sobered up again. I met Josh. We moved to Los Angeles. I established a successful practice. Josh left me for Steven. I closed my practice to find myself and discovered I was a lawyer. Steven died and Josh got sick. I went back to work handling criminal appeals out of my house so I could take care of Josh. Josh died. And that's how I'd spent the last decade.

Back in my office, tropical fish danced across the screen of my desktop. Piles of transcripts were stacked on the floor, spilling out of file cabinets, representing the fifty-odd cases on appeal I was handling. On makeshift bookshelves lining the walls were my law books, reporters, treatises, digests. Somewhere in the room was my degree from Stanford and a yellowing copy of my student law review note: "Recent Developments in Fourth Amendment Jurisprudence." On my desk was a picture of Josh I'd taken on a weekend trip to San Francisco shortly after we'd met. He was twenty-two, a little, beautifully made man with olive skin, a wild frizz of black hair, and eyes like wounds. He had only recently told me he was HIV positive. He was still afraid I would abandon him. In time, he'd learned to trust me and the wounded eyes healed. And then they'd closed for good. I took the picture from its frame, turned it over and scribbled on the back his name and dates and a line from Emily Dickinson that had been running through my head for months: "Parting is all we know of heaven and all we need of hell."

I DON'T KNOW how long I sat there looking at his picture before I was roused to the front door by the doorbell. I peered through the peephole at my friend Richie Florentino, his fist poised to bang on the door. I opened it.

Tall and thin, his long face was framed by a luxuriance of thick, wavy dark hair and he had the square-jawed glamour of a forties movie star, a look he carefully cultivated. Always draped in the latest fashions, he was wearing a burnt-orange sports coat over a linen shirt of paler orange, a silk tie the color of new grass and cream-colored linen trousers. On his large feet were lime-green suede loafers with brass buckles forming by the letters GV, Gianni Versace, his favorite designer. Richie lived in an apartment in West Hollywood that had once belonged to Jean Harlow and edited a magazine called *L.A. Mode* that catalogued the antics of the rich and famous. His lover of twenty years, Joel Miller, was a studio executive. Richie claimed descent from the de Medicis and a family fortune going back five hundred years. His friends knew never to question his veracity, but simply assumed that, out of any ten statements, Richie had made up nine of them.

"Good, you're home," Richie said, sweeping past me in a flood of Guerlain's Derby. "Oh, honey, it's so hot in here. Turn on the air-conditioning."

"You've been here before," I said. "You know my house isn't air-conditioned."

"But I keep hoping." He flung himself into an armchair and lit a Marlboro Light. "You don't mind, do you?"

"Would it matter if I did?"

He pretended to think it over. "No."

"I'll find you an ashtray."

"You like the coat?" he shouted. "It's Versace."

"Who would've guessed?" I replied, slipping, gratefully, into his mocking locutions. I handed him a saucer for his cigarette.

Richie was the kind of friend who touched down in my life like a whirlwind, rearranged the landscape and then blew on. I wasn't always happy to see him, but today I was glad because whatever he wanted—and it was always something—would, at the very least, drive me out of my grief.

He picked up the saucer, scrutinized it, pretended to weigh it in his palm. "Baccarat?"

"Cost Plus," I said. "It's good to see you, Richie. How are you?"

"Not dead yet," he said, blowing smoke out of the corner of his mouth like Bogart.

"No, really."

"Really? I feel great, Henry."

Richie had AIDS ("But darling," he liked to say, "all the best people do.") I'd met him at a hospital where I'd gone to visit Josh. Richie came into Josh's room, trailing his IV behind him, an unlit cigarette clamped in his mouth and excused himself to the small balcony off the room where, with Josh's permission, he could light up. At one point, he'd been so sick that he'd planned his memorial service, but then he'd bounced back and now he was on a regimen of protease inhibitors, the new miracle antivirals that were bringing so many people with AIDS back from the brink of death.

"My viral load is almost undetectable," he continued. "My T-cells have gone from fourteen to eight hundred and they're still climbing." He had dropped all affectation and there was awe in his voice. "If this isn't cured, Henry, I don't know what cured means."

"I'm happy for you," I said.

"It could all change tomorrow," he replied. "I know people the drugs stopped working for, or never worked for, and no one knows about their long-term effectiveness, but I've never lived in the long term. I'm sorry Josh didn't get to try them."

"I am, too," I said. "He was like the soldier who gets killed the day before armistice."

"I think about the people who didn't make it—Mario, Steven—and wonder, why me?"

"Every lawyer knows you never ask a question of a witness to which you do not already know the answer. It works in life, too. How's Joel?"

"Three things in life are certain," Richie grumbled. "Death, taxes and

Joel Miller." He grabbed one of the transcripts piled on the coffee table. "People versus Bailey. Pearl? Beetle? F. Lee?"

"None of the above. It's an appeal from a murder conviction."

"Oh," Richie cooed, excitedly. "Was the victim famous?"

"No, a domestic dispute. Mr. Bailey killed his wife."

"Breeders are so literal-minded. Hasn't anyone explained to them you can torture your spouse without ever laying a finger on them? Every fag knows that." He lit another cigarette. "Of course, I blame it on the schools. Instead of forcing high school kids to read *Romeo and Juliet*, they should assign them *Who's Afraid of Virginia Woolf?* Because, really, Henry, which one of those two great works of literature do most marriages resemble? I'll give you a hint, Liz Taylor played me in the movie."

I grimaced. "I know it's considered liberated to throw around the words 'fag' and 'faggot,' but they're still hate words to me."

He stiffened slightly at the correction. "People can pack as much hate into 'gay' as they can into 'fag.' "

We had covered this terrain many times. Richie's lacerating wit was more often than not directed at other gay men with a contempt that would have infuriated him had it come from a straight person. He never saw the contradiction. I did.

"Let's not argue," I said. "Not today." I pointed to the mantel. "Today, Josh came home."

He went to the fireplace, picked up the urn. "You beat his parents in court."

"It wasn't a battle I would have chosen."

"They picked it," he said, putting the urn on the mantel.

I smiled. "No, actually I think Josh did by not telling them he wanted to be cremated."

"You're so right about that," he said, lighting another Marlboro.

"What do you mean?"

"I was in the hospital with him, Henry. He was always worse after his parents visited him, especially that father of his." He made a face. "Like Charlton Heston in *The Ten Commandments*, that one. He laid the guilt on so thick the room had to be fumigated."

"Josh never mentioned that to me."

Richie arranged himself on the couch. "He thought you had enough to worry about."

I didn't know whether he was telling the truth or inventing what he considered a consoling story. But the story was not consoling if true, and if not, it was a terrible thing to say. At such moments I remembered that Richie was not, as he liked to say, "your old Auntie Mame." His wealthy family had institutionalized him when he was a teenager to cure him of homosexuality. When that failed, they cast him from the hearth and paid him to stay away. The experience left him with a corrosive rage.

"If I were you," he was saying. "I would've taken Josh's ashes and thrown them in his parents' faces."

I remembered Selma Mandel's piteous "Oh," when the judgment was announced. "Jesus, Richie. They aren't evil. They loved him."

"That's always the bottom line, isn't it?" Richie said, venomously. "Your family fucks you up seven ways to Sunday, but it's all right because they love you."

I shrugged, changed the subject. "Is this just a social visit, Richie?"

"I have a friend who needs a lawyer," he replied, abruptly all business.

"Because?" I prompted.

"Because he was arrested last week for something with a gun."

"Something with a gun?"

"I have the arrest report," he said, reaching into his breast pocket.

It never failed to impress me how quickly Richie could shuck aside the queeny manner when it no longer served his purpose. Even his posture changed, the languid pose abandoned as he leaned emphatically forward.

"Does the client have a name?"

"Alex Amerian," he said, handing me the arrest report.

I scanned the cover sheet. The charges were PC sections 245 and 12022.1; assault with a deadly weapon and possession of a concealed firearm. According to the arresting officer's narrative. Alex Amerian (twenty-nine years old, Caucasian) had been picked up by a security guard while wandering through the shrubbery on the grounds of a hillside mansion in Los Feliz belonging to someone called Cheryl Cordet.

I looked up at Richie, "Cheryl Cordet? Why do I know that name?"

Richie did a Mae West roll of his eyes. "Because last month she became the first woman ever to win an Oscar for best director?"

"Oh," I said and returned my attention to the report.

Amerian had pulled a gun on the security guard who managed to wrest it from his control and call the police. Amerian was arrested. He declined to make a statement.

"What do you think?" Richie asked when I raised my head from the report.

"What's his version?"

"He told me he was coming home from a party when his car broke down in front of Cheryl Cordet's place. He jumped the fence to see if she'd let him use her phone to call the auto club. The security guard caught him and they got into a scuffle. The guard called him a faggot. Alex lost control and waved the gun around. The guard knocked him down, got the gun away from him and called the cops."

"Why was he carrying a gun?"

"For protection. Six months ago he was gay bashed and got the shit beat out of him."

"Did he mean to shoot the guard?"

"No, he panicked."

"He didn't try to explain this to the cops?"

"He has an attitude about the police," Richie said.

"Why?"

"He was attacked on the streets of West Hollywood by some teenage punks with baseball bats who left him crawling in his own blood to a pay phone to dial 911. It took forty minutes for the sheriffs to show up and when they did, they refused to take a report."

"How do you know this guy, Richie?"

"The magazine ran a piece on violence against gays and lesbians a couple of months ago. Alex was one of the people we interviewed."

"*L.A. Mode* did a story about gay bashing? Who photographed it? Herb Ritts?"

"Bitch," he replied. "I'm a serious journalist, Henry."

"Between fashion spreads," I replied. "Alex Amerian sounds like one angry guy."

"Wouldn't you be if you'd gone through what he did?"

"Not to the point of stupid."

"He's not stupid, Henry. He was traumatized by the attack on him, and when he got into a scuffle with this security guard, who called him a queer, he thought it was happening again."

"Post-traumatic stress syndrome?" I said skeptically.

"What's so fucking unbelievable about that?" he asked, angrily. "What fag—gay person—hasn't been traumatized by someone's hatred? When we do fight back, this is what happens."

"All right, Richie. Calm down. I'll talk to him."

He leaned back and drawled, "I knew I could count on you, honey."

Something in his tone gave me pause. "Richie? Is there something you're not telling me?"

"Henry," he said, "after everything we've been through together—you, me and Josh—how could you even think that?"

"Sorry."

"You help Alex, you'll be doing a *mitzvah*. You can redeem it for a thousand years in Purgatory after you die."

"Is that why you do good deeds, Richie? To shorten your time in Purgatory?"

"Oh, honey," he said, brushing lint from an orange sleeve. "I'm going to hell. That's where the action is."

chapter 2

I CALLED ALEX Amerian after Richie left and agreed to meet him at five-thirty at his apartment in West Hollywood. At five, I came down the canyon and battled rush-hour traffic as I headed west on Sunset toward the gay ghetto, Boystown. The air was as brown as the curling edges of a burning book, and the palms that lined the road looked combustible. The only people on foot were the homeless and dazed tourists in search of a Hollywood that existed only in their imaginations.

I often felt like a tourist in Los Angeles myself, a temporary inhabitant, but then I suppose it felt like that to most of the millions who lived there. It was a completely invented city, a flimflam town that owed its existence to sunshine, cheap land and the movies. You could still see the sun most days, and there were parts of town where the land was still cheap, though you wouldn't want to live there. As for the movies, they thrived, and if the studio executive whose picture I had seen in the *Times* was to be believed, the Industry, as it was called, was poised to take over the world.

Long ago, as a literary-minded undergraduate, I had read a short story by the Argentine writer Borges called "The Babylon Lottery" that imagined a city in which each of the inhabitants partook of a secret lottery every seventy days that determined his or her fate until the next drawing. "Babylon," the narrator wrote, "is nothing but an infinite game of chance." That was my uniformed idea of Hollywood, an infinite game of chance that everyone could play and anyone could win; a permanent boomtown where the surging, naked energy of dreams alternated with the violence of rejection and despair.

This was also true of West Hollywood, the gay Mecca of southern California. I turned down Crescent Heights and then took a right onto Santa Monica Boulevard, West Hollywood's Main Street. Even to the unobservant, it was obvious that this was a lavender neighborhood. Rainbow flags hung limply from the small businesses on either side of the street, and the businesses themselves, antique stores, bars, an adult bookstore, coffeehouses where shirtless young men sipped iced cappuccinos at small tables on the filthy sidewalk, were unmistakable. Some signs were subtler, apparent only to the cognoscenti. Posted on the side streets off the boulevard were signs that forbade cars from making turns between the hours of midnight and 6 A.M., a seemingly bizarre injunction imposed by the city at the request of residents driven crazy by the heavy nighttime traffic caused by men cruising each other from their cars or picking each other up in the city's alleys. There was a stretch behind the storefronts on the boulevard between La Jolla and Harper streets that was so notorious it was dubbed Vaseline Alley, but, at night, after the bars closed, all the city's dark places teemed with hunters.

Most of them were hunting for sex, a few for love, all for some kind of completion that would repair the damage that, as Richie had observed, most gay people carried through life. They bore the affect of the hated, a vulnerability, a deep grief for the families that had cast them out, the childhoods and adolescences spent in hiding. Believing that safety lay in numbers, they created places like West Hollywood, the Castro, the Village. Yet ironically, the existence of these ghettos made them easy targets for the haters. Every year there were more and more violent attacks on gay men in the city's backstreets, some culminating in murder. Maybe that's why West Hollywood made me so uneasy. It might just have been my projection, but the air around Boystown sweated ambivalence — it dripped from the fronds of the palm trees that memorialized the AIDS dead — and the boys had in their eyes, behind the flickering lights of lust, the gentle, torpid look of animals being led to slaughter.

I pulled up to the curb beside Alex Amerian's house, which, like its neighbors, was a single-story whitewashed building with a red-tile roof, thick walls and arched windows. There was a plaster escutcheon above the front door: crossed swords and fleur-de-lis. I rang the bell, heard the shuffle of bare feet across a wooden floor and then the door was opened by a pretty, long-haired girl with beautiful but spacey eyes, wearing Levi cutoffs and a tee shirt that advertised a gay disco. Her pale skin was flawless but waxen, a drug addict's pallor.

"Hello," I said. "My name is Henry Rios. I'm here to see Alex."

She glanced at my wilted seersucker suit and surmised, "You're the lawyer?"

"Yes, is Alex here?"

"Uh-huh. I'm Alex's roommate, Katie." She offered me a damp, firm handshake. "Come on in."

The small, sunny living room was furnished with a futon, a ficus tree and two director's chairs. Rice-paper blinds on the windows diffused the light. On one wall was a framed poster advertising the Chicago Film Festival: a coy photograph of a nude elaborately muscled man and an equally sleek woman. The room was slightly musty, as if rarely used, and cobwebs clung to the corners. Katie called Alex's name, and a moment later, from the back of the house, down a long, dim hall, came a young man in a white linen shirt and gray slacks. His skin was olive-colored, his hair was a toss of damp, black curls and his face had a delicate, Mediterranean masculinity, like the face of an archaic Apollo. His eyes were black and gleamed like dark water. He had the rumpled air of someone who had just awakened. There was a second, as he emerged from the shadows, when I felt the stunned certainty of someone witnessing a miracle, that the young man approaching me was Josh, alive again. But then Josh's face melted into Amerian's features and was gone.

"Uh, Mr. Rios," he said, his extended hand unshaken. "Are you okay?"

I took his hand, shook it. "Yes. Glad to meet you, Alex."

I released his hand, but could not look away from his face. My eyes reported that his resemblance to Josh was nothing more than a matter of height and coloring and bone structure, but there *had* been something else, a flicker of Josh that had briefly illuminated this other man like a light passing beneath his skin.

He exchanged a nervous glance with the girl, who blurted out, "You want a beer or something?"

"A glass of water would be fine," I said, looking at her. When I looked back at him, the spell was broken. "Is there somewhere we can talk, Alex?"

"It's cooler in the courtyard."

I followed Alex down the hall, across a narrow dining room furnished with a picnic table and out through French doors to a shaded courtyard between his house and the adjoining house. The courtyard was paved with bricks and covered by a trellis overgrown with morning glory. The bricks were loose in the mortar, the trellis sagged beneath the weight of the vines. In the corner was a dry fountain. The wrought-iron table was dusty and in need of a new coat of paint. We sat down. I opened my briefcase and removed the police report, a pad of paper, a pen. I felt his eyes on me, and when I looked up I half-expected to see Josh again, but there was only an anxious young stranger on the other side of the table.

"It is cooler out here," I said. "Are the two houses joined or do they just share the courtyard?"

"They just share," he replied. "They were built by the same guy, for his family. You can see they're falling apart. With rent control, the landlord doesn't have much incentive to keep the place up."

"You've lived here a long time?"

"Two years," he said.

At that moment, Katie emerged from the house with a glass of ice water and two beers. "You're sure you just want water?"

"Yes, thanks," I said.

"Should I stay or what?" she asked.

"She already knows everything," Alex said.

"Do you want her to be called as a witness against you?"

"I'll be inside," she said. "Call me if you need me."

After she left, I said, "Tell me about the night you were arrested."

He repeated, without significant deviation, the story that Richie had told me, while I scribbled notes.

"Let me see if I understand this," I said. "You tried to explain to the security guard that all you wanted was a phone, but you say he got aggressive with you."

"Yeah," he said, peeling back the label on his bottle of beer.

"What did he do exactly?"

"He was screaming he was going to call the cops and then he shoved me a couple of times."

"What did he look like?"

"He was a big guy, six something, beefy. Fat neck."

"You shoved him back and then he knocked you down?" I asked, consulting my notes.

He nodded. "It was a reflex when I shoved back. I wasn't trying to pick a fight with him because I knew he could beat the crap out of me, but then he laid into me and knocked me down . . ."

"And called you a faggot. Do you have any idea why he called you that?"

"I guess it was the worst thing he thought he could call another guy."

"So it was just a general insult, but because you'd been gay bashed, you didn't hear it that way, right?"

He nodded. "He was standing over me, calling me a faggot, and it was like a flashback to those punks with their baseball bats. I thought, any second now and he'll start kicking me, so I pulled my gun . . ."

"Where was the gun?"

"In my waistband," he said.

"What happened then?"

"I got the gun out but before I could point it at him, he stepped on my wrist and I dropped it. He kicked it away. Then he rolled me over and got me into handcuffs. He pulled me to my feet and locked me to the fence until the cops came."

"You're sure you didn't point the gun at him."

"I didn't have a chance."

"Tell me about when you were attacked. How serious were the injuries?"

"Six broken ribs and a concussion, plus I was black and blue for weeks."

"And the psychological damage?"

He frowned. "I'd like to find those punks and kill them."

"Richie said the police wouldn't take a report. Is that right?"

He nodded. "That's right."

"So there's no record of the attack."

He stared at me. "You don't believe me?"

"If I'm going to be arguing to the DA or a jury that you pulled the gun on the security guard because you were in fear of your life based on the previous attack, they'll want evidence."

"Incredible," he muttered. "This was a misunderstanding, that's all."

"Misunderstandings that end up as felonies take on a life of their own."

He brooded into his beer. "What about the article about me in Richie's magazine? Is that evidence?"

I thought about it. "It depends on whether the reporter corroborated your story. Do you have a copy of the article?"

"I have lots of copies," he said. "I've been sending them all over the place. My congressman, the mayor, the sheriff. No one writes back."

"Where were you treated for your injuries?"

"The emergency room at Cedar-Sinai."

"Then there are those records, too," I said.

"What's going to happen to me, Mr. Rios? I don't want to go to jail behind this. It's not fair."

"The problem is the gun," I said. "Where did you get it?"

"It's not hard to get a gun in LA."

"I assume the cops kept it."

"As far as I know," he said.

"Would you agree to its destruction?"

"What do you mean?"

"If I can find a sympathetic DA, I might be able to work out a deal because, based on what you've told me, this isn't the kind of case a prosecutor's going to want to take to a jury. I can't guarantee you no jail time, but it's pretty unlikely unless you have a record. Do you?"

"I've never been in trouble before," he said, quickly.

"Then that's not a problem," I replied. "You want to get me a copy of the magazine piece?"

While he was gone, I went over my notes. Alex had provided a sympathetic and plausible account of the incident, one I could easily sell to a jury if it came to that. Was he telling the truth? Most of my clients lied to me, people in trouble usually do. Over the years I'd developed an intuition about how much was being concealed. My bullshit detector had twitched a couple of times with Alex, but no major alarms had gone off. I thought he might be lying to me about whether he had a rap sheet, but that was easy enough to check. One other thing bothered me, and when he returned, I asked him about it.

"Did you carry this gun with you everywhere you went?"

"Yes," he said, passing me the article across the table.

"But the attack was six months ago?"

His eyes were cold. "Have you ever been gay bashed, Mr. Rios?"

"No."

"I thought I was safe in West Hollywood," he said, "but once I was attacked I knew I wasn't safe anywhere. I had to protect myself."

I nodded. "And if I run a rap sheet on you, I'm not going to come up with any surprises."

He was more wounded than angry. "No."

"I have to make sure. I don't like surprises."

A dusty leaf drifted from the vine and settled in his hair. He was drenched in cologne. I recognized the fragrance—it was popular that year—but I couldn't remember what it was called.

"You looked pretty surprised when you first saw me," he said. "What did Richie say about me? Did he tell you I was crazy?"

"It wasn't anything Richie said. You reminded me of someone."

"Someone you liked?" A note of flirtation crept into his voice.

"My lover," I said. "He died a few months ago. I still think I see him sometimes, walking down the street, sitting in front of me at the movies, but of course it isn't him, just someone who looks like him a bit. I had one of those moments when I first saw you." I sipped some water, warm now that the ice had melted. "I didn't mean to stare."

The black eyes gazed at me. "What was his name?"

"Josh," I said. "Joshua."

"Joshua," he repeated. "I like that name."

"Yes," I said. "It's a nice name." I gathered up my papers. "I'll see if I can't straighten this out with the DA tomorrow."

He laid a hand on my sleeve. "I'm sorry about Josh, Mr. Rios."

Each time he said Josh's name, I felt a pang in my gut, like hunger.

"You will have a record after this," I said, not looking at him. "You should be aware of that. It might affect your future employment."

"I'm an actor," he said. "I don't think it will matter."

"A working actor?"

"If you're worried if I can pay you . . . ," he said, frowning.

"No," I interrupted. "I'm doing this as a favor to Richie. I was just curious, but it's none of my business."

"I support myself," he said.

He walked me to the front door. "Thank you," he said. "I'll be in touch."

I READ THE L.A. Mode article when I got home. Alex's was one of four gay-bashing incidents discussed in the story. According to Alex, he'd been attacked on his way home from a bar called the Gold Coast at two in the morning on a side street off the boulevard. He managed to get to a phone and call 911. Half an hour later an ambulance and a sheriff's patrol car arrived. As he was being loaded into the ambulance, he attempted to report the attack to a deputy sheriff. The deputy had refused either to take the report or to explain why. The writer claimed the reason was that by refusing to take hate-crime reports in West Hollywood, the sheriffs could then claim no such crimes occurred. A former deputy was quoted, anonymously, in support of this assertion. Asked for a comment, the captain of the West Hollywood station denied this was the sheriff's policy and declared Alex's allegation was "without merit."

Though there wasn't much direct corroboration of Alex's story in the piece, the claim that the sheriff's office was deliberately refusing to take hate-crime reports was potentially incendiary in a city where police were increasingly regarded with suspicion and hostility. In a trial, it was the kind of information that could have what some local defense attorneys were now calling "the Fuhrman effect," after the LAPD cop who'd been used by the defense to turn the Simpson trial into a referendum about racism in the department. If I could find the right person in the District Attorney's office to give this information, I might be able to leverage a plea in Alex's case.

The right person: a gay or lesbian deputy DA. There were a number of them in the DA's office, something that still seemed remarkable to me because when I had begun practicing, most prosecutor's offices were the preserve of people to whom homosexuals were, at best, a colorful part of the demimonde, like whores and junkies. I suppose it was progress that now some of us were deemed fit to put people in jail, and I wasn't above appealing to gay solidarity if it helped me on a case.

THE NEXT MORNING I made an appointment to see Serena Dance, the head of the DA office's Hate Crimes Unit. I'd known Serena casually for a couple of years, since we'd been on a panel together at the state bar convention to discuss the impact of the then newly enacted hate-crime statutes. At the time, she'd been the director of the Gay and Lesbian Law Project, and she'd been instrumental in assuring that crimes against gays and lesbians were included in the hate crime legislation. When the DA set up the Hate Crimes Unit, he hired her to run it, to much fanfare, but then it and she had faded from public view.

Her office was on the eighteenth floor of the Criminal Courts Building, the same floor where the DA had his suite. I gave my name to the black marshal who sat at a desk in the dim corridor and waited while she tracked Serena down. A few minutes later, she emerged from a side door. In one of the many profiles that had appeared after her appointment by the DA, I'd read that Serena had played on the women's pro-tennis circuit after college, and she still looked the part. Rangy and tall, she had the short, no-nonsense hair and sunburned face of a jock, and retained a kind of the stub-nosed collegiate cuteness. When she moved, it was with an athlete's self-confidence and economy.

She fixed me in her bright blue gaze, extended a muscular hand and said, "Henry Rios in the DA's office. I'm surprised you didn't turn into a pillar of salt when you stepped off the elevator."

"You used to be a radical lesbian lawyer," I said. "What happened? Have you gone native up here, surrounded by all these career prosecutors?"

"Come on back."

I followed her through the door to a corridor lined with cardboard boxes, file cabinets and discarded pieces of furniture, past a warren of small windowless offices, until we reached her office. It was a ten-by-twelve cubicle with metal walls, a dirty brown carpet and steel furniture finished in faux-wood grain, but it did have windows and a view of the roof of the building across the street. The city was, as usual, wreathed in smog.

"Nice view," I said, going to the window. "That's the roof of the old Hall of Justice, isn't it?"

She came up beside me. She was wearing scent. Something herbal; rosemary or lavender. "Yeah, there was a jail on the top floor and the roof was the inmate's recreation yard. Now it belongs to the pigeons."

"The sky is filthy."

"Like the scum around a toilet bowl," she said, going to her desk. "Have a sit."

I moved a stack of Supreme Court advance sheets from one of the two chairs in front of her desk and sat down. A boom box on a bookshelf was tuned to the same big-band station I listened to when I was working. Billie Holiday crooned a junkie version of "Lover Man" in a voice like velvet over barbed wire. On Serena's desk was a half-eaten egg-salad sandwich, a crumpled bag of Fritos, piles of case files, a laptop and a framed photograph of Serena, her lover, Donna, a therapist, and their five-year-old son, Jesse.

"How's business?"

"Close the door," she said.

I tipped the chair back, reached behind and pulled the door shut. "So, what's up? People stopped hating each other?"

"Nope, there's still a big market in hate in this town, but the DA's priorities have changed. Hate crimes are out, three strikes is in."

"What does that mean to you?"

"When I started, I had four deputies and a secretary. Now it's just me and a secretary I share with three other assistants. I may not survive the next budget."

"The DA can't get rid of you. There'd be a big ruckus."

She tossed a stack of papers across the desk. "The latest hate-crime statistics," she said. "Crimes against persons and crimes against property are both on the rise, especially against Jews, blacks and gays, with Latinos running a close fourth. Where's the public outcry? The *Times* will bury this report on the inside pages of the Metro section. The broadcast media can't be bothered." She slouched in her chair. "We're becoming habituated to hate. Maybe we're even becoming addicted to it. There's nothing like it for that adrenaline rush."

"That's a pretty grim prognosis."

"What does it say about a society that needs hate laws in the first place?" she replied. "You didn't drop by to hear this. What can I do for you?"

"I wanted to talk to you about a case."

She straightened up, all business. "What case?"

"It's a little complicated," I began, and launched into my spiel.

When I finished, I gave her a copy of the *L.A. Mode* piece. She flipped through it, frowning. "Yeah, I read this when it came out," she said. "Anonymous sources, uncorroborated claims and no one bothered to talk to me. Not stellar journalism."

"The attack on Alex was real enough," I said. "Cedars verified he was treated in the emergency room last November. I've subpoenaed his records."

"I'd like to see you get them in," she said. "They're not exactly relevant to an ADW six months after the fact."

"No? What if a woman was raped and then found herself in a situation where she thought it was going to happen again and tried to protect herself? There isn't a judge on the bench who would exclude evidence of the rape. It goes to the reasonableness of self-defense."

"Okay, decent analogy," she conceded. "But what does that have to do with me?"

"Doesn't it bother you that the sheriff has a policy against taking hate-crime reports from victims of gay bashings? I think it would bother a jury."

Her face hardened. "One, it's not true . . ."

"Are you sure? I did a little research on the sheriff's attitude toward gays. A couple of years back, he advised any gay or lesbian deputies to stay in the closet because he couldn't guarantee their personal safety. What kind of message does that send to the troops?"

"Unlike most politicians, the sheriff learns from his mistakes," she said. "Look, I'm not going to defend the entire department, but I've personally trained deputies in West Hollywood and they know it's their asses if they fail to investigate incidents of gay bashing. There is no contrary policy."

"Obviously at least one deputy didn't get the message."

"What are you going to do, Henry, put the sheriff's department on trial to deflect attention from your client?"

"If I have to," I said, "but this is not a case that needs to go to trial. My client was victimized, first by the guys who attacked him and then by the deputy who blew him off. Can you blame him if he goes in for a little self-help? He gets into a situation where he misreads the cues and overreacts. Is it right to throw him into jail for that?"

"He should've come to me six months ago."

"Your mandate is to protect victims of hate crime. That doesn't always mean prosecuting their assailants."

"What are you looking for?" she asked after a moment's thought.

"He pleads to misdemeanor assault and the gun charge. He agrees to the destruction of the gun, a fine and three years' unsupervised probation."

"Does he have a record?"

"I checked," I replied. "He's clean."

"He'll have to agree to counseling as a condition of probation."

"I don't have any problem with that."

"All right," she said. "When's the arraignment?"

"Monday."

"I'll make a note on the file," she said.

"Thanks."

She shrugged. "I might as well do someone some good while I still can."

A WEEK LATER, I was standing at sidebar in a crowded master calendar court while a young assistant DA named Campion explained to an impatient judge the deal Serena and I had worked out on Alex Amerian's case.

"Your Honor," Campion was saying, "we've agreed to a disposition on People versus Amerian."

"Am I supposed to guess?" the judge asked, rifling through a stack of files.

"The People will dismiss the charge of assault with a deadly weapon and the defendant will plead to simple assault and possession of a concealed firearm."

"Sentencing recommendation?" she asked impatiently.

"A thousand-dollar fine and thirty-six months' summary probation, with counseling," the DA said.

"The gun bothers me," the judge said. "Any prior record on this defendant?"

"No, Your Honor," I said. "As for the gun, Mr. Amerian was the victim of a vicious attack a couple of months before this incident, so he decided to arm himself. Not the smartest decision in the world, but understandable."

"Who attacked him?" she asked. "Is there a connection here?"

"It was a gay bashing, Your Honor," I replied. "It has nothing to do with this case."

"Is that right, Mr. Campion?"

"Yes, Your Honor. The defendant's agreed to the destruction of the gun. We're satisfied that this was a one-time thing with him. He's not a threat to public safety."

"You'd better be right," she said caustically. "The court accepts the disposition. Let's just take the plea."

At counsel table, Alex asked, anxiously, "Everything okay?"

"Yeah, she accepted the deal. No jail time."

"In the case of People versus Amerian," the judge said, "the defendant is present in court with his counsel, the People are also present. There has been a disposition. Mr. Campion."

"Yes, Your Honor," the DA said, "the People move to amend the complaint to allege as count three a violation of Penal Code 242. Upon the defendant's plea to counts two and three, the People will dismiss count one in the interests of justice."

The judge cast a reptilian gaze at me. "The defendant agrees?"

"Yes," I said. "We agree."

I waited until Alex had made arrangements to pay his fine, then went out into the corridor with him.

"I don't know how to thank you," he said.

"Stay away from guns," I replied.

He hugged me and brushed his lips against my cheek in what might have been a kiss. This time I recognized his cologne from magazine inserts. Obsession. I was aware that people were staring at us, and I could feel vibrations of hostility and disgust, but it was like holding Josh again and I kissed him back hard.

"I'm sorry," I said, breaking away from him. "I didn't mean to do that."

"Don't be sorry," he said. Then he kissed me back.

"We don't need to be seeing this," a black woman shouted from a bench along the wall.

"Goodbye, Henry," Alex said.

"Makes me want to puke," the woman was complaining to her neighbor.

I had another case on calendar. I went back into the courtroom.

chapter 3

BY MID-MAY, the city was drifting into summer, a season of muggy, overcast mornings followed by days of asphalt-melting heat and nights when the air was filled with grit and smelled of gasoline. From the parched hills, the houses of the rich looked down upon a burning plain, where the metallic flash of sunlight in the windshields of a million cars was like the frantic signaling of souls. I was working twelve-, fourteen-, sixteen-hour days. I justified the hours with a caseload that included three active death-penalty appeals, but there was a maniacal quality to my busyness I recognized from past experience as flight. When I was still drinking, it preceded a binge. Now that I no longer drank, I didn't know where it would take me.

Late at night, when I couldn't read another line of transcript or compose another sentence of argument, I got into my car and started driving. By two or three in the morning, Los Angeles had settled into a restless sleep beneath a red, starless sky. The labyrinth of freeways that arced above the city was as deserted as it ever got and I sped east to west, north to south, with the windows down and wind rushing through the car. Grief drove me, but this grief was a shape-shifter that often felt like other things. Like anger or fear or, surprisingly, like lust. I was as guiltily horny as a teenager, looking at other men with the same abashed eyes as when I was fifteen, tormented by the same fantasies. I felt like an animal slamming itself against its cage, as if my body was reacting in terror to Josh's death, with a frantic desire to generate or, failing that, for living flesh.

One night I found myself parked on a back road of Griffith Park, watching other men slip out of their cars and disappear into the brush. This was a dangerous spot for a lawyer—it teemed with undercover cops—and public sex had never appealed to me. I knew I was acting self-destructively but, for once, knowing was not enough to stop me, and all those years of disciplined sobriety counted for nothing against the emptiness in my gut. On a hill in the distance was the graceful hulk of the Griffith Observatory and somewhere in the hills behind me the Hollywood sign. A car pulled up beside me, a top-of-the-line Land Rover with tinted windows and a sun roof. The window on the passenger's side slid low enough to reveal a shiny pate and a set of intense, arrogant eyes. They took me in and rejected me, the dark window closing. A moment later, a different man, this one small and compact, got out of the driver's side and headed down the trail. By then I had concluded my own internal debate and went down the path behind him.

The trail dipped into a valley between a shaggy wood of shrubs and low growing trees. The shadowy figures of men moved among them. I plunged into the wood and waited beneath a eucalyptus tree. The little man whom I'd followed had been swallowed by the darkness. I heard a rustle and then a young Asian smoking a cigarette appeared at my side. He flung the cigarette down and ground it into the dust. Behind me, I heard a deep, cajoling voice whisper to someone else, "Come on, my car's parked on the road. We can party inside." The young Asian took my hand, guiding it to his crotch. I touched him, then pulled my hand away.

"What's wrong?" he asked.

"I made a mistake."

He looked at me. "Married guy, right?"

"No, I thought I was into this. I'm not."

He rolled his eyes. "Whatever. You better get home to the wife and kids." He zipped up and moved away.

I retraced my steps to my car. The little man had returned to the Land Rover with another man. I wondered if they were the two I'd overheard. They got into the backseat. A moment later, the second man jumped out of the car, slamming the door behind him. He was a boy, nineteen or twenty, a dusty-haired blond in a tank top and jeans. Hard blue eyes. He saw me, grinned spitefully.

"Troll," he said, jerking his thumb at the Land Rover.

"What?"

"The bald guy in the car. Scary." He'd come close enough to get a good look at me. His eyes glazed over. "See you around."

"Whatever," I said, getting into my car.

The little man emerged from the backseat and looked in my direction. I could not make out his features clearly, but a dark handsomeness registered that made me think of Alex Amerian. He smiled, shrugged and lunged back down the trail. I started up my car and pulled into the road. I noticed the plates on the Land Rover: PROUDJD. Another distinguished member of the profession.

MY LATE-NIGHT meandering sometimes found me in Alex Amerian's neighborhood, slowly driving past his house. If the lights were on, I'd park across the street and think about getting out, but what would I say to him? I'm obsessed with you because the first time I saw you I thought you were my dead lover? Not much of a pickup line. But I was obsessed, to my embarrassment, and conspicuous enough that one of Alex's neighbors, who pegged me as a cruiser, came out to my car one night and warned me off with, "Don't you guys ever give it a rest? Get out of here before I call the cops." I felt demeaned and out of control, but I couldn't keep him out of my thoughts or my fantasies. I would awaken from an erotic dream not sure whether the image fading into my unconsciousness was Josh or Alex.

I had learned with Josh that as much as you may want another human being, you don't really get to have them, not in a possessory way. You don't own, you absorb them. You adopt a gesture or a figure of speech or a preference for a certain color or kind of food. Then the transfer becomes subtler, a way of seeing things, a way of thinking, feeling. Eventually you can't tell where they leave off and you begin. One day, the part of Josh I'd absorbed into myself would fade into memory, but for now this shadow Josh inside of me continued to project itself onto the world of the living. It had projected itself onto Alex and because it kept Josh alive, I couldn't let go. But I wouldn't humiliate myself, either, by giving in to the obsession and calling Alex. So I buried myself in work, suffered my aging, lustful body and waited for it all to go away.

I WAS SITTING at home one hot night at the beginning of June, leafing through the sex ads of a gay newspaper, when the phone rang and it was Richie on the other end asking, "Do you have clean underwear?"

"What are you talking about?"

"Because if you don't, you can bring them with you when you pick me up and wash them at the laundromat."

"Are you on something?"

"Just a deadline, honey. You know that page in the magazine where we cover the trend du jour? Well, the latest thing is called the PLF, the Poet's Liberation Front. They want to bring poetry to the people." He paused for breath. "They give readings on buses, in shoe stores, with your rigatoni. Tonight there's one at a laundromat in Silver Lake, and you know Mother never ventures east of La Brea unescorted. You have to come. I'll buy you dinner afterwards."

"Why me, Richie?"

"Who else? You were a lit major and you live in the neighborhood."

It was like Richie to remember that English was my college major. He filed away facts when you didn't even think he was paying attention and then surprised you with them at a strategic moment.

"Why not?" I said. "I'll be at your place in fifteen minutes."

RICHIE LIVED IN the neighborhood of West Hollywood just below the Sunset Strip, where the black hearses of the Grave Line Tours ferried tourists to the sites of celebrity suicides, murders and hauntings: the carport on Holloway, where Sal Mineo was stabbed to death; the sidewalk outside of the Viper Club on Sunset, where River Phoenix died in convulsions. Richie's building was on the tour as the last domicile of Bette Davis, by whom it was said the building was haunted. Richie claimed it was true, that he had seen her ancient, wasted figure tottering through the halls whispering, "What a dump." It was a five-story brick building, whitewashed with green shutters. The dark-haired, handsome doorman sat in a little office beside the gate to the garage, waiting to be discovered. A brass plaque by the front door attested to the fact that the building was on the national register of historical places. The apartment Richie shared with Joel Miller was in the back of the building on the first floor, just past the unused swimming pool where I always half-expected to find William Holden floating facedown in the water.

The walls of Richie's apartment were pink and blue, the colors of a decadent nursery, and decorated with Fragonard-like murals of tubby gods and goddesses mistily seducing each other. Above a seventeenth-century French writing table of inlaid woods, a blunt black-and-white drawing by a prison artist depicted one tattooed gang member going down on another. A hundred-year-old Mexican reliquary held a plastic vial which, according to Richie, contained a bit of fat removed from Elizabeth Taylor's thighs by liposuction. On the walls of the dining room was a triptych of black-and-white photographs of Greta Garbo, Joan Crawford and Marlene Dietrich taken by George Hurrell, framed in heavy silver; "my mothers," Richie explained to bemused guests.

I rang the doorbell expecting to be admitted by Javier, the silent, dignified houseman Richie employed, but Joel Miller let me into the apartment. He was a plump, unprepossessing man whose face had been lifted, peeled and collagened to the smoothness, if not the innocence, of an infant. The expensive, baggy sweats he wore to hide his bulk only made it more obvious.

"Hello, Joel," I said. "Where's Javier?"

"It's his night off," he said. "Richie's getting ready."

"How are you?" I asked, following him into the living room.

"Busy," he said. "I have a lot of calls to make."

He disappeared into the library, and a few minutes later I heard him screaming at someone over the phone. Joel was a studio executive at Universal Pictures, vice-president in charge of something or other, but it was not clear to me what he actually did, no matter how often Richie explained it to me.

But then, Richie maintained that no one in Hollywood really knew what they were doing, and that pictures got made at all was an accidental by-product of deal-making. Joel, I gathered, was in the business of making deals. He rarely volunteered any information about himself. He could scarcely get in a full sentence without incurring Richie's ridicule, so he retreated into an aggrieved silence. The few times I had made an effort to talk to him away from Richie I sensed a rage beneath his platitudes I usually associated with the violent criminals I defended, a bottomless fury against the world. When I mentioned to Richie that Joel seemed to be a pretty angry guy, his eyes narrowed and he whispered, "Don't ever let him know you know." They'd been together for almost twenty years. Richie joked that he and Joel had an old-fashioned gay marriage: "It's based on mutual contempt."

Richie emerged from the bedroom, dressed entirely in black except for a necklace of large, fake pearls. "What do you think?" he asked, preening. "I call this Jack Kerouac meets Barbara Bush."

"No hat?"

He whipped a black beret out of his coat pocket. "I'm way ahead of you, Daddy-o. Where's Joel?"

"He said he had to make some calls."

"Did he offer you anything to drink? That asshole."

"I'm not thirsty. Shouldn't we be leaving?"

"Joel," Richie banged at the library door. "You shit. I know you're doing drugs in there. You better have 911 on redial because I won't be here when you OD."

Joel cracked the door open. "I'm on the phone, Richie. Working. Do you mind?"

"Just wanted to give you a kiss, honey," Richie simpered, planting a kiss in the air in the vicinity of Joel's cheek. "Don't wait up, pumpkin."

"Have fun," Joel replied, and shut the door firmly.

"Now, I'm ready to go," Richie announced.

I FOLLOWED RICHIE'S directions to a bad stretch of Sunset in Silver Lake, a neighborhood that increasingly defined what Los Angeles was becoming. In the hills above the reservoir that gave Silver Lake its name, the terra-cotta, white-walled houses of the affluent sprawled like a Mediterranean village, while down in the flats stood the graffiti-covered tenements of the poor. For a while, cheap rents in the flats had drawn artists to Silver Lake where, briefly, storefront galleries and coffeehouses had flourished, but crime had driven most of them away.

Outside the laundromat, a photographer from the magazine was waiting for Richie. I went inside to find seats while they talked. A microphone at the back of the room faced a half-dozen benches occupied by twenty or thirty people, many of them dressed as severely as Richie in shades of black, minus the whimsy of his pearls. They were mostly young and conspicuously white, lank-haired, bristling with attitude, smoking furiously. In contrast were the Latino families who had come not to hear poetry but to wash clothes. They milled around, unable to sit, since the benches had been appropriated for the reading, mothers, fathers, children, too polite to stare at the interlopers who were too indifferent to take notice of them. The room smelled of detergent, sweat and clove cigarettes, the washers and dryers thumped and chugged above the murmur of English and Spanish. I made my way to the front of the room, the only dark-skinned person to cross the invisible line separating the two groups. The room was sweltering.

Richie sat down just as the first reader was announced by the "facilitator," a pale, red-haired woman dressed in a black brassiere and a black petticoat over black tights. The poet was a young woman in black jeans and, daringly, a white shirt.

"This is a poem about LA," she drawled in a Valley accent. "It's called, 'The Seventh Circle.' It's based on, like, the *Inferno?*" She paused, waiting, apparently for some kind of recognition. When none came, she said, rhyming the name with *panty*, "By Dante? Dante Alighieri?"

"Just read the fucking poem," a bearded hipster called out.

"Whatever," she sniffed, and began her declamation.

It was a long, bad poem, and well before she finished, the restless audience had drowned her out.

"Hey," she protested. "This isn't the movies. Shut up."

"Sit down, sit down," her bearded heckler yelled.

"Fuck you," she said, and went on reading her poem. There was scattered applause when she sat down. Richie nudged me and said, "Let's get out of here."

"I'm with you."

"What was that all about?" Richie laughed, when we were safely outside.

"I think she was trying to compare LA to hell," I said.

"Please," he said, lighting a Marlboro. "Hell is where you go when you want a vacation from LA. What the fuck's the seventh circle?"

"Have you ever read Dante?"

He stared at me. "I saw the movie. The Norma Shearer original, not the Debbie Reynolds remake. Of course I never read Dante. Have you?"

"In college. The *Inferno* gave me nightmares, it was scarier than anything Stephen King has ever written. The seventh circle is where Dante puts the violent, including homosexuals . . ."

"Violent fags? What did they do, mix stripes with plaids?"

"Dante was Catholic, of course, so he thought of sodomy as an act against nature and homosexuals as the violent against nature. The seventh circle was a plain of burning sand. The souls of homosexuals are forced to run around the perimeter of the plain for eternity while a burning rain bakes them."

We walked to my car in silence, past shuttered shops and a Mexican bar. From inside I heard a *rancheria* I recognized as one of my father's favorites.

"So let me see if I get this," Richie said. "You've got all these guys running on a track, so they're in good shape, and there's this burning rain that keeps them tan. Gee, Henry, that doesn't sound like hell to me. It sounds like Palm Springs."

We got into my car. "Where to, Richie?"

"Well, there's nothing decent here," he said, dismissing, with a sweeping gesture, the entire east side of Los Angeles. "Spago? No, it's Tuesday. No one there but tourists. The Ivy? Even I can't get us in without a reservation. Maple Drive's too 90210. I know. Musso's. I love their creamed spinach."

MUSSO AND FRANK'S was the oldest restaurant in Hollywood, a place of dark wood, high-backed booths, starched tablecloths, elderly white-jacketed waiters, lethal martinis and a menu that listed such antiquarian items as consommé and a salad of iceberg lettuce. It was on Hollywood Boulevard, not far from Richie's office, on the tenth floor of a high-rise that overlooked what Richie insisted on calling *Grauman's* Chinese Theater, long after everyone else had accepted its change of ownership and name to Mann's Theater. Such sites were holy places to Richie, who often said everything he knew about life he'd learned from watching old movies. And it was true that while he might not have read Dante, he could recite big chunks of Gloria Swanson's dialogue from *Sunset Boulevard* by heart or rattle off the filmography of Maria Ouspenskaya.

I understood Richie's childhood devotion to old movies, because I had been as devoted to books, which, just as his movies did for him, helped me escape the loneliness of being different by creating an alternative reality where I was not alone. Richie had once told me the only thing that had kept him alive in the private mental institution to which his parents had committed him when he was fourteen was creeping into the day room at midnight to watch the late show.

"THE LAST TIME I was here," Richie confided over his martini at Musso's, "Bob Hope came tottering down the aisle. His *hair*, Henry. Bright orange. And his face looked like it was carved out of tapioca."

"What are you going to say about the poetry reading?"

"Blah, blah, blah. I only need a couple of 'graphs. Did you get a look at that blond by the door? Yummy. Of course, he's an actor." Richie smirked. "I think every actor in town ought to wear a sign that says, 'I am not a real person, I am an actor.' "

Our waiter came, a fussy ancient whose six dyed strands of hair were carefully plastered across his bald pate. He moued his disapproval over my order of an omelet and a salad, but Richie made up for it, ordering filet mignon in béarnaise sauce, a baked potato, broiled mushrooms, creamed spinach, a Caesar salad and a half-bottle of Bordeaux. I knew from other meals with him that Richie would eat every bite, then demand dessert, and yet he never gained weight. "I'm blessed with a starlet's metabolism," he boasted when I pointed this out to him, but a likelier reason was that his father used to scream at him at the dinner table to act like a man until Richie was so terrified his throat closed up.

"Alex Amerian is an actor," I said, after the waiter left. "He seemed real enough."

Richie raised an eyebrow. "Don't tell me you're sweet on him."

"Could you be serious for a moment?"

He dropped the supercilious eyebrow. "What's wrong, Henry?"

"I think I'm cracking up here."

All affectation vanished. "Tell me," he said quietly.

I told him everything, about the frantic work and the aimless driving, the incident at Griffith Park, parking in front of Alex's house, the neighbor who'd run me off, the shame, confusion, grief. I trusted Richie to understand me despite our many differences, because when I lay in bed at night in a small town in California, reading about Achilles and Patroclus, while he sat in front of a TV set in suburban Ohio, watching Joan Crawford in *Rain*, we had been learning the same lesson about the impossibility of our desire; a lesson that, as grown men, we were still trying to overcome.

"Ask him out," Richie said, when I finished.

"Alex? Just like that?"

"That's what people do when they're interested in someone," he said, signaling the waiter for another drink.

"It's all mixed up with Josh."

"Alex isn't Josh. You'll see that when you spend some time with him."

"What if he says no?"

Richie said, "He won't."

Dinner arrived and we talked about other things. We were drinking coffee when Richie's eyes widened at something or someone behind me. A tall, thickly built man in a beautifully tailored suit passed our table, with a thin woman on his arm. He nodded acknowledgment at Richie.

"Who is that?" I asked.

Richie dabbed his mouth with a napkin. "Are you serious? That's Duke Asuras."

"And he is?"

"The head of Parnassus Pictures, Henry."

"Oh, he's the guy who said Hollywood's going to take over the world," I said, telling Richie about the article in the *Times*.

"Don't think he can't do it," Richie said.

"Who was that woman with him? His wife?"

Richie snorted. "He's not married. That was Cheryl Cordet."

I was trying to place the name. "Isn't that—"

Richie stood up, again dabbing his mouth on a napkin. "I'll be back in five minutes." He returned in three. "Come on."

"Where?"

"Duke asked us to join them for a drink." He threw some money on the table. "You mind?"

"No, I've never met a movie mogul before."

I followed Richie through the restaurant to a remote booth that was further protected by a curtained doorway. He poked his head in, mumbled something, and then pulled the curtain back and said to me, "Hop in."

I slid into the booth. Richie followed and drew the curtain shut. The booth was very cold. Asuras and Cordet sat across from us, their backs to the wall. A wall lamp cast a pinkish light. A candle flickered on the table. The remains of a shrimp cocktail lay between them. Asuras was tanned to the color of mahogany. His bright blue eyes were the liveliest feature in a bullet-shaped, bull-necked head. He was bald except for patches of side hair which were shaved to salt-and-pepper stubble. Thick eyebrows, a flat nose and a wide mouth conveyed power and appetite. His shoulders were massive beneath the crepe-like material of his black suit—a weight lifter's shoulders—but his jowl had begun to sag. He conveyed a combination of strength and self-indulgence, and his heavy, imperious face recalled profiles of a first-century Caesar on an ancient coin.

Cheryl Cordet was a thin woman, with pale skin and a frizz of graying blond hair. She had a strong, plain face and small, shrewd eyes. Her black sheath dress was made for someone younger and more opulent and it hung on her gracelessly. She radiated nearly as much authority as he did and, despite the intimacy implied by the candlelit booth, the shared food, romance was distinctly not in the air.

When Richie finished making introductions, Cheryl Cordet said, "You never returned my calls, Henry."

"I beg your pardon?"

"You defended the guy who was accused of killing the gay judge. His boyfriend? You got him off. I had my people call you to discuss selling the rights to his story."

I had a vague recollection of talking to someone about the movie rights to the Chandler case. I remembered that the caller's eagerness to buy the story had been exceeded only by his ignorance of the events.

"I wasn't interested." I said.

"I remember that case," Asuras said. "I don't know, the gay angle would be a problem."

"We could change that," Cordet said. "Soften it. Maybe make the boyfriend a girl? What do you think, Henry?"

The conversation was so ludicrous, I didn't know what to say.

"Speaking of gay," Asuras rumbled, in a voice so deep I thought he had bronchitis, "I read that piece in your magazine about attacks on homosexuals, Richie. Kind of an unusual piece for you, wasn't it? You're not the *Advocate*."

"We cover the news," Richie said.

"I guess you checked to make sure what those people in the piece said was true."

"Yeah," he said. "Of course. I'm a serious journalist, Duke."

Asuras grinned. "Come on, Richie. As a journalist you're somewhere between Liz Smith and the *National Enquirer*."

"Well, in the interests of accuracy, Duke," Richie said, "is it true the board of Parnassus Company is still trying to get you fired?"

Asuras turned a slow, angry gaze on him. "I better not be reading that in your magazine."

"Is that a denial?"

"You ought to know better than to play games with me," he said.

Cheryl Cordet glanced at her watch and said, "God, Duke, it's almost eleven and I've got be on the set at five. Mind if we cut this short?"

RICHIE AND I stood outside, waiting for the valet to bring my car. He was uncharacteristically quiet.

"Maybe I don't understand the nuances here," I said, "but did you just get into a pissing match with that guy because he criticized your gay-bashing piece?"

"That's not the piece he's worried about," Richie said.

"What do you mean?"

"Do you know anything about Duke Asuras?"

"No," I said. "Hollywood's your obsession, not mine."

He lit a cigarette. "That's right," he said. "I love the movies and I'm not going to let Duke Asuras destroy them."

"I don't know what you're talking about."

The car came. The valet opened the passenger door and Richie deflated into the front seat. "Let me give you a crash course in the Industry," he said. "The first thing you need to understand is that Hollywood isn't one place, it's two. LA, where the studios are and the movies get made, and New York, where the companies that own the studios are headquartered. It's been that way forever, moviemakers versus moneymen, art versus commerce." He blew a smoke ring. "Movies are risky investments. When they pay big, they pay really big, but when they flop, they can take a company down with them, like *Heaven's Gate* killed United Artists. Every year, the cost of making movies climbs higher and higher until now, a medium-sized, medium-budget, no-big-name movie is costing a studio like Parnassus around fifty million to make."

"That's astonishing."

"The moneymen try to contain the costs of their investment in case it goes down the toilet. The moviemakers complain that the only thing the penny-pinching accomplishes is to make sure the movies will suck and lose money. It goes back and forth between New York and Hollywood on almost every movie that gets made by the big studios."

"Is that why you asked Asuras about his board?"

"Yeah. Duke runs Parnassus Pictures, but he doesn't run Parnassus Company in New York. He answers to the president, Allen Raskin, and Raskin answers to the board of directors, and most of them are Wall Street types who know shit about movies. Raskin does. His grandfather was one of the original producers at Parnassus, back in the thirties and forties. His dad was an exec at Parnassus. When he became president, the company was about to go under because of the idiot they had hired to run things before him. He brought Duke back from the dead and made him studio president. That was four years ago. Now Parnassus is the most successful studio in town."

"Then why would the board want to fire Asuras?"

"Because he's a crook," Richie replied.

"What does that mean?"

"It means he's a crook, Henry. He steals."

I pulled up in front of Richie's building. "Steals what?"

"Money," Richie said. "Duke started out as an agent representing some big names. He perfected the art of packaging, putting together stars with directors and writers and forcing them all down a studio's throat while he picked up multiple commissions. One of his clients was Twila Rhodes. You remember her?"

"No," I said.

"I'm not surprised," Richie said. "She was a second-tier actress with a drug problem. Duke forged her name on twenty thousand dollars in checks."

"He couldn't have borrowed it?"

"He didn't need it. The guy was clearing a couple of million a year."

"Then why did he do it?"

"Why does a dog lick its balls?" Richie said. "Because it can."

"That's it?"

"Look up 'greedy,' 'stupid' and 'arrogant' in the dictionary," he said, "and you'll find pictures of studio executives and movie agents. Of course, Duke told a much more complicated story when he was found out. He said he had a nervous breakdown, that it was an act of self-sabotage. You know, the diminished-capacity defense."

"Did the jury buy it?"

"It didn't get that far," Richie said. "Twila Rhodes overdosed and there was no one left to prosecute. But the scandal drove Duke out of agenting. He laid low for a while then started up an independent production company that had a couple of big hits before he suddenly quit and left the country to 'find himself.'"

"I can hear the quotation marks in your voice."

He flicked his cigarette out the window. "The rumor is that his partners caught him embezzling again and gave him the option of resigning or going to jail."

"And then Raskin brought him back from the dead?"

"From Thailand, actually," Richie said. "In any other business he'd be considered a criminal. In Hollywood, he's a victim, but not to the Parnassus board."

"Moral scruples?"

"Give me a break," he scoffed. "With Duke as head of the studio, Parnassus's stock has never done as well as it should have, given the company's earnings. The board thinks it's because Wall Street doesn't like a crook at the till. They've been looking for a reason to get rid of him, but as long as he was making them piles of money, they were stuck. Last year, he lost money, ten million, not much, but it was all the board needed to start screaming for his head. When Raskin refused to fire him, they started threatening him."

"What happened?"

"Raskin and Duke decided to counterattack."

"How?"

"That's the piece Duke's afraid of." He opened the door. "Goodnight, Henry. Remember Mother's advice. Call Alex."

I didn't give Richie's account of the nefarious goings on at Parnassus Company any more thought that night, and when I woke up the next morning, the details were already receding. The gist of it seemed to be crooks versus assholes, which more or less summed up Hollywood as far as I could tell. But I did call Alex.

chapter 4

"HELLO, ALEX? IT'S Henry. Rios."

"Mr. Rios?" Alarm crept into his voice. "Is there a problem with my case?"

"No, nothing like that," I replied, as reassuringly as my own nervousness permitted. "This is a social call, to see how you are."

"Everything's great."

In the pause that followed I wandered into the dining room and caught my reflection in the gilt mirror—a gift from Richie—that hung on the wall. There I saw a tall, thin man in khakis and a denim shirt with a long face and prematurely—well, at forty-five maybe not so prematurely anymore—white hair. Dark-skinned, the face unmistakably *mestizo* and clearly middle-aged. What did Richie say? After thirty-five, gay men aged in dog years.

I temporized, "That's good, Alex." Then, in a rush, "I was wondering if you'd like to have dinner sometime, take in a movie?"

A pause. "Are you asking me out on a date?"

My face was on fire. "Something like that."

"That would be great. When?"

I was so invested in rejection, it took me a minute to respond. "What about—are you free on Friday?"

"Friday's cool," he said.

We made arrangements to meet for dinner at a restaurant on Third Street and then take in a movie at the Beverly Center called *Letters*. I put the phone down and took another look at myself in the mirror. I had mysteriously become better-looking.

ACCORDING TO THE *Times* movie critic, *Letters* was a "postmodern remake of Agatha Christie's book, *The ABC Murders*," a description I couldn't begin to fathom except that I gathered it was a lot grislier than Dame Agatha's original, which I vaguely remembered having read as a teenager. It was playing to sold-out houses, so on Friday morning I drove to the Beverly Center as soon as the box office opened and bought two tickets for the nine o'clock show. I spent the morning downtown at the county law library, and the afternoon in Santa Monica with my accountant, trying to figure out how to pay my taxes. Josh had had no health insurance, and his parents, who were retired and lived on a fixed income, could not shoulder the burden. I had picked up the tab for everything Medicare refused to pay, including the twenty-four-hour nursing care that allowed him to die at home instead of a hospital. The bills had pretty much exhausted my savings, and caring for him had played havoc with my practice, leaving me, basically, broke. The IRS was not sympathetic. I resolved the crisis by emptying my last retirement accounts. I promised Marty, my accountant, that I would try to pay myself back as soon as I could, because, as he reminded me, "You're not getting any younger, Henry. You're going to need that money."

Back at home, I took a shower then stood at the closet for a long time, water puddling at my feet, looking for something to wear in a wardrobe that seemed to consist either of dark suits or blue jeans and tee shirts. In the recesses of my closet, I found a black motorcycle jacket, the grain of the leather carefully distressed by the manufacturer. I lay it on the bed. A bright green sticker over the right breast proclaimed ACT UP FIGHT AIDS. The coat had belonged to Josh, a souvenir of his days as an AIDS activist, when he was still well enough to sit through hours of Act Up meetings or spend the night in jail after being arrested at demonstrations at the federal building or the county hospital. He had met Steven at one of those demonstrations and left me for him to join the army of lovers battling for a cure for AIDS, trying to save their own lives. I remembered what Richie had said about wondering why he had survived while others had died. I wondered that, too, from time to time. I ran my hands over the jacket; maybe we survived to remember the ones who hadn't.

I went back into the closet and found a white, banded-collar shirt I had bought in an attempt to update my clothes and had yet to wear. I paired it with my least-faded Levis, a black belt with a silver buckle and black shoes. For a second I considered wearing Josh's jacket, but it would've looked absurd on me. I threw on a black linen blazer, and studied the result in the gilt mirror. The combination of the collarless white shirt and black blazer made me look like a priest. Not exactly the effect I was after. I tossed the coat aside and headed out.

I DROVE TO the restaurant with the windows down, a warm breeze blowing through the car. The air was drenched in a cantaloupe-colored light that faded things to the hues of an old, hand-tinted postcard. I had never really been on a date. In high school and college I watched from afar as straight friends performed the dance of courtship while I buried my head in books and ran distance on the track team. When I finally stumbled into a world of men like myself in San Francisco in the sexually liberated seventies, a date was the hour or two you spent drinking before you found someone to go home with. Josh and I had not so much dated as collided in the midst of a murder case in which he was a witness. Dinner and a movie was a first for me.

Alex hadn't arrived at the Trattoria and the host sat me a table to wait. The restaurant was a single large room partitioned by a concrete wall with rectangular openings across it. The floors were also concrete, as was the ceiling with its exposed pipes and track lights. The walls were sponged a marmalade orange. The distant overhead lights and the candles flickering in brass wall sconces cast a low, flattering light over the sleek clientele, but with nothing to absorb the sound and an exposed kitchen, the room was also noisy and hot. The fashionable men and women fanned themselves with menus and shouted at each other over their fancy risottos. Fading sunlight seeped in through tall windows that looked out on Third Street to a car wash, a vacant lot and a store that sold secondhand clothes once worn by movie stars. I ate crusty bread, was glowered at by a movie star I happened to notice and declined the waiter's offers of wine.

Alex arrived a half-hour late. I saw him at the door wearing white jeans, white sneakers, a sky-blue La Coste polo shirt. He spoke to the host, who bent forward to listen and then pointed in my direction. Alex looked and nodded. Approaching me, he smiled. He had been so much the subject of my fantasies that it was as startling to see him in the flesh as it had been to see the movie star. He was shorter than I remembered and more muscular, and he moved with a confidence I didn't recognize, but of course the last time I'd seen him was in a courthouse, a place that tested most people's confidence.

"I'm sorry I'm late," he said, kissing my cheek, a gesture that went unnoticed in that crowd. He was still using Obsession.

"Traffic?"

"I walked," he replied. "It was a lot farther than I thought. I'm so used to driving I can't get the hang of distances without a car."

"Your car break down again?"

He looked at me blankly. "It was blown up."

"When did that happen?"

"Didn't I tell you? About six weeks ago, right in front of my house."

"Good God. Do you know who did it?"

He shook his head. "It was in the middle of the night. I think it must have been a gay bashing, because I had one of those bumper stickers that said, 'How dare you presume I'm straight.' I was always getting flipped off on the freeway."

"Do you really believe people go around blowing up cars because they disagree with the politics of someone's bumper stickers?"

He mopped his forehead with his napkin. "It's happened to other cars in my neighborhood, too. They all had some kind of gay bumper sticker," he said. "You don't live in West Hollywood; you don't know the kinds of things that go on."

"Did you report it to the police?"

"The police," he said contemptuously.

"You should've called me. I could've done something."

He smiled. "I like that shirt on you. Every other time I've seen you, you were wearing a suit."

"Every other time you've seen me, I've been working."

"You don't have to work tonight," he said. "Let's forget about my car. I'm starved. What's good here?"

Over dinner, he told me he'd been raised in Foster City, outside of San Francisco, and gone to San Francisco State where he began as a business major to please his father, but then switched to drama, his true interest.

"How did your parents react to that?" I asked.

"My dad told me I was throwing away my life," he said, pulping the peas on his plate. "That was ten years ago. He and my mom have come around. Kind of."

"They know you're gay?"

He smiled. "Our family invented 'don't ask, don't tell.' "

"How did you get to LA?"

"After I graduated, I spent a couple years at the American Conservatory Theater in the city. An agent from down here saw me in *Ah, Wilderness!* and said I had what it takes to be a movie star. I moved here and called him. He didn't remember me." He sipped some wine. "I found another agent. She got me a couple of commercials, a couple of walk-ons, then nothing."

"The competition for work must be brutal."

"Yeah," he said, "I never knew how many ways there were to fail until I moved here."

"I don't understand."

"Hollywood's like a staircase that gets narrower and narrower," he said. "Everyone starts out together, but at each step there's less room and at the top step there's only room for one. Meanwhile, a fresh crop is always starting out at the bottom, younger and prettier."

"What do you do to keep climbing?"

"Whatever I have to," he said. "Have you always wanted to be a lawyer?"

"Yeah, since I was a kid."

"Why?"

"I had this idea that lawyers helped people."

"Not to get rich?" he asked with genuine curiosity.

"Very few criminal-defense lawyers get rich," I said. "Anyway, making money's never been a priority."

"What is?"

"Living life on my own terms, I guess. What about you?"

"I want it all," he said. "I want to be rich and famous."

I touched my water glass to his wine glass. "Good luck."

"You must think I'm pretty shallow."

"No, I don't," I lied.

"Because I *am* pretty shallow," he said, smiling. "You should know that about me, so you won't be disappointed."

"Why should I be disappointed?"

"I'm a hustler, Henry," he said. "That's how I support myself while I wait to be discovered."

I let it sink in that the object of my obsession was a prostitute; that instead of anguishing over how to approach him for the last month and a half, I could simply have bought his services. I couldn't repress a harsh laugh, at my foolishness. I saw the anger in Alex's eyes and apologized.

"I'm sorry," I said. "I'm not laughing at you."

"Then what's so funny?" he asked, unmollified.

"I confused you with someone else."

"Josh," he said. "Your lover. You said I looked like him."

I nodded. "Yes, I confused you with Josh and I imagined I had feelings for you that I had for him."

"And you think it's funny now because I'm a hustler?"

"I'm sorry, I don't mean to be an asshole. Your business is your business. I'm not judging you. Josh is gone and he's not coming back. If I didn't laugh, I'd cry."

His anger faded. "You know why I said yes when you asked me out, Henry?"

"No."

"Because of the way you kissed me when we were at the court. You kissed him that way, didn't you?"

I nodded.

"That's what I thought," he said. "I could feel all that emotion in you for him. You know, it was really beautiful, Henry." The waiter came and cleared our plates. After he left, Alex said, "I want to be him for you tonight."

"You can't."

"There's no charge."

"That's not what I meant."

"Listen to me, Henry," he said. "I'm not a lawyer like you, so I don't get to help people — not that I want to most of the time. I've got my own problems, but you helped me."

"You don't owe me for that."

"I wouldn't care if I did," he said, "but there's something about the way you treated me, the way you looked at me, that made me feel better about myself. It doesn't matter that it was because when you looked at me you saw him. I felt the love." He touched my hand beneath the table. "One time, no strings. Let me be Josh."

I looked at him. "It's too weird, Alex."

"Believe me, Henry," he replied. "Compared to most of the things I'm asked to do, it's really sweet."

"HOW DID YOU get from acting to . . ."

"Hustling?"

We had decided to skip the movie and were on our way to my house. The long summer dusk was holding in the sky, the violent pinks and oranges fading slowly into a gunpowder gray above the spindly palm trees.

"It's all the same thing," he was saying. "You act a part."

"I meant . . ."

"I know what you meant," he said. He turned on the radio and changed the dial from the classical station to a dance station. "It's not complicated. I needed money so I posed for a gay skin magazine. After the magazine came out, I got a call from someone who said he was a friend of a big agent who had seen my picture and wondered if I'd like to come to a party at his house in Malibu." He smirked. "A pool party, of course. When I showed up, it was a bunch of twenty-five-year-olds posing around the pool in their Speedos and four middle-aged guys sort of pointing their fingers like, 'I'll take you and you and you.' "

"The agent was one of them?"

"It was the agent, a director, a producer and a guy who had just bought a studio. You've heard of them," he said, and told me their names.

"The boys were all actors, like you?"

"Porno stars mostly," he said. "I found out that these guys basically use porn movies and skin magazines like catalogues. Anyway, the agent picked me. I was with him for a while, then with the director. After that, there were other people. I didn't ask for money at first because I still thought I was using these guys to help me with my career, but one day I realized, this was my career, so I better get something from it."

"How long have you been at it?"

"Going on three years," he said. "That's a long time, but I'm small and I look younger than I am. That kid brother look. Guys go crazy for it." He smiled. "Doesn't it bother you that we're talking like this? Doesn't it ruin the fantasy?"

"It's like you said at the restaurant, Alex, I don't have to work tonight. You don't, either."

"I'm getting out of the life," he said quietly.

"I've heard it's hard," I replied.

"You don't know how hard," he said. "Most of the guys who hire me hate themselves for being gay, so they take it out on me."

I DIDN'T UNDERSTAND how literally he meant that until I saw the bruises on his back when he removed his shirt. We were in the bedroom. He had stopped me when I reached for the light, and the room was filled with the shadows. I was standing at the foot of the bed. He was facing me with his back to the mirror and I saw in the murky glass the angry slashes across his smooth dark skin. He kicked off his shoes, unbuttoned his pants, removed them, stood naked, approached me.

"What happened to your back?"

He stopped, saw Josh's coat on the bed. "Was this his?"

"Your back."

He slipped the coat on. "Do I look like him?"

I forgot about the bruises. "Yes."

"Come here, Henry," he said. "Remind me what it feels like when someone loves you."

I slipped my hands beneath the coat and stroked his back.

WE MADE LOVE in darkness and in silence. It had been such a long time for me that at first it felt awkward as if my body was remembering the taboo against the nakedness of another man that had once kept me locked in my desire like a prisoner. I emptied my mind and let myself feel the body beside me, at once familiar and mysterious, mouth, chest, penis, thigh, until touch dissolved the barriers and we were one body. And then I became aware that the damp sheets beneath him smelled of Josh. I said, "Josh?" He opened his eyes and smiled at me. "It is me, Henry," he said. It was Josh's voice, and the eyes that held me in their gaze were Josh's eyes. "How?" I asked. He lifted my hand to his lips, kissed it, and murmured, "This feels so good. Don't stop." I buried myself in him, closed my eyes and came in a scalding orgasm, a cauterizing orgasm that closed a wound inside of me. When I opened my eyes again, Alex was looking at me. I lay down beside him, afraid to speak.

"He was here," Alex whispered. He touched his chest. "I could feel him here."

"I thought I saw him in your eyes."

He shivered. "This is so spooky."

I held him. "Are you afraid?"

"Not of Josh," he said. "Because he's gone, Henry. This time he's really gone."

"I feel that, too. But you are afraid, aren't you?"

"I saw something."

"What?"

"It was like he opened a door as he was leaving," Alex said. "And just for a second I saw death."

"IS THIS HIM?" Alex asked. We were in the living room, waiting for his cab. I sat on the couch in a bathrobe, watching him pick up the urn with Josh's ashes from the mantel. He was jittery, pacing the room, avoiding my eyes.

"Yes," I said.

" 'Joshua Scott Mandel,' " he said, reading the plate on the urn. "Are you going to keep them like this, on your fireplace?"

"It's a long story."

He returned the urn to its place, glanced at his watch. "Where's that fucking cab?"

"You could stay here," I said, repeating an offer I'd made earlier, but his mood made me less enthusiastic.

"I have an appointment."

"With the man who left those marks on your back?"

"Maybe," he said, his eyes suddenly cold. "Not that it's any of your business."

"Why are you so angry, Alex?"

"Did I say I was angry?"

"It's like you're punishing me because you felt something in there," I said, gesturing to the bedroom.

"Hey, don't get carried away," he said, impatiently. Outside, a car horn honked. "I'm not the one who was doing the feeling in there."

"What do you mean, 'don't get carried away'?"

He moved toward the door. "Remember what I told you, Henry. Acting and hustling are the same thing. You play a part."

I restrained him as he reached for the door. "It didn't feel like you were acting."

He shook himself free. "You got off, didn't you? That's the important thing."

"Don't say that."

He half-closed his eyes and murmured, " 'It is me, Henry. It's Josh.' "

"That's not what it sounded like."

"You were two seconds from coming," he said. "You heard what you wanted to hear."

I stepped back, stared at him. "You asshole."

He laughed. "Oh, come on, honey. I gave you the ride of your life and I didn't even charge you."

"Get out of here."

"Okay, but next time you want to fuck your boyfriend, baby, call La Toya's psychic line."

I grabbed him by the back of his collar and threw him against the door. He slumped to the floor, holding his hand over his nose. Blood seeped from between his fingers.

"Fuck," he said, getting to his feet. "I think you broke my nose."

"Jesus," I said, appalled. "I'm sorry. Let me get you a towel or something."

"Don't touch me." The cab honked again. He grabbed at the doorknob with bloody fingers and yanked the door open. "Man," he said, shaking his head. "Are all you fags crazy?"

He slammed the door behind him. I heard him say something to the cab driver and then the car sped off, wheels squealing. A drop of his blood dripped from the door knob to the floor.

I FELL ASLEEP on the couch, and when I woke up, late the next morning, a bitter sourness puckered my mouth. My head throbbed. The house was silent, but it was more than the usual morning stillness. This quiet was as dusty and thick as a tomb. Dazed, I wandered from room to room. There were dirty dishes in the kitchen sink, mold in the shower, a layer of powdery film over the furniture, and the air was rank. In the bedroom, the sheets were stained with semen and a bottle of lubricant had fallen on its side and spread a puddle of goo on the floor. A condom floated in the toilet bowl. I opened the medicine cabinet, searching for aspirin, and was confronted by row after row of Josh's medications. Pills, syrups, ointments, hundreds, thousands of dollars' worth. I picked a bottle at random: Xanax, prescribed for the anxiety attacks that consumed him when his head cleared from all the other drugs long enough for him to realize he was dying. I poured the pills into the sink, then grabbed another bottle, Prozac for depression, and then an ointment I had rubbed on the parts of his body where his flesh had begun to necrotize. I didn't stop until the medicine cabinet was empty.

"ARE YOU ALL right? You look like you're suffering from sunstroke."

I looked at the woman who had spoken, puzzled by the inflections in her voice that were both Southern and English. She was sitting on the stone bench in the courtyard of the Columbarium of Radiant Destiny, with the messy remains of lunch beside her: an apple core, balled up wax paper, a rind of bread. She was wearing a white blouse, a foamy, flowered skirt, Birkenstock sandals and a red straw cowboy hat over messy gray hair. Her face was pitted with small, deep scars and deeply seamed but the architecture of her bones was beautiful. Her eyes were sky blue.

"Sit down," she said. There was a green mesh bag at her side with a thermos in it. She reached for it. "Have some tea."

I sat down, still clutching the map I'd been given when I had driven into the cemetery.

"Thank you," I mumbled, accepting a plastic glass of cloudy liquid.

"It doesn't do any good if you don't drink it," she said kindly.

I took a swallow. It was cold, strong and sweet. "This is good."

"My mother was English," she explained. "She taught how to brew real tea, though it would've killed her to see me drink it cold. Ah, well, one must adjust. Are you visiting someone?"

Three of the walls of the Columbarium of Radiant Destiny held rows of niches where the ashes of the dead were interred behind marble plaques. The fourth wall, behind us, was a doorway that led out to the other vaults and columbaria of the Courts of Remembrance and from there to the green hillsides of Forest Lawn with its view of the freeway and Warner Brothers.

"No," I said. "I was looking for someplace to put my friend's ashes."

"Oh, he'd like it here," she said. "My husband does." She pointed a bony finger. "That's him."

"Gregory Slade," I read.

"Yes, and I'm Amiga."

"Amiga?"

"I know it's an odd name, but as I said, my mother was English. She married a Texan, who took her to live in a small town down by the Gulf where people were terribly prejudiced against the Mexicans, but my mother thought they were wonderful people and that Spanish was the most beautiful language she had ever heard." She squinted at me. "You're of Mexican descent, if I'm not mistaken. Finish your tea. There's more."

"How do you know your husband's happy here?"

"I know," she said.

"I don't think the dead are either happy or unhappy," I said. "They're just dead."

"If you truly believed that," she replied, "you wouldn't care about your friend's ashes. You really do look unwell. Are you sure you're all right?"

"There's a religion that believes the world was created by the devil, that this is hell."

"Of course, it's hell," Amiga Slade said cheerfully. "It's also heaven. It depends entirely on how you look at it." She touched my hand. "Whatever you think you've done, it's not so terrible that you deserve to be condemned to hell."

"I'm a homosexual."

"What does that matter to God? He made you."

"My friend died of AIDS."

"I'm so sorry," she said, grasping my hand. "I am so sorry."

"I can't let go of him."

"But Henry you don't have to," she said. "You can put him here with Greg, and the four of us can visit."

"I didn't tell you my name," I said.

She touched the center of her forehead. "I have second sight. Another gift of my English mother." She reached into her mesh bag and brought out a slab of yellow cake wrapped in wax paper. "You're hungry," she said. "Eat this."

It was dense and moist and sugary. I wolfed it down. "What do you do?" I asked her between bites.

She smiled, "I'm a fortune teller at a coffeehouse in Venice. Madame Helene. The kids love me. One of them even designed a Website for me."

I licked the crumbs of the cake from my fingers. "What's my fortune?" "Nothing that can't be survived," she said, "but be careful who you trust." It was late in the afternoon when I returned home. After I had left Amiga Slade and Forest Lawn, I looked at the adjacent Jewish cemetery, Mount Sinai, but I wasn't sure that interring Josh's ashes there wouldn't strike his parents as adding insult to injury. At any rate, by the time I pulled into my garage, it no longer seemed as urgent that I dispose of Josh's ashes as it had when I'd left, after dumping his medicines and cleaning out the closet of the last of his clothes. I was still unable to think about the previous night without remorse and shame. I had lost myself in this obsession for Alex the same way I had once lost myself in a bottle. Sitting in the Columbarium of Radiant Destiny with Amiga Slade, I had had a revelation that the death I was running from wasn't Josh's but my own. For two years I'd watched him die, cell by cell, and in the murk beneath consciousness it had awakened my own terror of death. My maniacal busyness was a kind of prolonged anxiety attack and now that I understood that, maybe the real grieving could start.

THE MESSAGE LIGHT was flashing on my answering machine. I played back the messages, three of them, all from Richie, each more urgent than the last. I picked up the phone and dialed his number. He picked up on the first ring.

"Henry?"

"Hi, Richie. What's so important?"

"Where have you been all day?"

"Looking at cemeteries. Why?"

"Alex Amerian was with you last night, wasn't he?"

"How did you know that?"

"That's not important. When did he leave your house?"

"I don't know, between eleven and midnight. Why?"

"He's been murdered. They found his body in a Dumpster in Vaseline Alley."

chapter 5

"ARE YOU SURE?"

"I heard it from one of the cops at the scene," Richie said. "What happened last night?"

From where I was standing I could see across the breakfast counter into the kitchen. There was a rag in the sink with Alex Amerian's blood on it.

"Do you think I killed him?"

"No, of course not," Richie said. "It must have happened after he left you. Did he say where he was going?"

I had walked into the kitchen. I picked the rag out of the sink and carried it into the pantry, where I tossed it into the washing machine.

"Henry?"

"He didn't say. I assumed it was a john."

There was a pause. "He told you he was a hustler."

Something clicked. "You hired him last night."

"That's crazy. He didn't come here."

"No," I said. "You hired him to go out with me."

"I was only trying to help you get over this thing you had about him and Josh."

"With what, a sex exorcism?" I asked bitterly.

"He wasn't supposed to tell you."

"It was part of his act," I said. "The hardened pro with the heart of gold. Was that your idea, too? Well, it didn't work, Richie. He couldn't keep up the act. His mask slipped and it got a little ugly at the end."

"What happened?"

"I shoved him, he hurt himself."

"How bad."

"A bloody nose."

"That doesn't sound like you, Henry," he said.

"Maybe my mask slipped a little, too."

Richie said, "He kept an appointment book. Your name will be in it for last night."

"Then so will the name of his last appointment."

"You were supposed to be his last appointment," Richie said. "I paid him for an all-nighter."

The bloody rag, my name in his appointment book. I felt a surge of panic. "Have you talked to his roommate?" I asked. "Katie?"

"The speed-freak fag hag? I've been calling all day. The line is busy."

"Maybe he told her where he was going last night after he left here."

"She deals drugs, Henry. If she gets wind that Alex is dead and the cops are coming, she'll split."

"Then I'd better get to her first," I said.

THE MOMENT I got into my car, I went into lawyer mode. I'd had sex and then scuffled with Alex Amerian hours before he was murdered. I knew exactly how those circumstances would look to a cop and what they would do with them. Once they focused on a suspect, the object of their investigation was to establish guilt. It was up to me to find exonerating evidence now, before I was incriminated. Meanwhile, I kept a lid on my feelings about Alex's murder.

I parked across the street from Alex's house where I'd so often kept nocturnal vigil the past few weeks. There were no signs of cops in the vicinity. I got out and walked to his front door. When no one responded to the bell, I tried the door. It was unlocked.

"Katie, are you . . . ?" The words died in my mouth. I saw why Richie had been getting a busy signal when he called. The phone had been yanked from the jack and left in the hall. I saw no other immediate sign of disturbance, but the air was charged. I proceeded down the hall, glanced into the kitchen. There were dirty dishes in the sink. I made my way to the bedrooms in the back of the house. I deduced from the contents of the closets which room was Alex's and which was Katie's. In his room was a king-sized bed, a TV and VCR and a dresser. On top of the dresser was some change, unopened bills, a stack of men's fashion magazines, Detour, GQ. No sign of an appointment book.

She slept on a mattress on the floor and kept her clothes in cardboard boxes. She had fashioned a desk from two sawhorses and a piece of particle board. On the table were pay stubs from a temp agency. There was also a computer monitor, a keyboard and a printer but no computer. As I stared at the monitor, I realized there were no personal papers of any kind in either room, no letters, address books, Rolodexes. The rice-paper shade that covered her window stirred. I rolled it up. The window was open, the screen had been removed. The signs were subtle, but it looked like someone had entered the house and removed things. Her computer, Alex's appointment book, other papers of a personal nature. Unless, of course, the computer was being repaired, and he had taken his book with him, and there were no personal papers.

I slipped one of the pay stubs into my pocket and went out in the hall. At the other end of it, the door was thrown open and two uniformed sheriffs burst into the living room with their guns drawn.

"Put your hands way up in the air," one of them shouted at me.

I raised my hands. "I'm not armed," I said.

"Stay put," the first cop said, while the second one came toward me, gun still drawn, and patted me down.

"He's clean," he shouted to his partner. "You can put your hands down, but keep them where I can see them."

"What's going on here?" I asked.

A third man had entered the house. He was in plainclothes but unmistakably a cop. He had thinning silver hair, a big gut and a face like a mound of mashed potatoes. He was wearing mirrored sunglasses. As he approached me, he removed them revealing small, shrewd eyes that brought his soft, pale face into sharp relief, like a blurred movie image that comes suddenly into focus. I saw intelligence, caution, cynicism.

"I'm Sergeant Odell," he said. "Is that your black Accord parked across the street?"

"Yes," I said.

"And what's your name, sir?"

"Rios. Henry Rios."

"You want to step outside with me, Mr. Rios?"

"Why? What's going on here?"

"Well as near I can tell, you're trespassing."

"I know the people who live here."

Odell smiled. "It doesn't look like there's anyone here but us chickens."

"The door was unlocked. I was concerned. I came in."

"Why don't we talk about it outside," Odell said, taking me by the elbow. I shook him off. He stepped back and let me go ahead. The two uniformed deputies had holstered their revolvers but their postures warned me against sudden movement. I stepped out onto the porch, where another deputy was standing with a man in civilian clothes who looked remotely familiar to me.

"That's him," he said excitedly, pointing at me. "He's been parking in front of my house two, three times a week in the middle of the night, just watching this place. I told him if he didn't quit, I'd call the cops. Good thing I wrote down his license plate."

Odell breathed heavily beside me. A fat man's breath. "Good thing, huh," he murmured.

"I know the man who lives here," I told him. "His name is Alex Amerian."

"Uh-huh," Odell said. "Last night someone killed him, Mr. Rios. I'd like you to come down to the station and answer a few questions."

"You can question me here," I said.

"I'm not the man you need to talk to," he said. "That would be Detective Gaitan from Homicide and he's at the station." When I didn't immediately respond, he added quietly. "I could arrest you for trespassing and take you down in handcuffs. It's up to you."

"You don't have to do that," I said. "Let's go."

I WAS ASSISTED into the back of a patrol car. Odell got in beside me and we were driven down Santa Monica Boulevard the dozen or so blocks to the West Hollywood sheriff's station at San Vicente. It was Saturday afternoon and the carnival that the city became on weekend nights had already begun. The windows of Twenty-Four Hour Fitness, the block-long gym just west of La Cienega, were filled with young men diligently racking their muscles on chrome-and-steel machines. The boutiques and coffeehouses were filled with weekend gays who gave away their tourist status with clothes and haircuts that were six months behind the times. Skinny twentysomethings paraded around shirtless, revealing elaborate tattoos and piercings. An old-fashioned queen in a white caftan and painted eyebrows walked a brace of poodles, swaying slightly right to left as if acknowledging applause only he could hear. A teenage Latino boy in the passenger seat of the car in front of us stuck his head out of the window and screamed, "Motherfuckin' faggots!" at two suburban-looking men holding hands in front of a hamburger stand.

"Pull that kid over," Odell said to the deputy driving the car. He turned on the siren and flashed his lights at the car, a beaten-up low rider. It pulled to the curb across the street from the low brown-brick building that housed the sheriff. We came to a stop behind it.

"Now what, Sarge?" the deputy asked.

"Bring him back here."

The deputy got out, approached the car, talked to the driver. A moment later, the kid who had yelled the epithet got out of the car and was sullenly escorted to the patrol car. He was a skinny kid in a plaid shirt and jeans that were a half-dozen sizes too big for him hanging off his hips. A gang-banger. Odell rolled down his window and gestured to the deputy to bring the kid to him.

"I'm Sergeant Odell," he said. "What's your name, son?"

"I didn't do nothing," the kid replied.

"We'll get to that," Odell replied. "I asked you your name."

"Jimmy," he said sullenly. "Jimmy Saldana."

"Where you headed, Jimmy?"

"Venice."

"Where you coming from?"

"Boyle Heights."

"West Hollywood's a little out of your way, Jimmy," Odell said. "What are you doing here?"

The kid shrugged, stared at his feet.

"Come to look at the fags, huh?" Odell said.

Jimmy lifted his head and apparently thinking Odell was an ally, smiled. "Yeah, the freaks."

"Well, let me tell you something, Jimmy," Odell said, in a voice filled with quiet menace. "This is my town and these are my people. I keep a list of punks that come in here and now your name's on it. If I catch you again, I'll haul your sorry *cholo* ass to jail, where you'll get to meet the real freaks. Now get out of here and tell your partner to take the 10 next time he wants to go to Venice."

Furious but frightened, the boy shuffled off with as much dignity as his sagging pants allowed.

"That was an illegal detention," I said.

Odell looked at me. "You a lawyer?"

"Yes."

He smiled. "Interesting."

WE PULLED INTO the parking lot behind the station where the patrol cars were parked and came in through the back entrance into a corridor. Behind a glass wall were a set of holding cells and an office where the jailer sat. The station was bright and clean and looked relatively new. The deputies in their khaki shirts and tan pants looked more like forest rangers than cops. But Odell's detention of the kid had reminded me that among the defense bar the sheriff's department had a worse reputation than LAPD for violating suspects' rights, because sheriff's deputies began their training at county jail, where they were vastly outnumbered by the inmates and developed a siege mentality they carried into the streets.

"You mind waiting here for a minute, Mr. Rios?" Odell said.

"I'd like to get this over with."

"I'll be right back," he said.

The deputy who'd driven us to the station departed and I was left alone in the corridor. It would have been easy enough to slip out the back door, and for a minute I considered it. I was not in a good position here. Anything I said would sound incriminating, but refusing to say anything would be equally incriminating. There was no innocent explanation of how I knew Alex, and the story of how I came to spend the last evening of his life with him would have made me suspicious of myself.

Ten minutes later, Odell beckoned me from the other end of the corridor. "Mr. Rios? This way please."

THE ROOM WAS furnished with a table and four chairs. There was a video camera mounted on the wall in a corner and a wall phone next to the door. A burly Latino cop in a short-sleeved shirt, shiny trousers and a K-Mart tie was waiting in the room when Odell and I entered. The man's shabby clothes did not disguise his authority. He was fairer-skinned than me, but as unmistakably Mexican: round face, thick salt-and-pepper hair, blunt eyebrows, black eyes. A hard alcoholic paunch. Strong hands, with fingers thick as *chorizo*. Late thirties, I guessed, but showing signs of heavy wear. He reminded me of my father. It was not a pleasant association.

"Mr. Rios," he said. "I'm Detective Gaitan. Homicide. I want to ask you a few questions about Alex Amerian. You knew he was murdered last night."

"Sergeant Odell told me," I said.

"Sit down, Rios," Gaitan said, pulling a chair out for himself. "Make yourself comfortable. We're going to be here for a while."

"That's up to me," I said. "I'm here voluntarily."

Gaitan slowly lifted his eyes from the manila folder on the table in front of him and stared at me. It was the prison-yard stare with which inmates tried to terrorize each other when no other weapons were at hand. It darkened his eyes with hatred and menace, extinguishing the human light in them. One of my recidivist clients had called it the mirror of death. I knew better than to look away.

"Maybe Odell didn't mention that I'm a criminal-defense lawyer," I said. "I have clients on death row, Detective. You're not going to intimidate me with a jailhouse stare."

"Then take a look at these," he said, and opened the folder, spreading its contents across the table. A half-dozen black-and-white photographs of Alex Amerian.

I sat down. Slowly, I picked up the first photograph and studied it as carefully as if it were a trial exhibit, to stave off the horror of what it showed: Alex's naked body folded into a recycling bin shoved against a cinder-block wall spread with a bougainvillea vine. His head and shoulders, upper chest and legs were visible. The left side of his face had been smashed into pudding, the eye missing from its socket, a fragment of jawbone protruding below what remained of his ear. There were sharp lacerations in the broken flesh that looked like stab wounds. His head had been nearly hacked from the rest of his body. A bougainvillea blossom had fallen into his exposed esophagus. On his chest were what at first looked like deep scratch marks but, in a second photograph, a close-up, were revealed to be letters spelling out the words: KILL FAGS.

I flipped through the other pictures, close-ups, full-body shots, all taken at the scene, ticking off mental notes as if I were preparing a cross-examination. Besides the blows to his face and throat and the carving in his chest, there were other bruises and welts on his body, but they were nonlethal, even superficial. I remembered from the bruises across his back that he was in the business of being beaten up, at least sometimes. Had this begun as an S&M scene that had gotten out of hand? What had he told me? Most of his clients hated themselves for being gay and took it out on him. Something else about the body seemed odd; it was slightly bloated, as if it had been submerged in liquid. And there was something odder still.

"There's no blood."

From behind me, Odell said, "What say?"

"He was hacked to death, but there's no blood in these pictures." I looked at Gaitan. "He wasn't killed in the alley."

"Then where was he killed, Rios?" Gaitan asked. "You should know. You did it."

I pushed the pictures back into the folder. "I want to call my lawyer."

"Let's talk and then you call your lawyer," Gaitan said.

Before I could answer, Odell said, "You heard the man, Mac. He wants to call his lawyer."

Without looking away from me, Gaitan said, "Why don't you take it outside, Lucas? I'll let you know if I need you."

Odell slapped his palm against the table. Gaitan jerked his head toward him.

With the same soft menace with which he'd addressed the gang-banger, Odell said, "In my station when a suspect requests a lawyer, questioning stops."

Suspect?

AFTER I MADE my call, Odell escorted me to the holding cells.

"I can't tell whether you and Gaitan were playing good cop/bad cop back there or if he really pissed you off," I said.

Odell tapped the sally port to get the jailer's attention and said, "You have more important things to worry about, Mr. Rios."

"He doesn't work out of this station, does he?"

The jailer buzzed us in.

"The homicide unit's downtown," Odell said. "He's here as a courtesy. Hey, Tim, Mr. Rios is going to be your guest for a little while, 'til his lawyer gets here."

"I'll take care of him," the slight, fair-haired jailer said. He got up and went to the door that opened to the holding cells. When he asked, "You prefer the Presidential suite or the honeymoon suite?" I detected the camp cadences of a gay man.

"Which has better room service?" I asked.

The jailer grinned; a best-little-boy-in-the-world kind of grin. A brother for sure.

"I'll leave you to it," Odell said.

"Sergeant," I said. "You know you can't hold me much longer."

"I can still arrest you for trespassing."

"A misdemeanor? You'll have to cite me out."

He smiled. "Not necessarily, counsel. The way we work it here is, when you arrest someone you fill out a PCD form and ship it to a judge, who has forty hours to either sign off on it or we kick the suspect."

"PCD? That's a new one on me."

"Probable cause determination," he said. "I'll let you know when your lawyer gets here."

"So, Deputy Tim," I said to the jailer. "Do these cells come with conjugal rights?"

He blushed.

FORTY-FIVE MINUTES later, Inez Montoya, wearing a blue power suit and sneakers and carrying a tattered briefcase, bustled into the jail, with Odell trailing behind her, and demanded of the jailer, "Release my client."

"Let him out," Odell said. "You can talk in the interrogation room."

He took us back to the room where Gaitan had showed me the pictures of Alex and left us there. Inez yanked a chair from beneath the table and plopped herself down. Her heavy bangs fell across her round, cherubic face. She pushed them away impatiently and said, "What the fuck is going on, Henry? I was on my way to dinner with the Governor when my office forwarded your call."

My friendship with Inez Montoya went back almost twenty years, to when we'd both been public defenders. I'd stayed in criminal law while she'd gone into politics, eventually serving on the Los Angeles city council and two terms in Congress. From the House, she'd gone to HUD, where she spent three years as the assistant secretary. A few months earlier, she'd resigned and returned to Los Angeles. Currently, she was cooling her heels as a partner in a politically powerful Westside law firm while she plotted her race for mayor a year hence. Inez was fierce in everything, including loyalty to old friends, even one like me whom she had long ago written off as a loser.

"I think I'm being held as a suspect in a murder," I said.

"*Madre de Dios*," she muttered. "What are you talking about?"

"It's a long story," I said, and explained.

She listened without expression until I finished, then crushed her cigarette on the floor and said, "That was too lame to be made up."

"You think I would make up something that makes me look like such a schmuck?"

"You stalk this guy until he agrees to go out with you, then you find out he's a whore but go to bed with him anyway, then you get pissed off because he was a whore, so you beat him up before sending him off his merry way to get murdered," she said. "Jesus, Henry, I thought you gay guys were supposed to be different than straight guys."

"I didn't exactly stalk him," I said, trying not to explode at her. "And I didn't exactly beat him up, and I certainly didn't know he was on his way to get killed."

She leveled a warning look at me. "Watch your tone."

"For Christ's sake, Inez. I got no sleep last night, I spent the afternoon at Forest Lawn shopping for a grave for Josh, and then I come home to find out that someone murdered my date and now I'm sitting here suspected of the crime. How would you feel?"

She dug into her briefcase for her cigarettes.

"I don't think you can smoke in here," I said.

Ignoring me, she lit up and puffed furiously for a few minutes. "You're going to have to tell the cops the truth," she said.

I had reluctantly come to the same conclusion myself while I was waiting for her. "I know," I said, "but it won't exonerate me. Not in their eyes. I'll still be a suspect."

She ran an exasperated hand through her heavy hair. "*Pues,*" she said. "Who else have they got? But since you didn't do it, they'll eventually give up on you."

"Not before my reputation is destroyed," I said.

"That's the least of your worries," she said. "What's the name of the cop from homicide?"

"Gaitan," I said, "but bring the other one in, too. Odell."

"Odell's just the watch commander," she said. "It's Gaitan's investigation."

"Gaitan's a macho prick," I said, and told her how he had attempted to question me after I'd requested a lawyer. "Odell stopped him."

"All right," she said. "But remember, Henry, you tell them everything, no matter how embarrassing it is for you."

"You're not enjoying this, are you, Inez?"

"Not really," she said. "It's kind of disgusting. You deserve to be convicted of poor judgment, if nothing else."

I MADE MY statement into a tape recorder that kept malfunctioning, so that every few minutes I'd have to repeat a sentence.

"I said, the reason I parked across the street from his house was because I was working up my courage to ask him out on a date."

A look of comic disbelief flashed across Gaitan's face. "You wanted to date him? Are you a homosexual?"

"Yes, Detective, that's what I'm saying. I'm gay."

The disbelief shaded into disgust. "But you're Mexican, man."

"Let's move on," Inez said.

I felt Gaitan's silent contempt, as I described my date with Alex and then going back to my house to have sex.

"Sorry," Odell said. "The machine. Can you repeat that."

I looked at my hands. "We went to my house and had sex."

Across the table, Gaitan muttered something.

"What's that, Mac?" Odell asked. "You want to put something on the tape?"

He shook his head slowly in a gesture of disgust.

"Afterwards," I continued, "as he was leaving, we got into a scuffle. I knocked him down. Gave him a bloody nose, I think. There was a cab waiting for him outside. He left, to another appointment, he said. That was the last time I saw him."

"Why did you beat him up?" Gaitan asked.

"He said something disrespectful to me," I said, hoping it was enough.

"What?" Gaitan persisted. "How could he dis you, Rios?"

"Inez," I said.

"It's not important," she said. "The important thing is when the man left my client's house he was still alive."

"If Rios is telling the truth," Gaitan said, "how come you were at the vic's house this afternoon?"

"The man who introduced me to Alex called me and told me he'd heard Alex had been murdered. I went to his house to talk to his roommate to see what she knew."

"Name of the man who introduced you?" Odell asked.

"Richard Florentino. He lives on La Cuesta Way, here in West Hollywood."

"And how did he know about Amerian?" Gaitan asked.

"He said he'd heard it from one of your deputies," I said, looking at Odell.

"He say which one?" Odell asked.

"No."

"Who is this roommate you're talking about?" Gaitan said.

"Her name is Katie Morse."

"What did you think she was going to tell you, Rios?"

"I thought she might know where Alex was going after he left my house."

"Why?"

"Because of this," I said. "I knew as soon as you guys found out that I'd been with him last night you'd be all over me. I wanted to be prepared."

"You don't trust us to do our job?" Gaitan asked.

"I know you guys go in for the obvious answers."

"That's because most of the time they're the right answers," Odell said.

"Not this time," I replied. "If you want to know who killed him, find out where he went after he left my house."

Gaitan tipped his chair back, looked at me with undisguised distaste, and said, "You know what I think, Rios? I think you two had a lover's spat and you killed him."

"I've cooperated with you completely," I said. "The only way you're going to keep me here is to arrest me, and not on some bullshit trespassing charge."

Odell said, "Will you consent to a search of your house and your car, Mr. Rios?"

"Now? Tonight?"

"If you didn't do it, you shouldn't have anything to hide," he said.

"That's right, Rios. You want to clear yourself, don't you?"

"I want a minute with my lawyer."

The two deputies left the room. "Listen to me, Henry," Inez said, "I'm the lawyer here. We do this my way."

"What are you talking about?"

"That macho crap, daring Gaitan to arrest you."

"We all know there's no probable cause."

"He'd do it just to harass you," she said. "Good thing that other cop is here."

"Do you think they could obtain a search warrant?"

"In a heartbeat. You have something to hide?"

"I told you, I bloodied his nose. They'll find traces of his blood at my house and his fingerprints all over my car."

"You explained all that," she said. She narrowed her eyes. "You're not holding out on me, are you, Henry?"

"You don't think I did it, do you?"

"Some judge somewhere will sign a search warrant," she said. "I think you should cooperate. Let them have their search."

"That doesn't answer my question."

She had to think about it. "Of course not," she said, after a moment.

IT WAS FOUR in the morning before the sheriffs concluded their search of my house. They had impounded my car for a later search, so Inez drove me home and remained with me until the last deputy left. I showed them where I had shoved Alex against the wall, pointed out the bloodstains, retrieved the bloody rag from the washer. Gaitan seemed particularly interested in my bathtub.

"You have a hot tub?" he asked me, emerging from the guest bathroom.

"No," I said.

One of his deputies broke a glass in the kitchen. Gaitan wandered around the living room, stopped, looked at the urn on the mantel.

"What's that?"

"It contains my lover's ashes," I said.

"Open it."

"Don't be ridiculous," I said.

He picked it up, shook it. "You could hide a knife in here."

"I won't open it."

By now, attracted by our rising voices, Inez had come over. I explained the conflict.

"I could come back with a search warrant," Gaitan said.

"Forensics can take it and x-ray it," Inez said. "But you can't open it."

"I won't agree to that," I said.

"We're cooperating here, Henry," she said. "Remember?"

Odell had joined us.

"I want it back tomorrow," I said.

"I'll see to it," Odell said.

"WELL, THAT'S OVER," I said to Inez, after the cops had left. "For now."

She lit the last of her cigarettes. "I'm going home, Henry."

"Thanks for coming to my rescue," I said.

She waved it off. "Don't thank me yet. You're not in the clear."

"I'm sorry you missed dinner with the Governor."

Anger and pity flashed through her eyes. "When we were starting out, you were the one with all the promise. What happened, Henry?"

"I don't know what you mean, Inez. I'm still here, sober, working, alive."

"You were supposed to do a lot more."

"We don't live in the same world anymore, and in my world, where a lot of guys are dead or drunk, those are major achievements."

"Well, then, do me a favor and hang on to them. Stay out of trouble."

I opened the door. "Trouble finds me."

"Only because you advertise," she replied, and drove away.

THE NEXT DAY, a deputy returned Josh's ashes to me. The seal on the urn had been broken.

chapter 6

"THESE NIGHTMARES," I said. "They're like something out of Bosch. I wake up shouting because I've dreamed that something is in the bed with me eating my flesh. Or I dream of the police pictures of Alex Amerian's body. Or Josh at the end. Wasted to his skeleton."

"You've had a series of traumas," Reynolds said. "It's not surprising they've invaded your dreams."

His pudgy face wore its usual beneficent expression. His gray-and-beige office was quiet except for the ticking of a grandfather clock in the corner. Above his desk a discreetly framed degree testified to his doctorate in psychology. It had been a long time since I'd sought out Raymond Reynolds, but I hadn't slept in the three days since Alex's murder, because when I closed my eyes I was plagued by nightmares. My waking hours were not much better. When I looked out the windows, I saw a police surveillance car parked at the curb. Every time the phone rang, I thought it was Inez calling to tell me the cops were on their way to arrest me. I felt like I was choking in my own skin.

"It's more than trauma. I feel implicated in Alex's death."

He shifted uneasily in his chair. "You don't mean . . ."

"Calm down. I didn't kill him."

"Then what do you mean, Henry?"

"This guy killed Alex in a particularly intimate way. He used a knife, the classic sex-crime weapon, an instrument of penetration and rage. . . . You should've seen the pictures. And afterwards, he bathed the body carefully. All that touching of Alex's naked body wasn't inadvertent or incidental. The killer got off on it. You know what that means?"

The clock ticked. "No, what does it mean to you?"

"It means he'll do it again," I replied. "I sent Alex off to a serial killer."

"And that's why you feel implicated?" Reynolds asked. "Because you didn't stop him?"

"No," I said. "I feel implicated because I understand the mind of the man who killed him. He's gay, Raymond, like you and me, but he can't deal with it, so he works out his ambivalence on the bodies of other gay men. I'm almost positive Alex wasn't his first victim."

"Why do you understand about the way his mind works, Henry?"

"I understand that it takes so much energy to resist the hatred so many people feel toward us," I replied. "It wears you down. You begin to wonder, if that many people are convinced you're evil, maybe there's something to it and that gives you license to behave as if you were."

"To kill other gay men?"

"I admit that's an extreme case," I said, "but look at how gay men treat each other, look at the nastiness and bitchiness of so much gay life. Isn't that a kind of acting out that most of us engage in?"

"There's another side to it, Henry."

"I knew you'd say that," I replied. "That's why I came here. What is the other side?"

"I think what frightens people about us isn't that we're different but that we're free, in a way."

"Free? Free to do what? Use each other?"

"I'm not talking about the freedom to do what you want, but to be who you are. To act on your deepest self-knowledge. Almost everyone feels trapped in their lives, but they're afraid to change. They're afraid to know themselves. We are forced to know ourselves."

"We're not a bunch of bodhisattvas, Raymond," I said. "Take a drive down Santa Monica Boulevard and tell me those boys are free."

"I said we've been forced to know ourselves, I didn't say we liked it. For most of us, that self-knowledge stops when we come out of the closet and then we build other closets. The ghettos. Addictions. Codependent relationships. Places to hide from ourselves. But the thing is," he continued, "once you begin to know yourself, it's very hard to stop the process for good. Even your killer must know somewhere in some corner of his mind that no matter how many gay men he kills, he will never kill the gay man inside."

"But how many others will have to die before he sees that?" I asked.

FROM REYNOLDS'S OFFICE in Beverly Hills, I headed east on Sunset to Hollywood to meet Richie for lunch. In the rearview mirror was another police surveillance car. I'd been followed more or less constantly since being questioned about Alex's death. Approaching La Brea, traffic came to a dead stop, though the distant signal light was green, entombing me in my car. Sunlight smeared the windshield. Car horns began their pointless cacophony. A toothless man in rags, carrying a cardboard sign that said WILL WORK FOR BEER pressed his sunbaked face against my window. I looked away and he moved on, weaving between the cars like one of the damned. A fragment of a poem passed through my head, "I myself am hell; nobody's here." Where was that from?

A horn blasted behind me. The road had cleared while I was trying to remember the poet. Robert Lowell. Part of that generation of poets who went crazy or killed themselves or both. Plath, Berryman, I put the gear and moved forward, winging the intersection as the light changed from yellow to red, turning north on La Brea toward Hollywood Boulevard. Off on the curb I saw the cause of the delay. Two paramedics were lifting a gurney into an ambulance. On the gurney was a body, covered with a bloodied sheet.

I pulled into a parking lot off Hollywood and walked to Richie's office. A heat wave had descended on the city, causing an inversion. The smog hung in the motionless air, like the respiration of a great, unseen beast, a dirty veil that curtained the city and left its inhabitants to stew in their own filth. The sidewalk on Hollywood Boulevard glittered with some shiny mineral ground into the concrete to suggest the sparkle of Hollywood, but the bronze stars of the "Walk of Fame" embedded in it were like gravestones. Across the street from Richie's office, in front of Mann's Chinese Theater, tourists photographed each other standing in the footprints of dead stars. As I entered his building, I looked over my shoulder, but for now I'd eluded my police escort.

Except for the framed magazine covers that lined the walls of the reception room, the offices of *L.A. Mode*, from the industrial gray carpet to the blonde faux Scandinavian furnishings, were as functional and unadorned as a dental office. The receptionist, a tousle-haired blond with capped teeth, apparently mistaking me for a movie agent, greeted me with a big smile.

"Hi, can I help you?"

"I'm having lunch with Mr. Florentino. My name is Rios."

"I'll let him know you're here." He whispered into the phone for a minute, then said, "He said to go on back to his office."

I made my way down the gray carpeted hallway, past the utilitarian cubicles that housed editorial and production. The decor of Richie's corner office was inspired by the Chinese Theater across the street. The walls were painted the color of coagulated blood, satiny gold drapes billowed across the windows, and a gold-and-crystal chandelier hung from the acoustical ceiling. Richie ran the magazine from behind a massive, inlaid, Biedermeier desk. A table and six chairs in the same ponderous style sat on a faded blue-and-white carpet of Chinese design. A large vase held a bouquet of huge wilted peonies giving off the scent of vegetable decay.

He was sitting at the table reading a long fax, a MontBlanc fountain pen in one hand, a cigarette burning in the other, wearing an avocado-green shirt and a blue tie patterned with orange and yellow tulips. A linen blazer the color of cornflowers hung neatly from a hanger on the coat rack by the door. He looked up at me with red-rimmed eyes.

"Asshole," he said, with weary irritability. "The cops have been here for the last two days questioning me about the murder. I've got a magazine to run. Why did you give them my name?"

I pulled out a chair. It was stacked with folders. When I moved them, a picture of Duke Asuras, fluttered to the floor. I sat down. "Because I was about three inches from being arrested."

He waved his hand dismissively. "That's ridiculous."

"Goddammit, Richie," I shouted, tearing the fax from his hand. "I've got cops following me everywhere I go, waiting to catch me chopping up someone else. They tore my house and car apart and my own lawyer looks at me like I could've done it."

He put his cigarette out in a crystal bowl. "What do you want me to do about it?"

"What did the cops ask you?"

"They wanted to know about your relationship with Alex."

"What did you tell them?"

"I said as far as I knew you'd just gone out with him once."

"As far as you knew?" I said. "Richie, you know I only went out with him one time, because you paid for it. Or did you forget to mention that to the cops?"

"I didn't see that it was relevant."

I looked at him. "This is not a game. Cops don't believe in the presumption of innocence. You feed them weasel words like 'as far as I know' and they're going to draw adverse conclusions."

"Did you kill him, Henry?" he demanded, fishing for another cigarette.

"You know I didn't."

"Then what the fuck are you worried about?"

"I'd like to be spared the humiliation of being arrested for murder and the trouble of having to clear myself," I replied. "The only way I can do that is by offering up the cops another suspect. I think Alex was killed by one of his clients. You told me he kept an appointment book. When I went to his house after you called me Saturday, I didn't see an appointment book, but it did look like someone had broken in and removed some things."

"What things?"

"A computer, papers. Maybe the book. And what about the roommate?" I said. "Katie Morse. As far as I know, she's still missing. You knew Alex. You must have some ideas about who killed him."

He shook his head. "Boys like Alex have been coming to Hollywood by the busload for eighty years because someone back in East Jesus told them they ought to be in the pictures. In Alex's case, it was some agent he blew for his card. The straight ones get married, go to work for the phone company and move to the Valley. The gay ones end up strung out on crystal or peddling their asses on Santa Monica. Alex got a break. Someone important liked him and passed him around to his friends."

"And one of them killed him."

"Oh, please, Henry," he said. "We're talking about rich and powerful men."

"Who are also closeted."

"You think they paid Alex with personal checks or posed for pictures with him? These guys could teach the Mafia something about *omertà*. Besides not even the tabloids are interested in stories about gays in Hollywood. Their readers don't care about cocksuckers. They want to know how Oprah keeps the weight off."

"Some of his clients were into S&M," I persisted. "Could this have been a scene that went too far?"

"You want to know who killed Alex. I'll tell you," he exhaled a plume of smoke. "Over lunch."

WE CROSSED THE street to the Hotel Roosevelt, where Richie had a standing lunch reservation at Theodore's, the hotel restaurant. In exchange for his patronage, he was allowed, discreetly and illegally, to smoke at his table. The Roosevelt, as Richie rarely failed to remind me, was the site of the first presentation of the Academy Awards. After years of neglect, it had been refurbished as part of the city's bid to revitalize Hollywood. The face-lift had succeeded, and the Roosevelt of the 1920s was recreated down to every last potted palm in the cathedral-ceilinged lobby, but the rest of Hollywood continued to resist the efforts of the city planners. As a result, the elegant old hotel was surrounded by tee-shirt shops, falafel stands and wig shops that served the needs of Hollywood's legion of transvestite prostitutes.

Theodore's was a calm, beige space separated from the lobby by a large plate of etched glass. Pale light suffused the room from tall, narrow, heavily draped windows. It was like walking into an earlier time, and I never entered there without expecting to find it filled with the shades of deceased movie stars raising ghostly cocktails to their pale lips. Instead, it was virtually empty and as quiet as a mausoleum, because Hollywood had long since decamped from Hollywood, leaving it to the drag queens and the tourists.

Richie inspected the purple napkins at the table, and frowned. "Whose idea was this?" he demanded of the waitress, a slight, dark girl whose name plate identified her as Isabel from Mexico, DF.

"Pardon," she said, so flustered by him that she gave the word its Spanish pronunciation.

"Purple napkins? What is this, a Puerto Rican wedding? Bring me a martini. And an ashtray."

"You have a theory about Alex's murder," I prompted.

Richie was contemplating the empty room. He inspected the flatware and disdainfully removed the little vase with its two wilted carnations from the table.

"I don't know why I give a fuck about Hollywood. It certainly doesn't give a fuck about itself."

"What are you talking about?"

"I'm working on the biggest story of my career," he said. Isabel brought his martini and his ashtray. He tasted the drink and smacked his lips. "At least the bartender can still pour a decent martini."

After she took our orders and left, I asked him, "I came to talk about Alex."

"I'm talking about the death of Hollywood," he said, with a regal wave of his hand. "The murder of Hollywood. It's a damn sight more tragic than the murder of Alex Amerian."

"Maybe to you," I said.

"Absolutely to me," he said. "I couldn't have survived the crazy house without it."

"Watching movies after lights out. I know. You've told me," I said, impatient to get back to Alex's murder.

He narrowed his eyes. "But you don't know, Henry, because I never told you how they treated homosexuality back then at the Chase-Levinger Hospital in Battle Creek, Michigan. Have I?"

"No," I sat back. Richie was on a tear. There was nothing to do but wait it out.

"They attached electrodes to my body and then showed me gay pornography and when I responded, they sent an electric current through me." He took a long swallow of his drink. "They called this aversion therapy. I was fourteen years old. I'd never seen pornography before. My fantasy was to hold hands with the football captain between classes. They showed me pictures of men doing things I didn't know were physically possible. Of course I responded. I couldn't help myself. They kept increasing the voltage until I had to be treated for second-degree burns. This went on week after week for almost two years. It's amazing I don't have some weird sexual fetish involving cable jumpers." He tried to smile, but it came out a twitch. "Sometimes I tried closing my eyes, so I wouldn't see the pictures, but then they'd shock me harder. You see, they wanted me to look. They wanted it to hurt to be a fag. I could've told them it already did. I thought they were going to kill me. So I taught myself to dream with my eyes open, to look at those pictures and see other things."

"What things?"

"Scenes from movies. They'd show me porn but I'd be seeing Bette Davis rooting around in her garden in *Dark Victory*, or Norma Shearer flashing her jungle-red fingernails in *The Women*. I stopped getting hard-ons. They decided the treatments were a success. But they kept me there until I was eighteen and they had to release me legally. Four years, Henry, that's how long my family had me institutionalized. I spent the last two years giving blow jobs in the bathrooms to the orderlies. I learned my technique from watching their porn, so I guess the therapy was successful."

"That's gruesome."

The waitress delivered our food. He ordered another martini.

"I don't want your pity," he said, after she left. "I told you that story so you'd understand what movies mean to me. My case was extreme, but there were a lot of other gay boys like me who survived their childhoods because Hollywood gave them something else to dream about. That's why I'm going after Duke Asuras."

"You lost me, Richie."

"Do you know who James Longstreet is?"

"Of course," I said. "Every gay person in America knows who he is. What about him?"

"Fundamentalist evangelical asshole," Richie spat. "He was staying here at the hotel once and got caught in the middle of a gay rights demonstration. When he got back to Buttfuck, Virginia, he sent out a fundraising letter that claimed the fags were pounding at his door, like wild animals, ready to tear him limb from limb." His face darkened to apoplectic purple. "I wish someone would kill the fat fuck. Don't you?"

"I don't wish anyone dead," I said. "On the other hand, there are definitely people I wish would shut up and he's one of them."

"He's a murderer," Richie said. "Think of all those little gay boys and girls out there trapped in so-called Christian families, forced to listen to him week after week tell them how God hates fags and AIDS is their punishment. Every time one of those kids commits suicide, the blood's on his hand."

I sipped my tea. "What does this have to do with Hollywood?"

He gulped his martini. "He wants to make movies."

"Who? Longstreet? According to him, Hollywood's on God's hit list."

"If you listen carefully," Richie said, cutting into his steak, "beneath the fire and brimstone is the whining of a would-be player. Longstreet runs a billion-dollar media empire, including two cable networks. He's cash rich and he's looking to expand into Hollywood, and those fuckers at Parnassus are going to open the gates."

"Asuras?"

Richie chewed and nodded vigorously. "I told you that Asuras and Allen Raskin, his boss at the Parnassus Company, have been feuding with their board of directors. Apparently, they decided the way to solve their problems was to find a white knight, either to buy out the major shareholder or to launch a takeover fight that would let them stack the board with their own people."

"Longstreet is their white knight?"

"That's what it looks like," he said. "You can't breathe a word of this to anyone, Henry."

"Who would I tell?"

"I mean it. People could get hurt."

"I'm not in your world, Richie. This isn't important to me."

He swallowed another chunk of meat. "You should care. If Longstreet pulls this off, he'll get mainstream respectability. You know what that means for us?"

"You're talking about making movies."

"Where did your dreams come from when you were a kid, Henry?"

"My dreams came out of books," I said.

"In another generation," he said, "the only books are going in museums."

"That's a scary thing for a magazine editor to say."

"It's true, Henry. You know Asuras gave a speech at the Academy Awards and said Hollywood was taking over the world. He wasn't joking. People don't have to know how to read to go to movies." He touched his napkin to his mouth. "Do you want Longstreet making the movies that people are going to watch in Bombay and Lagos? I don't, and I'm going to stop him."

"My problems are a little closer to home. You had something to tell me about Alex."

"I think Alex was killed by an anti-gay hit squad."

"What do you mean a hit squad?"

"Did you know his car was firebombed?"

"Yeah, he told me."

"I think the same people who attacked him and blew up his car also killed him."

"He also told me there were other car bombings in his neighborhood."

"That's right," Richie said. "And in each case there was something on the car that identified its owner as gay, a bumper sticker or Pride flag decal."

"That doesn't prove the owners' identities would've been known to the bombers," I said. "The bombing of Alex's car could've been a coincidence."

"But it wasn't," Richie said. "It happened right after I ran the gay bashing piece. He was the only victim we interviewed who agreed to use his real name. He made himself a target by going public."

"That's all conjecture."

"I heard from my source in the department that 'kill fags' was carved on his chest," Richie said. " 'Kill fags.' "

"So?"

"Gee, Henry, if a black person was attacked by white racists and went to the media and then his car was blown up and then he was murdered by someone who carved 'kill niggers' on his body, wouldn't it occur to you that there might possibly be a connection?"

"Touché." I said, "But, Richie, gay bashings are random and impulsive. I saw the police pictures of Alex's body. His murder was deliberate and methodical."

"Since when are gay bashings impulsive?" Richie asked, disbelievingly. "These punks deliberately come into West Hollywood and stalk us. Is it so hard to believe they'd carry it a step further?"

"Did you mention any of this to the cops when they came to see you?"

"I told you, they were only interested in you," he said. "Besides, I think the cops are in on it."

"Now you're in Oliver Stone territory."

He drained his drink. "You think so? Come back to the office with me."

Back at Richie's office, he had his assistant dig out the file on the gay-bashing piece that had featured Alex Amerian. Among the drafts and notes was a series of photographs of toilet stalls. On the walls were graffiti. Close-ups revealed the messages "Kill all fags" and "AIDS = Anally Inserted Death Serum."

"Nice," I said. "What's their relevance?"

"These pictures were taken in the men's bathroom at the sheriff's department headquarters in Monterey Park," he said. "I think they pretty much sum up the sheriff's attitude toward gays."

"I'm no fan of the cops," I said, "particularly at the moment, but if this is supposed to prove that deputies in West Hollywood are collaborating with gay bashers, it doesn't. It only proves that some cops are bigots, which is, believe me, no surprise to anyone who has to deal with them."

He threw his hands up theatrically. "Well, I give up, Henry. You asked me if I knew who killed Alex, but you don't believe me, even after I've connected all the dots."

"It isn't that I don't believe you," I said. "It's a plausible theory, but it's just a theory."

"I have to tell you, Henry," he said. "If you were a reporter, you wouldn't last here very long."

"I'm just glad I'm not your libel lawyer."

FROM RICHIE'S OFFICE, I drove to Century City for a meeting with Inez Montoya. I turned Richie's theory over in my head, trying to come up with a precedent for it. I remembered a case from Texas a couple of years earlier in which a gay man had been abducted from a public park in Houston and taken out into the country and shot. The prosecutor had successfully argued that transporting the victim showed premeditation, and a jury sent the man's murderers to death row. Why couldn't something similar have happened in Alex's case? Maybe after his last appointment, as he was returning home, he'd been abducted by the same men who'd attacked him and blown up his car. Maybe this murder was exactly what it appeared to be: a hate crime. Yet part of me still dismissed this scenario as Richie's paranoia. This was partly a survival mechanism, because if I actually believed that hit squads were murdering gay men, I might become so consumed by rage or fear I'd be immobilized. But there was another reason, too. As I'd explained to Reynolds, people who inspire such homicidal hatred in others can come to believe they deserve it, subliminally if not consciously. Richie had nailed me on that. I realized it was easier for me to believe one of Alex's closeted gay clients had hacked him to death than that he'd been murdered by a bigot, because even I struggled against this hatred of gays. And if it was true of me, how much easier would it be for the cops who were convinced they'd found the murderer. Me.

INEZ WAS IN a rumpled white linen suit behind a cluttered desk in her twenty-eighth-floor office in the south tower of the two Century City towers that dominated the skyscape of the westside of the city. Her windows looked south and west, and on clear days, she boasted, she could make out the bluish outline of Catalina Island on the horizon. The walls of her spacious office were bare and her personal belongings stacked in boxes that bore such labels as "Awards and Mementos." With the mayoral primary coming up in less than a year, it was clear that she planned to do her unpacking downtown in City Hall.

She was on a call when I entered her office. She gestured me to a chair and masticated a piece of gum while she listened to her caller, interrupting with an occasional "Uh-huh," or "No way."

"Yeah, yeah," she said, ending the conversation. "I'll talk to you later. I've got a client." She hung up and spit her gum into a tissue. "The cops still following you?"

"Mostly they park outside my house. I guess they're waiting for another victim to arrive so they can nab me in the act of beheading him."

"Good to know you haven't lost your sense of humor," she remarked sarcastically. "I have the preliminary report from the search."

"And?"

"No surprises," she said. "They found the victim's prints in your house and your car. They matched the blood on the doorknob and the rag to his blood type, but DNA testing will take weeks, so for now that's inconclusive. . . ."

"I admitted it was his blood," I reminded her. "Are they going to arrest me?"

"Not on this evidence," she said. "Except for the prints, your car was clean, and there were no other bloodstains anywhere in your house except where you said they'd be. They can't arrest you until they can explain how you carved the guy up and transported him in your car without leaving a trace."

"The body was bloated, like it had been submerged in water."

She nodded. "That's why Gaitan was so interested in your bathtub. There was water in the lungs, chlorinated water, as it turned out."

"A swimming pool?"

"Or hot tub," she said. "The killer soaked the body. It was as clean as a whistle."

"All the cops have got to do is find his pool-cleaning service. They must know it's not me."

"Detective Gaitan has a hard-on for you and I don't mean that in a good way."

"That's good because he's not my type," I said. "Reminds me of my father, and I don't mean that in a good way, either. Maybe the words malicious prosecution would help him overcome his animosity."

"His investigation hasn't crossed that line yet," she said. "We're just going to have to hang on for a few more days until Gaitan admits you're a dead end."

"What if we offered the cops an alternative to me?"

"Who are you thinking of, Henry? They executed Gacy."

"Just listen." I laid out Richie's theory.

"Do the cops know any of this?" she asked angrily, when I finished. "Because if they did and they didn't tell us, I will sue their asses for malicious prosecution."

"You think it's a plausible theory?"

"Plausible? Henry, I was one of the authors of the federal hate-crime law. You wouldn't believe the things we heard at the hearings. Gay bashing is practically a Saturday-night pastime in some places. And the cops, Jesus, the gays have as much to fear from them as their attackers." She dug a cigarette out of her purse. "It's the same place we were at with rape twenty years ago. When the victims go to the authorities, they get victimized all over again."

"You may want to take a look at these," I said, slipping her the pictures of the toilet-stall graffiti. "Richie loaned them to me. He says they come from the deputy's bathroom at sheriff's headquarters."

"Un-fucking-believeable," she said, flipping through them. She stuck her cigarette in the corner of her mouth and reached for her phone. "I'm going to get Gaitan's ass down here now."

I restrained her hand. "Wait, Inez. I have a better idea."

She put the phone down. "Such as?"

"If Gaitan is the asshole he appears to be, I doubt whether he's going to be impressed by anything we have to tell him. But the watch commander, Odell? He might be, especially since all this activity was going on in West Hollywood. And there's one other person we should bring into this: Serena Dance."

"Serena Dance," she said, frowning.

"You know her?"

"Oh yes," she said. "The hate-crimes unit. But you're right. If we can convince her, she'll call off Gaitan. I'll set up a meeting at the West Hollywood station as soon as possible."

"You have something against Serena?"

"That's not important," she said. Her phone buzzed. "I have to take this call. I'll be in touch."

IT WAS DARK when I returned home. My neighbor Jim Kwan came out of his house and across my yard, with a worried look on his round, good-natured face. Kwan was the head of neighborhood watch for our street, an easygoing, low-key guy, so I knew immediately something serious was up.

"Hey, Henry," he said. "Got a minute?"

"Sure, Jim. What's wrong?"

"I thought you should know a detective came over to my house earlier tonight and wanted to ask me and Sharon some questions about you."

My heart sank. "What kind of questions?"

Kwan looked at his shoes. "You know, Henry, what you do in the privacy of your house is no one's business."

"Jim, what did he ask you?"

"It wasn't so much what he asked," Kwan said, "as what he told us. He said you were a suspect in a murder case and the victim was a male prostitute. He showed us pictures . . ." His voice trailed off. "He wanted to know if we saw or heard anything last Friday night. Jesus, Henry, what's going on?"

"The detective's name was Gaitan, wasn't it?"

He reached into his shirt pocket and removed a business card. "Yeah, Montezuma Gaitan," he said, reading the card.

"I did have company on Friday," I said. "He was a prostitute. And he was murdered. The rest is a fabrication. Did Gaitan talk to anyone else in the neighborhood?"

"Just the Cohens," he said, referring to the neighbors on the other side of my house. "Fred came over after Gaitan left and told me he was sure it was all a mistake." He clamped my shoulder. "I'm glad to hear it is."

"I'm worried about my reputation on the block."

"Leave that to me," Kwan said. "Listen, you eaten dinner yet? We're just about to sit down. There's plenty."

In the seven years we'd been neighbors, I'd never been invited to his house for a meal.

"Thanks, Jim. I need to get some work done. Can I take a rain check?"

"Anytime, Henry," he said. "I'll let you know if Gaitan shows up again."

"I'll take care of that," I said.

CUSTOMARILY, ONE OF the first things a defense lawyer seeks to discover from the prosecution in a criminal case is whether the officers involved in the investigation have had any citizen complaints lodged against them for excessive force or other misconduct. There was even a name for the procedure, a *Pitchess* motion, after the state appellate case that authorized the disclosure of such records. I went into my office, pulled out my Rolodex and started calling every criminal-defense lawyer I could reach at home. The next day I called the offices of those I'd missed, asking all of them the same questions, "Have you run a *Pitchess* motion on a sheriff's homicide detective named Montezuma Gaitan? If so, can I have your file on him?" It was a distinctive name, and more than one of my colleagues remembered it quite well. My fax worked overtime.

chapter 7

I WOKE UP on Friday morning, a week after Alex's murder, feeling as irritable and fatigued as if I'd had no sleep at all. The sky was overcast in the window, coastal fog that would clear up before noon to reveal another flaming day in mid-June. I got out of bed, wrapped myself in an old flannel robe that was at once too hot, and stepped on a tack as I made my way into the kitchen, leaving drops of blood on the carpet. At the sink, I poured water into the coffeepot and looked out the window at the unmarked police car parked across the street in front of the Hercus's house. Inez had arranged the meeting with Odell and company for later that morning, so I was hopeful this would be the last day I would be watched by the police, though the curious stares of my neighbors might continue for a long time to come. While the coffee brewed, I got the paper from the porch. Scanning the headlines, I saw the usual collection of calamities and scandals. My horoscope spoke of confusion and secrets.

I poured a cup of coffee and went out to the deck. My house was perched on the side of a small canyon and my property declined steeply into a brambly wilderness that was home to raccoons, skunks and the occasional deer. There was a road at the bottom of the canyon and, on the other side, far grander houses. When I'd bought the house, I had imagined the canyon was an escape from the city, a green and rustic place, but the city was inescapable. The green was as flat as painted scenery and the air was stale and exhausted. One night recently, I'd heard shots, and the next day word filtered up that a family of three had been murdered during a robbery two blocks down the hill. There was now a movement afoot to gate our neighborhood and, in effect, secede from the city, as if that would make any difference.

I rinsed my cup at the sink, watching the police car. I could make out a man at the wheel. Gaitan? Probably not. This was drudge work. And then, suddenly, the car sped off without so much as a backward glance at me.

ON MY WAY into West Hollywood for the meeting, I stopped at a book store and found a copy of the *Inferno*. I parked my car on Larabee Street and went to the coffeehouse to wait for Inez before proceeding to the sheriff's station across the street. I reread Dante's account of meeting his beloved teacher,

Ser Brunetto, among the sodomites on the burning plain and my glance fell upon this passage:

> "*. . . a troop of souls ran up beside the dike*
> *peering at us, each one, the way at dusk*
> *men eye one another under a new moon . . .*"

I remembered that Dante's description of the burning plain reminded Richie of a gay resort in Palm Springs. A desert setting; tanned, fit men forever circling each other, peering into one another's faces. What were we looking for? I closed the book. The morning mist had cleared and now the air was still like steel wool. The pair of ficus trees in front of the coffeehouse were wilted and dusty. I saw Inez turn the corner, remove her sunglasses and push open the door to the coffeehouse. She came over to my table, an odd, questioning expression on her face, as if she didn't completely recognize me.

"Inez? Are you all right?"

"There's been another killing," she said, and for a split second I read the question in her eyes.

"Sit down," I said. "Tell me about it."

THERE WERE FIVE of us cramped around Odell's desk on folding chairs in his windowless office. From where I sat, I faced a framed photograph of Odell and a young woman in the uniform of LAPD. Glowering at me from the other side of the desk was Gaitan's dark face as he popped antacids. Serena Dance sat between him and Odell, Inez next to me. The tension between the two women was almost as thick as it was between Gaitan and me, Inez's cold, "Hello, Serena," having elicited an equally frosty, "Inez." Only Odell, with his snowman's face and sharp eyes, seemed impervious to the currents of hostility that crossed the room. He saw me looking at the photo on his desk, smiled and said, "My daughter."

"Let's get down to business," Inez said. "There was another killing last night. Same MO. Young gay man beaten and stabbed, dumped in the alley with a hate message carved on his body. Since you've had my client under constant surveillance for the last week, you know he had nothing to do with it. Now maybe you'll stop harassing him and find this guy before he kills again."

"Who told you about the second killing?" Gaitan demanded.

"I did," Odell replied calmly.

Gaitan addressed him angrily. "So much for the blackout."

"The blackout applies only to the media," Odell responded. "Ms. Montoya had a right to know, since it affects her client."

"This is my investigation," Gaitan said. "I decide who needs to know what and when."

"These murders are happening in my town," Odell responded. "I want them stopped."

"You could have prevented them," Inez told him.

Odell cocked his head back. "I beg your pardon?"

"Our information is that Alex Amerian was the victim of two hate crimes before he was murdered, and neither the sheriff nor the DA either properly investigated or prosecuted those crimes. Then he was murdered under circumstances that suggest another hate crime. How much clearer does it have to be before you people get it?"

"Get what, ma'am?" Odell asked, dangerously.

"Alex Amerian wasn't just murdered, he was assassinated by the same people who beat him up and torched his car, and when you had your chance to prevent it, you sat on your hands." She laid out the details of our theory of Alex's murder.

"There was no corroboration that Amerian was gay bashed," Dance said, when Inez finished. "Furthermore, the sheriff investigated his claim that a deputy had refused to take his report, and decided it was untrue."

"I know that's the company line, but you thought there was enough truth in Amerian's claim to cut him a deal on an ADW charge," Inez reminded her. "You weren't so sure then a jury would believe the sheriff. After looking at these pictures, I can't blame you." She threw the toilet-stall pictures across Odell's desk. "These were taken at department headquarters in the deputies' bathroom."

"What is this supposed to prove?" Serena asked.

"That your faith in the sheriff may be a little misplaced," Inez replied.

Odell examined the pictures. "Anyone who put anything like this on the walls of my station would find himself out of a job before the ink dried."

"You still deny that one of your deputies refused to take a report from Alex Amerian when he was gay bashed last year?" I asked him.

Odell shifted in his seat. "It was investigated."

"Did you also investigate the firebombings that occurred last winter?" I asked him.

"Those are still open cases," he replied.

"Six months later and still no arrests," I said.

"And two murders," Inez chimed in. "It should be clear by now that you've got some kind of hate group operating in this city, but instead of going after them, you harass my client."

"Harass?" Gaitan broke in. "Rios was the last person to see the victim, he admits he beat him up. That makes him a righteous suspect."

"You only have those facts because he cooperated with you," Inez said. "Don't forget that, and don't forget you haven't found a shred of independent evidence that connects him to Amerian's murder and now you've got another body on your hands."

"A copycat," Gaitan said dismissively.

"No," Inez said, "it's not a copycat killing and you know it."

"How can you be so sure?" Serena asked.

"Because when the sheriff's department briefed the media on the first killing, it withheld the fact that there was a hate message carved on the victim's chest. Isn't that right, Sergeant Odell?"

"Yep," he said.

"But the second victim also had a hate message carved on his chest," she said. "What was it? 'Dies 4 Sins.' "

Gaitan shrugged. "Someone could've leaked the information." He glanced at Odell. "Maybe one of your gay deputies."

"What the hell is that supposed to mean?" Odell growled.

"Things get out," Gaitan said. "People take care of their own. All in *la familia*, right, Rios?"

I glanced at Serena. In a voice of controlled fury, she asked Gaitan, "Did you have Rios under surveillance when the second victim was killed?"

"So?" Gaitan begrudged.

"Therefore, he's in the clear."

"Hey," Gaitan complained. "The body's still warm. No one's in the clear. Besides, his lawyer's wrong. We have other evidence that connects him to Amerian."

"What evidence?" Inez demanded.

"I'll let you know when I arrest him."

Serena said, "You'll let all of us know now."

Gaitan stared at her. "I don't take my orders from you, lady."

"Cut the crap, Mac," Odell said. "We're here to solve this thing."

"I don't take orders from you, either."

"Don't make me get my captain," Odell said. "Don't make get on the phone to yours. Again."

"I doubt if that would impress him," I said. "Detective Gaitan has a long record of insubordination, reprimands and suspensions. Don't you?"

"What is this?" he hissed at me.

"I've been doing some investigation of my own, Gaitan," I said. "I have enough paper on you to put you on trial. Excessive force complaints going back to when you worked county jail and roughed up inmates in the queens' tank. A three-day suspension for the time you called a black suspect a 'nigger.' Repeated accusations that you planted evidence when you worked Narcotics. A couple of times, a judge dismissed a case just because you were the investigating officer. You want to arrest me? Go right ahead. I'll match my reputation against yours in front of a jury any time."

"Your reputation? As what, a drunk?" He looked at Inez. "You know Rios was suspended from the state bar for drinking? Up in San Francisco, your ex-colleagues tell me you were a blackout drinker. You was drinking the night Amerian was murdered. The waiter says you went through a bottle of wine, plus who knows how much more later. I think you killed him in a blackout. Is that how it happened?"

"My last drink was eight years ago," I said.

"I've got the waiter from the restaurant."

"I've heard about your interview technique from my neighbors," I said. "You tell them what you want them to say. You hear what you want to hear."

Odell cleared his throat. "That's enough. This is degenerating into a pissing contest."

Gaitan got up. "Yeah, you're right. I've had enough. I'm going back to work." He looked at me on his way out and spat. "*Desgraciado.*"

"What did he say?" Serena asked.

"There's no English equivalent," I said. "It's a kind of Mexican tribal curse."

"I want him off this investigation," Inez told Odell.

"I'm not his commander. Anyway, it sounds like he's got something on your client that deserves a little more looking into."

"What, that I killed Alex in a blackout? That's ludicrous."

"You're a lawyer," Odell said. "You know how it works. This is standard operating procedure."

"Let me tell you something that isn't," Inez said, gathering up her papers. "If my client isn't cleared by Monday morning, we'll call a press conference on Monday afternoon to talk about the sheriff's record on hate crimes in this case and why you're wasting time and money investigating an innocent man while there's a murderer on the loose."

Flushed, Serena said, "You can't make demands like that without allowing us to investigate . . ."

"You should have investigated when Amerian was still alive."

"Inez, can I have a minute with you?" I said. We went out into the hallway. "Press conference? What are you talking about? I can't admit I'm a suspect, even to deny it, because we both know what people will remember."

"Relax," she said. "They'll cave."

"Just in case they don't," I said, "you've got to give them more time. I have an argument on Tuesday in San Francisco in front of the state Supreme Court. I'd rather not show up as a suspected felon. Can we keep a lid on it until I get back?"

"Fine," she said. "We'll give them a week. To next Friday."

"And what happens if they won't clear me? We're not going to go through with a press conference."

"We worry about it then."

We returned to Odell's office, where Inez gave him and Serena our ultimatum. As I walked Inez to her car, I asked, "What's with you and Serena Dance?"

"She's a fanatic," she replied, unlocking her door.

"What do you mean?"

"When I was in the House working on the federal hate-crime bill, she was part of a group of gay lobbyists who threatened to out any closeted legislator who refused to support putting gays and lesbians in the statute," she said. "One of the people they threatened was a friend of mine. A married man with kids from a conservative district in the Midwest. They put him through hell."

"Was he gay?"

She crushed her cigarette beneath a fire-engine red high heel. "That's not always the point, Henry. Things can be a little more complex than that."

"Maybe," I replied. "But I get tired of doing double duty for all those closet cases who want to have their cake and eat it, too. The ones who claim being gay is a bedroom issue, not a civil rights one. Maybe they're the ones who need a lesson in complexity."

She shook her head. "You could lose a lot of friends with that attitude."

"I've already lost a lot of friends, Inez," I told her, as she slipped into her car. "Like Josh. They're not coming back. It's hard for me to get excited about a few ruined political careers."

"Whatever happened to tolerance?"

"Tolerance is a luxury."

"Watch what you say doesn't come back to bite you."

BY EVENING THE media blackout on the second murder had apparently been lifted, because the local TV stations were running the story with lead-ins like "Serial Murder Stalks West Hollywood Gays." I surfed the channels until I found the least offensive station. On the screen was a black-and-white photograph—obviously a mug shot—of the second victim, a twenty-six-year-old man named Jack Baldwin. The camera cut to footage of male hustlers on Santa Monica Boulevard while the voice-over narrator said, "Baldwin, a known male prostitute, who was last seen by friends getting into a taxicab two nights ago near the intersection of Santa Monica Boulevard and Formosa Avenue in West Hollywood. His nude body was found yesterday in a Dumpster behind this restaurant." The screen showed a fast food Mexican restaurant that the reporter pointed out was only a block from the sheriff's station. "According to the medical examiner, Baldwin was stabbed and beaten. Only a week ago, another man, twenty-nine-year old Alex Amerian, was also found in a Dumpster in the alley behind Santa Monica Boulevard with similar injuries. Police refuse to speculate on whether the murders were connected, but the young male residents of West Hollywood, who are predominantly homosexual, are convinced there is a serial killer on the loose." The camera went to a tank-topped kid who expressed concern for his safety and his belief that the sheriff's department did not do enough to protect him. "Furthermore," the reporter continued, switching to another talking head, "according to Victor Frenza at the Gay and Lesbian Community Services Center, these killings may be part of an upsurge in hate crimes against homosexuals, which increased by fifty-five percent last year in the county." The camera recorded Victor Frenza's thoughts on hate crimes, then returned to a helmet-haired reporter standing in front of the sheriff's station. "West Hollywood doesn't have its own police department. It contracts with the sheriff's department to provide police services. Relations between the department and the city's gay residents have frequently been rocky in the past. In response to criticism from gays and lesbians, the department has started an aggressive campaign to recruit gays into its ranks. A year ago, a new captain, Walt Sturges, was brought in to command the West Hollywood station. Sturges has required mandatory sensitivity training for his deputies, brought in gay and lesbian deputies, and designated as his liaison to the gay community Sergeant Lucas Odell, a twenty-three-year veteran of the department, whose daughter, Layne, is one of only six openly lesbian officers in the LAPD. Sturges has received high marks from the gay community for these moves, but all that could be threatened if these murders continue. This is Linda Frye . . ."

The phone rang. I picked it up and switched the TV off.

Richie said, "I hear from inside the department the second victim had the words 'Dies 4 Sins' carved across his chest."

"Apparently. They didn't show me crime-scene pictures this time."

"They can't still suspect you," he said. "It's got to be a Christian hate group."

"Why Christian, Richie?"

"Sin? That's them all over."

"The detective in charge of the case still likes me," I said. "But I don't think he has much credibility with the deputies in West Hollywood and it's their turf."

"I don't understand," Richie said. "Is he an outsider?"

"Yeah, in the sheriff's department the homicide bureau is centralized, and detectives are rolled out as needed. Gaitan's an old school cop who wears his contempt on his sleeve. Clearly not a fan of gay people. He's creating problems for the West Hollywood command."

"What are you going to do?"

"Inez Montoya gave the department until next Friday to clear me before she goes to the media and accuses the sheriff of harassing an upstanding, innocent member of the bar instead of investigating the hate-inspired attacks on Alex that preceded his murder."

"Tell her not to forget to give the magazine credit for breaking the story."

"I hope it doesn't come to that," I said. "I don't need that kind of publicity."

"Any publicity is good for business."

"It's never good for business for a lawyer to be named as a murder suspect."

"I know this must be making you crazy," he said. "Is there anything I can do? If you'd like to get out of town, you can use the condo in Montecito. It's right on the beach."

"Thanks for the offer, but I have business in San Francisco on Tuesday, so I'm flying up tomorrow and making a long weekend out of it."

"San Francisco? Take plenty of latex."

"Jesus Christ, Richie, you're still living in nineteen seventy-eight."

"And you're still living in eighteen seventy-eight," he replied, and hung up.

THE NEXT MORNING, I boarded a flight for San Francisco, and as soon as the plane was in the air, I felt tension in my shoulders ebb. By the time I caught sight of the city's skyline, fifty minutes later, I had almost forgotten I was a murder suspect in my excitement to be there. San Francisco and I went back a long way. When I was a boy growing up in a dusty town in the Central Valley, it was the golden city of my imagination. Much later, as a law student at Stanford, it was also the city of eros. AIDS changed all that. There was a time when walking through the Castro, the gay neighborhood, was like walking through a graveyard. But even that had changed, and the last time I'd visited, Castro Street was thronged and for the first time in a decade, the living again seemed to outnumber the dead.

I was met at the gate by the friend with whom I was staying, Grant Hancock. We'd been classmates at law school and boyfriends, briefly. After law school, he'd married and fathered a son. "Dynastic pressures," he explained later, a reference to the old and distinguished San Francisco family he'd been born into. Now he lived with his lover, Hugo Luna, in a working-class neighborhood of the city not even visible from the Pacific Heights mansion where he'd been raised.

"Welcome home," Grant said, greeting me with a bear hug.

His blond hair had faded to dusty gray. He was still broad shouldered, but he had acquired a patriarchal belly and the tailored suits from Wilkes Bashford he'd worn as an associate at the law firm his great-grandfather had founded had long since been exchanged for blue jeans, flannel shirts and work at a public interest law firm that provided legal services to the people with AIDS. He and Hugo both had the disease.

"You look great," I said.

"And you look exhausted," he said. He grabbed my garment bag. "Is this it, or do you have other luggage?"

"Just this."

"Great, let's go."

It was a blue and beautiful day as we drove north on the 101.

"How's Hugo?" I asked.

He frowned into the rearview mirror. "Hugo's in Arizona."

"The custody case?"

Grant nodded.

Hugo, like Grant, had a son from an earlier marriage, but unlike Grant and his ex-wife, Marcia, who amicably shared custody of Charley, Hugo's wife had taken their son back to the small desert town in Arizona where she'd been raised and obtained sole custody of the boy on the grounds that Hugo's homosexuality rendered him an unfit parent. For the past two years, the case had been up and down the state court system.

"Still? I thought he won on appeal."

"The trial court judge is an old friend of the wife's family," he said. "So he just ignored the appellate decision. Hugo's lawyer went up on a writ. Oral argument's on Monday."

"Why didn't you go with him?"

Grant shrugged. "Hugo's worried that if his male lover shows up in court with him, he'll lose. I told him that's not the way the law works, that he deserves to win on the merits of his case." He smiled. "He reminded me that the law didn't prevent the trial judge from taking his son away from him."

We turned off the freeway at Army Street, recently renamed Cesar Chavez Boulevard. The signage lagged behind the sentiment. A few minutes later, we pulled into the driveway of the hillside house Grant and Hugo shared.

"Oh," he said, fumbling for his key, "Charley sends his love. He's studying Spanish in Cuernavaca this summer. So it's just you and me in the house." He unlocked the door and was set upon by a small, yappy mutt. "And Good Boy, of course."

GRANT IMPROVISED LUNCH from odds and ends in his refrigerator and we went out on the deck to eat. Good Boy lay poised at our feet, ready to spring at any dropped scrap of food. Tangos played over outdoor speakers mounted on the wall. Grant poured himself a glass of wine and dug into his cold burrito. The view from his deck embraced the entire city from the Golden Gate to the Bay Bridge.

"I never get over this view," I said.

"I can see my family's entire history," he replied. "All six generations. When I was younger, it embarrassed me that I was such a small-town boy. . . ."

"Some small town."

"But it is," he replied. "Now I feel incredibly lucky that I never had to leave my home to live my life. Unlike Hugo, or you."

I ate a forkful of Thai noodles, gazed out at the crowded hills of the city and wondered how it felt to belong to a place. My homosexuality had exiled me from my own hometown, where the local prejudices would have kept me in the closet had I remained. When I was younger, I was relieved to have kicked its dust from my shoes; but with fifty only five years away, rootlessness was quickly losing its appeal. What would it be like to die in the same place where you were born, to grow old with people you knew as children, to be compared to your grandfather or grandmother by people who had actually known them?

"Once you leave your hometown," I said, "every other place feels temporary, no matter how long you live there."

"Every place is temporary," Grant said. "Ultimately."

I looked at him. He dabbed sour cream from his chin and smiled at me. "How's your health, Grant?"

"These protease inhibitors are miracle drugs," he replied. "Hugo's talking about going back to work." He sipped some wine. "For me, the miracle may have come too late. We're trying different combinations of drugs, but so far the effects are transient."

"The longer you can stay alive, the better your chances that something will work," I said.

"I know," he said. He unbuttoned his shirt and pulled it open, exposing his pale skin. "Feel the sun, Henry. Isn't it wonderful?"

"Are you afraid to die?"

He squinted at me. "I'm not in any hurry but five generations have gone before me, so I'll have a lot of people waiting at the dock when I get there."

"There? You think we survive death?"

He set his plate on the ground for Good Boy and said to the dog, "Don't tell Daddy." To me, he said. "Of course I believe in an afterlife. Don't you?"

"In heaven and hell? No."

He put his arm around me. "Heaven and hell? You're just like Hugo. He can only imagine heaven if there's a hell. Well, you're both Catholic, after all. Me, Henry, I think it's all heaven. Great food, good weather, hunky guys."

"You're describing San Francisco," I pointed out.

"Why not? Why shouldn't it be like this, but without the suffering?"

"Even for those who inflict suffering?"

"We all inflict suffering, honey," he said. "And we all suffer. Why not a world where everyone forgives everyone else for good?"

"Not everything can be forgiven," I said.

He shook his head. "That's why you worry about hell."

I SLEPT MORE soundly at Grant's house than I had for months. On Tuesday, I took a cab downtown to the courtroom of the Supreme Court, where I was arguing a death-penalty appeal. The justices listened to my arguments like seven sphinxes, although one of them, a judge I'd known in LA, winked recognition at me when I first rose to speak. From the court, I took a cab to Grant's, collected my belongings and went on to the airport. Waiting for my plane, I bought an *LA Times*. On the front page of the Metro section, just beneath the fold was the headline: "Police Question Suspect in W. Hollywood Slayings." I began to read: "Police have been questioning a suspect in the recent murders of two West Hollywood men, the *Times* has learned. The suspect, 45-year-old attorney Henry Rios, was initially questioned after police discovered the body of the first victim, 29-year-old Alex Amerian, in an alley off of Santa Monica Boulevard . . ." I folded the paper, tucked it into my briefcase, and went to find a phone to call Inez.

" '. . . EVIDENCE CONNECTING RIOS to the first victim the night of the murder was discovered in a search of his home,' " I read into the phone. " 'After the body of the second victim, twenty-six-year-old Jack Baldwin, was found under circumstances similar to the first victim, Rios was again questioned by sheriff's deputies. The detective in charge of the investigation, Montezuma Gaitan, declined to either confirm or deny that Rios is a suspect in the murders and would only say that the investigation is continuing.' "

There was an explosive, "That asshole," from Inez.

"Gaitan?"

"Who else?" she said. "His way of retaliating. What time do you get in?"

I glanced at my watch. "Around one."

"Come straight to my office."

IT SEEMED TO me that everyone on the plane was reading the *Times*, and even though the piece didn't carry my picture, inwardly I cringed. I knew only too well that the mere mention of someone's name in the media in connection with a crime was all the proof of guilt that most people needed. Remembering the tabloid coverage of the second murder by local TV news, I could only imagine what they would do with this new development. The media was like the Red Queen in *Alice in Wonderland*: first the execution, then the trial. I had images of TV vans lining the street outside my house, and my befuddled neighbors cornered by lacquered-haired reporters demanding, "What kind of man is he?" And it wouldn't take much research to discover that much of my practice consisted of cases on which I was appointed by the appellate courts on behalf of indigent criminal defendants. I could guess how that would play: public money pays murder suspect to defend other criminals. In fact, it wouldn't take much research to get a pretty full picture of my life, to discover I was gay or had been treated for alcoholism, exactly the kind of information that could be spun to create a media monster, another Andrew Cunanan. By the time the plane touched down in Los Angeles, I saw my life collapsing around me.

chapter 8

"ALL I KNOW," Inez explained in her unpacked office, the lights on her phone blinking urgently, "is that in politics, when your opponent goes negative you hit back hard and fast. Same thing here."

"I'm not running for anything," I replied.

"You're running for your reputation," she said. Her phone buzzed. "Let me get this."

I went to the windows. A bronze cast to the late-afternoon light gave the city a solemn, funereal look. The smog was so deep it reminded me of the fog I'd watched roll in over Twin Peaks the previous afternoon at Grant's house. Out over the ocean, the sun inflamed the wispy clouds. The little stucco houses were lined up in neat rows as far as the eye could see, like modest grave markers. An eastbound jet crossed my field of vision and I was filled with the urge to run.

"That was the sheriff's PR guy," Inez said. "They questioned Gaitan. He denies being the leak."

I turned back to her. "Duh."

"They tried the reporter. She climbed on her First Amendment high horse." Inez lit a cigarette, using a wooden kitchen match from a box on her desk.

"I assume that means no retraction."

She flicked the match into an ashtray. "The sheriff backs up Gaitan; the paper stands by its story."

"The sheriff backs up Gaitan? Gaitan's a cowboy at best. At worst, he's dirty."

"From your perspective," she said, blowing smoke out of the corner of her mouth. "To the sheriff, he might just be a very zealous cop."

"Who hates blacks and gays and plants evidence in drug cases."

"All unproven allegations," she reminded me. When I didn't answer, she continued, "I know you don't want to turn this into a media circus, but now that they have your name, they're going to hound you until you respond. Let's do it in our way and on our turf." She smiled. "Trust me, Henry. I know what I'm doing."

I looked at her. Years earlier, when we were both young public defenders, she told me the only part of trial she really enjoyed was the summation, when she knew the jurors were transfixed by her every move, hanging on her every word. We were deep in our cups—I was still drinking—and I remember she leaned against me, her heavy, scented hair falling against my cheek, and giggled, "I love it when they watch me. It's better than sex."

"You should consider what effect this might have when you run for mayor," I said now.

"I'm only defending an old friend's reputation from police excess."

"An old friend you thought might be a murderer."

Her eyes were hard and bright in her expensively madeup face. She crushed her lipsticked cigarette in the ashtray. "In politics it pays to assume the worst about everyone," she said. "You're rarely disappointed. I'm sorry if I hurt your feelings."

"Thanks," I said, wondering if she would have been so anxious to stand beside me if I had been guilty.

"Don't be childish," she said. "Amerian was a whore. You slept with him. If you consort with lowlifes you've got to expect complications."

"All right," I said. "We'll do it your way. We'll meet the press."

"I do the talking," she said, reaching for the phone.

INEZ HAD DEPLOYED an associate from the firm to drive past my house. He reported four TV vans parked outside, so I checked into a hotel under a false name, ordered in a pizza and called voice mail. Eighteen messages from friends, colleagues and clients. Most expressed concern, but some had phoned in the same spirit that makes people slow down at the site of a traffic accident. I didn't return those calls. By the ten o'clock news, KPRA had obtained a picture of me that I got to watch appear on the screen behind the broad shoulders of a male-model anchorman above the caption: SERIAL KILLING SUSPECT. I turned the TV off and worked on my statement for the press conference the next morning. At around one, after a final cheerleading call from Inez, I turned in.

I woke up an hour later, freezing. The air-conditioning had gone on overdrive. I shut it off and drifted back to sleep, but woke up a second time, drenched in sweat. I opened a window that looked out on a courtyard. The red night sky seemed to pulsate, as if lit by a distant fire. A draught of ocean air rustled through the banana trees and fluttered the still, blue surface of the pool. Anxiety knotted my stomach when I considered the prospect of

pleading my story to an audience of skeptical reporters. The feeling was similar to the anxiety I experienced when I told someone I was gay for the first
time, never knowing whether the response would be acceptance, repulsion
or something in-between, polite and noncommittal. It occurred to me that
my empathy for my clients must come from my own half-submerged feeling
of being constantly on trial and having to establish my normality over and
over in the face of the presumption that gays are freaks or monsters. The
irony was that my sympathies were with the freaks and monsters, just as it
was with my clients and not the hypocritical good burghers who passed judgment on them. I returned to bed and lay awake staring at the ceiling, where
lighter shadows danced across the darker ones. What had the old psychic
told me at Forest Lawn when I asked her to predict my future, nothing you
can't survive? Cold comfort at four in the morning.

THE PRESS CONFERENCE was held in the public meeting room of the shopping center that adjoined Inez's office building. It had been a slow summer
for scandal, and we had a packed house. After associates from Inez's firm
handed out copies of the photos from the deputies' bathroom at sheriff's
headquarters, she read a statement explaining away the evidence of my connection to Alex's murder and pointing out that no evidence connected me
to Baldwin's killing. "In fact," she continued, "because the police had my
client under surveillance the night of the second murder, they know beyond
any doubt that he is innocent, but they continue to harass and defame him
because of a pervasive homophobia in the sheriff's department personified
by the lead detective in the case, Montezuma Gaitan. Because of this bias
against homosexuals, the sheriff has ignored the obvious fact that these murders were hate crimes. We informed the sheriff some time ago that the first
victim, Alex Amerian, was gay bashed, not once, but twice in the months
before his murder and . . ."

It had been a long time since I'd seen Inez in action and I'd forgotten
how good she was at this. She wore an authoritative blue suit and she had
tied her hair back in a schoolmarmish bow. Standing beside her, I watched
some of the reporters begin to nod agreement as she tore into the sheriff's
department, not even aware they were doing it. I spotted Richie at the back
of the room. He gave me a thumbs-up.

". . . will file a malicious prosecution action if the department does not
immediately issue a statement that my client is not and never was a suspect in these tragic killings. Furthermore, ladies and gentlemen of the media, now that you are aware of the true facts of this case, I must also warn

you that we will take legal action against any news organization that continues to refer to my client as a suspect. And now, Mr. Rios will say a few words."

I went to the podium, looked at the sea of hardened, curious faces, and said, "It's unfortunate that simply by being gay, one can become a suspect in a murder case, but that's what happened here. There was a time when police didn't bother to investigate the murders of gay people or, for that matter, blacks or Latinos, because one more or less of us was not considered anything to get excited about. Even today, it still seems that police bigotry plays a bigger role in their investigation of hate crimes against gays than the actual evidence. The sheriff's department knows by now that I am innocent of these crimes. I call upon the department to exonerate me and give me back my reputation. That's all."

When the press conference was over, there was a rush to the door and, presumably, across town to sheriff's headquarters. Only Richie remained behind.

"You were fabulous," he told Inez. "You had them eating out of your hand."

I began to introduce them. Inez said, "I know Richie. His magazine profiled me when I went to DC. You two are friends?"

"I'm Henry's imaginary friend," Richie replied. "The one who slipped him the photos of the little boy's room at sheriff's headquarters."

"Sorry I didn't mention the magazine," I said.

He brushed it aside. "I'm already working on the press release."

"How do you think they'll play the story?" Inez asked him.

"Listen, you did for Henry what Johnny Cochran did for O.J.," he said. "The press will be all over the sheriff with those pictures. By the time they're finished with him, no one's going to care or remember that Henry was a suspect."

"Unlike O.J. Simpson," I reminded him, "I didn't kill anyone."

"That's not the point, anymore," Richie replied.

THE PRESS CONFERENCE was on Wednesday morning. That afternoon, the sheriff declined comment on Inez's allegations, but a liberal member of the board of supervisors called for a special commission to investigate them. The story dominated that night's news broadcasts, with follow-ups the next day, but by the weekend it had gone into suspended animation, as everyone, including me, waited for the next development. I used the time to call my clients and reassure them I was not going to jail for murder. By and large, the cons were more amused than concerned about my situation, because they knew how the cops could be once you made their shit list. They all had stories about rousts and hassles and some of them were even true. Many were more surprised by the news I was gay. A couple demanded another lawyer; one propositioned me.

A week after the press conference, I called Inez to ask whether she'd heard anything from the sheriff.

"Nothing," she said, unworriedly.

"What do you think is going on?"

"The sheriff's an elected official," she reminded me. "He can't afford to alienate anyone, that's why he's not commenting. My guess is that he'll lay low and hope all this blows over."

"Will the press let him do that?"

"Until something else happens, there's no story," she said. "Even the media doesn't make things up. Yet."

"Where does that leave me?"

"They'll never admit any wrongdoing, but I bet you've seen the last of Detective Gaitan."

"Everyone's waiting for another murder, aren't they, Inez?"

"Just make sure you're far away when it happens."

LATE FRIDAY AFTERNOON, there was a knock at the door. I assumed it was a solicitor, but when I looked through the peephole I saw two uniformed sheriff's deputies and a patrol car pulled into my driveway. I turned around, went to the phone and dialed Inez at home. Her machine picked up. I left a message and answered the door.

"Yes, what can I do for you?" I asked them.

One was white, one Latino, but otherwise they could have been twins, six-two or three, square-jawed, crew-cut, pneumatic muscles bulging beneath their uniforms. They weren't wearing badges.

"You Henry Rios?" the Latino cop asked.

"That's right. Who are you?"

"We have a warrant for your arrest," the white one said. He had wet blue eyes, a saint's eyes.

"On what charge?"

"Auto theft," he said. "Two counts."

"Is this some kind of a joke?"

"You see anyone laughing?"

"Let me see the warrant."

The white cop handed me the arrest warrant. The defendant had my name, but according to his birthdate was twenty years younger than me.

"Wrong Henry Rios," I said. "If you'll let me get my driver's license, I'll show you . . ."

The Latino cop pulled his cuffs from his belt and said, "Put your hands behind your back."

Trying to remain calm, I said, "This Henry Rios is twenty-three years old. I'm forty-five. You can see I'm not the man you're looking for."

The white cop grabbed my shoulder, flipped me around and slammed my face against the wall. The other one cuffed me.

"Turn around."

I turned, tasting blood in my mouth. "What the hell's going on here?"

The Latino cop grinned and said, "We're taking you for a ride, counsel."

I looked at him and understood immediately what was happening.

"Gaitan put you up to this."

The white cop pushed me down the steps to the patrol car. "Let's go."

WE DROVE OUT of the city on the 5 North into the vast unincorporated areas of Los Angeles that were the sheriff's domain. The cops ignored my questions about our destination. An hour out of the city, they turned off the 5 onto the 114, the road into the high desert. Dusk had fallen. The landscape, familiar from thousands of Westerns, was mountainous and austere, the ground covered by low growing vegetation, creosote and burro bush, broken only by solitary Joshua trees. We got off the freeway and headed toward a blur of city lights. We drove down a road as brightly lit as a carnival midway with fast-food restaurants and car dealerships. Drivers in other cars glanced at me and then looked quickly away. The glittering road trailed off to a row of shuttered businesses. It was getting darker. We turned off the main road to a bumpy side street. A splintering sign read: WELCOME TO ROYAL PALMS HOMES. We turned again. Around me the frames of unfinished houses rose against the deep blue desert sky. Abruptly, the car stopped. The Latino cop cut the lights.

"Where are we?"

"You'll find out," he said.

The white cop hauled me out of the backseat and pushed me toward one of the houses. The air was cold and dry. There was a stack of four-by-fours on the ground. The wood was old, decaying. The houses had been abandoned. I staggered forward until the cop behind me, the one with the saintly eyes, yanked at the handcuffs and ordered me to stop.

"Get down on your knees," he said.

I looked over my shoulder. His partner had come up beside him. Their faces were lost in the gloom.

"What are you doing?"

"I said, get down on your knees," he said, sliding his service revolver out of its holster. A Beretta nine-millimeter semiautomatic. Standard issue. He laid his finger on the barrel, regulation-style. He only had to slip it onto the trigger and squeeze.

"What's the problem, Henry?" the Latino cop said. "Ain't that where you fags spend most of your time?"

I spat, "Fuck you" at his smirking face.

The white cop grabbed the cuffs, kicked my legs out from beneath me and forced me down. He scowled, not from anger but concentration, and lowered his revolver to the level of my eyes. I looked up. His eyes had disappeared into shadow but when he stooped down to murmur, "Face the other way," I saw them again, mournful still.

"Don't do this," I said.

"Turn your head," he said, louder, irritated.

I turned my face away from him and stared through the doorway of the skeleton house to a purple ridge between two mountains where a quarter moon was rising. I felt the gun gently probe my neck. Cold tears began to drip down my face.

"Think pretty thoughts," the Latino cop said.

I drifted out of myself. I could see us there, a man kneeling before the bones of a house, two big men standing shoulder to shoulder behind him, one with his arm outstretched, the gun grazing the neck of the kneeling man. The bare terrain, the dark mountains, the big sky tumbling around them, the stars as watchful as eyes, as tremulous as souls. The man with the gun lifted it slightly until it pressed against the skull of the kneeling man. The kneeling man screamed, "No!" As his echo died, the man with the gun, instead of shooting, turned his hand and slammed the barrel into the back of the kneeling man's head.

I toppled forward. The Latino cop stepped in front of me, sliding his nightstick from his belt. The sad-eyed white cop came around the other side. I curled into the fetal position just as I had as a child when my father cornered me. After a few minutes, I could no longer tell whether it was his voice or theirs that called me queer and *maricón*.

I WOKE UP handcuffed to a hospital bed. My body resisted consciousness and I soon knew why. The smallest movement was an electric jolt. Even my hair hurt. The left side of my body throbbed dully. The room swam slowly into focus. Cinderblock walls painted nausea green, an old-fashioned air conditioner in one window, steel bars in the other. A closet, a bathroom. Across from the bed, a steel door with a narrow, horizontal window in it. A stripe of face appeared in the glass. Eyes, nose, hair. There was a clank and then the door opened to reveal Inez Montoya, a sheriff's deputy and a woman in a doctor's white jacket.

"Why is he handcuffed?" Inez demanded.

"He's under arrest," the cowed deputy explained.

She shoved a paper at him. "This is a court order for his immediate release. Uncuff him." The deputy gingerly stepped past her and complied with her demand. To the woman behind her, she said, "Can he be moved?"

"There are no broken bones," she said, "but he's probably in a lot of pain."

"No probably about it," I said weakly. "I hurt like hell. What happened?"

Inez came to the side of the bed. "I don't know. They found you sitting in the lobby last night in cuffs. You told the jailer to call me. Do you remember anything?"

"They hauled me out to the desert and put a gun to my head. Sheriff's deputies."

"Gaitan?"

"No, some thug friends of his. Shit, I hurt."

"I know," she said, touching my hand lightly, "but, Henry, while they had you in custody last night there was another murder in West Hollywood."

I lay back in bed and laughed until I choked on the pain.

THE THIRD VICTIM'S name was Tom Jellicoe, twenty-seven, a sales associate at Barney's in Beverly Hills. He was last seen getting into a cab by the bouncer of the after-hours club which he had just left. The next day, his body was found behind a discount shoe store that fronted Santa Monica Boulevard. He'd been tossed naked into the Dumpster, beaten and stabbed, the words FAG—AIDS etched across his chest. I studied his picture in the *Times*. Streaked hair, pudgy, smooth-faced. Cute but only just. Nothing special about him except the manner of his death.

The *Times* characterized the murders as "puzzling to police" and went on to say that "one man had been questioned in connection with the earlier murders, but no arrests have been made." The paper's libel lawyers were more cautious than the TV stations. They continued to broadcast my name and picture in their reporting of Jellicoe's murder, albeit also running clips from the press conference. Anticipating this, Inez had wanted to hold another press conference on the steps of the hospital, but I asked for a few days for the swelling to go down, both physical and psychological, before we made any statements. She quickly agreed, making soothing noises about my need to rest and recover from the trauma of the assault, and I let her believe that was all the damage there was. I couldn't tell her that what had really happened out there was when the cop had pressed his gun against the back of my neck and I knew I was going to die, in the last second, after I shouted "No," I felt not terror but relief. Maybe it was no more than a chemical reaction of the body to ease the inevitable moment of death, but it bothered me how easily prepared I was to let go. Had Tom Jellicoe felt something similar in the last seconds of his life? Was he glad to be done with it? I tossed the paper into the recycle bin.

The doorbell chimed. I hobbled to the door in my bathrobe, on a sprained ankle, and put my eye to the peephole. My visitor was wearing a flowered shirt and khaki shorts that showed thick, pale legs, but the mirrored sunglasses still made him look like a redneck cop from the wrong side of the bayou. Odell. When I opened the door, his glasses reflected my bare, battered torso.

"Jesus," he said.

"But no broken bones," I said, my refrain to everyone who had seen me in the past three days. "I'm guessing from your get-up this isn't an official visit."

"I heard what happened," he said, removing the mirrored glasses.

"Really?" I said, leading him into the living room. "Maybe you can explain it to me because I'm still not sure."

"What I heard was secondhand. Hearsay. I'd like to hear your version."

"Why, Sergeant? Why should I talk to you?"

"Because I have information that could help you if you decide to take some kind of legal action against the department," he said.

"Off the record, of course."

His small, bright, intelligent eyes met mine. "That depends."

I told him what I remembered. "At some point as they were working me over," I concluded, "I passed out. I came to in the jail ward of the local hospital where they'd dropped me off, charged with resisting arrest."

"What were their names?"

"They weren't wearing shields."

"What about the booking sheet?"

"I was never booked. They left me sitting on a bench in cuffs. There's a note in the jailer's log with my name and the charges beside it, but he swears he didn't write it. He claims he didn't even see them bring me in."

"Would you recognize the deputies if you saw them again?"

"I don't know. Most of the time I was staring at the backs of their heads. When the one cop pulled his gun on me, his face got so big I could've counted the hairs in his eyelashes, but now it's fading. My doctor says I have a mild concussion, and between that and the painkillers, my memories are sketchy." I yawned. "You work for the sheriff. Do you know who they were?"

He seemed to study my injuries before he spoke. "Six, seven years ago," he said, "there were rumors about a paramilitary group inside the sheriff's department. Maybe you remember?"

"Vaguely."

"It was supposed to be centered out at the Antelope Valley station. There's a lot of crazies out in the high desert, survivalists, militia-types, white supremacists." He grinned. "It's a little bit of Idaho right here in Southern California. A lot of deputies live out there."

"The Simi Valley syndrome," I said, referring to the distant suburb of LA county that was home to many LA police officers. It was famous as the site of the first Rodney King trial in which a white jury's verdict acquitting the cops who beat King precipitated a riot.

He shrugged. "Something like that. The sheriff wanted to get to the bottom of things, so he sent a couple of deputies in kind of an undercover capacity. I was one of them."

"You worked Internal Affairs?"

"Not officially," he replied. "The sheriff just figured I'd fit in."

I nodded, easily imagining Odell in the role of a bigot. "Is there a militia inside the department?"

"It was more like twenty guys getting together in a bar once a week, complaining about how the world's going to hell in a handbasket and how they would take care of business if they were in charge, and then one day a light goes on and they realize, hey, we're police officers. We are in charge, at least out there on the streets."

"Every cop eventually has that revelation."

"These guys were more organized about it," he said. "They put themselves in positions where they could give each other cover."

"You mean cover-up," I said. "For what?"

"Excessive force, illegal searches, falsified police reports, planted evidence," he said. "Everything you defense lawyers claim we do, these guys did, and they protected each other."

"Was Gaitan one of them?"

He nodded. "He was four years out there after he did his stint at the jail."

"What happened with your investigation?"

"We got the goods on six of 'em."

"Including Gaitan?"

"No, but we knew he was involved. Deeply involved."

"And the ones you caught?"

"Five were allowed to resign to avoid criminal prosecution. The last one, he pleaded no contest to one count of falsifying reports and served nine months. Another dozen, including Gaitan, were reassigned."

"That's not even a slap on the wrist."

"The sheriff wanted to break things up, not send deputies to prison. Bad for morale."

"Not to mention public relations."

"LA is the hardest place in the country to police," Odell said. "People here want it both ways. They expect us to put our lives on the line for them but they dump on us every chance they get."

"Whose fault is that?"

"I'm not going to argue the point," he said, the softness of his voice concealing steel.

"So why are you here?"

"I think the men who came to your door were two of the guys who resigned."

"Where'd they get the gear?"

"From their buddies in the department," he said. "We didn't catch all of them and some who were reassigned have drifted back. I hear on the grapevine they've started meeting again. I'd be surprised if their attitudes toward law enforcement have changed."

"Police vigilantes," I said. "Does the sheriff know they're back?"

"He does now."

"Gaitan was behind it, wasn't he?"

"That's gonna be hard to prove. Mac's much smarter than you give him credit for."

"Smarter? He's just a thug."

"That press conference of yours was a provocation."

"To him or to you?"

"It hurt all of us," he said, emphatically. "Good cops and bad. I've personally worked real hard to build up trust with the gay community in West Hollywood. You destroyed that."

"Blame the bigots in your department. Besides, how do you think I felt about having my name appear in the media as a murder suspect?"

"That was Gaitan working freelance."

"It doesn't matter. I had to respond. My reputation was on the line."

"We could've worked something out," he said.

"Not according to your boss, the sheriff," I replied.

"He listens to me."

It occurred to me that while Odell might look like a corpulent southern sheriff, he had the soul of a frontier lawman; Gary Cooper's heart in Andy Devine's body.

"I thought you worked for him."

"Chuck Ramsay and I go back a long way. We have our understandings."

"Why aren't you running West Hollywood if you're so tight with him?"

"I do," he said. It was a simple declaration of fact. "I'm not still a sergeant because I can't get promoted. I choose to stay in the field."

"If everything's copacetic with you and the sheriff, why are you giving me ammunition to sue the department?"

"I don't like what happened to you."

"That's touching," I said, "if not entirely convincing."

He shrugged. "Believe what you want. There's a problem in the department. I want to see it solved."

"You're an insider, Odell," I said. "Someone like you doesn't tell tales out of school unless you've already been to your friend, the sheriff, and he blew you off. Is that what happened?"

He got up to go. "I did what I came to do," he announced. "The ball's in your court." On his way out, he paused and said, "But I'd keep an eye on your lawyer."

THE NEXT MORNING, while I was still pondering Odell's warning, Inez turned up at my door with a bag of *pan dulce* and a box of *Abuelita* cocoa. She removed her pinstriped jacket and went into the kitchen, where she went about making the cinnamon-laden hot chocolate. Refusing my offers of help, she clattered through the shelves and cupboards, cursing when she couldn't find what she was looking for. I had never seen Inez in a kitchen before. It was unnerving.

"Whenever I was upset, my mother always served me *pan dulce* and

Abuelita," she said, running her finger along the rim of a serving plate. "Look at the dust on this. When was the last time you cleaned in here?"

"I don't dust my dishes. Wouldn't it be easier if I did this?"

"You're sick," she said. "Fuck! I burned my hand on the fucking pot. Don't you have pot holders?"

"On the rack under the sink. And I'm not sick, Inez, I'm battered."

She turned from the stove to me. I was wearing drawstring pants and sandals. "You look better than you did in the hospital."

"They were very careful how they hit me," I said. "Soft tissue damage only."

She poured the chocolate into mugs. "Here, you take these. I'll bring the pastries. Let's sit outside."

It was a musty midsummer morning, the air dry and stale. The canyon was more brown than green. Fire season. We sat down at the picnic table. The chocolate burned my tongue while the *pan dulce*, a little mound of bread topped with squares of crumbly sugar, was flavorless. So much for Inez's home remedy. My mother gave me chicken soup when I was sick.

"I've been talking to the sheriff," Inez said. "I think we've worked out a deal."

"A deal? Three days ago you wanted me to show my wounds to the world."

"The sheriff disclaims any responsibility for the men who abducted you," she said, through a mouthful of pastry. "He says they were impersonating deputies."

"I know," I replied. "Odell told me."

"Odell?" she said, narrowing her eyes. "When did you talk to him?"

I told her about his visit, leaving out his warning at the end.

"He should've come to me," she huffed when I finished. "Still, I guess it doesn't matter as long as you understand why it would be a bad idea to sue the department."

"I don't understand," I said. "I want to sue the department. I want to crucify the department. Those men were acting under color of authority whether or not they were employed as deputies."

"Do you know how hard that's going to be to prove?" she asked, blowing across her cup. "Or how long it's going to take? Years, Henry. Not to mention the expense." She sipped her chocolate. "I've been acting as your lawyer as a favor, but if you take on the sheriff, the firm will expect to be paid for my time and I'm not even sure I'm the best lawyer to handle this kind of case."

"Inez, I was kidnapped, threatened with a gun and beaten," I said. "I want those punks punished, and if Gaitan is connected, I want him punished, too. I don't care how long it takes or how much it costs."

"I understand," she said. "You feel victimized, but think about it as a lawyer for a minute. You'll be in discovery for a decade just to figure out the identity of the men who kidnapped you, and you'll spend another ten years arguing over whether the department was liable for the action of a couple of rogue cops or ex-cops. Are you ready to depose every deputy who works or ever worked out in Antelope Valley? Subpoena every piece of paper? Because that's what it's going to take to get answers, if you can get answers. We both know cops and cons don't snitch."

"One of the many ways you can't tell them apart," I said. "Odell will cooperate."

"I wouldn't count on him," she said. "He may have a hair up his ass now but he's a company man. He'll come around. Besides, what about that daughter of his in LAPD? They find out the old man's a snitch and they'll make her life miserable."

I was exhausted and my body ached. Inez had covered all the angles and she was right about everything. The case would be complicated and difficult even if Odell cooperated and if he didn't, I could forget about it. If Inez bailed, I faced the further difficulty of finding a lawyer who would work on at least partial contingency. Unless I represented myself, but I was a criminal lawyer, not a civil one, and I would be over my head from day one.

"You said you cut a deal with the sheriff," I said, wearily. "What kind of deal?"

She perked up. "He agrees to issue a statement completely exonerating you from any suspicion in the West Hollywood murders and apologizing for the leak to the press. He also agrees to launch an internal investigation into whether anyone in his department was involved in your abduction, and if they were, he'll turn their names over to the District Attorney for prosecution. Finally, he agrees to a cash settlement. A hundred thousand dollars."

I laughed incredulously. "He denies any responsibility, but he's willing to buy me off."

"He denies legal responsibility," she said. "But he knows he's got a problem with his people out in the desert, so he accepts moral responsibility."

"Accepting moral responsibility is the last refuge of politicians. It's meaningless," I said. "Plus, Inez, how does he propose to get the board of su-pervisors to approve a hundred thousand dollar settlement on a claim that doesn't officially exist?"

"That's his worry," she said. She licked a crumb from the corner of her mouth. "Deal?"

"What's his quid pro quo?"

"We keep our mouths shut."

"About the settlement or what happened out there in the desert?"

"Both," she said. I looked at her. She met my eyes and gazed back at me. There was a lot of history in that back and forth. "I've given this a lot of thought, Henry. It's in everyone's best interest."

"Does this buy the sheriff's neutrality in the mayor's race or his endorsement?"

Her face slowly darkened and she pulled herself up from the table.

"That's it. You go tilt at your fucking windmills alone."

"No, wait," I said, laying a restraining hand on her arm. "Don't leave, Inez. I'm sorry. I'm not in the best frame of mind."

"I know what happened to you out there," she said, "but you have to be reasonable."

"You're right," I said. "I should be reasonable. A messy case like this could eat up the next five years of my life. Ruin my practice, bankrupt me. Drive me crazy. I just hate that Gaitan will get away with humiliating me."

"That's playground thinking."

"I can taste his hatred in the back of my throat."

"Maybe you're tasting your own," she said. "What do you care? He's an asshole."

"It was guys like Gaitan who expelled me from la raza for being gay."

"You let them," she said. "They tried to run me out because I'm a tough broad. I fought back. So could you."

"It's too late," I said. "I don't belong anymore. I don't want to belong."

"So you're happy with this life?" she said, gesturing toward my empty house. "Your boyfriend's ashes on the fireplace. Dusty dishes in the kitchen. Wake up, Henry. Josh is dead, not you."

"You are a tough broad," I said, smiling. "Why aren't you a lesbian?"

"*Diosito mio*, I get so sick of you men sometimes, I wish I was a dyke," she replied. "What can I say? I like boys. Do I have to tell you why?"

"Make the deal," I said. "We'll split the money."

"You need it more than I do."

"Please, leave me with a shred of male dignity."

She kissed my forehead maternally. "I'll take care of it. You get better. 'Bye, *m'ijo*."

I SAT ON the deck for a long time after Inez left. Letting Alex Amerian into my life had brought me one disaster after another, and I should have been relieved that it was finally over. But I wasn't. There was a man out there venting his hatred for people like me on the bodies of young men. Some of those entrusted to find him shared his hatred for his victims. It was hard to say from whom the rest of us had the most to fear.

chapter 9

AT THE END of July came a series of breathtakingly beautiful days. Desert winds swept the air clean and the light had a purity and intensity reminiscent of an earlier time, when the city was still half orange grove and street cars shuttled back and forth between downtown and the ocean. The San Gabriel mountains, seldom visible between May and December, appeared so suddenly it was as though they were advancing on us like a herd of ancient behemoths. The shiny leaves of the ficus trees were an even glossier green, the throats of the cawing bird of paradise a deeper purple, and the white walls of the stuccoed city blazingly bright. At Forest Lawn in Hollywood Hills the light ricocheted off the marble surfaces of the Courts of Remembrance and the air smelled of cut grass, eucalyptus and roses. I sat in the Columbarium of Radiant Destiny, on the bench where Amiga Slade had shared her tea with me, and contemplated the brass marker that recorded Josh's name and dates and beneath them the words BELOVED SON & BROTHER and, beneath that, LITTLE FRIEND. There were fresh flowers in the vase beside the marker, white carnations. They weren't from me. I wondered who, among his friends, had come to visit. Who among them was still alive? After I had interred his ashes, I'd gone through his address book and sent out notes to let his friends know where he could be found. They were still coming back to me, marked "Deceased." I'd written his parents, too, and half-expected them to return the letter unread. I was glad they hadn't. Glad for Josh. I still hadn't forgiven them. But sitting there in the shade, I remembered that Grant had told me heaven was nothing more than a world where everyone forgave everyone else, and my anger thawed, for a moment.

I got up to go. On my way to my car, I saw a fresh burial mound and wondered whether the police had ever released Alex's body or those of the other victims of the killer the media had briefly christened the Invisible Man. Briefly, because since Tom Jellicoe's murder almost a month earlier there had been no others and the story had faded from public attention. My involvement had ended with the sheriff's statement that I was not nor had I ever been a suspect and apologizing for any misimpression. Privately, I agreed not to sue the department and accepted the settlement Inez had negotiated.

Up to the last moment, I'd considered backing out of the agreement and going ahead with a lawsuit. Part of me still very much wanted vengeance, especially against Gaitan, but I knew Inez was right about my chances of prevailing in an action against the department, so I reluctantly let it drop. When I signed the release, Inez reminded me that the sheriff was conducting an investigation of my kidnapping, but I could've predicted the result and I was not surprised when a letter came from county counsel exonerating the department. Other than that, my last contact with anyone in the department had been with Odell, who told me off the record that the investigation had been cursory, as if I hadn't already guessed that. I paused for a second at the mound of drying dirt that covered the new grave. Now that the murders had apparently stopped, the cops would have no incentive for solving them, and the case would be as dead as whoever lay here. And anyway what were three more unsolved murders in this city, where each year hundreds were killed? It was like a war out there, and in war you didn't stop to count every casualty, much less determine the cause of every death. In war, the bottom line was who was winning. The cops knew it wasn't them. Violence was escalating in the city, rising like the temperature in a kettle on a low flame, so gradually and inexorably that before we knew what was happening we'd all be boiled alive.

A COUPLE OF days later, the weather reverted to its usual summer pattern of smog and heat. I was working at my desk when the phone rang. When I picked it up a woman said, officiously, "Please hold for Mr. Nick Donati." I didn't know any Mr. Nick Donati, so I hung up.

A moment later, the phone rang again. This time when I picked it up a deep, authoritative male voice asked, "Mr. Rios? Did you just hang up on my secretary?"

"Are you Mr. Nick Donati?"

"That's me," he said.

"Then, yes, I did hang up on your secretary."

"Why did you do that?" he asked, with apparently genuine curiosity.

"Because I've never heard of you."

His chuckle, like his speaking voice, was too deep to be natural. "I'm sorry, Mr. Rios. In my business, you never pick up the phone and just call someone, because no one wants to deal with you if you actually have time for them."

"What is your business, Mr. Donati?"

"Nick," he said. "I'm the head of the legal department at Parnassus Studio. We have a problem here involving one of our people and I thought you could help us out with it."

"A legal problem?"

"Yes."

"I'm not an entertainment lawyer. I'm in criminal defense."

"I know that," he assured me.

"What happened? One of your actors get picked up for driving under the influence?"

"It's a little more complicated than that," he said. "You know about the Invisible Man murders in West Hollywood." It wasn't a question.

"What about them?"

"The police suspect one of our people of being the killer."

The screen of my computer went momentarily blank and then tropical fish drifted across it. "An employee?"

"Yes," he said. "His name is Bob Travis. He works on a TV show called *Nights in Blue.*"

"*Nights in Blue,*" I said. "The cop show?"

"Yeah, the studio coproduces and it's filmed on the lot. We get a lot of cooperation from LAPD and the sheriff's department. That's what's so ironic about this situation."

"Why do the police suspect Mr. Travis?"

"I didn't call you at random," he said. "I know the police questioned you about the murders and I watched your press conference. Your lawyer, Ms. Montoya, claimed the police were going after you because they were biased against gays. Bob Travis is gay and I believe something similar may be happening here."

"What makes you think that?"

"I'd really prefer to discuss this face to face."

"Customarily, Nick," I said, "it's the suspect who calls the lawyer."

"There's potential studio involvement," he said.

"So who's the client here?"

"The studio wants to hire you to represent Bob. You've already dealt with these people once, on your own behalf. We'd like you to deal with them on his. And ours."

"These people?"

"The sheriffs," he said. "Detective Gaitan."

I let this sink in. "Gaitan's still on the case?"

"He seems to be in charge of it," Donati said. "He's kind of a tough customer, but you probably know that."

"When do you and Mr. Travis want to meet?"

"This afternoon? Around four? I'm sure you know where we are. Just come to the front gate and give the guard your name."

"I'll be there."

PARNASSUS STUDIO WAS not only Hollywood's oldest studio, it was the only one actually located there, occupying four square blocks on La Brea between Beverly and Melrose. Like a medieval fortress, it was enclosed by a high wall. Nothing was visible from the street but a water tower emblazoned with the studio's logo, a mountain crowned with a laurel wreath representing Mount Parnassus, which, in Greek mythology, was the abode of the Muses. This was the studio that Duke Asuras headed and which Richie claimed was in danger of being sold to Reverend Longstreet, the anti-gay crusader. As I pulled up to the famous front gate, a replica of Hadrian's Arch—which was Roman, not Greek, but this was Hollywood—and gave my name to the female guard who consulted a list, handed me a map and waved me through, I wasn't thinking about Asuras or Longstreet. All I was thinking was that fate had handed me another chance to tangle with Gaitan. I pulled into a parking lot and got out expecting to see extras parading around in costume, but the only other people around were two Japanese businessmen hunched over a map, conversing in Japanese.

The parking lot was enclosed by two- or three-story stucco buildings painted beige with brown trim. Looming in the distance were enormous barnlike structures. I consulted my map and found the administration building where Donati's office was located. My path led me across a perfectly trimmed patch of grass where perfect flowers grew in identically proportioned flower beds reminiscent of the grounds at Forest Lawn. The surrounding buildings were in an architectural style that combined the sleek lines of Art Deco with the baroque ornamentation of Spanish Colonial. I stopped to examine an exhibit case that held shelves of Academy Awards. Some went back to the early thirties, for best movie or best actor or director. All of them bore the inscription on their base: DUPLICATE FOR STUDIO USE. I walked on, unnoticed by the men and women in suits who came in and out of the buildings, briskly purposeful, their eyes hidden behind Oliver Peoples sunglasses. The administration building was newer than its neighbors. Inside was a vast lobby, the walls of which were faced in brown marble and bare except for a dozen framed movie posters. The stainless steel walls of the elevator I took to Donati's office on the fourth floor made me think of an autopsy table.

NICK DONATI SAT at a big desk in a double-breasted charcoal suit that, upon closer inspection, sported the subtlest of pinstripes. I hadn't spent all that time around Richie without picking up a thing or two about fashion, so I was pretty sure the suit was Armani and had cost at least a grand. I felt pretty dowdy by comparison in my old olive drab Brooks Brothers sack suit. Donati's dark hair was crisply barbered and threaded with gray and his light blue eyes were searching and intelligent in a bony, handsome face. I judged him to be about my age. As his secretary ushered me into his office, he flashed a flawlessly white smile and came around his desk, hand extended. Then the shock. He was child-sized, no more than five foot three, even in his discreetly lifted loafers. On the slender column of his neck, his big head was like an unwieldy monument. He stopped about a foot and half away from me, grasped my large hand in his delicate one and squeezed firmly. Later it occurred to me that the reason he'd stopped short was because, had he come any closer, instead of discreetly tilting his head forward to meet my eyes, he would've had to look up at me. It also occurred to me that he was not aware of doing this, that it was second nature to him.

"Henry," he said, his deep voice as incongruous as his big head. "Thanks for coming. Have a seat. Can I get you something to drink?"

"Coffee," I said, masking my surprise at his appearance. "Black."

He settled into his chair and directed his secretary to bring in the coffee. I glanced around his office. On the wall behind him were ornately framed degrees from his undergraduate and law schools, Cornell and Columbia. On the credenza were a half-dozen framed photographs of Donati in black tie with similarly dressed people, including a movie star or two, of whom I recognized Tom Hanks and a Baldwin brother at what were clearly social functions. In each of them, he maintained his height-leveling distance. Off to the side, prominent in its isolation, a snapshot showed him standing in a park with two small sleek dogs on either side of him.

"Pablo and Paloma," he said, following my glance.

"What are they?"

"Italian greyhounds," he replied, his eyes lingering on the photograph. "Do you have pets, Henry?"

"I've never had time for pets."

"You should make time," he said, reluctantly looking away from the picture. "Studies prove that people who have pets are happier and live longer than people who don't have them."

"Why not just take vitamins?"

He grinned. "You're really not a pet person."

His secretary trundled in with the coffee, which had a rich, expensive smell.

"Where's Mr. Travis?" I asked Donati after she left.

"He'll be here," Donati replied. "I wanted to talk to you privately first."

I sipped the excellent coffee. "About what?"

"This is the most publicity-conscious business on the planet, Henry. Hollywood's not a fishbowl, Henry, it's a shark tank. I'm trying to keep the scent of blood out of the water."

"People in your business have a pretty exaggerated sense of their own importance."

With one of his small, delicate hands, he made a subtle gesture of disagreement. "No, it's not really about vanity. Making movies isn't like making widgets. Every movie is a huge financial gamble. Plus, the people who make the movies, like creative people everywhere, tend to be a little more unstable than your average factory worker. It's a volatile mix where perception is reality and rumors have incredible power, so naturally we all tend to be a bit hypersensitive about appearances."

"What does this have to do with me?"

"If you agree to represent Bob, I have to be able to count on your discretion," he said. "I need for you to try to keep the studio out of this. There are things going on, high-level stuff, that would be seriously impacted by adverse publicity."

I wondered if he meant the Longstreet deal. "Other than the fact that Travis works here, how could Parnassus possibly be involved?"

"The police think studio property was used in the murders."

"Why don't we start at the beginning," I suggested.

Donati nodded. "A couple of weeks ago, Detective Gaitan showed up here, asking whether we had ever used a picture car . . ."

"A what?" I interrupted.

"A picture car," he said. "A prop car. Gaitan was looking for a blue-and-white cab with the logo Lucky's Taxi Service painted on the side. He said the car had been connected to one of the murders and a deputy of his thought he remembered seeing it when he was working location for *Nights in Blue*. I told Gaitan I'd have to check, but if I found it we'd cooperate any way we could."

"Was it one of yours?"

"Yes. It was used on the *Nights in Blue* set."

"And you turned it over to Gaitan and he found something?"

"Here's the complication," Donati said, gingerly. "Once I discovered the cab, I talked the situation over with my boss and we decided I should . . . ," he paused and seemed to grope for the right word, ". . . look the car over before we gave it to the police."

I lifted an eyebrow. "You searched the car before you turned it over to the police? That's obstruction of justice, Nick."

His eyes froze. "I wasn't planning on destroying evidence. I just wanted to know if there was anything that could incriminate the studio."

"What would you have done if the backseat was covered in blood?"

"It wasn't," he snapped. Smiled. "Fortunately."

"What did you find?"

"Nothing," Donati said. "We called the sheriffs and let them impound the car to conduct their own search. They also asked to talk to everyone who had had access to the car since the beginning of June. We gave them a list of twenty-two people, including Bob. I sat in on some of the interviews. Basically, the police wanted to know whether anyone had driven the car off the lot. Of course, a number of people had when the show went out on location shots . . ."

"You'll have to explain that to me," I said.

"*Nights in Blue* supposedly takes place in Detroit," he said, "but except for the opening montage, it's all filmed here in LA, mostly at the studio on the New York street set. Occasionally, the producer likes to go off the lot and shoot around the city. When he does that, he takes his picture cars with him, including the Lucky taxi."

"Why not use real cabs?"

Donati raised his eyebrows. "I'll tell you about the teamsters sometime."

"What about Travis? Did he work on location shoots?"

"Yeah," he said. "Bob is the assistant production designer on the show."

"Like a set designer in the theater?"

"More or less," Donati said, then smiling, asked, "Were you in theater, Henry?"

"I was in my junior high school's production of *Arsenic and Old Lace*," I said. "I played the evil brother. Cast for my height, not my talent."

"I wanted to be an actor when I was a kid," he said.

"What happened?"

"I stopped growing." He sipped some coffee. "To answer your original question, Bob did go out on location to touch things up, give them the right look. You know, add graffiti, toss some garbage around, change street signs, bring in snow, whatever it takes for downtown LA to resemble downtown Detroit."

"Would he have driven the cab?"

"Absolutely not," Donati said, emphatically. "The union's very touchy about that. No, Bob didn't drive the cab on the set, but he did remove it from the lot for his own personal use and without anyone's permission."

"Why?"

"Earlier this summer, his car had major mechanical problems that he couldn't pay for. While he got together the money for the repairs, he borrowed some of the picture cars, including the cab."

"He drove off the lot in a fake cab and no one stopped him? What about the guard at the gate."

"The guards' job is to keep people from getting onto the lot. They don't pay much attention to people leaving. You just smile and wave and they open the gate."

"Wouldn't a cab be conspicuous?"

"To the contrary, people are always arriving here by cab from the airport for a meeting or something. The guards didn't know the cab was a picture car. That's one reason Bob took it."

"There's no paperwork when you take a car off the lot?"

"Only if you do it legitimately," Donati said. "Bob didn't. He waited until shooting was over for the day, then took the keys from the pegboard and drove off. He was careful to return the car before the next day's shooting began."

"All right," I said, "so Travis borrowed the car. That's a long way to making him a murder suspect."

"When the police searched the car, they found evidence."

"What kind of evidence?"

"They're not saying until they can talk to Bob again."

"What do you think they found?"

"I don't think they found anything," Donati said, meeting my eyes. "I searched that car, Henry. It was clean."

"You're suggesting the cops are bluffing?"

"I think they planted evidence."

"That's a very serious charge."

"I spent a couple of hours with Detective Gaitan," he said, "and while I'm no criminal-defense lawyer, even I could tell the man has a bad smell to him."

"Anything specific?"

"I gathered he was under a lot of pressure to close this case," Donati said. "It didn't seem to me he cared all that much how he did it."

"So you're basing your suspicion on the fact that he found evidence where you didn't after he'd indicated he was in a hurry to close the case."

"That, and the fact that of all the people he interviewed, Bob's the one he suspects."

"Why is that significant?"

"Because," Donati said, "as I told you over the phone, Bob's gay. In fact, he was the only gay person of the twenty-two Gaitan interviewed. I think you know how Gaitan feels about gay people."

"This isn't about me, now," I said. "It's about Bob Travis."

"No," Donati said. "It's about Detective Gaitan." At that moment, his phone buzzed discreetly. He picked it up. "Yeah, okay. Send him in." He put it down and said, "See for yourself. Bob Travis is here."

HAD THERE BEEN a homosexual Everyman for white, urban gay males, he would've looked very much like the person who now entered Donati's office. Bob Travis had the average dimensions of an ordinary man in his early thirties, but he was skillfully renovated so as to appear somehow taller, thinner and better-looking than he was. He wore black rayon pants, a thin black alligator belt, a white linen shirt buttoned to the neck and a red, gold and black striped silk vest. The slight orangish tint to his skin suggested his tan was the result of lying in a machine rather than sitting in the sun. His clothes were tight around his chest, arms and thighs where his body was pumped from the gym, but the muscles conveyed effort rather than physical strength and contrasted oddly with his soft, slightly flabby face. His mouth was a long, thin line and his small, perfect nose was too obviously the result of rhinoplasty. Beneath sparse eyebrows his eyes were his best feature, china blue, quick and bright. His pale hair was buzzed to trendy stubble to disguise incipient baldness. I could smell his cologne from across the room—Eternity. From a distance, he was handsome, but as he approached, a worried smile bending the nearly lipless mouth, I was conscious of how much work had gone into the package, the painful effort to raise himself a notch or two on the scale of male pulchritude.

"Mr. Travis," I said, shaking his hand after Donati made formal introductions.

"Hi," he said, his eyes flicking up and down my body in the reflexive ten-second sexual appraisal men give anything that moves. "I'm very happy to meet you."

"Henry has a couple of questions for you," Donati said.

I leaned toward him, forcing him to meet my eyes. "Did you kill those three men?"

He licked the corner of his mouth with a pointed tongue, but his eyes stayed on mine. "I didn't kill anyone, Mr. Rios," he said.

"Why do you think the police suspect you?"

"It was the car," he said. "The cab. I took it off the lot when my car was in the shop, but it wasn't that hard, Mr. Rios. Anyone could've taken it."

His eagerness to please, to be helpful, bordered on self-abnegation, and for a moment I saw the good little boy he must have been.

"You must make a decent living," I said. "Why didn't you rent a car while yours was being repaired?"

He glanced anxiously at Donati. "I have some debts."

"Tell him everything, Bob," Donati said.

"Okay, financially I'm way over my head. Maxed out on all my credit cards. I didn't have the money to fix my car when it broke down and I couldn't afford to rent one, so I took cars off the lot."

"Why the cab?" I asked him. "Why that particular car?"

"Because it was easy to get it off the lot," he said. "I put on my sunglasses and a baseball cap, slouched down and the guards actually thought I was a cab driver. They let me in and out without questioning me. And it was kind of a kick to cruise around in a cab. People flagged me down for rides."

"Did you pick any of them up?"

"No," he said, the good boy again. "I'm not licensed to drive a cab. I didn't want to get into trouble."

"Did you know Alex Amerian?"

"No."

"Jack Baldwin?"

He licked his mouth again, shook his head.

"Tom Jellicoe?"

"I didn't know any of them, Mr. Rios. Look," he said, "I'm gay. I live in West Hollywood. I was as scared as anyone else when I started hearing about those murders."

"Where in West Hollywood do you live?"

"On Flores Street, just below Fountain," he said.

"That's within a couple of miles of where all the bodies were discovered."

"Tell me about it," he said. "I stopped going out after eleven."

That he lived in the neighborhood where the bodies were found was an additional circumstance supporting Gaitan's decision to go with him as a suspect. One Donati hadn't mentioned.

"When did you use the cab?"

He frowned. "The police asked me that, too. My car was broken down most of June, but I only took cars off the lot on weekends or if I needed to get around to do errands. I guess I took the cab maybe three or four times until I finally borrowed the cash to fix my car."

"I'm interested in dates," I said.

"I don't remember dates," he said, snippily.

"Try."

"I'll have to look at a calendar," he said.

"The cops told Nick they found evidence in the cab linking it to the murders," I said. "You drove it. What did you see?"

"Nothing," he said. "I can't imagine what they're talking about."

"Do you know how often it was cleaned?"

"It all depends on the look the director's going for," he said. "Sometimes you want it to look grubby."

"When you borrowed it, did you clean it before returning it?"

"No, I snuck it back on the lot in the same condition I took it out. I would've been in big trouble if anyone knew I'd borrowed it."

"You're in pretty big trouble now," I observed.

"Tell me about it," he said. Beads of sweat were forming on his upper lip despite the air-conditioned chill in the air.

"What happened when you talked to Detective Gaitan?"

At the mention of Gaitan's name, the crease between his eyes deepened. "At first he was sort of friendly, but when I told him I lived in West Hollywood, he asked me if I was a homosexual. That's the word he used. I said, 'Well, I'm gay, if that's what you mean,' and after that his entire attitude changed. He started calling me Bobby, but it was sarcastic, not friendly."

"What kind of questions did he ask you?"

"The same ones you asked," he said, "about the cab, and my financial situation but it wasn't like he was asking questions because he was interested in my answers. It was like he already knew the answers and was testing me."

"He was trying to catch him in a lie," Donati said.

"You were there?"

"I sat in on Bob's interviews," he said. "The tone he took with Bob was different than with anyone else. Total contempt. I finally intervened."

"What did you say?"

"I told him that some of his questions seemed inappropriate," Donati said. "The guy was asking Bob about his sex life."

"What did Gaitan say?"

"He said he would decide what questions were appropriate and told me to get lost, basically," Donati replied. "So I threw him off the lot."

I smiled. "You did what?"

"I reminded him that I was the studio's lawyer, that he was at the studio as a courtesy and then I told him he'd worn out his welcome. I asked him to leave."

"And did he?"

Now Donati smiled. "Oh, yes. He left. And later that day I had my boss call the sheriff and complain."

"Your boss is . . ."

"Duke Asuras," he said. "The head of the studio."

I nodded, turned my attention to Travis. "Gaitan wants to question you again?"

"Tomorrow. He called me and said if I didn't show up, he'd arrest me."

"I assume that's bullshit," Donati said to me. "I don't remember much criminal law, but if the police have probable cause to arrest, they don't usually invite you to come and discuss it with them, do they?"

"No, they don't," I said. "I'd like to talk to Bob alone for a few minutes."

He glanced at his watch, nodded. "Sure, I have a meeting with my boss so you can stay here and talk. If I'm not back when you're done, I wonder if you'd wait for me, Henry."

"All right."

Travis's anxiety level soared after Donati left the room.

"You seem very anxious, Bob."

"I'm terrified," he blurted out.

"I can see that," I said. He'd gone white beneath his salon tan, and sweat stained the armpits of his expensive shirt.

"Nick told me about you," he said. "He said you were a suspect for a while. He told me you're gay, too."

"That's all true," I replied.

"Then you know about Gaitan. I moved here to get away from people like him. People that stare at you like you're something they stepped in. He made me so nervous I would have confessed just to get away from him."

He would've made a bad interview, I thought, dripping in his own sweat, alternately eager to please and frightened.

"I know better than you what kind of cop Gaitan is," I said. "He's a thug, but he's not stupid, and the fact is that you are a legitimate suspect based on what you've told me today, even without knowing what the evidence is he claimed to find in the car."

"I didn't . . ."

"Two of the three victims were last seen getting into an off-duty cab," I said. "Someone has obviously identified the cab as the same one you were driving around the time the murders were committed last month. Plus, Bob, you live in the neighborhood where the bodies were found. Based on that alone, I'd suspect you, too."

"Other people could've taken the car," he said.

"Someone obviously did. Who else could it have been?"

"I don't know," he said, "but it wasn't me."

"Tell me about yourself," I said.

"What?" he looked confused, suspicious.

"Let's just talk."

In the next hour I learned that Bob Travis was thirty-four but admitted to thirty-one and lived beyond his means in a two-bedroom apartment furnished with antiques and a closet full of designer clothes. He hit the bars on weekends, used drugs recreationally, mostly pot and occasionally Ecstasy, had never had a steady boyfriend and had gone into therapy to discover why. Travis was quietly but deeply dissatisfied with his life, and sometimes wondered if being gay was not the cause of his unhappiness, but felt guilty about this because he thought he was supposed to be proud of being out. He gave money to AIDS and gay organizations when he could and had volunteered at Project Angel Food, delivering meals to people with AIDS, but quit because it got too depressing. He enjoyed his work, but worried about advancing, got along better with his women coworkers than the men, but didn't see any of them socially. His small circle of friends was all other gay men, and while his family back in Maryland was "okay" with his homosexuality, he rarely saw or spoke to them. What he wanted most in life was a nice house, a stable career and a boyfriend.

By the time I'd finished questioning him, I had concluded that if he was the killer, he was an incredibly brilliant actor or completely psychotic to be able to fake such ordinariness. He didn't appear to be either.

As if he'd read my mind, he asked, "Did I pass?"

"The studio wants to hire me to represent you. Is that what you want?"

"Yes," he said, gratefully.

"All right," I said. "I'll call Gaitan and set up a meeting. In the meantime, you are not to talk to anyone about this case, especially the police. Here's my card. Refer any questions to me."

"What about Nick?"

"Nick represents the studio," I said. "I represent you."

Travis frowned. "But the studio's paying you."

"That doesn't mean I work for them," I said, "but of course I'll keep Nick informed so long as there's no conflict of interest."

"I really need to get back to work," Travis said apologetically.

"Go," I said. "We'll talk tomorrow."

I GATHERED MY things and prepared to leave, then remembered that Donati had asked me to wait for him. At that moment, his secretary came in and said, "Mr. Rios? Mr. Donati asked me to bring you to Mr. Asuras's office. They'd like to have a word with you."

chapter 10

ASURAS'S SUITE OCCUPIED the top floor of the administration building. After a five-minute wait in an austere anteroom that featured as its
sole decoration a gigantic bronze temple gong, his male secretary led me in
to the inner sanctum. The room was arctic, so cold I shivered. It was also
very large, and decorated in a style that was supposed to evoke the paneled
library of an English country house, but the books which filled the bookshelves seemed chosen for size and color rather than content, and instead of
hunting prints there was a series of odd, brilliantly colored framed wall hangings filled with floating Buddhas and fanged Asian monster gods. New Agey
music seeped quietly into the cold air and I detected the smell of sandal-
wood. At the far end of the room was a massive and unoccupied desk. Off
in a corner a hard round pillow lay on the floor in front of a kind of altar
that held candles, a small Buddha, bells, a framed photograph of the Dalai
Lama, a vase of flowers. Through a bank of tinted windows I saw shirtless
construction workers swigging sodas from a roach coach. On the other side
of the room, Duke Asuras and Nick Donati were seated in front of a blazing
fire in an ornate fireplace, having tea. Asuras was as physically imposing as
I remembered him, while the diminutive Donati seemed like — I thought of
his greyhounds — the big man's lapdog.

"Over here, Henry," Nick said.

I walked across the room, conscious of Asuras's assessing gaze. He wore
a brown tweed jacket over a brown leather vest buttoned to his neck, a
banded-collar shirt, gray wool pants, highly polished boots. Not exactly summer in LA wear. Above the fireplace was the largest of the wall hangings. It
depicted a circle in the maw of a black demon. The circle was divided into
six segments, showing animals, humans, wraiths, demons, gods and warriors.
In the center a smaller circle showed a rooster devouring a snake that was
devouring a pig. I recognized it from visits with Josh to the New Age book
store the Bodhi Tree as the Buddhist Wheel of Becoming. Each of the six
segments represented a realm into which a soul could be reincarnated. The
three animals in the center represented ignorance, desire and malice. The
black demon was Yama, the god of death. Josh, who went to the Bodhi Tree

in search of spiritual sustenance, often stared at their poster of the Wheel and speculated into which realm he might be reincarnated. The goal, however, was not to come back at all.

"Sit down, Mr. Rios," Asuras said. "Have some tea."

I sank into a red leather armchair with brass studs. "No, thank you."

"Something else?" he asked solicitously. "Coffee? It's early, but if you'd like a drink."

"Nothing," I said. "This is quite a place. Are you a Buddhist or just a collector?"

"Both," he said. "You know about Buddhism?"

"It's the religion du jour, isn't it?"

Asuras frowned, formidably. "I'm sincere about my practice."

"I didn't mean to suggest you weren't."

"The hour I sit at my altar meditating is crucial," he said. "The liberating thing about Buddhism is that it teaches there is no right and wrong, just cause and effect."

"Karma?" I asked.

"And cause and effect," he continued, ignoring me, "are themselves illusions."

"So what does that leave?" I asked.

He grinned. "Perfect freedom of action. And once you understand that," he droned on, "you can go out into the world as a warrior. Free to risk everything, to lose everything, because nothing matters but the act."

Nick Donati discreetly stifled a yawn. I imagined such theological ruminations must become tiresome after a couple of thousand times, and it seemed from their obvious ease around each other that they'd had a long and intimate association.

"That's very interesting," I said, politely. "Nick's secretary said you wanted a word with me."

Asuras put his cup down. "Is the man guilty?"

"I beg your pardon?"

"Was I unclear?" he asked. "I want to know if we have a murderer on the lot."

I turned to Donati. "Do you want to explain attorney-client privilege, or should I?"

"No one needs to explain anything to me," Asuras said. "I have a law degree from Yale University. Let me explain something to you. The studio's paying your fee and that makes you a studio employee."

Donati broke in. "Henry, you have to understand. This isn't just a legal situation, its a public-relations problem. As soon as the press gets wind of this story, they'll be camped out at the studio gates."

"Presumably you have people who know how to give non-answers to the press," I said.

"It would help if they knew which non-answers to give," Donati said.

"You took the same oath I did, Nick, to uphold the laws and represent your clients to the best of your ability. That precludes telling their secrets to third parties."

"Mr. Rios," Asuras said, in a soft rumble. His voice, I noticed, was even lower than Donati's. Together they were like a duet in testosterone. "I run a billion-dollar-a-year business. Thousands of people depend on the studio for their livelihoods. I need to know when something is going to have an adverse effect on them."

"I don't understand," I said. "An hour ago Donati was telling me he thought Bob was being framed, and now you're asking me if he did it."

"I do think he's being framed," Donati said. "All we want is your professional assessment."

"After all," Asuras said offhandedly, "the man is a homosexual."

"And that means he's more likely to have done it?" I asked.

"It means he's feminine," Asuras said. "Ergo, weak."

"By that reasoning," I replied, "it's virtually certain he's innocent, since women don't go in for serial killing. It's mostly a male sport."

"So you don't think he did it," Asuras said. "You would know, being a homosexual yourself. What homosexuals are capable of, I mean."

I got up. "What this homosexual is capable of is walking out of this ridiculous and offensive meeting. The studio can keep its fucking money. I'll work something out with my client."

On my way out, I kicked the gong.

Donati caught me just as the elevator door slid open. "Henry," he said. "Wait." He got into the elevator with me and pushed the button to the mezzanine. "Duke asked me to apologize."

"Was he too busy meditating to come himself?"

Nick glanced at his watch. "Can you squeeze in a tour? I want to show you the lot."

"I'll take a rain check."

We were outside on the steps of the administration building. He put on a pair of sunglasses and said, "It'll help explain what happened up there. Come on. Not many people get my personal tour."

Grudgingly, I followed him down a narrow street toward the hulking buildings at the back of the lot. I noticed a couple of two-story wood-framed buildings with covered porches behind a row of tamarisk trees. Casually dressed people popped in and out of them. Those who recognized Donati were respectful rather than friendly.

"Those buildings look familiar," I said.

"They're where the studio used to quarantine the writers," he said. He stopped, pointed to a louvered door. "William Faulkner's office. Two doors down was Scott Fitzgerald. There was a movie about a screenwriter in the forties a couple of years back. It was filmed here, that's probably why you recognize the buildings."

"They filmed here? Aren't those working offices?"

He smiled. "They've filmed in my office. In Duke's. There's a parking lot over there," he said, pointing toward the water tower, "that was flooded and used as the Red Sea in a TV movie about Moses. Parnassus is the smallest studio in town, every inch does double duty, at least."

We were on a narrow street. A woman in dark glasses steered a black compact BMW carefully between trucks and trailers, while a young man whizzed by on a ten-speed and a sweatshirted technician shouldered a coil of heavy electrical cable. A suit came by in a golf cart. I asked Donati about a row of unlocked bikes.

"They're the quickest way to get around the lot," he explained. "Execs go by golf carts. You can see there's not much room for cars."

"What are all the trailers?"

"The little ones are makeup, the bigger ones for the actors. You wouldn't believe the negotiations over the size of a star's trailer," he said. "Or what we have to put inside of it."

The noise of saws and hammers blasted from the open door of one of the massive buildings that Donati identified as a soundstage. From the outside it was shaped like a barn or airplane hangar with a rounded roof. Inside, a construction crew was building the interior of a three-story Victorian mansion for a movie about vampires in San Francisco. The set didn't begin to fill the vast space. We stood and watched for a few minutes, then resumed the tour. Against the studio's back wall was a row of Quonset huts that housed graphics, carpentry, fiberglass fabrication and other shops.

"It's total chaos," I said, watching the swarm of workers darting in and out of the workshops.

"It would be if everyone didn't know their jobs," he said. "But everyone does, Henry. These people are incredibly disciplined and hard-working and competent."

"I can believe that," I replied. "What does it have to do with Asuras?"

Donati said, "Duke's no bigot, Henry. Especially not toward gays and lesbians. Parnassus was one of the first studios to offer domestic-partnership benefits. Duke's personally given a couple of hundred thousand to AIDS organizations over the years . . ."

"Then what was that all about?"

"You wouldn't believe the pressures he's under," Donati said, a fragile hand sweeping through the air. "He's responsible for everything that goes on here and he takes that very seriously. These people are more than his employees, they're family. It frustrates him that he's not entirely the master of his own house."

"What does that mean?"

"We're not a freestanding business here. The studio's owned by Parnassus Company in New York. The president of the company is Duke's boss and both of them answer to a board of directors. I can tell you that's not an easy relationship. It's especially tense now."

"Why particularly now?" I asked innocently.

"I can't go into details, but things are coming to a head between Duke and the company. Any adverse publicity for the studio would weaken his hand. This trouble with Bob is a potential disaster."

"You said Bob didn't do it."

"Anyway you look at it, it's a PR disaster," he said. "Duke has enough keeping him awake at night without one more thing to worry about. Look, Henry, the man drives himself to the limits and sometimes he crosses them and says or does something he regrets. That's all that happened."

"So you're saying he doesn't hate gays and women."

"Two of his key executives are women," Donati said. "His closest advisor is a gay man."

We'd been walking back toward the administration building. I paused and said, "And that would be you?"

"I'm not advertising my private life," Donati said. "I just want you to understand that we're not the enemy here."

THE GUARD WAVED me through the gate without so much as a second look and I reentered the real world, where a flashing sign on a savings and loan reported a temperature of 89 degrees, and left the land of make-believe, where Duke Asuras sat beside a New England fire costumed as a country squire and Nick Donati cultivated a voice at least six inches taller than he was. Then I remembered the hive of purposeful activity that went on at the studio outside the executive suites, and thought I was probably being unfair to most of the men and women who worked at the studio. I doubted whether the carpenters or set designers confused the illusions they helped create with the reality of their own lives. Possibly I was being unfair even to Asuras, about whom I had formed my opinion based on Richie's catty stories. Donati's explanation of the pressure his boss was under was plausible enough. After all, Asuras was trying to sell the company behind the backs of its present owners to the kind of man whose cultural politics must be repulsive to him. Dancing with the devil was bound to produce a certain amount of anxiety and stress. The last thing Asuras needed was the cops accusing one of his employees of using studio property to commit a series of gruesome homosexual murders. Who was I to blame him for an off-the-cuff politically incorrect remark? He was standing beside Travis after all.

Anyway, Asuras's mental health was outside my bailiwick. I hadn't told Donati how much I knew about Gaitan's rogue past when he'd told me he thought the cops had planted evidence against Bob Travis because I might need his testimony and I couldn't afford to taint him with my own prejudices. Also, I reminded myself, it was important for me to keep an open mind as to the possibility that the evidence was legitimate. But when Travis described Gaitan's interrogation of him, I felt in my gut that Donati was right and Gaitan was up to his old tricks. What cinched it for me was Bob Travis. Between the lines of our interview, I read rejection by his family, loneliness and dissatisfaction with his life. I guessed he was someone for whom coming out had been so traumatic he expected to be rewarded for it, and was disappointed to discover that all he had won was the right to be ordinary. He was a victim who felt responsible for his victimhood, eager to please, fearful of disapproval and easily shamed. A perfect candidate for police bullying, the kind of suspect who could be confused, intimidated and coerced. Gaitan must've picked up on that right away. Embarrassed by his debacle with me, under pressure to close the case, faced with someone he could crumple with a stare, I could easily imagine he had decided to help things along.

I felt an adrenaline rush when I imagined the expression on Gaitan's face when I walked into his office with my client. No, not his office. I would make him meet us at the sheriff's station in West Hollywood. Then I realized I'd lose the element of surprise if I talked to him directly, so when I got home I called Bob Travis and had him set it up. Afterward, I ran an errand I'd been meaning to get to for weeks.

———

THE FOLLOWING MORNING I pulled up to the apartment house on Flores Street where Bob Travis lived. The Santa Anas had returned and the tall trees that lined Flores swayed wildly as if they were trying to uproot themselves. Travis lived in an old courtyard building that had managed to escape the wrecker's ball when the rest of the neighborhood went condo. A few such buildings still dotted West Hollywood, some of them once inhabited by movie stars. Travis's was a typical specimen. A white stucco wall enclosed a U-shaped, two-story building. The roof was tiled with terra-cotta tiles. The center courtyard was filled with a wild tangle of shrubs and flowers that spilled into a reflecting pool. A lotus drifted in the turbid water, and here and there was the flash of silver at the bottom of the pool, coins tossed in with a wish. Scattered around the courtyard were broken-down bits of patio furniture, rusted iron tables and wicker chairs in need of recaning. The elephantine leaves of a banana trees fluttered in the dry wind. A ginger cat reclined in the sun.

I entered a dark hallway, found the door with Travis's name on a card taped to it and rang the doorbell.

"Coming," he shouted, and a moment later opened the door. "Mr. Rios, am I glad to see you." His almost handsome face was panicked. He was in his underwear. "Come inside."

"What's wrong Bob?" I said, stepping inside. "Why aren't you dressed?"

"I don't know what to wear," he said.

Thinking I'd misheard him, I said, "What?"

"It can't be too faggy," he said. "Maybe a suit? Dark colors? What?"

"Bob, take a deep breath."

He inhaled, exhaled. "I'm so nervous I could shit my pants."

"Another breath, please."

After the fourth one, something like calm had returned to his eyes. "I'm sorry," he said. "I didn't get much sleep last night."

"Everything's going to be fine," I said. "Go get dressed. I'll wait for you."

He disappeared through a door off the hallway. The living room was lighted by two large windows. Frosted glass kept the room light but cool. The room was crammed with a disorderly mix of antiques, Shaker chairs, Art Deco lamps, Chinese cabinets, an ornate Louis the something desk, all of it shoved around the room in no discernible pattern, like a warehouse. In all the clutter, there was nowhere to comfortably sit, so I wandered around pausing at the Louis desk. There was a pile of threatening notices from a half-dozen credit-card companies and collection agencies. Beneath the bills was a brown leather picture frame laid facedown. I dug through the bills and turned it over. It contained a photograph of Travis and Nick Donati on a beach. Travis lay on his back, his head in Donati's lap. Donati frowned at the camera, plainly displeased at having his picture taken. I heard footsteps and put the picture back where I'd found it, just as Travis emerged from the hallway. He was wearing a navy blue suit, a white shirt and a silk tie with horizontal burgundy and gold stripes. He looked more like a lawyer than I did.

"Is this okay?"

"You look fine, Bob," I said, then, indicating the room, asked, "Do you deal in antiques?"

"No," he said, "I just buy. And buy, and buy. My sponsor says I'm the most compulsive shopper he's ever met."

"Your sponsor? Are you in AA?"

"DA," he said, straightening a cuff. "Debtor's Anonymous. But I've been to AA, too, and CA, NA, SCA and Al Anon." He shrugged. "I guess shopping's not the only thing I'm compulsive about."

"Do you have a problem with drugs or alcohol, Bob?"

"No, like I said yesterday, I drink socially and I only do drugs when I go out to the clubs." His face reddened. "The only reason I went to AA was because someone told me it was a good place to meet guys."

"Did you?"

He walked to the desk and picked up the bills. "Oh, yes, I met someone. Went out with him for three months. I'm still paying for it."

"We should go," I said.

"YOU KNOW WHY my relationships never work out?" he said, as we left his apartment. "I'm always apologizing for things that aren't my fault. Guys get tired of me saying I'm sorry."

WHEN WE ENTERED the lobby of the sheriff's station ten minutes later, Lucas Odell was standing behind the counter, talking to the deputy on duty. He stopped midsentence and raised his pale eyebrows.

"Don't you ever go home?" I asked him.

"Think of what I'd miss if I did," he said. "You here to see me?"

"No, Mr. Travis and I are here to see Detective Gaitan," I said. "Is he around?"

A slow smile of comprehension spread across his face. "Yeah," he said. "He's back there drinking up my coffee. Let me bring you to him."

The deputy buzzed us through the door into the back of the station. We went down the bright, clean corridor, past Deputy Tim and his jail, to the interview room. Odell stopped short and gestured for us to wait. He went to the doorway, rapped the wall and said, "Hey, Mac, got someone here to see you." He looked at Travis. "What was your name, son?"

"Bob Travis."

"Young man named Travis," Odell spoke into the room. "And his lawyer."

From inside the room, Gaitan groaned, "His lawyer? Shit." A chair skidded across the floor and then he stepped out into the hall and saw me. His eyes went dead. His face turned to stone. "Rios. What the fuck are you doing here?"

I smiled. "I represent Mr. Travis."

I DEMANDED A tape recorder, and for good measure insisted that Odell be present when Gaitan questioned Travis, so it took a few minutes before we were arranged around the metal table in the bare room. Gaitan was on one side, Travis and I on the other, Odell in the corner rocking on the back legs of his chair, hands folded on his big gut.

"So, Rios," Gaitan said, "is this a coincidence or what?"

"If we're getting started, turn on the tape."

He flicked on the recorder, gave the date, time and the names of those present.

"To answer your question," I said, "I'm here because after you questioned my client at Parnassus studio, he and the studio's legal counsel figured you needed someone to keep you in line."

Gaitan started to speak, glanced at Odell, then said, formally, "We can connect your client to two of the Invisible Man killings."

"Everything's connected in the great scheme of things. I assume you have something more specific."

Ignoring me, he said to Travis, "So, Bobby . . ."

"Address my client as Mr. Travis, please."

Gaitan glared at me. "Okay, Mr. Travis, the last time we talked, you admitted taking a—what do you call it—a 'picture car' off the lot at Parnassus studio." He shuffled some papers from a manila folder in front of him and withdrew three pictures, which he laid in front of us. They showed a medium-size, two-toned American car, blue and white, with a taxi light on the roof and the logo Lucky's Taxi Service painted on the passenger doors. "Is this that car?"

"Yes," Travis said. "I borrowed it while my car was in the shop."

I leaned toward Travis and said, "Answer his questions yes or no. Don't volunteer information."

"I'm going to give you some dates," Gaitan said. "I want to know whether you had the car on any of those dates." He read from a sheet of paper three dates in June, the dates of the murders. "What about it, Mr. Travis?"

After a whispered conference between us, he said, "I don't remember the dates."

"Well, did you use the car during the month of June?"

"Yes."

"On weekends?"

"I don't remember."

"You don't remember if you used the car on a weekend in June?"

Travis stole a glance at me, but I was also interested in his reply, so I nodded at him to answer.

"Maybe I did. I'd have to look at a calendar."

A gleam came into Gaitan's eyes. "You saying you didn't use this car on weekends?"

I stopped Travis from speaking. "No," I said, "what he said is he doesn't remember. I want to clarify something. My client used a couple of cars during the month of June while his car was in the shop, including this cab. Right, Bob?"

"Yes," Travis said. "Three that I remember."

"And that was because the cab wasn't always available, isn't that right?"

"Yeah, I . . ."

"Stop right there," Gaitan said. "This isn't a goddamned trial. I ask the questions."

I said, "I want the record to be clear that you were told up to twenty-two people had access to this car, but my client is the only one you've brought back for questioning. He's also the only gay person in that group. Coincidence, Detective?"

I wished, looking at Gaitan's expression, that I'd requested a video camera.

"No one's arrested your client, Rios, so his Miranda rights haven't kicked in yet and I could throw you out of here."

I felt Odell spring to attention.

"If I leave," I said, "he goes with me."

"On my say-so," Gaitan said.

"If you keep him here against his will, then he is under arrest, whatever you call it, and entitled to counsel. You can't have it both ways, Detective.

You dragged him down here because you said you had evidence connecting him to the murders. What is it?"

For a long moment, Gaitan stared and said nothing.

"Fibers in the trunk of the cab match fibers from Amerian's body," Odell said, amiably. "Also I think there was a paint transfer on the fence in the alley that forensics connected to the car. That right, Mac?"

Gaitan turned his head slowly to Odell, furious. "You're interfering in a homicide investigation."

"I'm moving it along," Odell said.

"That's it?" I asked. "That's your evidence?"

"We have eyewitnesses that saw your client driving the cab when the Baldwin kid and Jellicoe got into it," Gaitan said. "Plus a bloodstain in the trunk that matches Baldwin's blood-type and your client's prints all over the place."

I felt the icicle of Travis's silent terror.

"Is that all?" I asked.

I thought I heard Odell suppress a chuckle.

"What do you mean 'is that all'?" Gaitan said.

"At best, your so-called evidence connects the car to the murders, but that's a given. None of it incriminates my client. Of course his prints were in the car. He admits using it."

"Maybe you didn't hear me right," Gaitan replied. "We have witnesses who put Baldwin and Jellicoe in the cab with your client driving."

"Then arrest him," I said.

Travis gasped.

Odell whistled, "Wooee."

"If your witnesses can really put him in the car with the victims, that gives you probable cause to arrest. So arrest him."

"What kind of lawyer are you?" Gaitan sneered.

"The kind who's familiar with your interviewing tactics," I said. "Do you remember telling me in this room that you had a witness who told you he saw me drinking the night Alex Amerian was murdered? A waiter from the restaurant."

"What about it?"

"I talked to him last night," I said. "He didn't tell you he saw me drinking. In fact, he told you he didn't see me drinking, but you badgered him until he admitted he wasn't watching the table every second. Apparently, your idea of an eyewitness is someone who doesn't see something."

"Get out of here," he said.

"That's what I thought. Come on, Bob."

Passing Odell, I shrugged, but he was deep in thought and didn't respond.

TRAVIS AND I didn't speak on the short drive from the station to his apartment, but when I pulled up in front of the building and he started to get out, I said, "Wait, Bob."

He settled back into his seat. "What were you doing in there telling that prick to arrest me?"

I looked at him. He was still white. "After I heard his evidence, I knew he didn't have enough on you, but you were really terrified, weren't you?"

"Of course I was," he said. "My own lawyer is saying arrest him."

"Is that really what scared you?" I asked. "Or was it what they found in the car?"

"There wasn't anything in the car," he blurted.

"What did you say?"

He took a steadying breath. "Nick told me he looked."

I nodded. "When did he tell you that?"

"After Gaitan questioned me the first time," he said, but his eyes didn't match his words.

"Not before?"

"No," he said.

"All right, Bob," I said. "Let's keep in touch the next few days. Gaitan will be deciding what to do. If he tries anything with you, call me immediately."

He opened the car door. "Mr. Rios," he said. "I don't know what you're thinking, but I didn't kill anyone."

He said it with such conviction that I had to believe him.

LATER, AS I sat on the terrace watching the sky darken, I thought about Gaitan's evidence. Fibers, paint transfer, a bloodstain. All evidence that could easily be faked: a few fibers combed from Alex's body scattered in the car; a surreptitious drive to the alley in the cab once it had been impounded to scrape it against the fence; a drop of blood preserved from Baldwin's autopsy smeared in the trunk. It was only a little more sophisticated than dropping a gun in a suspect's car to justify a search, or planting drugs on him to justify an arrest, activities that Gaitan and his gang in Antelope Valley were known to have engaged in. As for Gaitan's eyewitnesses, if what they had seen didn't amount to probable cause to arrest Bob Travis for murder, it wouldn't convict him of it, either. But what exactly had they seen? And what were the circumstances under which Gaitan's investigation had turned up the physical evidence? I got up, went to the phone and dialed the West Hollywood station.

"Is Sergeant Odell still there?" I asked the deputy who answered the phone.

"I'll check," she said. "Who's calling?"

"Henry Rios."

A couple of minutes later, Odell said, "Mr. Rios. You wanted to talk to me?"

"I'd like to buy you a cup of coffee when you get off duty," I said.

"That's never," he said, "but if you want to meet me in about a half hour I could give you a few minutes."

"Where?"

"There's a Denny's on Sunset around Genesee, you know it?"

"I'll find it," I said. "Thanks."

"Don't thank me yet," he said.

chapter 11

SUNSET BOULEVARD WAS littered with palm branches torn from the trees by the Santa Ana winds, and signals were out from Vermont to Highland. The restaurant was near the intersection where Hugh Grant bought a blow job from Divine Jones, one of the many women who worked this part of the boulevard. Tonight they huddled in doorways to keep the dusty wind from ruining their hair and makeup and ran to the curb like giggling schoolgirls when there was a rush of traffic. I pulled into the parking lot, narrowly missing a trash can that went rolling into the street. Inside, the cheesy cheerfulness of the orange vinyl booths and bright yellow walls contrasted bleakly with the handful of customers, working girls stopping in for a burger between tricks, a couple of tattooed twentysomething malcontents, a foursome of old people tucking into the senior specials. Odell was at a back booth, his face reflected in a darkened window, hunched over a dinner of pancakes, eggs and bacon, like a figure in an Edward Hopper painting.

"Odell," I said, sliding into the booth.

He looked up, wiping syrup from his chin. "Mr. Rios. You hungry? My treat."

I glanced at the greasy food on his plate. "Thanks, I'll pass."

"Suit yourself," he said.

"I was surprised you were still at the station," I said, while he smeared pancake into egg yolk. "You really don't go home, do you?"

"No point," he said, chewing. "My wife divorced me ten years ago, both my kids are grown." He signaled the waitress for coffee and when she came, said, "And he'll have a cup, too, darling."

"I'm not your darling, mister," she said, filling our cups.

He watched her go. "It doesn't take much to piss people off these days, does it, Mr. Rios?" He dumped three packs of sweetener into his coffee. "You wanted to talk to me."

"Gaitan's trying to frame Bob Travis for the West Hollywood murders."

"You mean the 'Invisible Man Murders'," he said, pronouncing the phrase with disdain. "Invisible Man, Night Stalker. Who thinks up that shit?" He sipped the coffee. "Tell me about Gaitan."

"You know better than I do what kind of cop he is," I replied. "I think he planted the evidence he found in the cab."

"Why do you think that?" he asked, meeting my eyes.

"I'm going to level with you."

"Good idea."

"Before the studio turned the cab over to Gaitan, someone there conducted his own search and didn't find anything to connect it to the murders. Gaitan gets possession of the car and suddenly there's fibers, there's bloodstains, paint transfers."

He frowned. "It's a felony offense to interfere with a police investigation."

"I'm not defending the studio," I said. "Travis is my client. Don't you think it's pretty fishy that Gaitan discovers evidence where there was none?"

He took a couple of quick bites of food, washed it down with coffee. "You want to know what I think, Mr. Rios? I think you should get off this case."

"Why is that, Odell?"

"You had your crack at Gaitan. You didn't take it. Let it go."

"This isn't about what happened to me out in the desert."

"Sure it is," he said. "You were humiliated. You want to get even. Avenging insults is part of the code for you Mexican guys."

"That's a fairly primitive analysis of what's going on here."

He smiled a yolk-stained smile. "We're primitive creatures, Counsel." He belched softly. "What if I told you I think your client's dirty?"

"I'd have to question your judgment. Bob Travis is a mouse."

"I watched him today. He's hiding something."

"He spent the first twenty-five years of his life in the closet," I said. "That leaves a mark. A kind of furtiveness. The smell of mothballs. That's all you're picking up."

He shook his head. "My daughter's gay," he reminded me. "Some of my deputies. People I work with in the community. I know the difference between nervous and guilty."

"I know a little bit about gay people, too," I said. "The man who committed those murders is a violent, twisted closet case who is also extremely intelligent and methodical. Travis is a set designer who lives in an antique-filled apartment, pines for a boyfriend and can't pay his bills. He's no more the killer than I am. Except to Gaitan who equates gay with criminal. That's why he went after me, that's why he's going after Travis."

"You must be really good in front of a jury," Odell said.

"Hear me out," I said, and explained how I thought Gaitan might have planted evidence in the cab.

"You've got this all figured out," he said.

"You have to admit, with the right motivation, it could be done."

"Sure," he said. "It's no trick to get evidence out of booking, especially in a case like this where there's lots of people bringing in little pieces of this and that and things are going back and forth from forensics. It could have happened the way you say."

"I need to get my hands on the police and lab reports," I said. "They'll show chain of custody."

He grinned. "If Gaitan's smart enough to plant evidence, he's smart enough to cover it up."

"Still, I need those reports."

"And that's where I come in?"

"I can't get discovery unless Travis is charged," I said. "In the meantime Gaitan may be manufacturing other evidence."

"Did it ever occur to you that he found the evidence in the car just like he said he did?"

"I told you, someone else looked before he did."

"Maybe he didn't know what to look for," Odell said. "When you talk about things like fibers, you're talking small."

"Do you know that for a fact in this case?"

"No," he conceded.

"Me, either," I replied. "I won't know until I get the analysis from hair and fiber."

Odell grunted a noncommittal, "Uh-huh," and returned to his meal.

"I don't understand, Odell, a couple of weeks ago you came to my house and wanted me to bring a lawsuit against the department to stop Gaitan and his friends. Have you had a change of heart?"

"That was a different situation," he said, slugging down the last of his coffee. "You could've forced some real change in the department."

"That's your job, not mine. My job is to defend my client."

"Is that what you're doing? Or are you going after Gaitan?" He shook his head. "Mac might be a bigot, but even a bigot can be right sometimes."

"You won't help me."

"You don't need me," he said. "If you want to talk about the evidence against your client, call Serena Dance. She's running the task force on the murders."

"Since when?"

"Since the sheriff had to apologize to you," he said, pulling his wallet out of his pants pocket. "He needed cover with the gay community, so he agreed to let her run the show from the DA's office." He laid some bills on the table. "Of course, that don't mean Gaitan is telling her everything he's doing, but she knows more about the evidence than I do."

"Why didn't you tell me that before?"

"I wanted to warn you."

"About what? Staying on the case?"

"You've made up your mind about that," he said. "Just don't let your prejudice against cops blind you to the obvious. And watch your back."

EARLIER, I'D LEFT a message for Donati to call me. There was a return message from him on my machine when I got home from my meeting with Odell. I phoned him, reached an answering machine and started to leave a message, but then he picked up.

"I was working," he explained.

"It's almost eleven."

"A typical day for me starts at six and ends at midnight," he said, "but you didn't call to hear about the sad life of a studio lawyer. What happened with the police?"

"You haven't talked to Bob?"

"He's your client, now," he said. "I don't want to interfere in your relationship."

I hesitated, then asked, "Am I interfering in yours?"

"I'm not sure I understand, Henry," he replied, cooling.

"There's a picture at Bob's house of the two of you on a beach. You know which one I'm talking about?" When he didn't immediately answer, I said, "I'm not asking out of idle curiosity, Nick. The nature of your relationship to him is relevant to why you searched the car before you turned it over to the police."

"What do you mean?" he asked in a tight, angry voice.

"Maybe you were trying to protect him."

He made a contemptuous sound. "I did it to protect the studio, not Bob. I didn't even know the police were going to question him again. All I knew is that they wanted the car."

"But after you searched it, you told him it was clean."

"No, I didn't," he said firmly. "I never told him that."

"He says you did."

"He's wrong," he said, anger creeping back into his voice. "Whatever he told you, he's wrong."

"Were you involved with him?"

"It was a while ago," he said, "and it was a mistake. Bob's one of those gay boys with a little job, a little apartment, a little circle of swishy friends. Living for the weekend, looking for Mr. Right in the bars. I hated the smallness of his life. It was suffocating."

"Unlike the closet?"

"I don't live in the closet," he said. "I live in the real world. In the real world, people don't advertise who they fuck, and who they fuck is no one's business."

"You're going to a lot of trouble for someone for whom you feel such contempt."

"I told you, my only concern is the studio."

"Married to your work?"

"Is this really why you called?"

"The cops found a bloodstain from the second victim in the trunk of the car, along with fibers that matched fibers taken from the first victim's body," I said. "They also found prints they've matched to Bob and paint from the car on the wall of the alley where one of the bodies was dumped. You searched the car. Any of this sound familiar?"

"Well, obviously I couldn't have seen fingerprints," he said, "but I know for a fact the interior and exterior of the car were clean."

"You're sure of that?"

He hesitated. "It's complicated," he began. I'd begun to realize when he used that word, it meant trouble. "There's something I didn't tell you yesterday."

"What?"

"I didn't find anything when I searched the car," he said. "But afterwards, I drove it off the lot to a car wash and had it washed and vacuumed from top to bottom."

"You what?"

"I swear, I didn't see anything in the trunk or anywhere else."

"Then why did you have it cleaned? In case you missed something?"

"I accept full responsibility," he said, stiffly.

"What the hell is that supposed to mean?"

A dog barked in the background. He shushed it. "Isn't the important thing that the police found evidence where clearly there couldn't have been any?"

"Are you prepared to testify to that and expose yourself to prosecution for tampering with evidence?"

"Obviously, you have to figure out a way to keep the case from coming to trial," he said, adding airily, "Make a deal with someone."

"You don't seem to understand the gravity of the situation."

The deep voice was peremptory. "This is what I understand, Counsel. I've given you hard proof that the police planted evidence against Bob. A first-year law student could take that to the bank."

"With no way to prove it."

"If you want off the case, just tell me," he said.

"I'll stay on the case," I said, "but I'm warning you, Nick, I will put you on the stand if I have to, whatever the risk to you."

"If you do your job right, it won't come to that."

"I can't do my job if you keep withholding information."

"I've told you everything," he said. "I swear."

I HUNG UP, astonished by the conversation. If Donati was any indication, Hollywood was as lawless as Gaitan's cohort in the sheriff's department; but I understood police corruption. Nick Donati was something new.

SOMETIME DURING THE night, a transient who'd been in and out of mental hospitals most of his life poured a gallon of gas over a patch of scrub in the hills above Sierra Madre and put a match to it. By dawn, the wind had blown the fire out of control. When I went downtown to the Criminal Courts Building to see Serena, soft gray flakes of ash were falling from the smoky sky and the acrid air burned my eyes. Office workers walked between the government buildings with handkerchiefs covering their mouths and noses. Looking northeast from Serena's eighteenth-floor window I could see a funnel of smoke rising from the vicinity of Pasadena.

I hadn't seen Serena since she'd turned up at the West Hollywood station where Gaitan was questioning me about the Baldwin murder. Her face was pale with fatigue. She twisted the gold band on the ring finger of her right hand as I began my pitch for access to the evidence reports. Two sentences into it, she stopped me.

"Henry, why are you doing this?"

"Doing what?"

"Taking on this case," she said. "I mean, besides the potential conflict of interest, don't you feel any moral qualms about representing someone who preys on gay men?"

"What conflict?"

"I could call you as a witness in the Amerian murder."

"To testify to what? I wasn't a percipient witness to anything."

She frowned. "You were the last person to see him."

"No," I corrected her. "His killer was. My testimony wouldn't be relevant to anything except possibly establishing the time of death, and the medical examiner can do that."

She twisted the ring. "The relevance of your testimony is a matter for the court to decide. If you persist in representing Bob Travis, I'll move to disqualify you."

"Gaitan put you up to this, didn't he?"

She glared at me. "No one put me up to anything, least of all Mac Gaitan."

"If you charge my client, and if the case gets to trial and if you subpoena me, I'll get the subpoena quashed on the grounds that any marginal value I might have as a witness is clearly outweighed by my client's constitutional right to counsel."

"The right to counsel," she said, "is not a right to a particular counsel."

"I can pretty convincingly demonstrate that he needs me to establish a defense of police misconduct."

"What are you talking about?"

"Why is Gaitan still running this investigation?"

Her face reddened. "He isn't running it," she said. "I am. This case is a lot bigger than one deputy. There are homicide units from the sheriff and LAPD working with me. Even the FBI's assisting."

"Gaitan's still out there riding the range like a cowboy," I said.

"I don't understand your obsession with Gaitan."

It occurred to me she hadn't heard about the incident in the desert. I told her.

After I finished, she looked at me silently. "How can you be sure Gaitan was behind it?"

"I can't, obviously," I said, "but the circumstantial evidence is pretty compelling."

She sank back in her chair with a complicated expression on her face. "What do you want, Henry?"

"I want to examine the evidence against my client."

"Your client hasn't been charged. If he is, you can file a discovery motion. Until then, he's not entitled to anything."

"The evidence is already tainted by Gaitan's involvement in the case," I said.

She sighed. "Can you be more specific?"

"I think he's planted the evidence recovered from the Parnassus studio prop car."

"I have an eyewitness who saw the second victim get into that car. The same with the third victim, Jellicoe. The actual search was conducted by forensics."

"Who brought the cab in?"

"I don't know," she said, exasperated.

"According to the studio lawyer, it was Gaitan. How much time passed between when he brought the car in and forensics searched it?"

"Shouldn't you be saving this for a jury?"

"I'm telling you Serena, I have information that will prove the evidence was planted."

"What information?"

"I can't disclose that without jeopardizing my defense."

"You've just told me your defense."

"Then believe that I can prove it," I said. "Look, we can resolve this now before it goes any farther, or play it out in front of a jury and embarrass your office."

"You're that sure," she said, wavering.

I decided to play my trump card. "I'm so sure that if you'll agree to let me preview this evidence, I'll submit my client to a lineup with your eyewitnesses."

She cocked an eyebrow. "A lineup?"

"Do we have a deal?"

She thought about it. "All right. Deal. I'll messenger you this afternoon."

MY CAR PHONE rang. It was Richie Florentino on the other end saying, "You're holding out on me, Henry."

I was stopped at a light on Sunset just outside of town. Ash rained down on my windshield. A plume of black smoke unfolded in the gray sky like a wing. The light went green and I lurched forward behind an exhaust-spewing, nearly empty bus.

"I'm very busy, Richie," I said.

"I know you are," he replied. "Working for Parnassus. My spies say you had a meeting with Nick Donati."

"How could you possibly know that?"

"If I tell you, will you tell me what you talked about?"

"No," I said. Out of the corner of my eye, I saw an enormous, filthy woman lift her voluminous skirts and squat in a weed-choked lot.

"I've got the dish on Donati," he said.

On my right, a banner in a gay-porn store just outside Silver Lake advertised XXXXX-rated videos. "Richie, what do you think an XXXXX-rated gay video could possibly show?"

"Restraint?" he ventured. "Good taste?"

"That would be shocking," I agreed. "I'm not interested in your dish on Donati."

There was nothing like indifference to goad an inveterate gossip like Richie.

"He's so far in the closet, you can't see him for his suits," Richie said.

"He told me he was gay," I said, stretching the point.

"He did?" Richie was astonished. "What else did he tell you?"

"I went to see him on a professional matter," I said. "I can't say anything else."

"A professional matter? You mean as in the police are after him?"

"No," I said, adamantly. "The police are not after him."

"Can I quote you on that?"

"Quote me? What are you talking about?"

"I have to say something in my piece on Parnassus about a big-time criminal-defense lawyer showing up for a secret meeting with the head of legal," he said, adding a disingenuous, "don't I?"

I pulled out of traffic and stopped in front of the Vista theater.

"This is extortion."

"All I know," he said, "is that I'm waiting for Asuras to try to close the Longstreet deal so I can run this story, and suddenly everything stops and I can't find out why."

A light went on. "Does Donati know about the Longstreet deal?"

"He's Asuras's shadow. Take away Asuras and Donati's an empty suit with a two-hundred-dollar haircut."

"How far would Donati go to protect Asuras's interests?"

"As far as Asuras tells him. So I'm right," he said triumphantly. "Your meeting with Donati had something to do with the delay in closing the

Longstreet deal." His mood changed to anger. "How could you double-cross me when you know how important this story is to me?"

"I'm not one of your spies, Richie," I said. "I can't violate attorney-client privilege to help you win the Pulitzer prize or whatever it is you're running for."

"This isn't about any fucking prize," he huffed. "It's about protecting Hollywood from a homo-hating bigot. Whose side are you on?"

I waved away a tattered man who was trying to clean my windshield with a soiled rag. He muttered a stream of invectives and wandered off.

"I'm doing my job," I said.

"That's what the Nazis said at Nuremberg," he shouted.

"Richie, calm down," I said, thinking fast. I knew how destructive he could be when he was enraged. "Let's make a deal."

"I don't make deals with collaborators," he fumed, but he was listening.

"I can tell you this much," I said. "Donati's not the client. The client's a low-level studio employee who's suspected by the police of a serious felony. I personally don't think this has anything to do with the Longstreet deal."

"It has to," Richie insisted. "Everything just stopped."

"The police are at the point in their investigation where they either have to arrest him or let him go," I said. "I expect a decision within a few days. Either way, I'll call you and you can decide for yourself if it had anything to do with the deal."

"So you're saying it's a routine case."

"Exactly, it's just a coincidence that it's at Parnassus."

"If it's routine, why can't you tell me about it now?"

"I'm at a very delicate place in my negotiations with the District Attorney," I said. "If the story gets out prematurely, it could jeopardize them."

There was a long silence. "I don't know how much longer I can sit on this piece before Duke finds out about it."

"What does that matter?"

"Are you kidding? He's famous for killing books and stories about him," Richie said. "Just last year he got an unauthorized biography literally pulled off the presses by his libel lawyers."

"Haven't your libel lawyers vetted your piece?"

"You let me worry about my lawyers," he said. "I have a week to deadline for the September issue. If I don't hear from you before then, I'm running with what I've got."

"Richie, I'm speaking as a friend, here. If you make any statements implying I met with Donati because he's the target of a police investigation you're courting a libel suit."

"I have a friendly warning, too," Richie said. "Before you get too cozy with Donati, remember, everyone in Hollywood is either a flake or an asshole."

"You don't have to worry about me going native."

"Just remember," he intoned ominously. "A flake or an asshole."

chapter 12

IT'S FOUR IN the morning, I'm writing this letter . . .

Wearily, I reached over and switched the radio off on Leonard Cohen's lament, and got up to stretch. It was a little after two in the morning. The dining table was covered with police and lab reports, forensic texts, legal pads. For the past eight hours I'd been plodding through the Invisible Man files, paring down my throughts and impressions to a couple of pages of notes. I put my pen down and read them.

1. Time. Gaitan impounds prop car at studio at 4 pm; search conducted the following day starting at 9 am. Seventeen hours enough time to plant evid. *Follow-up:* When was car booked, where? Who had access?

2. Fiber evidence. Hair and Fiber Unit match fibers combed from Alex Amerian's body hair to fibers found in the trunk of the cab. Fibers identified as cashmere, light blue in color, between half an inch and an inch in length. Found everywhere from the hair on his head to the hair on his legs. Examiner says: body was wrapped in a cashmere blanket and transported from the murder site to the alley. Half-a-dozen fibers found in the trunk, which was lined with a short, gray industrial-type carpeting. The match was ninety-five percent certain. Fiber samples from body booked into crime lab.

Nota bene: A. Donati says trunk vacuumed before Gaitan gets it;

> B. Fibers should shed in pattern of how body positioned, should be numerous if entire body wrapped and stowed. Here only *six* fibers found;
>
> C. *Query:* why no fibers found on bodies of other two victims if same car used to transport?

2. Blood evidence. Dime-sized bloodstain in the trunk of the car matches blood type of second vic, Baldwin. Type O positive, most common blood type. Sample sent out for DNA analysis to confirm blood Baldwin's. Results not in.

NB: A. Medical examiner takes blood sample from body for toxo analysis; booked into crime lab;

> B. Without DNA confirmation, bloodstain could belong to anyone with O pos blood with access to car (22 at least, per Donati);
>
> C. Even if DNA confirms Baldwin, proves only he was in the car (eyewit says he saw him get into car; x-ref statement of Willie Wright);
>
> D. *Only* blood of any vic found in car. How hard to borrow sample from Baldwin autopsy and drip it in trunk?

3. Paint transfer. Paint found on the fence in alley where Amerian's body was dumped matches paint on the car from scratch on front bumper. The Materials Unit says match is ninety-nine percent certain.

NB: A. Gaitan has plenty of time to drive to alley in car, scrape fence;

> B. How common is paint? A hundred cars with same color? A million? May match this car but can't prove for sure if many others also painted same shade of blue.

4. Fingerprint evidence. Prints from inside glove compartment, trunk, seat match Travis through his DMV print of thumb. (Wish Donati cleaning a little more thorough.) So what? Admit he used car. Trunk prints a problem? No, could've put groceries back there.

NB: Prints hard to plant.

5. Eyewitness statements:

> A. Willie Wright. Hustler. Sees cab pull up to corner on Sta. Monica Blvd. where Baldwin working. Remembers logo, Lucky, because that's one of his street names. Sitting at bus stop twenty five feet away, about 1 a.m. Says cab off-duty. Sees Baldwin approach and interior light go on. Driver's profile visible: white, "old," baseball cap, dark glasses. Light goes out, Baldwin gets in. Total time elapsed: "couple of minutes."
>
> B. Parker Gray. Bouncer at sex club. Stationed in parking lot. Sees third vic, Jellicoe, leave club and cross street. Sees cab cruise street. Remembers logo; *his* nickname also Lucky. Cab stops beneath streetlight fifty feet away. Describes driver: white, fair hair, thirties. No baseball cap,

glasses. Jellicoe approaches. Talks to driver. Gets in. Total
time elapsed: 2–3 minutes.

NB: A. Both descriptions vague; even so, don't match up.
B. Gray description stronger. Could fit Travis, could
fit anyone who looks like Travis.
Conclusions: 1. Gaitan had opportunity to plant
blood/fiber evidence. Only question is his access to crime-
lab blood/fiber samples. Fibers *very* suspicious.
2. Only direct evidence linking Travis to car, his prints. No
big deal, we concede he used it.
3. Eyewitness evidence, negligible.

I tossed the pad on the table and went out on the deck for air. Except
for the distant drone of traffic, it was completely still in the canyon. The
dry, eviscerating desert wind had blown itself out and though the air still
smelled of smoke and ash from the Sierra Madre fire, it was also damp and
cool. Birds fluttered through the undergrowth, perched on the branches of
stunted trees and sang. The big houses on the other side of the canyon were
dark as tombs. I breathed in the wet, smoky air and remembered the moment
in the desert when I had kneeled with a gun pressed to the back of my head
and felt relief. Life is a kind of exile and we all long to go home. Who said
that? What that the cause of my relief, that the bullet which would end my
life would also send me home?

Behind me, in the house, the phone started to ring. Startled, I went in
and picked it up, expecting, at that hour, a drunken wrong number, but it was
the fax machine in my office and not the phone I'd heard. I went in to investigate. Two pages appeared, the first a cover sheet from Nick Donati's office
at Parnassus on which he'd written: "Attached declaration re my search of
picture car. Use it at your discretion to help Bob." The second page was a
declaration by Donati signed under penalty of perjury admitting both that
he had searched the car and had had it cleaned.

I picked up the phone and dialed his number.

He answered with a slurred, "Hello."

"Nick, it's Rios. I just got the declaration."

"Why are you still up?" he asked, definitely under the influence.

"Working. Are you all right?"

"I'm drunk," he announced.

"Big night?"

He laughed. "Yeah, big night. My declaration okay with you?"

"It's fine. Unexpected."

"To help Bob," he muttered. "But try to keep me outta jail."

"To help Bob? I thought you only cared about Parnassus. Why the change of heart?"

He breathed heavily into the phone, as if collecting his thoughts. "Let's say I have a guilty conscience and let it go at that. Too much conscience, Henry. Lawyers shouldn't have 'em. You Catholic?"

"I was raised Catholic," I said.

"Me, too. Italian Catholic. I don't believe in any of it anymore except—" he giggled—"I still believe in hell. Strange, huh? Hell made a big impression on me."

I thought of my copy of Dante's *Inferno* gathering dust on the bedside table. "From all accounts, the Catholic hell is a lot livelier than the Catholic heaven."

"I always pictured the devil as this sexy older guy," Donati said. "Big muscles, dark skin, like my grandpa. A ditchdigger. Old country *paisan*. Jesus? Forget about it. Goody Two-shoes, never told a lie. Or is that George Washington? I'm babbling here . . ."

"Maybe you should get some sleep."

"You talk to Bob today?" he asked, suddenly alert.

"No," I said.

"He has something to tell you," he said, drifting off again. "About the case." He yawned. "'Scuse me. He started to tell me, but I told him to save it for you."

"I thought you weren't talking to Bob at all," I said.

"He's here," Donati said. "Upstairs. Asleep. Think I'll join him."

He hung up.

I MEANT TO call Travis later in the morning, but just before dawn I woke up, grabbed a legal pad and began scribbling the revelation that had come to me while I was asleep.

"THANKS FOR COMING by on such short notice," I said.

Odell grinned. "I wouldn't miss it, Mr. Rios. You're always full of surprises."

"Why is Lucas here?" Serena asked, smiling at him to take the sting out of the question. "I mean, you're not part of the investigation, not officially."

The three of us were seated around my dining table.

"He's here because I trust him," I said. "Let's start. I went over the investigative material you sent me, Serena. It proves Gaitan planted evidence in the cab."

"I'm listening," she said. "But I'm dubious."

"All your evidence suggests that the killer—Mr. Invisible Man—is driving around West Hollywood in a fake cab picking his victims up at random. Right?"

She nodded. "Yeah, so?"

"You even have eyewitnesses who saw the second and third victims actually getting into the cab," I continued. "But there's a missing link. No one saw Alex Amerian get into the car."

"The physical evidence puts him there," she said.

"I'll get to that in a minute," I said. "My point is that no one ever identified the car Alex drove away in from this house the night he was killed. The only reason we assumed it was a cab was because he told me he'd called one, and that's what I told the cops. This morning, I looked at my June phone bill. There were no calls made from my house after seven that night."

"That just means he arranged it earlier."

"That's what's impossible, Serena," I replied. "He couldn't have called Lucky Taxi Service, because it doesn't exist. The only way you can put him in that car from here is if you believe the killer was cruising the neighborhood and happened to spot Alex standing outside waiting for the cab he'd called."

The point clearly worried her, but she said, "Why not? We don't know the killer's patterns."

"I was here," I reminded her. "I saw what happened. Alex waited in the living room until he heard the car pull up and the driver blew his horn."

Odell, who has been listening intently, now said, "You know there's another way he could have left here in that car."

"I know," I said, nodding. "He could have arranged for that particular car to pick him up, but that means he knew the driver. The murderer. Travis says he never met Alex." I tapped the stack of papers at Serena's elbow. "There's nothing in any of these witness interviews to contradict him. Besides, if Alex knew the driver, that contradicts your theory that the killings were random."

Serena shrugged. "It's obvious what happened. Amerian left here by whatever means, went wherever he was going, left there and then ended up in the Lucky cab."

"The evidence won't support that," I said. "He left here at midnight. The medical examiner says he was killed sometime between one and six in the morning. A five-hour window. The manner in which he was killed, the events that preceded his murder and the way his body was disposed of would've taken at least that long."

"There's no evidence of what happened before he was killed," she said.

"No direct evidence," I corrected her. "But between circumstantial evidence and my own recollections, I can infer the sequence of events."

"And what was that?" Odell asked.

"According to the medical examiner, Alex was drunk when he was killed, but he was sober when he left here. When Gaitan showed me pictures of his body, I noticed superficial marks and welts that I didn't see earlier that night and were clearly not part of the beating that killed him later."

"S&M?" Odell guessed.

I nodded. "He told me some of his clients were into that," I said. "Obviously, he left here, went to a client, had some drinks, had sex with him, and only after that was he murdered. That all took time. Plus, after he was killed, 'Kill Fags' was carved into his chest and then his body was carefully cleaned to erase any evidence. Not just wiped off. Bathed, bundled up and transported. There's no time in this scenario for Alex to be running all over LA in the middle of the night. Wherever he went from here was his last stop. The question is how he got there. The answer is not by Lucky Taxi Service."

Serena tossed her head back and looked at me. "I thought you told me you weren't a percipient witness."

"I didn't think I was until I reviewed your evidence."

"Well, you can't have it both ways, Henry. You can't represent Bob Travis and also expect to call yourself to the witness stand and testify, 'I know the victim didn't have these marks on his body because I slept with him a few hours before he was murdered.'"

"If it comes to that," I replied, "I'll withdraw as Bob's counsel. I asked you here to stop this thing before we end up in a courtroom."

"I'm not convinced," she said. "It's still your conjecture versus my physical evidence."

"Evidence that was planted."

"That's not even conjecture," she said.

"What if I can prove the car was cleaned inside and out before Gaitan impounded it and the evidence was discovered?"

"What if," she said, dismissively.

"Take a look at this," I said, slipping Donati's declaration across the table to her.

Odell put on reading glasses and peered over her shoulder. Her mouth constricted into a thin, angry line.

"This is unbelievable," she said, rattling the paper. "Obstruction of justice, evidence tampering, and he's a goddamned lawyer . . ."

"I'm not defending him," I said. "You can go after him for all of that, if you want. But the point is, the car was clean when Gaitan got it."

"We're talking about things like fibers, practically microscopic . . ."

I flipped through the forensics reports, found the fiber analysis and quoted, " 'Between half an inch and an inch in length. Light blue in color.' Hardly microscopic, Serena." She opened her mouth to retort, but I cut her off. "Just listen to me." I explained shedding patterns and the disparity between the location and amount of fibers combed from Alex's body and those found in the trunk.

When I finished, she said, "The point is the fibers match."

"The question isn't whether they match, but how they got into the trunk."

"There was other evidence beside the fibers," she said, leafing through the crime-lab reports.

"A paint transfer from the car to a fence in the alley," I replied. "That's easy to explain. Gaitan had seventeen hours to drive the car to the dump site and scrape it against the wall before the crime lab folks examined it."

"They can tell a fresh scrape from an old one," Odell observed quietly.

"I bet no one asked them to," I said. "I bet the materials analyst was told there's paint on the fence in the alley that's the same color as the car. Match them if you can. End of story."

"The department's crime lab is one of the best in the country," Odell said, in the same thoughtful voice.

"I'm not accusing any of them. The planted evidence was already in the car when they searched it."

"But if you're right, Mac got fiber samples from the lab because that's where they would've been booked."

"You said it yourself the other night, Sergeant. It's a complicated case. Little bits of evidence coming and going all the time."

"You believe this, Lucas?" Serena asked.

"Tell her about Antelope Valley," I said.

Odell shrugged. "Gaitan's been accused of planting evidence in the past. Never proved."

"Come on, Odell. You told me he was involved."

He looked at me. "You're the lawyer, Mr. Rios. You know prior bad acts can't be used to prove present misconduct."

"No one doubts Gaitan's an asshole," Serena said impatiently, "but I'm not convinced he planted evidence."

"What about you, Sergeant?" I asked Odell.

"You've given me a lot to think about," he said.

"You may not be convinced," I told Serena, "but reasonable doubt is still the gold standard. As it stands, you don't have sufficient evidence even to arrest my client, but if at some point you think you do, you should consider how a police-misconduct defense will play in front of a downtown jury."

"What are you looking for, Henry?"

"Gaitan off the case. My client exonerated."

She shrugged, "I don't have any control over who the sheriff assigns to a case."

"Even with this information?"

"You're crazy if you think I'd go to the sheriff with all this conjecture."

"Not conjecture, inference."

"Whatever," she said. She chewed her lip. "I can't do anything about Gaitan."

"I thought you ran this investigation."

"Shouldn't you be more worried about your client than about Gaitan?"

"I said I wanted my client exonerated."

"The deal is he comes downtown for a lineup," Serena said.

"You know your eyewitnesses can't ID him," I said. "Their descriptions are vague and contradictory."

"If they can't ID him," she said, "then as far as I'm concerned, that eliminates him as a suspect."

"And Gaitan goes scot free."

"Jesus Christ, Henry," she said. "Will you back off? This is a murder investigation, not an internal-affairs probe. If you want to bring misconduct charges against Gaitan, go to the appropriate forum." She got up. "Now if you'll excuse me, I've got to get back to work."

"When do you want to do the lineup?"

"Day after tomorrow. Friday. Ten o'clock. Bauchet Street."

AFTER SHE LEFT, Odell said, "You pushed her buttons."

"What do you mean?"

He grinned. "She's a figurehead. Mac's still calling his own shots."

"Why is that, Odell?" I asked, putting the reports into order. "Why, after the press conference and what happened to me in the desert, is Gaitan even on the case?"

"Remember Willie Williams?" he asked. Williams was the black cop who'd replaced Daryl Gates as chief of LAPD after the King riots, but was then himself replaced after a single term.

"What about him?"

"The public loved him," Odell said. "The *L.A. Times* loved him. They all thought he was doing a great job, but when it came time to renew his contract, the city council gave him the boot. You know why, Mr. Rios?"

"I listen and learn."

"His own people in the department did him in. The union, the career brass, the lifers. Sheriff Ramsay's like you. He listens and learns, too. Every chief's got two constituencies, the public and his own people. Williams paid attention to the wrong one. Chuck won't make that mistake. Keeping Gaitan on the case was the sheriff's way of showing his people where his loyalties lie. But he's no Daryl Gates," Odell continued. "He knows he can't ignore it if someone calls his department homophobic or racist. That's why he agreed to let Serena run the task force." He smiled. "I'm sure he had a meeting with her and promised her his full cooperation. I'm also sure she's getting squat."

"You're sounding a little bitter, Odell," I said. "I thought you and the sheriff were tight."

"I understand that Chuck has to appease the good old boys in the department," he said, rising heavily to his feet. "Hell, I'm one of them, but when you start to turn a blind eye to criminal activity in the ranks . . ." He shrugged. "I don't like the exclusionary rule any more than the next cop, or Miranda or knock and notice, or any of that shit, but it's the law. If you're a cop, you follow the law. Period. No picking and choosing."

"What about that kid you rousted the first time I met you?" I reminded him.

He looked puzzled, then smiled. "The little gangbanger? Sure I scared him. But I didn't drop dope on him or take him out to Antelope Valley and beat the shit out of him. Did I?"

"There's no such thing as violating the law a little," I said. "An illegal detention is an illegal detention, with or without the trimmings."

He patted my shoulder. "We all draw the line somewhere, I guess. I can live with mine. You know, it occurred to me, listening to you, that that first murder is a lot different from the other two."

"I know. I've thought about that, too."

"Yeah," he said. "Interesting. Take care of yourself."

BOB TRAVIS HAD agreed to meet me for dinner to discuss the developments in his case. That evening I drove into West Hollywood, to a restaurant called the French Marketplace which occupied the bottom floor and terrace of a faux New Orleans mansion; painted brick, green shutters and fancy ironwork. The terrace fronted Santa Monica Boulevard. Wrought-iron tables were lined in two rows, one against the wall and the other against the railing, a narrow aisle between them for pumped-up waiters in skin-tight black trousers and little red aprons to deliver big plates of bad food to an equally pumped-up male clientele. The smells of grease and designer cologne hung in the stale air as I came up the steps to the restaurant and scanned the terrace for Travis. I was cruised in a bored sort of way by a streaked blond picking slices of mandarin orange out of his Chinese chicken salad. Behind me, a bus rumbled by, spraying exhaust. A thin, handsome waiter with a French accent offered to seat me, but then Travis came out of the building. His clothes, a yellow knit jersey and tight, faded jeans, seemed chosen to advertise his progress at the gym. He looked relaxed and happy, and I saw he was, in fact, if not the great beauty to which he aspired, a pleasant-looking man with a firm jaw and gentle eyes. Had he been straight, he would've been a suburban dad with wife, kids, dog and Volvo. Instead, he was stuffed into clothes that were too young for him. He probably thought the fashion statement he was making was "Look at me," but to me his appearance called out "Find me."

"Mr. Rios," he said. "I had to make a call." He pointed to a table by the railing empty but for a glass of iced tea and crumpled napkin. "I'm over there."

We passed the blond who had made a little pile of orange slices on his bread plate and was now removing slivers of almonds from his salad. At the table, we perused oversize menus on which most of the items were prefaced with either "blackened" or "Cajun." I ordered a grilled cheese sandwich.

"I wanted to bring you up to speed on the case," I said, after the French waiter took our orders. I told him about my review of the evidence and my meeting with Odell and Serena Dance. I explained that I had agreed to submit him to a lineup. A furrow deepened in his forehead between his eyes.

"A lineup? Won't that incriminate me?"

"No, it'll eliminate you as a suspect," I said.

"You're sure?"

"Aren't you?" I asked, studying him. "I mean, if you weren't behind the wheel of the car when those two men got in, the witnesses won't pick you out. Right?"

"Right," he agreed quickly. "This is all kind of scary to me. Before this, the only trouble I ever had with the police was speeding tickets."

Our food came. A stream of grease oozed from his hamburger, congealing on the plate. My grilled sandwich was burned.

"I don't understand how this place stays in business," I said. "The food's inedible."

Travis grinned. "Look behind you."

I glanced over my shoulder. A man was walking toward us. He wore a pair of cutoff jeans and a black tank top. His thighs were rock hard, his thick arms corded with heavy veins and he could have crushed a beer can between his pecs. He cruised slowly past the terrace, looking straight ahead, seemingly unaware of the commotion at the tables, but then he stopped and stripped off his shirt. The hush that descended on the terrace was like the hush in a theater that precedes a standing ovation but there were only whispers and giggles as he walked on.

Travis said, "It's the best show in town, especially in the summer." He looked at me, gauged my expression. "Not your type?"

"I don't specialize," I said. "Isn't Nick Donati more yours?"

He blushed. "He said you knew about us."

"He led me to believe it was over between you."

"It's complicated," he said. Donati's phrase. "In the Industry, you can be out, but you can't be out out."

"Aren't you out at work?"

"Yeah, but I'm a production designer. I'm supposed to be gay. Nick's upper-level management. He has to keep it private."

"That mean no boyfriend?"

"It's hard because I really love him," Travis said. "I want everyone to know. I want to live with him. That's what most of our fights are about. We break up, we get back together. All this trouble has brought us a lot closer."

"That's one good thing, then," I said. We picked at our meals for a few minutes, talking about things unrelated to the case. Then I recalled what I meant to ask him. "Last night Nick said you had something to tell me about the case. What is it?"

He swigged his tea, put the glass down. "Yeah, remember you told me to try to figure out what weekends I was using the cab?"

"I remember. Did you?"

"Yes," he said. "I definitely did not use it the first weekend of June."

The weekend Alex was murdered.

"You're sure?"

"I was trying to reconstruct when my car broke down," he said. "I looked at the receipt from the mechanic. I didn't take it in until that Wednesday, so it must have been working over the weekend. Does that help me?"

It was further evidence he couldn't have been driving the cab the night Amerian was killed. "Yeah," I said. "It's very helpful. Bring the receipt to the lineup."

THE SHERIFFS CONDUCTED their lineups down at Bauchet Street, site of the men's county jail. Every new deputy sheriff started out as a jail guard at that squalid, violent and overcrowded pile of concrete. In a few cell blocks, the deputies patrolled from catwalks suspended between the rows of cells where they monitored the floor on closed-circuit cameras, rarely coming into contact with the prisoners. For the most part, though, they worked the floor, where they were vastly outnumbered and in constant fear for their safety, a combination that bred paranoia and encouraged brutality. I'd been in and out of a lot of jails and prisons, but there wasn't anywhere like the LA County Men's Jail; to step inside was to step into a funnel of rage. Bob Travis went chalk-white when I led him in for the lineup, and I think he would have grabbed my hand if some instinct for self-preservation hadn't stopped him.

"He's terrified," I said to Serena, as we watched Travis and five other men file into the room on the other side of the one-way mirror.

"He looks all right to me," she replied, plainly understanding the purpose of my remark.

"If this wasn't pro forma," I said, "I'd object to proceeding with the lineup until he calmed down."

"Why don't we get started." She went to the door and said, "Mac, the first witness, please."

"Mac?" I said. "You can't mean Gaitan."

Before she could answer, he swaggered into the room, followed by a child. When our eyes met, I think we would have snarled if we could. My gaze flicked past him to the child who, I quickly realized, was not a child, but a young man. Willie Wright. The hustler who'd seen Jack Baldwin climb into the Lucky Taxi. He had a soft, spoiled prettiness and glanced around the room glassy-eyed.

"Are you ready, Willie?" Serena said.

From the depths of whatever drug he was on, the boy said, "Yes, ma'am," in a soft, hillbilly drawl.

"Mac," she said to Gaitan. He read the standard admonition. "You understand?"

"Yes, sir," Willie said, a bit more firmly. "Yes sir, I do. You want me to tell you if one of those men took Jackie."

"That's right," Serena said. "Take a look, Willie."

"You have to be positive," I said.

"Just tell me if you recognize any of them," Serena said, throwing me a warning look.

Willie Wright went to the window, standing so close his breath fogged the glass. "No," he said.

"Take as long as you need," Serena said.

"That's coercive."

She made a sour face. "That's absurd."

Willie turned slowly from the window. "Jackie was my friend. I'd tell you if I saw the man. He ain't one of them. They're too young." The little speech seemed to exhaust him. "Can I go now?"

"All right," Serena said. "Thanks, Willie. Mac?"

"I did see him once," Willie drawled, as Gaitan tried to usher him out of the room. "In the paper . . ."

"Wait a minute," I said.

"Let him go, Henry," Serena said, bristling. "He didn't ID your client and he's obviously under the influence."

They left the room.

"What is Gaitan doing here?"

"He interviewed these witnesses," she said, "and he asked to be here. I didn't see any reason to say no."

"After what I told you about him?"

"Let's just get on with it, all right?" she snapped, jaw quivering.

"What's with you?"

She went to the door. "Mac. Mr. Gray, please."

Parker Gray, the sex-club bouncer, was turtle-necked and gargantuan in his pressed walking shorts and red, white and blue tank top with an American Gladiator logo. There were heavy patches of acne on his big shoulders, a side effect of steroids. He studied the men on the platform carefully.

"Could they please turn to the side?" he asked, with the faintest of lisps. "Thank you." He knotted his hands behind his back and examined them. "No, I'm sorry. I can't be sure."

I skipped a breath. "Do you mean you think you recognize one of them?"

"The man I saw looked something like these men," he explained apologetically, "but none of them look exactly like the man I saw. Does that make sense?"

"In other words," I said, "you don't see that man here today."

"No, I guess not."

"That's a miss," I told Serena.

"I'm not so sure," she said. "Do you need more time, Mr. Gray? Would that help."

"No," he said, surer now. "I don't see him."

"Thank you," she said. Gaitan let him out but didn't leave with him. I heard Serena draw a deep breath and said, "There's one more witness."

"What?"

"The investigation's ongoing," she said stiffly. "Another witness has stepped forward."

"When did this happen?"

"A couple of days ago. I didn't mention her because we hadn't taken a statement from her until yesterday." I watched her glance at Gaitan. "Was it yesterday, Dectective?"

"That's right."

I exploded. "You bring me down here with my client and forget to mention you have a third eyewitness? This is bullshit."

"You agreed to the lineup," she said defensively.

"I didn't agreed to be sandbagged by you and this—" I stared at Gaitan. "This scumbag." He took a step toward me. "Just try it, you asshole."

"*Maricón* . . ."

"Stop it," Serena said, jumping between us. "Get out of here, Mac."

I felt his breath on my face. He told her, "You better remember whose side you're on, lady."

"I said get out."

He backed off. "I'm bringing her in," he said.

Serena went to the intercom and instructed the deputy in charge of the line-up to clear the room. "You won't do anything until I tell you to," she told Gaitan.

He raised his hands. "Whatever. You're the boss."

After he left, I said, "What's going on, here?"

There was a door opposite the one from which Gaitan had exited, "Come with me," she said. "There's a conference room over there. We need to talk."

"I'll say."

chapter 13

I FOLLOWED HER into yet another windowless room with scuffed walls and a battered table. The kind of room where I seemed to spend a lot of my life. She tossed her briefcase on the table and removed a file from it. Without looking up at me she said, "Here's a copy of Ms. Schilling's statement. She's the new witness."

I grabbed the two handwritten sheets from her. "Why didn't you mention this when I first got here?"

Nervously, she smoothed her skirt. "I hoped one of the other witnesses would ID your client."

"But if not, you had this in reserve," I said. "And if you'd told me any sooner, you know I would've walked. You played this wrong. We're leaving anyway."

"At least read the statement," she said, in a voice that was halfway between imperious and imploring.

I started reading. Joanne Schilling lived in an apartment two blocks from the alley where Alex Amerian's body had been found. At around five-thirty A.M., on the morning Alex's body was found, she was out walking her dog when a blue and white cab exited the alley at a high rate of speed and nearly ran her over. The driver stopped just in time to let her cross, then sped off. She got a good look at his face. The description she gave matched Bob Travis down to pale eyebrows.

"Gaitan took this statement?"

Serena colored. "Don't start, Henry. I've talked to the woman. She repeated her description almost verbatim."

"Bob wasn't driving the cab that weekend," I said. I showed her the receipt from his auto mechanic indicating his car had gone into the shop the Tuesday after the murder.

She studied the receipt, swallowed. "If I was going to kill someone," she said, returning the receipt, "I wouldn't use my car, either."

"Gaitan is using you to help him frame an innocent man," I said.

She scowled. "That's so incredibly offensive to me."

"You brought me down here under false pretenses," I replied. "That's more offensive."

"Look at these," she said, digging into her briefcase.

She slapped a stack of pink phone messages on the table. I glanced through them. They were all from either Mr. or Mrs. Jellicoe.

"I don't understand," I said.

"Tom Jellicoe's parents. They live in Colorado Springs. Their priest told them Tom's death was a blessing in disguise. After the newspaper ran the story of his murder, the Jellicoes got hate calls. Mrs. Jellicoe sent me Tom's baby pictures, his high school yearbook. She told me she wanted me to know who he was, so I wouldn't stop looking for his murderer just because he was gay." She slipped the phone messages back into her briefcase. "I make it a policy not to come out to victims or witnesses, but I came out to her so that she would understand that I understood. Now she calls me two or three times a day because she doesn't have anyone else to talk to. People in her town think this guy did her a favor by killing her faggot son. I hold the phone to my ear and listen to her cry. I promised her I would find the man who killed Tom."

"My client didn't kill anyone."

"Then let's finish the lineup," she said. "If he wasn't in the alley, she won't ID him. If he was, Henry, I want him off the streets today."

"You said she repeated the statement to you verbatim. That sounds like coaching to me."

She was about to answer when there was a knock at the door and then Gaitan entered the room.

"The lady picked his client," he thrust his chin at me. "She's positive it was him."

"What are you talking about?" I asked.

"I told you to hold off on the lineup," Serena said, angrily.

"I admonished her," Gaitan said.

For a moment, Serena and I were both too stunned to speak.

"You conducted a lineup of my client without telling me?" I said. I grinned at Serena. "You can kiss that identification goodbye."

She had turned beet red. "Goddamn you, Gaitan. Haven't you ever heard of right to counsel?"

"Miranda only applies to questioning," he replied.

"Not hardly," I said. "You can fill Gaitan in on the law later. Right now my client and I are leaving."

"I arrested him," Gaitan said.

"Then unarrest him."

"Cut him loose," Serena said wearily.

Gaitan looked at her and said, "No."

"The lineup was improper," she said, speaking slowly. "The ID won't hold up. Cut him loose."

"Lady," he said, "isn't it time you remembered whose team you're on?"

"What is that supposed to mean?"

"What are you, a DA or a dyke?"

She pushed past him to the lineup room. I followed her, Gaitan behind me. She grabbed the nearest deputy and ordered him to bring Travis to the room. He arrived in handcuffs, so pale I thought he would pass out from shock. She ordered the cuffs removed.

"Take him," she told me. "Go."

"He ain't going anywhere," Gaitan said.

"I'll escort you out," she said, ignoring him.

Gaitan grabbed her arm. "Let's knock this shit off."

She spun around, shaking him off. "You touch me again, I'll have you arrested for battery. I'm going to write you up as soon as I get back to my office. Why don't you shut your fucking mouth before you make it worse for yourself."

He looked as if he'd been slapped, then he recovered, grinned. "Hey, you're the Man. You want to cut this guy loose, it's all on you."

OUT IN THE parking lot, I sent Travis to the car and told her, "You did the right thing in there."

"Don't thank me," she said, snapping on a pair of sunglasses. "Gaitan fucked up, not me. I can still use Schilling."

"You'll never get her ID in," I said. "I'll argue that any future identification was tainted by what happened this morning."

"I'm talking about her statement," she said. "I can still use that."

Before I could ask her what she meant, she was striding across the lot. I got into my car, where Travis huddled in the passenger seat.

"Am I under arrest?" he asked, as I started up the car.

"No," I said. "Gaitan produced a last-minute witness who claimed she saw you in the alley, driving the Lucky Taxi, the morning Amerian was killed." When he didn't respond, I glanced over at him. "Bob?"

"Pull over," he gasped. I pulled the car to the curb. He opened the door and threw up into the gutter.

I WAS SITTING in Travis's antique-filled apartment waiting for him to come out of the bathroom, where he had been for the past fifteen minutes. I'd heard the tap run and then nothing. Finally, I called him. A moment later, he stumbled out. His eyes swam in and out of focus.

"What were you doing in there?"

He sprawled in a chair. "Relaxing."

"What are you on, Bob?"

"Quaalude," he said. "For my nerves."

"How many?"

His eyelids fluttered. "Enough."

"How many?"

"One, two," he said. "I'm tired. I want to rest."

"Don't fall apart on me."

"I'll be all right," he said, closing his eyes.

I sat with him, watching for signs of an overdose, but after awhile it became clear he was merely asleep. I shook him into consciousness long enough to get him to bed, then I went into his bathroom and searched it for other drugs. I found small dosages of everything from crystal meth to Percocet; party drugs, recreational drugs. I flushed them down the toilet and called Nick Donati. I caught him as he was leaving for a meeting, but there was more than impatience in his cold, "What do you want, Henry?"

"Something wrong, Nick?"

He was silent. "Say what you have to say."

"All right," I said. "Detective Gaitan has produced an eyewitness who said she saw Bob coming out of the alley where the first victim was dumped," I said, and recounted the morning's events.

"That's ridiculous," he said. "His witness has to be a fake."

"That's my working assumption, too," I replied, "at least until I interview her."

"So what's the problem?"

"The DA in charge of the case is operating under a different assumption. She talked to the woman, and she believes her. I'm pretty sure she's going to use the witness's statement to obtain either a search warrant or an arrest warrant. I wanted you to know this is about to escalate."

"Media?"

"If there's an arrest, I don't see how it can be avoided."

"Shit," he muttered.

"Meanwhile, Bob seems to be falling apart. I just flushed his pharmaceuticals down the toilet, but at the moment he's passed out on Quaaludes. I think someone should be here to keep an eye on him."

"Can't you stay?"

I glanced at my watch. It was nearly noon. "I've got a suppression motion in Torrance at one-thirty," I said. "If I don't show up, I'll be held in contempt."

"All right, I'll take care of Bob," he said. "I'll call you tonight. Meanwhile, don't talk to anyone in the media again."

"Again?"

"You heard me," he said, and hung up.

Puzzled by his peremptory tone, I put the phone down, checked on Travis, and left.

WHEN I GOT home that evening, I found a FedEx envelope at my door from Richie Florentino. I called Travis, but his line was busy, so I returned some other calls that had come in while I was in court. As I talked on the phone, I opened the package and out slipped the September issue of *L.A. Mode* with a note from Richie on a pink Post-It stuck to the cover. On the cover were pictures of Duke Asuras and Reverend Longstreet at their most predatory, under the headline: THE SECOND COMING: JESUS IN TINSELTOWN. The note read: *Couldn't wait to hear from you. R.* I shook my head and put the magazine aside while I finished my calls. I ordered some food from the chicken place down the street, and when it arrived I went out on the deck to eat and read Richie's big story.

It was essentially the one Richie'd told me weeks earlier, about the battle between Parnassus Studio and its corporate parent, Parnassus Company, over the direction of the studio and the distribution of credit and profit. Continually thwarted by the Company's board of directors, Asuras and his boss, Raskin, had conducted secret negotiations with Reverend Longstreet to buy a majority interest in the Company and stack the board with directors favorable to Raskin and Asuras.

There was nothing libelous in the first few pages of the article, which outlined the byzantine machinations of the parties. Although the studio had become wildly profitable under Asuras, the company's stock value had never completely reflected this profitability. A majority of the board of directors, led by its chairman, an investment banker named Adler, blamed this on Wall Street's continuing doubts about Asuras's personal honesty and integrity because of his record as a convicted embezzler. Adler and his allies had tried to force Raskin, who had final authority in personnel matters, to fire Asuras. Raskin refused, igniting a corporate civil war. Raskin himself could not be fired by the board, even had Adler had the votes, because there were two years remaining on his five-year contract. The article detailed acrimonious board meetings, venomous memos, leaks and counter-leaks, all of which were slowly eroding the studio's standing as Hollywood's "creative community" awaited the outcome of the power struggle. Projects that would have been offered to Parnassus were now shopped elsewhere first while other studios openly poached projects already in development there.

Asuras and Raskin had devised a plan to invite a third-party investor to buy Adler out and replace him and two of his allies with directors who would give Asuras free rein. The third-party investor would make Adler an offer he couldn't refuse: triple the value of his stock. If he did refuse, the investor would launch a public takeover of the company. To finance that kind of warfare, Asuras and Raskin needed deep pockets, a cash-rich investor with a burning desire to get into Hollywood. They found one in Reverend Longstreet, sole proprietor of a billion-dollar media empire anchored by his cable network FVTV or Family Values Television. FVTV alternated reruns of fifties and sixties sitcoms and self-produced religious epics with the most rancid hate-mongering on the public airwaves. In the margins of the story, Richie had quoted from Longstreet's writings and set them off in bold, oversized type: "God does not hear the prayers of Jews;" "God has ordained the family for the propagation of life and it is not a voluntary association"; and "God hates homosexuality today as much as he did in Lot's day."

"You can imagine the Reverend's movies," the writer noted, "Walt Disney meets Leni Riefenstahl. They'd make *The Sound of Music* look like *Last Tango in Paris*."

According to the piece, in a series of meetings between Longstreet and Asuras and Raskin conducted in secret at the home of Cheryl Cordet, a director Longstreet admired, the three men had plotted the takeover of the company, which was to be announced on September first. Longstreet was dispatched in a few paragraphs. The real venom was saved for Asuras. The section on him began: *"To call Duke Asuras soulless gives him too much credit. When someone asked him back in the seventies, during his earlier incarnation as a million-dollar-a-year agent (this was before he kited $20,000 worth of checks from a brain-addled, heroin-addicted client), what he wanted, Asuras summed himself up in a single word, 'More.' "*

I skimmed the account of Asuras's embezzlement conviction until my eye fell on the words *"Rios, a prominent criminal defense lawyer."*

"Richie, you didn't," I sputtered through a mouthful of cornbread.

"Adding to the studio's troubles, there are rumors that Duke might be up to his old tricks. Henry Rios, a prominent criminal defense lawyer, recently had a secret meeting with Parnassus's head lawyer, the incredibly shrinking Nicholas Donati. Rios would only say he'd been hired by the studio to represent an employee under investigation by the police for 'a serious felony.' Like embezzlement?"

"Richie . . ." I muttered. An accusation of criminal activity was slander *per se*.

"No one's saying, but negotiations between the two sides suddenly stalled and then the criminal lawyer appeared on his mysterious errand."

I suddenly understood why Donati had been so sharp with me when we'd talked earlier. He had obviously seen the article and concluded that I'd given Richie an interview because we were friends. The phone in my office rang. I tossed the magazine aside and went to answer.

"Mr. Rios?" as unfamiliar woman's voice asked.

"Yes, who is this?"

"I'm Kate Krishna from Eyewitness News on KVUE," she said. "I wanted your comment on a breaking story that involves a man named Robert Travis . . ."

I cut her off. "What story? What are you talking about?"

"Our sources tell us that Mr. Travis was arrested for the Invisible Man killings in West Hollywood earlier today, but then he was released by the District Attorney handling the case even after a witness identified him as the murderer. As his lawyer, you . . ."

"How did you find out about this?"

"Is it true?"

"Was it Detective Gaitan from the sheriff's department?"

"You were a suspect in this case yourself at one time, weren't you?"

"Yeah, and he probably leaked that to you, too," I said. "Doesn't that give you some idea of his reliability?"

"So you're saying your client's innocent?"

"Are you admitting your source is Gaitan?"

After an equivocal silence, she said, "Will you talk to me if I tell you my source was someone in the sheriff's office?"

"I'll talk to you after I've talked to my client."

"Okay," she said, "but we're running this on the ten-o'-clock broadcast."

I glanced at my watch. It was a quarter after eight. "You can run my denial," I said. "Oh, and remember Richard Jewell before you convict my guy on the air."

"Richard Jewell? Who's that?"

I hung up, called Travis and reached his answering machine. I was halfway through a message when he picked up, sounding groggy but sober.

"The press has got your story, Bob. I just got a call from a reporter from Channel Three."

"She called me, too," he said. "I didn't know what to say, so I hung up on her."

"That's all right," I said. "I talked to her. Have you heard from any other reporters?"

"Just Channel Three," he said. "Who told them?"

"Gaitan," I said. "He's trying to embarrass the DA who let you go this morning. She was already working on obtaining an arrest warrant. This will cinch it."

"An arrest warrant? I didn't do anything."

"The eyewitness, the woman who said she saw you in the alley . . ."

"I wasn't in the alley. I wasn't driving the cab."

"The judge they go to for the warrant won't know that," I said.

"Can't you tell him?"

"Unfortunately, the way it works is you don't get to challenge the warrant until after it's been issued." I paused. "I'm trying to tell you that you may be spending some time in jail until I can challenge the warrant."

"Oh, man, this is a nightmare."

"I'm going to call the DA and try to find out what's happening over there," I said. "If the cops come, call me at this number." I gave him my private, unlisted home number. "And Bob, I threw out all the drugs I found in your bathroom. If you have any others, get rid of them. You don't need a drug charge in addition to everything else. Has Donati called you?"

"No," he said.

"He said he would."

"I'll call him," he said.

"Good idea. Remember, if the cops show up, you call me, no matter how late it is. I'll be in touch."

I LEFT MESSAGES for Serena everywhere I could think of, but by ten o'clock I had still not heard from her. I turned the TV on to Channel 3 and pressed mute. The two anchors, an elegant black woman and a white-haired, crinkly eyed white man, sat shuffling papers importantly, and then on the screen behind them a graphic appeared showing a male outline and the words INVISIBLE MAN. The male anchor began to speak. I clicked on the sound.

". . . learned today that a suspect in the murders of three young men in West Hollywood last month was actually released from custody after he was arrested by order of the District Attorney handling the case. The suspect, thirty-three-year-old Robert Travis, was arrested this morning at the county jail, where he was reportedly identified by an eyewitness as the murderer but then released a few minutes later at the direction of assistant prosecutor Serena Dance. We go now to Kate Krishna, who's at the Criminal Courts Building where the District Attorney has his offices. Kate."

The camera cut to a beautiful Indian woman standing on the steps of the shuttered court building.

"That's right, Larry. Apparently the police actually had their man this morning in these brutal killings, but then they were told to let him go by Serena Dance, the head of the Hate Crimes Unit in the DA's office, and the prosecutor in charge of this investigation. I talked to Dance about an hour ago, as she was leaving the building on her way to a meeting about the case at the sheriff's headquarters."

The screen showed the reporter accosting Serena on the steps of the CCB. She looked exhausted. Her exhaustion changed to tight-lipped fury when Krishna asked her, "What do you say to the residents of West Hollywood when they wonder why you released this suspect back into their community?"

"This investigation is ongoing," she seethed. "I have nothing to say about it at this time."

"Can you confirm that Mr. Travis was arrested and then released?"

"I have no comment," she replied, batting the reporter away.

"What is the purpose of this meeting you're going to with the sheriff?"

"What part of 'no comment' don't you understand?" she snapped, and stormed off.

"Attempts to reach Travis were unsuccessful, but his lawyer, Henry Rios, denied that his client was guilty. We'll be following this story in the days to come. This is Kate Krishna at the Criminal Courts Building in downtown Los Angeles."

"Kate," the male anchor said, "before we lose you, is it true that the suspect was identified as the killer by an eyewitness just before the DA released him?"

Krishna frowned. "Well, not exactly, Larry. Apparently the suspect was identified by an eyewitness who reportedly saw him leaving the area where one of the bodies was found," she said. "As far as we know, there were no eyewitnesses to the murders themselves."

The camera went back to the anchor, who insisted, "But he was arrested for the murders."

"Yes," she said. "Of course, even someone who gets arrested still has to be convicted of the crime . . ."

He cut her off. "Which the DA made harder by releasing the killer," he said. "A shocking, shocking story. We will keep you informed. Now, in other news . . ."

A FEW MINUTES after the broadcast ended, the office phone rang. It was Serena Dance.

"I've been trying to reach you," I said.

"I heard," she replied. "I've been in a meeting."

"I know. I saw you on the news. What's going on, Serena?"

"Gaitan went to the media, I got screamed at by the DA and the sheriff, and your client is about to be arrested."

"You don't mean now?" I said. "It's after eleven."

"Judge Perez signed an arrest warrant and a search warrant twenty minutes ago," she said. "I'd expect the cops are arriving at your client's house right about now."

"This is scapegoating, pure and simple."

Wearily, she said, "Tell it to the judge, Henry. I'm going home."

Chastened, I asked, "How bad was it for you?"

"Bad," she said. "The sheriff accused me of giving preferential treatment to your client because you're gay."

"From Gaitan's lips to the sheriff's ear."

"The old boys," she sighed, then added, "You know, Henry, you're a little bit of an old boy yourself."

"I beg your pardon."

"You've patronized me since day one," she said. "You assumed I didn't know the reason I was in charge of the task force was to give the sheriff political cover with the gay community. You were wrong. I understood the score going in. I knew Gaitan was a cowboy. I knew he had the sheriff's ear."

"Then why did you take the job?"

"Because," she said, in a wrung-out voice, "I want the killer to be caught."

"So do I, Serena," I replied. "I just don't think it's my client."

"Maybe you haven't noticed, Henry, but since the sheriffs started focusing on your client, the killings *have* stopped."

She hung up.

WHEN NO ONE picked up at Travis's apartment, I pulled on a shirt and shoes and headed to West Hollywood. Friday-night traffic rendered the streets nearly impassable and I didn't reach Flores Street until a quarter to twelve. I was immediately aware of the lights, the flashing blue and red of squad cars, the flickering red of an ambulance, the white glare of TV cameras following cops going in and out of Travis's building. The cars created a cordon, so I pulled into a driveway and parked. A swarm of people on the sidewalk were being held back by sheriff's deputies. I approached one of the cops.

"My name is Henry Rios," I said. "I'm Bob Travis's lawyer. I need to get into to see him."

He gave me the cold cop stare, then called over his shoulder, "Hey, Detective, this guy says he's Travis's lawyer."

A moment later, Gaitan materialized out of the darkness, smoking a cigarette. "Rios," he said, grinning.

"I want to see my client."

He flicked the cigarette to my feet. "No problem."

The door to Travis's apartment was open and people were spilling out into the hall—cops, paramedics, crime-lab types. When I recognized a woman from the medical examiner's office, I got a bad feeling. Inside, two deputies were inspecting some of Travis's gewgaws, one of them lisping mocking commentary to the other. A sandy-haired paramedic was standing at the doorway to the bathroom, looking in. Gaitan asked him to move aside and then stepped back so I could see what he'd been staring at.

Bob Travis knelt in front of the toilet, his head completely submerged in the bowl, water and vomit spilling down its sides.

"What happened?"

Gaitan chortled, "He drowned, man. In his own puke."

STUNNED, I TURNED away from the sight and met Gaitan's eyes. They were amused and contemptuous.

"What do you mean he drowned?" I demanded.

He reached into his coat pocket and removed an evidence Baggie containing a brown prescription bottle. "Valium," he said. "Found the bottle by his bed, empty, and an empty fifth of vodka in the kitchen. He got loaded, got sick and passed out while he was puking. It happens, Rios. Remember Lupe Velez?"

"What are you talking about?"

"Actress in the forties, the Mexican Spitfire," he replied conversationally, as if the smell of vomit wasn't oozing through the warm air. "She decides to kill herself, right, so she eats a big Mexican meal and downs a bottle of pills. She gets all dressed up and lays down on her bed to die, like it was a movie, but the food makes her sick to her stomach, and she runs to the john, puking all over the place. She passes out with her head in the toilet, like your *compadre* here, and that's how they find her."

"Mexican Spitfire?" I said incredulously. "What the hell are you talking about?"

"You don't look so good, Rios," Gaitan said, following me out. "What are you doing here, anyway?"

I tumbled into a chair in the living room. "I wanted to be present when you arrested him."

"Who told you we were going to arrest him?"

"The DA."

He smirked. "Dance? I shoulda guessed. You people are tighter than the Jews. You queers." He bit off the word, then smiled. "That's right, isn't it, Rios? Don't you call yourselves 'queers'?"

The two mocking deputies fell silent.

"Knock yourself out, Mac. Call me whatever you want, if it makes you feel like more of a man. You can use all the help you can get."

In a single, swift motion he reached down, grabbed my jacket and pulled me to my feet. "What do you know about being a man? You stopped being a man the first time you let someone fuck you."

"How do you know what I do in bed? Or is that an offer?" I smirked. "Sorry, Mac. I'm a top, but I could probably set you up with —"

He threw me against the wall. "You make me sick."

"You might try therapy," I said. "Now let go of me, you asshole."

Rage flooded his face, rising in a red tide. He took half a step back, tightening his hands into fists. I got ready to swing back.

I heard Odell before I saw him. "What the hell is going on here?" He stepped between us. "This is a crime scene, not a schoolyard."

"Hello, Sergeant," I said.

"What are you doing here, Counsel?"

"I heard my client was going to be arrested. I wanted to make sure it was all aboveboard."

Odell said, "I wouldn't worry about it. The only place he's going to is the morgue. Take off."

I looked at him. "I beg your pardon?"

"I'll see to things here."

I shrugged. "I'll expect a thorough investigation into Bob's death."

"I'll be in touch," Odell said.

OUTSIDE ON THE street, the TV reporters were clustered around Serena Dance. I slipped past the cameras, disappearing into the crowd of spectators on the sidewalk, and looked for my car. Across the street was another knot of spectators. One of them broke loose and came toward me. Nick Donati. His expensive suit was wrinkled and he was tieless.

"Henry," he said. "What the hell's going on?"

I pulled him into the shadows. "What are you doing here, Nick?"

"I went to a screening this evening. When I got home, there was a hysterical message from Bob on my machine. I called him back and a policeman picked up the phone, so I came right down."

"Bob's dead."

"Oh, Jesus," he moaned. "How?"

"This isn't the place to talk about it," I said, indicating the press. "Didn't you tell me you live in Laurel Canyon?"

Dazed, he said, "Yeah."

I walked him to my car, unlocked the passenger door. "Get in," I said.

"What about my car? I'm double-parked."

"Worry about that later," I said, pushing him into the car.

As I drove away, the paramedics came out with Bob Travis's body on a stretcher.

chapter 14

I BACKED OUT of the driveway and drove to Sunset, then headed east to Laurel Canyon, the snaking road that connected the city to the valley. From Laurel Canyon, tributary roads forked into dark and wooded hills, where rustic bungalows elbowed million-dollar châteaux, and everyone locked up their pets at night to keep them from being carried off by coyotes. I turned off Laurel Canyon at Kirkwood. Donati directed me across a web of narrow, twisting streets to a cul-de-sac where his two-story house occupied the last lot, which backed up against the grove of eucalyptus trees. I pulled into the driveway. The fragrant trees perfumed the cool air and it was so still I could hear the rustle of small animals moving through the woods.

The ground floor of Donati's pillbox-shaped house was a wall of unpainted concrete, pristine and stark, partly covered by a sheet of corrugated metal. The upper floor was a wall of greenish glass, brightly lit from within, but of such distorting thickness it was impossible to see in from the street. The front door was made of hammered copper and it bore a sign that warned the house was protected by an armed-guard service. The sign seemed extraneous; the house was obviously a bunker. It took Donati a good five minutes to shut off the security alarms and let us in. Of course, his hands were shaking.

From a small foyer paneled in dark marble, metal stairs twisted up to the second floor. I glimpsed an office and a bedroom off the foyer as I ascended behind him. The upper floor was a single big room, anchored on one end by an open kitchen and on the other by a fireplace. The kitchen gleamed, as if it had never been used. Neutral area carpets were scattered across the concrete floor. The room was sparsely furnished with leather club chairs, a matching sofa, a scattering of occasional tables. The walls were a snowy shade of white, dominated by an enormous black-and-white abstract painting that looked very much like a Franz Kline. Over the fireplace were two Mapplethorpe photographs of flowers. Between them was a small engraving. The contrast between Donati's house and Travis's apartment could not have been greater. Travis's antique-cluttered apartment was pure camp. This room was as sour and penitential as a monk's cell.

"I need a drink," Donati said. He tossed his keys with a clatter on a lacquered dining table, the overhead light shimmering on its surface. "You?"

"I'll have a Coke," I said.

While he slammed through the kitchen, I took a closer look at the engraving on the mantel and recognized it as one of Gustave Doré's original drawings for the *Inferno*.

"The wood of the suicides," Donati said, coming up behind me. "From the *Inferno*."

"I recognize it," I said, accepting a glass.

In the *Inferno*, the suicides were consigned, like the sodomites, to the circle of the violent, having committed violence against themselves. They spent eternity encased in trees under attack by the Harpies, scaly, foul-smelling birds with iron talons and women's faces, who ripped bloody branches from the trees. The suicides could speak only as long as the blood ran from their amputated limbs.

"Did Bob kill himself?"

I remembered the scene in the bathroom. "Not according to the cops. Why do you ask?"

He downed his drink, slipped into a chair and filled his glass from the bottle of Chivas he'd brought from the kitchen.

"His message. It was crazy, desperate."

"Did you save it?"

He hesitated a moment, then shook his head. "It was too disturbing."

I sat down. "What did he say?"

"If he didn't kill himself, what did happen?"

"The police say they found him facedown in the toilet. They think he mixed pills and booze and passed out while he was vomiting, and drowned."

Donati's delicate fingers tightened around his glass until his knuckles went white. "He drowned in his toilet?"

"That's the theory. I won't know for sure until I see the autopsy."

"On the message, I could hear in his voice he was drunk," Donati said.

"When did he leave the message?"

"A little after nine."

"I spoke to him an hour earlier. He sounded sober."

Donati smiled grimly. "After around seven, Bob was never completely sober."

"Did he have a problem with drugs, too?"

Donati nodded. "Bob didn't like reality very much."

"What did he say on his message?"

Donati took a quick drink, looked past me. "I guess it can't hurt him now. He incriminated himself in the murders. That's why I erased the message. That's why I went to his apartment, to talk to him, to persuade him to talk to you."

"What exactly did he say?"

"He said he was afraid to go to jail for killing those men." He rolled his glass between his hands. "He said the police were about to arrest him. Is that true?"

"Yeah," I said. "They came with arrest and search warrants."

He swallowed more scotch, grimaced, and said, "I still can't believe he killed those men."

"You knew him better than anyone."

He looked at me wearily. "Not really."

"Wasn't he in love with you?"

"Oh, please," he said. "Men can't love each other that way."

"Which way?"

"The way men love women," he said. "The way women love men. Romantic love is for making babies. We're a different kind of biology."

"Bob didn't agree?"

Donati sprang to his feet and paced to the window. "He wanted us to live together, play house. I told him I wasn't interested. That was the first time he tried to kill himself. It was pathetic and disgusting. He was. You see why I don't advertise I'm gay."

"No, not exactly, Nick."

"Because I don't want to be confused with people like Bob." He tossed back his drink. "Drag queens, leather queens, all those sick fucks who parade around and make it impossible for the rest of us to have normal lives. You must understand that, Henry. You're a man, like me."

"The bigots don't make those distinctions," I said. "We're all the same to them."

"Why should we care what the fly-overs think?"

"The what?"

He went back to the table and poured himself another drink. "Everyone who lives between the coasts. The fly-overs."

"Does that include Reverend Longstreet?"

He narrowed his eyes. "What are you talking about?"

"Richie Florentino sent me a copy of next month's issue of *L.A. Mode* with his exposé of your boss."

"That issue will never see the light of day," he said, dismissively. "You shouldn't have talked to him."

"He quoted me without my knowledge or approval."

He nodded. "That pretty much sums up his ethics."

"But he has a point," I said. "Why give Longstreet another forum to express his hatred of us?"

"I'm not part of that 'us,' " Donati said, his eyes beginning to blur with drink. "That's what Bob never understood. I don't want to be part of any 'us.' "

"You were ready to face obstruction of justice charges to protect him," I reminded him. "When I called the other night, he was here."

"That was before I knew he was a murderer," he said.

"You must have felt something for him."

He swirled the scotch in the heavy glass. "My father committed suicide when I was thirteen. My older brother killed himself when I was twenty. Bob had already tried once. I was afraid he would try it again. I couldn't have another suicide on my conscience."

"I'm sorry," I said. "Why would it be on your conscience? People kill themselves of their own free will."

"Suicide is a message," he said. "A message to the people who survive."

"What message?"

He downed the rest of his drink. "You failed me."

I heard the scamper of small feet on the stairway and then two small dogs bounded into the room. They stopped when they saw me, tensed, sniffed the air.

"Pablo, Paloma," Donati called. "Come." The dogs jumped into his chair and licked his hands and face.

"It's late," I said, getting up. "I should get going."

"I want to know what happened to Bob," he said, as the dogs settled on either side of him.

I stopped, turned. "You care, but you don't care. What is that?"

"I'm not like Duke," he replied. "I believe in consequences. By the way," he continued, rubbing his temples, "tell Richie Longstreet doesn't hate gays. It's all an act, a marketing device."

"Well, that makes it all right," I said.

THE MEDICAL EXAMINER'S report arrived two days later, listing the cause of Bob's death as asphyxiation. There were high, though not fatal, levels of benzodiazepines and alcohol in his system. When he had passed out in the toilet, he managed to aspirate vomit and choke to death. Death by misadventure was the official verdict. The media, however, continued to report it as a suicide in a flurry of stories in which, no longer fettered by libel laws, he was anointed a serial murderer, or, as one headline had it: THE INVISIBLE MAN DISAPPEARS.

The day after I got the Medical Examiner's report, while I was the Criminal Courts Building on another case, I ran into Serena Dance in the grim little coffeeshop on the first floor. It was noon. She was sitting alone with a stack of files and a Styrofoam plate piled high with a salad of wilted greens and wrinkled vegetables. I sat down at her table. She looked up, flicked a stray hair from her face.

"I was going to call you," she said. "I got back some preliminary results from the search of Bob Travis's apartment."

"I'm surprised you bothered," I said, tucking into a greasy enchilada. "He's already been convicted in the press."

"This time they were right."

I paused, mid-bite. "What did you find?"

"There were blue fibers on his closet floor that match the fibers in the car," she said. "They were also found in the garbage chute and the Dumpster." She looked at me. "I think it's pretty unlikely Gaitan crawled down the garbage chute to plant them."

"A garbage chute is pretty much the man's natural habitat."

"There was a fast-food wrapper stuck to the bottom of one of Travis's shoes by a quarter-sized bloodstain," she continued. "The wrapper came from the Mexican restaurant where the second body was dumped. The blood stain is O positive, Jack Baldwin's type. I've sent it out for DNA testing, but I'm pretty sure it'll come back his." She ate a forkful of salad. "Ms. Schilling picked your client out of a photo lineup."

"You were thorough."

"I wanted to tell Mrs. Jellicoe we got the right man," she said.

"Did you ever doubt it?"

She pushed her plate aside. "God, this food is terrible. Yes, I did wonder. When you weren't impugning my integrity, you actually had me believing that Gaitan had planted evidence against Travis."

"I apologize if I impugned your integrity."

"You thought I was gutless because I wouldn't take Gaitan on, but my job was to find the killer. I wasn't interested in stroking your wounded male ego."

"Hey, it wasn't my ego his pals beat the shit out of out there in the desert."

She frowned. "You could've brought charges. You decided not to."

"I decided I was in no position to take on the entire sheriff's department," I replied. "But then I'm not the one who's working from inside the system."

"Don't lay that on me," she said. "I didn't come to work for the DA to sell out my principles, I did it to implement them. There are thousands of hate crimes in this city every year. The only reason that any of them get prosecuted is because of me. I need the cops. I can't be screaming police misconduct every time one of them pisses me off."

"Gaitan has more than just an attitude problem," I said. "He's a vigilante with a badge."

"Whatever Gaitan did or didn't do, your client was guilty. End of story."

THAT NIGHT, I stopped at the Mayfair on Hyperion to pick up something for dinner and saw a stack of the September issue of *L.A. Mode* beside the manager's counter at the front of the store. They were still in their shrink wrap. I had misplaced the copy Richie had sent me, so I went over to grab one from the pile.

As I tried to tear through the plastic, I heard someone say, "Excuse me, sir, you can't do that." It was the manager, an open-faced man who, even as he admonished me, smiled pleasantly. "I'm sorry, but those aren't for sale."

"Isn't this the new issue?"

"Yes," he said, "but we've been told we're not supposed to sell them."

"Why? They spoil?"

"It's on the advice of our legal department," he said. "I guess the magazine's been sued for libel."

"When did this happen?"

"I couldn't tell you," he said politely. "But I have to ship these back to the distributor in the morning."

"You can't spare even one copy?"

He hesitated. "I'm really sorry, but if I don't return the exact number I was sent, I could get in big trouble." He smiled again. "We have a lot of other magazines."

"Thank you," I said and went off to buy my Lean Cuisine.

As soon as I got home, I called Richie. Javier answered.

"Javier, hi, it's Henry Rios. Is Richie there?"

Javier was the master of silences, capable of imbuing them with many different kinds of meaning. This one was anxious.

"You haven't heard, sir?" he asked, finally.

"Heard what?"

"Mr. Richie was fired," he said. "He's not talking to anyone."

"Fired? When?"

Another silence. Doubt, reluctance.

"Yesterday," he said. "They changed the locks on his office. He had only one hour to pack and they watched him the entire time."

"Please, Javier, would you ask him if he'll talk to me?"

"Yes, sir."

A few minutes later, I heard a low, broken, "Henry."

"Richie?"

"Those fuckers," he raved in a tear-stained voice. "They hired a fucking armed security guard to keep me out of my office. Everyone stood there and watched, even the goddamned little fag receptionist knew. I gave that little prick the job." He started crying. "They took it all away."

"Richie, I'm sorry."

He breathed roughly into the phone. "When I started that piece of shit, they had forty thousand subscribers, Henry. Forty. Now there's two hundred thousand. I put them on the fucking map. I did. I could kill that cunt . . ."

"Who are you talking about?"

"The publisher," he said. "Alyssia Moran. Bitch. I even taught her how to dress. You should've seen the crap she used to wear before I got her into Armani." He sniffled. "And her makeup. What a disaster. She made Tammy Faye Bakker look like fucking Martha Stewart."

I couldn't help but laugh. After a brief, wounded silence, he laughed, too.

"What happened, Richie?"

I heard him strike a match and light a cigarette. "Asuras sued," he mumbled as he drew on the cigarette. "The day the magazine was going out, his lawyers served Alyssia with a TRO to keep us from distributing the issue until the case was heard."

"Wow," I said, "That's prior restraint. Asuras must have some really good lawyers."

"She had to pull every fucking issue," he said. "When I came in yesterday, she fired me."

"What did he allege was the libel?"

"He said I accused him of committing a crime."

"Embezzlement," I said, remembering the brief passage about my visit to the studio.

"Embezzlement?" Richie said. "He was convicted of that."

"Then what does he say you accused him of?"

"Murder," Richie said.

"Murder? I don't remember anything like that in the article."

"Well, his lawyers caught it," he said. I heard the doorbell ring. "Listen, honey, that's my shrink. I talked her into making a housecall. I'll call you back."

"All right. Let me buy you dinner."

"Sure, sweetie. Kiss, kiss." He hung up.

I waited two days for Richie to call, and when he didn't, I called him. His answering machine repeated this message: "This is Mr. Richie Florentino. I've left the country because I'm rich and I can. So fuck you."

WORRIED, I CALLED Joel Miller at Universal. After being put on hold by three different, but equally snippy, assistants, I reached him.

"Joel, it's Henry Rios. How are you?"

After a brief, petulant silence he said, "As if you cared. You want to know about Richie."

"I guess that's true. Sorry, Joel. I talked to him Monday, now his answering machine says he's left the country. I didn't know who else to call except you."

"I don't know where Richie is," he said, "and I don't really care. I moved out of the apartment three weeks ago."

"Three weeks? He didn't mention that."

"He didn't notice," Joel said bitterly. "You're like all his other friends. You don't know what he's really like. Richie's a failure. He was a nobody when we came to LA. I'm the one who got him his contacts, and then he turns around and treats me like shit. I only put up with it because I knew it was just a matter of time before he sabotaged himself. He's fucked up everything he's ever tried to do. He has to. He thrives on the drama. I put up with it for twenty years, but I'm through with him. And his goddamned friends."

He slammed the phone down.

Richie liked to say "In Hollywood, you're only as good as your Rolodex," and he bragged about his, but when I called around to some of the people in the Industry he'd claimed as friends, it became clear they all knew about the Asuras piece and Richie had become a non-person as a result of it. I wrangled their numbers from various sources and they were not happy to hear from me, most of the conversations beginning, "Who gave you my number?" A few of them hung up on me when I explained I was trying to find out if anyone had heard from Richie. Others stayed on the line long enough to say, "No, don't call again." Only a couple expressed their own concern about him, one of them a female producer who reluctantly took my call, but warmed to me when I told her it was about Richie.

"I talked to him the day after he was fired," she said. "It was ugly."

"I know, I talked to him, too."

"He took it very hard," she said. "I was afraid he might do something to himself."

I panicked. "You don't think he has, do you?"

She laughed. "Oh, no. If Richie was going to do away with himself, he wouldn't leave a note, he'd rent a billboard on Sunset."

"You think he actually just picked up and left the country."

"It would be a good career move for him. There's nothing for him here. You don't take on the head of a major studio unless you can bring him down. It was foolish of Richie to think he could."

"Why?"

"Richie ran a little fashion magazine, for God's sake. He's never had any weight around town. People kept him around because he was outrageous and funny, but no one took him seriously."

"He thought he was doing a public service by keeping Reverend Longstreet out of Hollywood."

"I know, I know. He explained it all to me in tedious detail. That really shows how little Richie understands about the Industry. Hollywood has a way of humbling people like Longstreet," she said, the name curdling in her throat. "As far back as Joe Kennedy and Howard Hughes, you have these magnates who want to make pictures their way, and who end up having their heads served to them on a platter. Look at the Japanese. They paid billions to get into the game and now they're unloading their studios at fire sale prices. Poor Richie. He thinks it's about making movies when it's only about making money."

"So Longstreet would have met his match in Hollywood."

She let out a throaty peal of laughter. "Remember Savonarola? The Florentine priest in the middle ages who persuaded all the wicked Florentines to change their ways and burn their dirty books and flashy jewels in a great bonfire? It was very exciting for a while, but then they got bored, and ended up burning him at the stake. Longstreet's nothing but a modern-day Savonarola. He'll ride into town on his white charger and everyone will cheer about the return of family values until his first picture bombs. Then we'll all line up to light the first match."

"Richie didn't know this?"

"Richie's outrageous, but he's not corrupt. Not like the rest of us. He has an odd kind of innocence, you know?"

"Yes, I know. I think it's what keeps him alive. I mean, that and his rage."

"Don't worry about Richie, Mr. Rios," she said. "He loves Hollywood. He'll be back. If you hear from him, give him my love and tell him to call me. And remind him that vice always overwhelms virtue and money trumps them both. Goodbye."

TEN DAYS AFTER Travis's death, I was summoned to Parnassus Studio for a final meeting with Donati. When I stepped into his office, I was met with a blast of bone-chilling air and then I saw Asuras, in his patriarchal wools and tweeds, at the head of the glossy conference table in a corner of Donati's office. Donati sat at his right hand. Asuras greeted me with a magisterial nod.

"I'm surprised to see you," I said, taking a seat at the end of the table.

"I'm responsible for everything that involves the studio," he said.

"The studio's involvement was always minimal," I said.

"Thanks to you," Donati said.

I shrugged. "I didn't go out of my way to keep the studio out of the case."

"You also didn't go out of your way to drag us in," Asuras said. "Most lawyers in this town would've tried to squeeze some personal publicity out of the case. The studio angle would've guaranteed headlines."

"It wouldn't have helped Bob to feed him to the press."

"We've been approached by a number of people representing the victims' families about whether we were interested in the movie rights to their stories," Donati said.

I said nothing.

"You're not interested in selling your story?" he persisted.

"Of course not," I said. "This case involved three gruesome deaths, four, including Bob's. I'm not interested in making money off of that."

"A principled lawyer," Asuras said. "Did you notice whether pigs were flying when you came in?"

"No, but it is a cold day in hell," I replied. "In this office anyway."

"We just want this thing to be over," Donati said.

"As far as I'm concerned, it is."

"Good," Asuras said, and then, after a couple of uncomfortable moments, asked, "There's no doubt in your mind that Bob Travis was the murderer?"

"That's what the evidence indicates."

Asuras smiled. It was a smile of great, fatherly charm. "You're not convinced? Something nags at you?"

"Serial killers usually start out as the kind of kids who pull wings off flies and torture the family cat," I said. "Travis didn't seem the type."

"Not evil?" Asuras asked.

"I don't believe in evil," I said.

Asuras arched a satanic eyebrow. "You don't believe in evil? In your business?"

"I don't believe in evil as a theological concept," I explained. "As some kind of innate depravity."

"You think it's all the result of bad parenting?" Asuras said derisively.

"No," I said, annoyed to be patronized by him. "I think it's in your karma."

"What do you mean?"

"Auden says it best," I said. "Auden, the poet?"

"I know who Auden is," he said, scowling.

"Then you probably know the lines I'm referring to, from his poem 'September 1, 1939,' " I continued, mocking him.

" 'Those to whom evil are done/Do evil in return,' " he quoted stentoriously. "Those lines?"

Abashed, I said, "Yes, those lines."

"Auden's not talking about karma," he said. "He's talking bad parenting. Karma is the accretion of all your acts in all your lives, the residue, if you will. Sometimes the residue is evil, pure and simple."

"I bow to your greater knowledge of evil."

Donati broke in impatiently, "An eyewitness saw him leaving the alley. The police found bloodstained shoes in his closet. That proves he was the killer."

"I know," I said. "I know what the evidence is."

"I can't quote poetry," Donati persisted, "but I know my Sherlock Holmes and he said if the facts compel an obvious conclusion, then the conclusion must be correct, however improbable."

"And the murders have stopped," Asuras said. "Isn't that the best evidence that Bob was the murderer?"

"Yes," I said. "The murders have stopped."

Donati said, "Well, thank you for coming by, Henry." He slid an envelope across the table. "Your fee."

I glanced in the envelope. The amount was outrageous. "You're sure you're not trying to buy my silence?"

"You earned it," Asuras said. "And if there's anything else I can do for you, just let me know through Nick."

"There is, actually," I said.

The two of them looked at each other as if the other shoe had dropped. "What is it?" Asuras asked, warily.

"You have a lawsuit pending against *L.A. Mode*," I said.

He frowned. "That's right. You're a friend of Richie's."

"Whom you've named as a defendant," I said. "I'll return your fee if you'll dismiss him from the case."

"Why should I?"

"You got the magazine pulled before it was distributed," I said, "so your damages are minimal and I'm sure the magazine will settle. There's no point in keeping Richie in the suit except to run up his legal bills."

"And teach him a lesson," Asuras said.

"He was fired from his job. No reputable magazine will ever hire him. His friends have dumped him. I think he learned his lesson."

Asuras studied me, then said, "Tell Richie I'll dismiss the suit against him in exchange for a handwritten letter of apology."

"Thank you."

"And keep your fee," he said, as if the hundred-thousand-dollar check was no more to him than a tip.

THAT NIGHT I dreamed I was standing on a promontory covered with grass greener than any earthly grass, overlooking an ocean upon which the light fell like sheets of glass. I turned away from the sea and saw, about fifty yards distant, an elaborate Victorian mansion with turrets and towers and gingerbread woodwork like something spun from sugar. It was framed by a sky of such profound blue I had to shield my eyes against it. A young man stepped out onto the verandah, looked in my direction and began walking toward me. My heart stopped. It was Josh. He was dressed in the clothes in which he'd been cremated but he was whole again. His flesh was supple, his hair shone and his eyes were clear, free of pain or fear. Wordlessly, he threw his arms around me and I held him so tightly I could feel his heart beating against mine. He smelled of honey and incense and ash and his body radiated a delicious warmth, a womb-warmth. He kissed me.

"My God, Josh," I whispered. "You're alive."

"No," he said gently. "I've come back, but just for a minute." He slipped out of my embrace.

"What do you mean, Josh? What is this place?"

"Come with me," he said, taking my hand. We walked to the edge of the promontory. He looked across the brilliant sea and said, "This is sort of a jumping-off point."

"Jumping off to where?"

He spread his arm above the ocean. "There. Henry, it's my time. That's why I came back, to say goodbye."

"I don't understand."

He stroked my hair. "It's hard to explain. After you die, there's a place, a place of judgment. Kind of. It's a place you've always carried around inside. It's what you imagine happens after you die. If you imagine heaven, that's what you get. If you imagine hell, you get hell." He clasped my hand tighter. "But the point is, they don't exist except in your imagination, and when you realize that, you're free to go."

"Go where, Josh?"

He released my hand and stared out at the sea of light. The look on his face was ecstatic. He whispered, "There are no words . . ." He seemed to burn from within, with a light of such intensity he became translucent, a rainbow aureole forming around his head. Without changing shape, he seemed to grow larger and larger, until clouds drifted across his eyes. His face shone like the sun and his legs were like pillars of fire. I could no longer look at him and cowered, afraid I would be consumed by his light.

"Don't be afraid," he said. "Look at me."

I looked and it was as if I saw through him, past the awesome light, to something indescribable. Later, I remembered it as a rose as vast as the universe, charged with intelligence, serenely folding and unfolding shimmering petals of fire.

"Oh," I said. "Oh, oh . . ."

And then it was over. The inhumanely radiant light faded, he shrank to his normal size and I could hold him in my eyes again.

He kissed me again with a mouth that tasted of apple.

"Goodbye, Henry," he said. "I loved you so much. More than either of us knew."

"Will I ever see you again?"

"Look into yourself," he replied, slowly seeping into the gloom of dreams. "We're the same person."

"Josh . . ."

I woke to darkness, tears running down my face.

chapter 15

BOB TRAVIS WAS cremated and his ashes returned to his family in Maryland. I knew this because I arranged it, in consultation with Donati and Bob's father, whom I spoke to several times on the phone. Mr. Travis — "Hey, call me Ron" — was a mail carrier, a gruff man whose response to his son's death was bafflement and shame; the same response, I suspected, he had had to Bob's life. He clung to the notion that Bob had been corrupted in Hollywood by "the gays." Out of respect for his loss, I kept my mouth shut about myself. To me, this was a variation of the all-too-familiar story of the son who left home to find himself only to be returned to his family years later in a coffin or an urn as a stranger. The twist in the story was that Bob hadn't died of AIDS. When I told his father how he had died, he said, "Oh, Jesus. Don't say anything to his mom." Fortunately, the West Hollywood murders had remained a regional story, which allowed me to emphasize, without contradiction, that Bob had only been a suspect at the time of his death. Fortunately, too, Ron Travis never asked me point-blank if his son was guilty, because I wasn't sure my euphemisms were equal to the question.

It was now August, and the city was basically uninhabitable. The downtown skyline simply disappeared for days at a time into the smog, only to reappear at night, brilliantly lit up against the red sky. The heat turned wet and I never left home without a spare shirt in my briefcase. At night I sat on the terrace in my boxer shorts reading the *Inferno* and swatting at mosquitos. I thought a lot about the dream I had had of Josh and the places of judgment we carry within ourselves and I wondered what mine looked like, my heaven, my hell. Of course, I realized they were not places at all, but feelings. A center of joy, a center of despair both so consuming only mystics or pyschopaths could set up permanent residence there. The rest of us brushed up against them only occasionally, most often through a death. Josh had died in pain and confusion, resentful at how little time he'd had, and I suppose I kept those feelings alive for him and created my own little hell. The dream invited me to release myself from those feelings but one did not simply walk away from the great darkness; you had to walk through it, and I felt I was not yet through. Perhaps that's why I so eagerly followed Dante to Cocytus, the ninth circle of his Hell where a three-faced Satan stood in a lake frozen into ice by the beating of his own gigantic, leathery wings:

> In every mouth he worked a broken sinner
> between his rake-like teeth. Thus he kept three
> in eternal pain at his eternal dinner.

Then, within a few days after I shipped Bob Travis's ashes to his parents, three things happened.

The first was an unexpected package that arrived one afternoon from Parnassus Studio. Inside was a videotape of a movie called *Letters* and a note from Asuras's secretary: "Mr. Asuras asked me to send this to you." I had no idea why he had sent it but the title was familiar and then I remembered. It was the movie I'd brought tickets to on my date with Alex. I slipped the tape into the VCR. The movie was a Parnassus production and because it was based on a book by Agatha Christie, I expected a period piece. Instead I found it was set in contemporary San Francisco and involved a series of grisly murders which had in common that the victims' names were in alphabetical sequence, from A to D. D was as far as I got, at any rate, because after that murder—in which the victim was beheaded, his chest carved open and his head shoved into the cavity—I turned the movie off. After twenty years of examining crime-scene photos, I knew most of what there was to know about how human bodies can be violated, so it wasn't that these images made me squeamish. What repelled me was their clear pornographic intent, as if this butchery was sex by other means. I assumed the gift was a gloss on our discussion of evil, but this wasn't evil, just appallingly bad taste.

THEN, LUCAS ODELL dropped by on a Sunday morning as I was lying in bed, wading through the *Times*, drinking tea because I'd run out of coffee. The doorbell chimed. I pulled on a pair of jeans and a tee shirt. Looking through the peephole, I saw Odell, dressed as casually as I was, holding a big white bag. I opened the door.

"Sergeant," I said. "You always arrive unannounced."

"This time I brought breakfast," he said, holding up the bag.

"Come on in," I said.

"You're not going to ask me why I'm here?"

"I'm sure you'll let me know in your own good time. Is that coffee I smell?"

By now he knew his way around my house and went directly into the kitchen, where he laid breakfast on the table: two large cups of Starbuck's coffee and four pastries, muffins, a cheese danish, a croissant. I poured orange juice, brought him milk and sugar for his coffee and we settled in at the table. He politely offered me the danish. I politely insisted we share it. I was surprised at how happy I was to see him because I thought I had long ago outgrown the need for father figures, but he stirred that longing in me. From the way he treated me, I saw he reciprocated the feeling, but neither of us spoke of it.

He was eyeing me with a grin. "You look like you just rolled out of bed."

I yawned, glanced at the clock. It was after ten. "I'm afraid so. I was out last night and didn't get back until late."

"You have a date?"

"Odell, what a question. No, I was out with a friend. Dinner, a movie."

"You're a good-looking young fellow, Henry," he said, through a mouthful of bran muffin. "You should get out more."

"I'll keep that in mind."

He chugalugged coffee. "I mean it. You'll be old and fat soon enough and no one will want you. Get it while you can."

"You give your daughter the same advice?"

He smiled. "Believe me, my daughter doesn't need my help in that department. She runs girlfriends hot and cold."

"Do you know what the phrase cognitive dissonance means?"

"Seeing ain't believing?" he ventured.

"Basically," I said. "That's how I feel when I talk to you. You look like Archie Bunker, but you sure don't sound like him. On the subject of gays, anyway."

"My daughter came out to me when she was seventeen, I had to choose between the things I was taught about homosexuals and what I knew about her," he said. "I'm a practical man. It wasn't a hard choice."

I thought about Ron Travis. "Not every parent feels that way about their gay kid."

He stuffed a bit of muffin his mouth. "Things are changing. Be patient."

"They're not changing fast enough for my friends who've died."

"Close friends?"

"The man I lived with," I said. "He died about a year ago."

He nodded, as if in confirmation. "I wondered why you were alone."

I shrugged. "I'm alone because I'm cranky and choosy."

He smiled. "You know Tim down at the station? My jailer? He's single."

"Are you trying to set me up?" I laughed. "Is that why you dropped by?"

"It's just a suggestion," he said. "It's not why I dropped by. I came to see you about Gaitan."

My mirth evaporated. "What about him?"

"I've been conducting a little unofficial investigation," Odell said, clawing a chunk from the second muffin. He popped it into his mouth. "You were right. He planted the fiber evidence in the cab."

"I'm listening."

"The fiber samples they took from Amerian's body disappeared out of the evidence locker at the crime lab after they were analyzed."

"How could they match the fibers they found in the car if the fibers were gone?"

"They did it on paper," he replied. "They analyzed the fibers from the trunk and matched them to the earlier analysis of the fibers from the body."

"No one bothered to mention to me the sample had disappeared."

"No one knew but the lab. I also called the FBI and talked to their fiber guy about your theory of how the fibers should've shed if the body was wrapped in a blanket in the trunk. He said you were right."

"Why did you call the FBI?"

"I wanted an objective opinion," he said.

"You don't trust your crime lab?"

He shrugged. "Someone in the lab removed the fiber sample and gave it to Gaitan."

"You know that for a fact?"

"There's no other way it could've been done, because the lab people are the only ones who would have had access to the sample."

"That's circumstantial, at best."

"Gaitan has an old partner from his Antelope Valley days. Jim Roca. Roca's brother-in-law works in the lab. Hair and Fiber. His name is Stan Bedell. He did the analysis."

"Gaitan and Roca still keep in touch?"

"They and a couple of other deputies own a cabin up at Big Bear."

"Was Roca part of the vigilantes you were sent to Antelope Valley to break up?"

"He was one of the ones that was transferred."

"What do you think happened?"

"Gaitan sees Bedell's name on the fiber report and calls his *compadre* Roca," Odell said. "Roca has a word with his brother-in-law. The sample disappears."

"Wouldn't Bedell have to account for it?"

Odell shrugged. "There's thousands of bits of evidence in the locker. Some of it gets lost."

"It was several weeks between the discovery of Alex's body and the impounding of the car. Did Gaitan hang on to the fiber sample all that time?"

"Yeah, waiting for his opportunity to use it," Odell said. "You see, I told you the good news first. There's bad news, too."

"What's that?"

"The bloodstain in the trunk they matched to the Baldwin boy, that wasn't a plant."

"You're sure?"

He nodded. "They drew blood for a tox screen," he said. "The remaining sample's never been tampered with."

"What about the paint transfer on the cab?"

"It's like you said, no one asked the lab how old the scratch was. The car's out of impound. There's no way of telling now."

"But it's possible that Gaitan planted the fibers and scraped the car against the fence at the same time."

"Yeah, it's possible," he said. He tore off a piece of the croissant. "Of course, there's that eyewitness who claims she saw Travis coming out of the alley where Amerian was dumped."

"A witness procured by Gaitan," I reminded him. "I never interviewed her. It seemed pointless after Travis died. Did I tell you he said he wasn't using the cab the weekend Alex was murdered?"

Odell was unimpressed. "What else was he going to say?"

"His alibi was that he used the cab after his car broke down. I saw a receipt that shows he didn't take his car into the shop until the Wednesday after Alex was killed."

Odell said, "All that means is that Gaitan planted the evidence in the wrong car, not that Travis didn't kill Amerian."

"If he did, it's inconsistent with the other two killings," I said. "Serial killers don't change their methods."

"The man's car broke down. He needed another vehicle to pick up his victims," Odell said. "I'm sorry, Henry, but just because Gaitan planted evidence doesn't make Travis innocent. Gaitan didn't make the case up, he made it stronger."

"What are you going to do about him?"

"I don't know."

"If Travis had lived and you had given me this information, he would've walked."

"Yeah," Odell said. "Maybe."

"Would you have told me?"

"If he confessed to you he was the killer, would you have told me?"

"It's not the same thing. A defendant has his fifth amendment right against self-incrimination. You have a duty to turn over exonerating evidence."

"It didn't exonerate him," he said. He eyed my untouched pastry. "You going to eat that?"

I pushed the plate across the table. "You would've let the man go to prison on falsified evidence?"

"The man was guilty," Odell said, munching the danish.

A COUPLE OF nights later, I was watching the local news when, on the screen, behind the anchorwoman's bland, robotic face, came a fuzzy picture, clearly from a driver's license, of a dark-haired girl. I hit the volume button.

". . . the remains of twenty-four-year-old Katherine Morse were found in a shallow grave in a remote section of Griffith Park this afternoon by two hikers. The woman's family in Fresno had not heard from her for several months, after she told them she was moving from the Bay Area, where she had lived, to Los Angeles. Police had declined to list the woman as missing, because she had been out of touch with her family before. Today, however, the mystery of her whereabouts was tragically solved. Now, on a happier note . . ."

Katherine Morse. Katie. Alex Amerian's roommate.

I GAVE IT a day before I decided the coincidence that both Alex and Kate had been murdered was worth looking into, if for no other reason than to assure myself it was a coincidence. Since her body had been found in Griffith Park, her murder was under the jurisdiction of LAPD, but I figured Odell could obtain a copy of the police report.

"Odell," he barked into the phone, when I reached him at the West Hollywood station.

"It's Rios," I said. "I have a favor to ask you."

"A favor?" he said. "Do I owe you?"

"Morally."

He laughed. "Shoot."

"A couple of hikers in Griffith Park found the remains of a young girl on Friday," I said. "Her name was Kate Morse. She was Alex Amerian's roommate. She disappeared the day after he was murdered."

"Yeah, I heard about that."

"Interesting coincidence," I observed.

"I remember the girl was heavy into drugs. That's a dangerous life-style."

"Did anyone actually follow up and try to find her at the time Alex was killed?"

"I couldn't tell you offhand," he replied.

"I'd like to look at the police report."

Silence. "Maybe I would, too," he said.

"Can you get it?"

"I'll call you back."

I HEARD FROM him the next morning.

"It's pretty straightforward," he said. "Cause of death was blunt force trauma. The medical examiner says her skull was smashed. She was buried in a shallow grave. No signs of rape, but there wasn't much left after the animals got to her."

"When was she killed?"

"Sometime in the last three months," he said.

"Nothing more specific?"

"The last time anyone heard from her was her brother in Fresno. She sent him a birthday card around the middle of June."

"The middle of June covers a lot of ground," I said.

"Amerian was killed the first weekend," he reminded me. "That's the beginning of June, no matter how you slice it."

"But you don't have a specific date."

"You must be real good on cross," he said. "No specific date."

"Didn't it worry her family that they hadn't heard from her in two months?"

"The father told LAPD Kate was a drug addict who left home when she was seventeen," he said. "Reading between the lines I'd say they didn't care if they heard from her or not. The brother tried to file a missing person's report with LAPD in July, but after they got the full story from the parents, they declined to accept it."

"What kind of substances did she abuse?"

"Ecstasy, Special K, plus stuff I'm sure there's no name for yet."

"Those are party drugs," I said. "She wasn't an addict, she was just a club kid."

"If you say so," he replied, the disapproval in his voice reminding me he was a cop.

"Do you think her disappearance is related to Alex's murder?"

"We don't even know when she disappeared," he said. "All we know is that she wasn't there the morning after."

"The place had been tossed," I said.

"Or maybe they were bad housekeepers," he replied. "Look, if she sent her brother a birthday card in the middle of June, she was still alive."

"Anyone bother to ask him if the card had a return address?"

"I'm sure LAPD is working on it."

"What's the brother's name?" I asked, reaching for a pen.

"Come on, Henry," he said gruffly. "You know I'm not giving you that information."

"It's relevant to Travis's case."

"Travis is dead," he replied. "You don't have a client, you don't have an interest."

"Will you at least tell LAPD about a possible connection?"

"Yeah," he said. "I'll pass that along."

ODELL WAS RIGHT, of course. I had no evidence Katie had disappeared the Friday Alex was murdered. She could simply have not come home that night. At the time, Richie claimed she was dealing drugs, and if that was true, fearing the cops, she might not have returned to the apartment at all once she heard Alex had been killed. But certain images of that morning disturbed me when I remembered them: the phone, pulled from the jack and left lying in the hall; the cardboard boxes in her room full with rumpled clothes; the missing computer; the screen that had been removed from one of the windows in the back of the house. Something had happened there that night. As I mentally walked myself through the apartment, I remembered taking a receipt of some kind from her desk, a pay stub. I found it in my wallet, tucked away with the two unused movie tickets to *Letters*. Until I held the tickets between my fingers, what I remembered about Alex Amerian was inextricable from the grotesque manner of his death. But now he came back to me, in vivid physical detail, and I relived again the shy hopefulness I'd felt when he agreed to go out with me, the surge of desire when he walked through the door of the restaurant. I remembered how we'd slipped into each other's nakedness and how Josh had seemed to inhabit him, and I remembered the ugly scene afterward, his blood dripping from the doorknob. My memories of Alex unfolded like a movie, from our first meeting to the jagged final images, the black-and-white photos of his mutilated body. The discovery of Katie's body was like an unexplained coda. I felt, without being able to say why, something crucial was missing.

I called the temp agency named on the pay stub. A brisk woman answered the phone with a clipped, "Temporarily Yours. This is Judy. How can I help you?" When I explained that I was calling about Katie Morse, she said, "Well, it's about time."

"I beg your pardon?"

"I called you last week, as soon as I saw the news." She paused. "You are the police, aren't you?"

I couldn't remember whether impersonating an officer was a misdemeanor or a felony, so, leaving myself wiggle room, I said, "I'm working with Sergeant Lucas Odell at the West Hollywood sheriff's station. Can you answer a couple of questions?"

"If you make it quick. I do have a business to run."

"When did Kate last work for you?"

"That's why I called you," she said, with exasperation. "On the news they said no one knew when she disappeared. I checked her time sheets. We placed her with a law firm in Century City on a nine-week job in mid-April. She worked through May and the first week of June, then she didn't show up and I couldn't get ahold of her. The firm was very upset."

"Was she a flake?"

"No, not at all," the woman said. "That's why I was worried, but when she didn't return my phone messages, I pulled her card from my Rolodex. I mean, let's face it, they don't call this temp work for nothing. People come and go. But I was surprised that Kate just disappeared."

"Could you fax me her time sheet?"

"Of course."

"Did she fill out any kind of application with you?"

"Yes, our standard agreement."

"Could you fax me that, too?"

"Give me your fax number and I'll do it right now, before I get any busier."

I gave her the number. "Did you know anything about her personal situation?"

"Honestly? No. She'd only been with us a couple of months and I really only saw her on Fridays when she picked up her paycheck. She was a nice girl, very pretty. I was sorry to hear about her."

"Can I call you back if I have any other questions?"

"Sure," she said. "Just ask for Judy. Who are you?"

"Detective Gaitan," I said. "G-A-I-T-A-N."

FIVE MINUTES LATER, I was looking over Katie Morse's employment application. The most interesting thing on it was under the heading PERSON TO BE NOTIFIED IN CASE OF EMERGENCY, where she had scribbled, "Rod Morse." Under RELATIONSHIP TO APPLICANT, she'd written "brother," but instead of an address or phone number, all she had provided was an e-mail address. That night I went on-line and sent a message to RMorse@Osiris.net:

> *Dear Rod, I'm an attorney in Los Angeles who knew your sister and her roommate, Alex Amerian. I would be interested in talking to you about her disappearance and death because Alex was killed around the same time and I'm wondering if there was a connection. Please e-mail or call me at* 213-555-4592. *Sincerely, Henry Rios.*

I checked my e-mail every day for the next week, but there was no response from Rod Morse, nor did he call me. I didn't think I could get away with another call to the temp agency, so I was reduced to checking the paper to see if the police had uncovered any new information about Katie, but she wasn't mentioned again. Her disappearance was complete.

"HENRY, ARE YOU there?" The voice on my answering machine was whispery and hoarse, as if the air had been squeezed from it, but still recognizable.

I picked up the phone. "Richie?"

He sneezed. "There's a special place in hell for queens who screen their calls."

"Are you all right? When did you get back?"

"Summer cold," he grumbled. "Just now."

"Where were you?"

"Here and there," he said, vaguely. "I got your message about Duke. Thanks, Henry. My lawyer is composing a groveling letter of apology." He coughed. "I'm all by myself. Come and see me."

"I was sorry to hear about you and Joel."

"All good things come to an end," he croaked. "Come for tea? Four-ish?"

JAVIER—RICHIE'S HOUSEMAN—let me in. He was a man of indeterminate age, somewhere between thirty and sixty, whom Richie had helped escape from El Salvador where, as a homosexual, he had been reviled by both sides in that country's endless civil war. There had been some trouble with INS, which refused to grant refugee status to immigrants who had been persecuted because of their homosexuality on the grounds that they were mere criminals. I represented him *pro bono* at the INS hearing, where he described how government soldiers had stuck bamboo splints into his urethra. When he was given his green card, he kissed my hand. I had never felt so humbled.

"Hello, Javier."

He smiled formally. "Señor Henry."

"Richie invited me to tea."

"He's in the living room."

I found Richie in the sky-blue living room, seated before the tiled fireplace, where a fire was burning, though it was ninety outside. The room was refrigerated. I thought of Duke Asuras and wondered whether fires in the summer was simply the latest trend among the rich; no quarter to nature given there. Richie was dressed like a character from a novel by Somerset Maugham set on the Riviera in a thick blue-and-white striped terry-cloth robe with a lavender silk scarf elaborately wound around his neck. He wore monogrammed espadrilles. At his elbow a lacquered table held a tea service, including plates of crustless sandwiches and fruit tarts. He was smoking and wheezing. I eased into the chair opposite him. His skin was yellowish and he looked fevered and ill.

"Darling," he murmured, in the same whispery voice he'd used on the phone. "You've come to see your old Maman." He shifted in his chair and his robe opened to reveal a thin, hairless leg. He sketched the sign of the cross in the air above my head. "Bless you."

"You don't look well, Richie," I said. "Is everything all right?"

"Let's see," he replied, touching a long finger to his chin. "My lover left me, I was fired, I was sued and no one will return my calls. Yes, everything's fine. Do you want black tea or green?"

"I meant about your health," I persisted.

"I told you, I picked up a virus somewhere. I mean, other than HIV."

"Have you seen a doctor?"

"Oh, darling, please, there will be time enough when we're seventy to discuss our little aches and pains. Believe me, I'm fine."

He exhaled a plume of cigarette smoke, then choked, coughing until he was red-faced and sweating. I rose from my seat to help him, but he waved me away. Javier stood vigilantly at the doorway. The coughing subsided, and his face went from red to white as he gasped for air.

"Water," he said.

Javier went into the kitchen, returning with a glass. "I should call the doctor," he said sternly, as he handed it to Richie.

"You should polish the silver and walk the dog," he said. "Or walk the silver and polish the dog. Go away now. I want to talk to my friend alone."

"Javier's right. You look seriously ill."

"If you both don't shut up, I will be seriously ill," he said in a fierce whisper. "Go, Javier." After Javier left, he poured me a cup of tea with trembling hands and gave me a plate piled with sandwiches. "*Mangia*, Henry. You're reed thin. I read about your serial killer. Drowned in the toilet? I always stay in the shallow end myself."

"He passed out from drugs and alcohol and choked on his own vomit," I said, biting into horseradish and beef.

"Charming picture."

I sipped the strong, sweet tea. "Do you remember the girl who lived with Alex? Katie Morse? They found her body in Griffith Park a few days ago."

"I saw that on TV," he said, lighting another cigarette. He cautiously inhaled.

"The cops think she disappeared shortly after Alex was killed."

"She was a speed freak," he said. "She ran with rough trade."

"That's what the cops think, too."

He exhaled, sipped his water. "You don't?"

I said, "By the time a case is over, it usually tells a pretty straightforward story but this one is all over the map. Travis was a completely unlikely suspect, the cops planted evidence, a witness turned up out of nowhere, Travis dies in this ridiculous accident, but then the police find evidence that definitely connects him to the first two murders. Just when it looks like all the loose ends are tied up, Katie Morse turns up murdered. You connect the dots. I can't."

"Back up," he rasped. "The police planted evidence?"

I told him about the fibers in the trunk of the car. "The ironic thing is that it was completely unnecessary since they found the same fibers in and around his apartment."

"Maybe Gaitan planted those, too," Richie said.

"There was other evidence," I said, explaining the bloodstained shoe, the fast-food wrapper.

"You're not suspicious enough," he said, stubbing his cigarette out excitedly. "Maybe they planted all of the evidence." He lit another cigarette. "You never did look into the gay-bashing angle I gave you."

"What do you mean, Richie?"

"Alex was attacked twice before he was murdered and the police didn't do anything about it."

"I don't see the connection between that and planted evidence."

He frowned. "Think, Henry. Whoever framed Travis had access to the evidence."

"Obviously it was the cops."

"But why?" he asked. "What was their motive?"

"They knew he was guilty and wanted to help things along."

"Or maybe," he said, "they were diverting attention from themselves."

I let this sink in. "Are you suggesting that the cops killed Alex and the other two victims?"

"Yes."

"But why, Richie?"

"Because they hate us."

"Oh, come on."

"They pistol-whipped you and you're defending them?"

"Eyewitnesses saw two of the victims get into the prop car," I said.

"All the studios hire off-duty police for security," he said. "It's a kind of payoff. Who's to say an off-duty cop didn't borrow the car?"

"An anti-gay death squad in the sheriff's department? Someone would've noticed."

"No one takes me seriously," Richie complained. "Everyone assumes I'm some kind of flake."

"The problem isn't with your conclusions, it's with your research," I said.

"Don't you start."

"You quoted me in that piece of Asuras without permission," I reminded him.

"I warned you I would," he replied.

"That's not exactly true," I said.

He bent his head over the tea table as he poured himself a cup of tea. The scarf around his neck parted slightly to reveal a patch of severely bruised skin.

"What happened to your neck?"

His hand went to where the scarf had come apart. He adjusted it so that the skin was again covered, sipped his tea and said, "Would you like a scone? They're from the La Brea Bakery. Lemon and ginger. To die for."

"Richie, your neck."

"I had an accident."

"What kind of accident?"

He put his teacup down. "I accidentally tried to hang myself."

chapter 16

"I HAVE TO be Someone," Richie said, delicately setting his cup on its saucer.

"You are someone, Richie," I said.

"No, Henry, I mean Someone, with a capital S. A star." He tapped ash from his cigarette. "That's the only way it means anything."

"I don't understand."

"Everything I suffered," he said, quietly. "The four years in that hospital, HIV, Joel. Being born a fag. It has to add up to something because if it doesn't, then the fundies are right, and God is a crazy bitter old queen who creates us just so he can torture us." He took a quick puff from his cigarette. "Think about it, Henry. If this God creates people in his image, that's got to include John Wayne Gacy and Jeffrey Dahmer, and what does that say about his personality? Hide the knives, that's what it says. Watch your back."

"Why didn't you call me before you tried to kill yourself?"

He patted my knee. "You've never needed to be a star. You don't understand what I would do to be one. Which is just as well, because you wouldn't like me very much if you did."

"What happened?"

"As I was hanging there, in the bedroom, from the lighting fixture, I heard a voice in my head that sounded a lot like Vivien Leigh say, 'There's always tomorrow. Tomorrow is another day.' Then I passed out. When I came to, I was on the floor covered with plaster. I'd pulled the fixture out of the ceiling."

"Is any of that true?"

"All of it," he said, crossing his heart. "I swear. Scarlett O'Hara saved my life."

THE SUICIDE ATTEMPT had injured his larynx, but according to his doctor, the damage would be temporary. For a while, however, he had barely been able to speak, so he had concocted the story that he was out of the country. No one knew of the attempt except Javier and now me. He swore me to secrecy.

In return, I made him promise not to commit suicide. He agreed, on the condition that I go shopping with him for new suits at Barney's when he felt better, "because if I have to keep seeing you in those Brooks Brothers muu-muus you wear, I will kill myself." On my way out, I slipped Javier my num-ber and asked him to call me should Richie's depression worsen. Inscrutable as always, he took the number. Only on the drive home did I allow myself to feel the weight of what Richie had confided to me and I pulled into my driveway, blinded by tears.

THAT NIGHT, I checked my e-mail, and to my surprise, there was a message from Rod Morse, but when I called it up it was incomprehensible, a single line, all in caps: RUKWERE? I printed it out. After checking various dic-tionaries without finding a word that remotely resembled it, I was about to write if off as an error in transmission when it occurred to me that the first two letters, R, U, formed the question alluded to by the question mark. Are you KWERE? I sounded it out several times before I got it. ARE YOU QUEER? It was impossible to discern the intent behind the question, but the fact he had encoded it was circumstantial evidence that it was not hostile, since such hostility is seldom veiled. On the other hand, the word queer was ambiguous; for decades it had been an epithet, but many younger gays and lesbians had co-opted the word and proudly described themselves as queer, in the same spirit that long-hair college students in the sixties used to call themselves freaks. But I knew nothing about Rod Morse, not his age, his sexual orientation or level of political sophistication. Still, he was my only hope for getting information about Katie, so, after mulling it over, I wrote back, YES. The following evening, I got a message in return in the same odd code. WILKAL. Will call.

THE PHONE RANG at midnight. I rolled over in the darkness and saw that the call was coming in on the office line. I picked up the phone.

"Will you accept a call to anyone from Rod?" a male operator asked.

"Yes," I said, turning on the light. I sat up and grabbed the legal pad and pen I kept on the bedstand to jot down ideas that came to me about my cases as I was drifting off to sleep.

"Hello, Mr. Rios?" It was a boy's voice, just this side of puberty.

"Rod? Rod Morse?"

"Uh-huh," he said.

"How old are you?"

"Sixteen," he said, a little defiantly. "I turned sixteen in June."

I heard restaurant noises behind him, the clatter of plates, shouted orders. "Where are you calling from?"

"All-night diner by the highway," he said. "I come here sometimes."

"Do your parents know?"

Silence. "I sneak out of the house. How come you're asking me all these questions? I thought you wanted to know about Katie."

"I expected you to be older," I said. "Why did you ask me if I was queer?"

"I figured if you knew Alex, you might be," he said.

"Did you know Alex?"

"I knew he was gay," he said. "Katie told me. All of Katie's friends were gay." He hesitated. "I guess that's how she figured out I am, too."

As soon as he said that, I understood the coded messages, this call.

"Your parents don't know."

"No one knew but Katie," he said. "Well, people on chat lines, but they don't count. She promised to get me out of here."

"What do you mean?"

"She told me I could come and live with her, that she would send me money to get down to LA."

"When was this supposed to happen?"

"Right after my birthday," he said. "When I didn't hear from her, I started to get worried."

"I understand you tried to file a missing person's report with the LA police department in July. What happened?"

"The policeman wouldn't do anything unless I let him talk to my parents," he replied. "My dad told him Katie was on drugs somewhere and not to waste his time looking for her."

"Why were you so sure she was missing?"

"Because she wouldn't blow me off. She knows what my folks are like. She knew I had to get out of here."

"When is your birthday, Rod?"

"June fifteenth."

"The police say you got a card from her. Do you remember when it arrived?"

"Yeah, it came the day after. Katie messed up and left off the zip code, that's why it took so long."

"Did you keep the envelope it came in?"

"Yeah, why?"

"I want you to look at the postmark and let me know when it was mailed from Los Angeles."

"Okay," he said. "What happened to Alex?"

"He was murdered the first weekend of June," I said. "I think Katie may have disappeared around the same time and I was wondering if there was a connection."

"Do you know who killed him?"

"The police had a suspect, but he died before they arrested him. I was his lawyer."

"I thought you were Alex's friend," he said, suspiciously.

"I was," I said.

"And you were the lawyer for the man who killed him?"

"The man who was accused of killing him," I said. "It wasn't proven. There's a long story behind this that I'll tell you another time. Right now I'm interested in when Katie disappeared."

"How did you know Alex?"

"What do you mean?"

"Were you, um, his boyfriend?"

"I went out with him once, but I wouldn't say I was his boyfriend."

Silence. "Did you pay him to go out with him?"

"No. How did you know that Alex was a hustler?"

"The disc," he said.

"What disc?"

"I have to go now," he said. "I'll e-mail you. You figure out my code?"

"Yeah, I think so. Rod, what disc?"

"Check your e-mail tomorrow night. Late."

THE FOLLOWING EVENING, after midnight, I got Rod's e-mail. I decoded it and printed it out.

Katie moved up to San Francisco as soon as she graduated high school. I was 13. She knew I was gay before I did because she had a lot of gay friends up there and I guess she recognized the symptoms: Like I don't play sports and I don't have a girlfriend and I like nice clothes and whatever. She told me I was queer when I was 14 and everything kind of fell into place. Since then all I want is to get OUT OF HERE. My parents are born-agains. They told Katie she was going to hell because she liked to party, so you can guess how they'd react if they knew about me. I'm pretty sure they know, because they are always asking me weird questions like what do I think about when I'm alone. Plus I have to go to church three times a week . . . It sucks. There's no place for gays here but a couple of bars and a park downtown. I can't get into the bars and the park's gross. I used to spend a lot of time in gay chat rooms, talking to other queer kids, but then someone at the church told my dad that there's child molesters on the Internet, so they installed this thing called a Cybersitter on my PC that tells them what sites I've been to so I had to stop going to the gay sites. I still e-mail some of the people I met, but I have to delete the messages and I made up this code. I don't know how much longer I can take this, now that Katie's gone . . . R.

Following this was a second message, transmitted a few minutes later:

Oops, I forgot. The disc. Katie sent me a computer disc with my birthday card and told me to keep it for her until she needed it. She said it was important. I'm attaching the file for you to download. I didn't tell the police about it. You'll see why when you read it. R. PS I looked at the envelope. The postmark says it was sent from LA on June 3rd. I told you she screwed up the zip code, right?

When I got the second message, I flipped my calendar back to June. The third was a Wednesday, two days before Alex was murdered. So Odell was wrong about when she'd sent the card. I downloaded the file Rod sent me, a long one taking nearly ten minutes, and saved it on Word. When I called it up, a title page flashed on my screen: *Scenes: Tales from the Hollywood S&M Sewer* by A. I printed out a seventy-page manuscript and read through it with growing astonishment and pity and disgust.

. . . J. came into the room wearing bondage apperral and tied me down to the bed with leather restraints. I was so out of it from the 'ludes I didn't understand what was happening until he started whipping me with a cat o' nine tails. I told him to stop but he kept breaking viles of amyl nitrate under my nose instead. After a while I figured, what the fuck and just went with it. He shoved a dildo in me and called me names. There was an opening in his leather chaps for his dick, but he couldn't get hard, no matter what he did to me. It was all the drugs, I guess. His 'ludes were pharmaceutical quality, not the street shit. Plus we did a lot of coke. Finally, he managed to dribble a little something out his dick. He untied me

and gave me $500 and invited me to clean up and go downstairs to his screening room and watch his new movie with him and his wife. She was their all the time we were upstairs! I sat between them and we watched the movie and ate popcorn. He played an FBI agent, he was pretty good but it was weird sitting there with them. That was my first time getting paid for S&M.

I consider myself bisexual but the truth is most people who are in to S&M are guys, so that was most of my clients. So I was surprised when I got a call from this woman who said she heard about me from T. She was a director who won an Oscar. I'll call her Judy. She lived in Los Feliz in a big white home with black shutters. She was skinny and homely but there was that Oscar over her fireplace. Her scene was bestiality. She had these big Greyhounds that she liked to watch have sex with people, boys and girls. I don't why she called me. I guess she figured if I'd do S&M I'd do anything.

Judy introduced me to my evillest client. He is a big studio executive. I'll call him Mr. King, because he's like a king of his little kingdom. He's used to getting his way. When it comes to sex, he doesn't have any limits. There was even rumors he killed some kid when he was living in another country. They say he just snuffed him and then recorded it to watch later. Like a lot of these S&M queens, Mr. King had a playroom, but it didn't look like a dungeon, the way most of them do. It looked like a room in a hospital where you do operations. He had this steel table with gutters that he said they used for autopsies. When I first met him, he was totally friendly. Plus, he paid the best. He became my best client. Our first scenes were pretty tame, but little by little, they got more crazy and I figured out he was breaking me in, testing my limits. He was a total manipulator and mindfucker. But, like I said, he paid me well and he gave me presents, including a car.

One night I was called to his house—he lives in Los Feliz in this old stone mansion that looks like a castle. It belonged to someone like Charlie Chaplin. There was already someone there, a big stud dressed from head to foot in a rubber suit. Him and King got me into the bathroom. The rubber guy pushed my head into the toilet while King pissed into the bowl. I thought I was going to drown. King pulled my head out and started beating me, really whaling on me, so hard the rubber guy tried to stop him. Even with all the drugs

we were taking I could feel the pain. It turns out he broke a couple
of my ribs. And my face—I couldn't go out for a week.

After that I stopping taking King's calls because I thought he was go-
ing to kill me. I guess Mr. King was not used to rejection and he took
his revenge. First, I got beat up one night when I was coming home
from a bar. While I was down on the ground, I saw King's car parked
across the street. A few days later, he called me and asked me if I'd
learned my lesson. I said, fuck you, if you don't leave me alone, I'm
going to the police. Of course, I wouldn't go to the cops, like they're
going to believe me over him. The next thing that happened was the
car he gave me was mysteriously bombed. That's when I decided I
had to do something. The cops were out, but I decided I was going to
write this book to expose King and all the other freaks in Hollywood.

They say Hollywood is a dream factory, but to me it's more like a
sewer. When I came here I was a young, struggling actor with big
ideas but big ideas don't pay the rent. I didn't want to be a waiter-
actor-whatever. The first time I got paid for sex I told myself why
shouldn't I get paid for doing something I was going to do anyway?
But it's not like that. It drags you down and you see people at there
worse. That's why I took more and more drugs and all my dreams
became nightmares. Today I'm off drugs, and I'm cleaning up my
act. Even though I'm still attracted to men, I also have a girlfriend,
Katie, and we're planning on getting married and having a family.
This is the only happy ending I want.

As soon as I'd finished, I e-mailed Rod to call me, collect. He phoned
within the hour. From the background noise—canned music and passing
voices—I knew he was at the diner.

"I was going to call you," he said. I could feel his anxiety like a blast of
hot air across the line. "My parents are going to do something bad to me."

"What's going on, Rod?"

"I found a book in their room about some kind of hospital in Utah that
says it can cure homosexuality."

"That's unbelievable."

"They can't do that to me, can they?"

"I don't know. Do you think this is going to happen soon?"

"I don't know," he said. "I'll run away."

I thought of the army of runaway kids that roamed the mean streets of

Hollywood. "Do you know for sure they're planning on sending you to this place?"

He hesitated. "No, I guess not."

"Then you don't have to do anything right now," I said. "If something does happen, you call me. I promise I'll do what I can."

"Can you stop them?"

"I'm not that kind of lawyer."

"There's no one else."

"I promise I'll help you, Rod."

"I guess you read Alex's book," he said.

"Are you sure Alex wrote it?"

"The disc had his name on it," Rod said. "What did you think of it?"

"It was pretty raw," I replied.

"When you called me and said you were a friend of Alex, I thought you might be one of the people he wrote about."

"No, I'm not into that kind of stuff."

"Me, either," he said. "I mean, if I ever have sex it won't be like that. I don't even know why you'd want to do stuff like that, with whips and tying people up. Do you, Mr. Rios?"

"It's a fantasy for some people," I said.

"It's sick," he said. "Do you think Alex really did those things?"

"I can't verify all of it," I said, "but some of it matches things I know about him."

"Does that have something to do with why Katie was killed?"

"Alex must have given the disc to Katie for safekeeping in case something happened to him," I said. "She sent it to you, so she must have been worried about her own safety. You said you didn't tell the police about the disc. Why?"

"I didn't know Alex was dead," he explained. "I wasn't even sure it was real. I thought maybe he made it up, and it was like, a porn book. Should I tell the police now?"

I thought about it. By itself, the disc explained nothing about Katie's murder without an elaborate exegesis, something to which I doubted the police would be receptive. Moreover, although the information on the disc shed a different light on Alex's murder, without further investigation and corroboration, it was all speculation.

"Listen, Rod," I said. "I'm going to ask you to trust me and not tell anyone about the disc until I can verify all of what's on it. Then, maybe, there will be enough to go to the cops."

"I trust you," the boy said. "I knew I could trust you from the first time you called me."

"You have my number," I said. "Call me any time, collect, for any reason. If I don't answer, leave me a message or e-mail me. Okay?"

"Yes," he said.

"You know, Rod, I also left home when I was a teenager. I went away to college and I never went back."

"My grades aren't good enough for college," he said. "I'm too busy trying not to get beat up to study very hard."

"All I mean is things will get better."

"They can't get worse," he said. Then, added hopefully, "Can I meet you someday?"

"I promise," I said. "You're not alone anymore."

WHEN ALEX WAS murdered, my first thought was that one of his clients had done it. As I reread the manuscript, I kept coming back to the long section about "Mr. King." The attack on Alex and the bombing of his car weren't the work of gay bashers but a spurned client. Could the same man have killed him? Why? Who was Mr. King? Studio executive. Foreign exile. Murder allegation. A libel right off the pages of L.A. Mode. I went out into the garage and dug through a stack of newspapers awaiting recycling until I found the issue of L.A. Mode that had got Richie fired. I flipped through the magazine to the cover story. The first time through I'd been distracted by Richie's having inserted me into the article without my permission and never finished reading it. Now I read it word for word. Toward the end, there was this:

"Briefly married twenty years ago, Asuras has been seen with some of the most beautiful women in Hollywood, but the operative word here is 'seen.' His most frequent escort is the not-so-beautiful-by-any-standards Oscar-winning director Cheryl Cordet, a well-known fixture at a bar called The Palms in West Hollywood that is euphemistically referred to as a 'women's bar.' As for Asuras, he's been reportedly seen at clubs frequented by the black leather set of all persuasions. Says one habitué of these clubs who claims to have "done a scene" with the studio head, 'S&M is the logical place for these guys to end up, the big execs and actors, the ones who spend their days pushing people around and getting paid for it. Needless to say, we're talking S's here, not M's.' Whatever his *tastes, Asuras has managed to keep his private life private except for the incident that got him banned from Thailand (see sidebar). Still, you have to wonder what Reverend Longstreet would make of the Vulcan Club, one of the places where Asuras was allegedly seen, where guests are greeted by the sight of a nude young man in a sling available to anyone who wants to . . ."*

The boxed sidebar was captioned *Duke's Servant Problem.* Three long paragraphs and a picture of Asuras standing outside his palatial residence in Bangkok. According to the piece, when a nineteen-year-old boy hired as a servant by Asuras had disappeared, his parents went to the police and accused Asuras of killing him. The police investigated the claim and cleared him. After Asuras left Thailand to run Parnassus, it was discovered that a second boy whom he had employed had also disappeared. Some months later, human remains were found buried in a park that abutted Asuras's property. The remains were too decomposed to be conclusively identified, even as to gender.

On these ambiguous facts, the writer implied that Asuras had murdered the two boys while having sex with them and had buried one of them in the park where the remains were found. I had to agree with Donati that the piece was slander *per se*, an accusation that the weakly circumstantial evidence could not begin to support. Even granting Richie's lax standards of journalism, his audacity in publishing the story was breathtaking. It was almost as if he was inviting a lawsuit. Was he counting on some last-minute corroboration?

For the next couple of days, I thought long and hard about Alex's memoir and what, if anything, I should do. Even if Asuras was the spurned lover who had had Alex beaten and his car destroyed, this was not proof he'd killed Alex, much less Jack Baldwin and Tom Jellicoe. On the other hand, it seemed an improbable coincidence that the vehicle used in at least two of the murders was a prop car from Asuras's studio. I began to reconsider the meaning of Asuras's solicitousness toward Bob Travis. Was he really concerned about Travis or even the studio, or was he worried about his own safety as a co-conspirator? And where did Donati, Asuras's trusted right hand, Travis's erstwhile boyfriend, fit in all this? What motive would either of them have had to kill Alex Amerian?

In retrospect, it was hard for me to believe I had actually puzzled over the question of motive when I had there in front of me Alex's memoir. An idea began to form in my head, and I started to make some connections, but they were all tentative, unsubstantiated. I knew better than to make Richie's mistake. I needed certainty before I was willing even to speak aloud the terrifying possibilities that had begun to emerge from my confusion.

A FEW MORNINGS after receiving Alex's memoir, I poured myself a cup of coffee, sat down with the phone at the dining table, opened the yellow pages to literary agents, and started calling. I posed as the executor of Alex's estate and told the dozen receptionists I talked to that I was trying to determine if Alex had secured representation for his book before his death. No one at the first seven agencies had ever heard of him. The receptionist at agency number seven had a record on her computer of receiving a manuscript from him which had been returned unread. At agency number eight, a junior agent had read the manuscript and passed on it. At agency ten, Eleanor Wyatt and Associates, I was put on hold for Miss Wyatt after I explained why I was calling. Five minutes later came a crisp, "This is Eleanor Wyatt."

I launched into my explanation of why I was calling.

"Yes," she said, cutting me off. "He came here. We talked. I told him I was interested but that it was obvious he was no writer. I suggested he find a ghost writer and I gave him the name of someone I thought would be appropriate."

"You read the manuscript?"

"Uh-huh," she said.

"And you actually thought it was publishable?"

She laughed. "Well, I wouldn't want to read it, Mr. Rios, but the fact is a similar book by a group of prostitutes describing their adventures in the Industry called *You'll Never Make Love in This Town Again* spent three months on the *New York Times* bestseller list. No one ever lost money overestimating the prurience of the American public."

"That's appalling."

"You can't be that appalled," she said briskly. "You wouldn't be interested if you didn't think there was money in it for the estate. How did he die, by the way? AIDS?"

"He was murdered," I said.

"Oh, really," she salivated. "Murdered? What happened?"

"Weren't you concerned about libel when you read Alex's book?"

"Believe me, an army of lawyers would have gone through it with a fine-toothed comb before it ever saw the light of day."

"Did Alex tell you the identities of the clients he was writing about?"

"He didn't have to," she said. "They were obvious. That was one of the problems with the manuscript."

"Mr. King, for example?"

She hesitated. "I told him that section would have to be cut."

"Why? Did you doubt his veracity?"

"I sell books to the studios," she said. "I can't afford to alienate someone like . . ."

"Duke Asuras?"

"That's right," she said. "I'm very busy."

"You remember the name of the ghostwriter you sent him to?"

"Wait a sec." I heard the faint rustling of papers. "Here it is. Rhodes Janeway."

"Do you know if Alex took your advice?"

"Well, Rhodes called me to talk about the project. I assured him it had commercial possibilities and told him to keep me informed. That was the last I heard from either of them."

"When was this?"

"I don't remember, exactly. Late spring, early summer. If he finished a manuscript before he died," she said, "I'm still very interested in representing him. Very interested."

JOHN RHODES JANEWAY had graduated from Harvard, a fact proclaimed by the framed diploma that hung above the toilet in the bathroom of his kitsch-filled Hollywood apartment. He lived a couple of blocks above Hollywood Boulevard on a street lined with junked cars, where guys with beepers dealt drugs from behind the banana trees in the yellowing yards of condemned houses. He was on the top floor of a three-story apartment dating from the twenties that looked from the outside like an Egyptian temple, complete with a bas-relief above the arched doorway depicting a winged sphinx. Inside, the resemblance was to catacombs; all murk and must and dusty silence. I rapped at the door numbered 333, heard the shuffle of footsteps, and felt myself being scrutinized through the peephole. Bolts slid, chains jingled, and the door was opened by a thin man of about forty wearing a stained silk bathrobe that emphasized his slightness over a dirty tee shirt and jeans. He had the wavy, tumbling yellow hair and the faded prettiness of a childhood sissy. Bitterness was cutting hard, deep lines around his Cupid's bow of a mouth, and beneath the cocked, mocking eyebrows, his pale eyes were fearful.

"I'm Henry Rios," I said. "I called you earlier about Alex Amerian? I represent his estate."

"Come in, Counsel," he said airily. "Before someone steals the suit off your back for crack." I followed him into a cramped living room, every surface piled with newspapers and magazines or folders and manuscripts. "Excuse the deshabille." He arranged himself in a chair. "Sit down. Just move whatever's in your way."

I moved a pile of *People* magazines from a corner of the couch. Along the walls of the room were shelves filled with bric-a-brac, collections of salt and pepper shakers, commemorative plates, Barbie dolls, autographed photos of old movie stars, paper fans, martini shakers. The shade was drawn over the window and the room was suffused with a pinkish light from a half-dozen small lamps burning pink light bulbs. The smell of cedar incense mingled in the still air with marijuana and bourbon. A kitchen table was visible in the next room and on it was a computer monitor and keyboard and a scattering of books and papers.

"I appreciate you seeing me, Mr. Janeway," I said.

"Rhodes," he replied coquettishly. "May I call you Henry?"

"Of course."

"I feel like I already know you," he continued.

"I beg your pardon?"

"I guess someone like you doesn't read the gay rags," he said, his voice tipped with sarcasm. *"Frontiers? Edge?"*

"No, not very often."

"The gay press is my bread and butter," he said. "It keeps me in this luxurious lifestyle you see around you." He smiled, but there was more grievance than good humor in the remark. "I know who you are, Henry," he continued. "And I know you're not anyone's executor. You were the lawyer of the man who killed the three gay boys this summer." He smiled again, poisonously. "Why did you lie when you called me?"

It was as if a friendly witness had suddenly turned against me in the middle of being examined, an unpredictable and dangerous situation.

"If you knew I was lying," I countered, "why did you agree to see me?"

"Obviously because there's a story here," he said. "The one you tell me or the one I make up. The rags will publish it either way."

"There might be a story," I allowed, "if you help me."

He narrowed his eyes. "I think I'm the one who should setting the conditions."

"Why is that, Rhodes?"

"Because I could ruin you," he said. "The rags didn't devote much space to the murders because their biggest advertisers are bars and sex clubs and they were afraid if they paid too much attention to boys getting stabbed to death in the alleys of West Hollywood, it would be bad for business. But if there's one thing the gay press really loves, even more than Madonna, it's running vendettas against prominent fags. Now that the killing's over, I think I could get them interested in why a gay lawyer was defending a gay serial killer."

"There's no need to threaten me. I told you, there might be a story here if we help each other and it's a lot bigger than any hatchet job you could do on me. If you're interested, let's talk. If not," I continued, playing a hunch, "I can take it elsewhere, the same way Alex did with his manuscript."

The soft pink light could not entirely conceal the deepening of the pinched lines around Janeway's mouth.

"Any agreement between us, I want in writing," he said.

"I assume that means you didn't get it in writing from Alex," I said.

He sipped his drink, the taut lines around his mouth relaxing. "He was an imbecile," he said scornfully. "Street trash who could barely spell his own name. I didn't think I had to protect myself against him."

No, I thought, I bet you didn't. "Eleanor Wyatt thought there was a book in Alex's experiences as a hustler. Did you?"

"Oh, yes," he said.

"So you believed his stories?"

"Of course I didn't believe him," Janeway said. "I asked him lots of questions. Names, dates, places, who was there, what was said, I made him write down all that stuff, plus I made him bring me pictures, receipts, notes, matchbook covers, anything that could prove his stories, then I did my own research." The lines of bitterness reappeared around his mouth. "I forced him to document the book and then he turned around and took it to someone else."

"What happened?"

"I made files from everything he brought me. He stole them."

"What happened?"

"He came over one night, we had some drinks, ended up in bed," he said. "I was too drunk to remember he was a whore. The next morning, he was gone, with the files."

"Do you know where he went?"

He smirked. "A couple of weeks after Alex ripped me off, I got a letter from *L.A. Mode* offering me five hundred dollars for my work if I signed a release giving up the rights to Alex's story."

"What did you do?"

"The rent had to be paid," he said. "Cocktails purchased. I took the money."

"Who did the letter come from at the magazine?"

"The queen bee herself. Richie Florentino."

chapter 17

THE TEN-MINUTE DRIVE between Janeway's tenement and Richie's gilded apartment cut straight through Hollywood, past Richie's sacred sites, the Chinese Theater, the Walk of Fame, the Roosevelt. I covered the distance in a fury. I wasn't certain of all the details, but clearly Richie had lied to me from the very beginning about Alex Amerian. I pulled up in front of his building and persuaded the sleepy-eyed doorman to buzz me in unannounced. I wanted to surprise the truth out of him. The white-and-gold lobby was empty, the courtyard deserted in the midday heat. He was in the solarium, a small, plant-filled room off the living room, enclosed on three sides by windows that looked out on the still pool. Sitting in a cane-backed rocking chair, a book in his lap, meditatively smoking, he emanated an aura of purposelessness. He wore white pants, a yellow sweater, a paisley ascot around his battered neck. Eyes closed, he raised the cigarette to his lips between two slender fingers, delicately inhaled, lowered the cigarette, exhaled question marks of smoke, sighed, fingered the book. I stopped at the door. He was so fragile. My anger melted away. Sensing me, he turned his head to where I was standing and croaked, "The door's unlocked."

I stepped inside the room, brushing past an enormous dracaena. "We need to talk."

"Obviously," he drawled. "Why else would you be here. Sit down, Henry. Do you want something to drink. Iced tea? A Coke?" He rocked forward and the book in his lap fell to the floor.

"No, nothing," I said, retrieving the book. "*How We Die*. Why are you reading this?"

"I'm trying to improve my mind," he replied, taking the book. "Don't worry, it's not a manual. It's something I've been thinking about since I was fired, what happens after we die. What do you think?"

I remembered my dream about Josh. "I think we create our afterlives in the same way we create our lives on earth, out of what we love and what we're afraid of."

"You've just condemned me to eternity in a drag bar," he said, putting out his cigarette in a butt-choked ashtray. "Sit down, Henry, you're blocking my light. What do you want to talk about?"

I sank into a red velvet armchair. "I read Alex Amerian's memoir, Richie, and I know he came to you with it. I think he tried to blackmail Asuras. Is that why he was killed?"

"He's dead," Richie said, dismissively. "Afterlife or not, it can't matter to him who killed him. It shouldn't matter to you." He smiled, quoted, " 'It's Chinatown, Jake.' "

"You involved me in this. You owe me the truth."

" 'The truth? You want the truth? You can't take the truth.' "

"Your Jack Nicholson needs work, Richie."

"Yes," he sighed, "I know. I should stick to the classics. Bette. Joan." He tilted his head to one side tremulously. "Katharine Hepburn."

"Are you finished? This isn't a movie."

He settled the crystal ashtray in his lap and lit another cigarette. "Now that's where you're wrong. This is a movie. A Parnassus release, called Letters. Have you seen it?"

The video Asuras had inexplicably sent me. "I don't know what you're talking about. I want you to tell me about Alex."

"You won't like what I have to say," he said. "Because you were part of it."

"Alex, Richie."

He sighed. "All right, but don't say I didn't warn you. The first time Alex showed up at my office, I listened to what he had to say about Duke and threw him out."

"You didn't believe him?"

"Oh, I believed him," he replied, "but I didn't care. I mean, it was interesting dish about Duke because there have always been rumors, but I wasn't running a tabloid. Besides, Alex was . . . Well, let's just say he was a whore, with all that that implies."

"Asuras raped him," I said. "Or don't you think whores can be raped?"

His smile was mocking. "You really fell for him, didn't you? I don't blame you, Henry. He was pretty and he could laugh or cry on cue, almost like a real person, but the only thing he ever felt was greed. I mean, come on, Henry, the first instinct of most people who are raped is not to write a book about it. And anyway, he didn't come and see me after the toilet episode, if that's the rape you're talking about. He came to me the moment he hooked up with Duke."

"Before he went to Rhodes Janeway?"

He took a final draw on his cigarette and said through a mouthful of smoke, "Harvard, class of 'seventy-eight Rhodes Janeway? Yes. He came to me first, wanting to sell his dirty little story about how Duke liked to beat up boys and then fuck them."

Outside, the light began to fade, as that rarest of meteorological events in LA, a summer storm, gathered in the August sky. The wind came up, abruptly slamming a door shut in another room.

"So when did you get interested in Asuras's sex life?"

"When I found out he was trying to sell Parnassus to the Antichrist," Richie said. He put his cigarette out, shifted the ashtray from his lap to a side table. "Look at the rain." The placid surface of the pool was hammered by fat drops of rain, shattering it. He watched meditatively for a minute before continuing. "I thought if Longstreet knew one of his potential partners was a sexual sadist, he might change his mind about buying into the company."

"If you wanted to screw up the deal, why didn't you go after Longstreet and avoid pissing off Asuras?"

"Because everything that can be said about him has been said," Richie replied, "and either people don't get that he's a Nazi or they don't care. That left Duke."

"So you got in touch with Alex."

He nodded. "By then, the other things had happened, *l'affaire toilet.* The beating, the car bombing, enough to ruin Duke. Even then, I hesitated."

"Attack of ethics?"

"Ethics? From a lawyer. I'm surprised the word doesn't burn your tongue. No, I wasn't worried about ethics, I was just plain afraid."

"Of Asuras?"

"I knew if I published this stuff and it didn't bring him down, I could kiss my ass goodbye. Joel's too, probably, because Hollywood's a small town and what goes around comes around. So I fired a warning shot."

"The gay-bashing piece," I guessed. "Even though you knew Asuras had had Alex beaten up, you made it sound like he'd been gay bashed."

"I wanted Duke to know that I knew about him and Alex."

"What happened?"

"Your friend Donati called me," he said. The rain slammed against the windows. "He asked, in so many words, what I wanted to keep my mouth shut. I told him I wanted Asuras to find another business partner. I reminded him that he was a fag, too. He hung up on me."

"That's when you decided to go ahead with your exposé?"

"Yeah, that's also where you came in."

"What do you mean?"

"Duke gave Alex a car, and when Alex stopped letting Duke beat him up for fun and profit, the car was mysteriously blown up. In retaliation, Alex decided to kill Duke."

"What?"

"I was surprised, too," Richie said. "I didn't think he had it in him, but he found a gun and went up to Duke's house to shoot him. A security guard stopped him and called the cops. They arrested him and hauled him off to jail. He called me."

"And you called me," I said. "But, wait, Alex wasn't arrested at Asuras's house. He was arrested at that director's place. What's her name . . ."

"Cheryl Cordet," Richie said. "No, not exactly."

"What do you mean?"

"She lives in Malibu. When she comes into town, she stays in a guest house on Duke's property."

"Is there anything you didn't lie to me about?"

"Well, sweetie, the truth was a little complicated." He finished his cigarette. "The sound of rain always reminds me of hospitals."

"You really played me, Richie," I said, angrily. "You embellished the story with that line about Alex carrying a gun because he'd been gay bashed. You wanted me to feel sorry for him, to be angry on his behalf."

"I wanted you to be motivated to help him," he said.

"Is that why you hired him to go out with me? For future legal emergencies?"

He raised his hands as if to shield himself from my outrage. "I hadn't counted on your becoming obsessed with him. You thought he was Josh, but he was a creep, a user. Someone had to burst your bubble. I knew if you spent time with him, you'd see through him."

"Instead I was nearly arrested for his murder."

"But you weren't, Blanche," he murmured as Bette Davis. "You weren't."

Outside, the rain had abated as quickly as it had come. The room was again flooded with light.

"Who killed him, Richie?"

"Asuras sent word he wanted to settle things with Alex after Alex tried to shoot him. A payoff."

"How do you know that?"

"The girl called me. Katie? She didn't trust Asuras, and she was afraid for Alex. Naturally, I was annoyed that the little shit planned to double-cross me after I'd paid him ten thousand dollars for his life story, such as it was. He agreed he wouldn't meet with Asuras until after we talked."

"Did you?"

"He was supposed to call me on the Saturday after your date."

"The meeting he was going to from my house, that was with Asuras?"

"No one will ever be able to prove it."

"Then who was Bob Travis? What was his part?"

He shrugged. "A bit player."

"Yeah," I said. "That makes sense." Things started to fall into place. "The line from Travis to Asuras runs through Nick Donati."

"There are no straight lines in Hollywood," Richie said. "And not many straight men."

"The last time I talked to you, you tried to convince me it was the cops who killed Alex."

"I wanted to protect you from Hollywood."

"That's a little melodramatic even for you, Richie."

"You don't know what you're up against," he said. "Think, Henry. If Asuras killed Alex, who killed the other two men? And why?"

"You tell me."

"*Letters*," Richie replied.

"What letters?"

"The film," he said. "You should go see it."

"I have it," I replied. "Asuras sent it to me after Travis died."

"That's so perverse, even for Duke."

"What are you talking about?"

"Go home and watch it," he said, rising slowly from his chair. "You'll understand. I'm all worn out, Henry. Excuse me, won't you?"

"What happened at the magazine?" I asked, also getting up. "You must've known you were going to get into trouble with some of the allegations you made against Asuras."

"Alex had files, the ones Rhodes Janeway put together. They were my corroboration. They disappeared from his apartment after he was murdered."

"Along with Katie," I said. "What about the stuff from Thailand? That didn't come from Alex."

"I sent a reporter over there, but Asuras's lawyers presented affidavits from the dead boys' families, claiming that my reporter made the story up. A patholgist submitted an affidavit that the bones found outside of Duke's property were a woman's and had been there for at least thirty years. Duke threatened to bankrupt *L.A. Mode*'s publisher if she distributed the magazine."

"She pulled the magazine and fired you."

"Afterwards, my reporter heard from a stringer he'd used in Bangkok. He said he talked to the mother of one of the boys. She told him Duke's Thai lawyer threatened to throw her into prison if she didn't retract her statements about her son's disappearance."

"What about the pathologist's affidavit?"

"How much do you think that cost Duke? Five hundred, a thousand? I know he killed those boys. I know he killed Alex."

"The perfect crime?"

As he walked me to the door, he said, "Unless Duke is as crazy as he seems to be."

"What do you mean?"

"The only reason Duke was discovered stealing money from his clients and his partners back in the seventies and eighties was because he started forging their names on checks."

"Are you saying he wanted to get caught?"

"No, I'm saying he wanted to show off. That's why he sent you the video."

"Is Longstreet still poised to take over Parnassus Company?"

"The board of directors bought him off. Greenmail."

"That must put Asuras in a difficult position."

"*Au contraire*," Richie replied. "Once Duke and his boss, Raskin, proved they had the muscle to sell the company right out from underneath the board, the directors suddenly got very, very cooperative. Duke's been given a brand-new long-term contract with a big raise, a lot more power, and millions of dollars' worth of stock options." He smiled grimly. "A happy Hollywood ending. Enjoy the movie."

WHEN I GOT home, I found the video and slid it into the VCR. I fast-forwarded through the part I had already watched and forced myself to sit through the rest of it. When it was over, I understood the message, the warning it contained. Buried beneath the slaughter and the fancy camera work, a jumble of images interspersed with snippets of portentous but empty dialogue, were the musty bones of Christie's book, *The A.B.C. Murders*. There were things I had missed on a first viewing, but I couldn't bring myself to watch the film again, so I drove to the nearest Barnes & Noble and bought the book.

The premise was simple: a series of murders occurred that had in common the alphabetical progression of the victims' names and the locations of the murders: Mrs. Alice Ascher was killed in Andover, Miss Betty Barnard in Bexhill, Sir Carmichael Clarke in Churston. While the police puzzled over the murderer's bizarre obsession with the alphabet, Poirot noticed inconsistencies between the first two killings and the last one, all the while issuing obiter dicta to the bemused English investigators. "Crime is terribly revealing," he announced at one point, and at another, "At the time of the murder people select what they think is important. But quite frequently they think wrong!"

His solution was that there had only been one intended victim, the last one, Clarke, whose fortune, upon his death, would pass to his brother, Franklin. With so obvious a motive to kill his brother, Franklin looked for a way to disguise his purpose and hit upon the ABC scheme. There was another element of the book I had forgotten. As part of his plan of diverting attention from himself, Franklin framed another man for the killings, a man named, conveniently enough, Alexander Bonaparte Cust.

I closed the book and pulled out my notes on the Travis case with Poirot's phrase bubbling through my head: *Crime is terribly revealing.* Somewhere I had started a list—where was it?—of the differences among the three murders that Travis had been accused of. Here it was. Wright, the witness in the Baldwin murder, said he saw Baldwin entering a cab driven by a middle-aged man; Gray, the witness in the Jellicoe murder, also saw the driver of the cab, but he described him as being in his late twenties to mid-thirties. Alex had been beaten and then stabbed, while the other two victims had first been stabbed and then, post-mortem, beaten. Alex's blood alcohol level was .20, twice the level of legal intoxication, but he had been sober when he left my house; no alcohol was found in the blood of either of the other two victims. Alex and Baldwin had marks on their bodies consistent with being whipped, but there were no such marks on Jellicoe's body. Blue cashmere fibers were combed out of Alex's body, but not from the other two.

I had started this list intending to use these minor dissimilarities to argue there was reasonable doubt that the murders had been committed by the same person, notwithstanding the greater and more dramatic similarities that seemed to connect them. Now a different pattern emerged. In a typical murder investigation the cops begin with the victim and deduce the killer from what they learned about the victim's life. Had Alex been the only victim, the investigation would have proceeded in that manner and the police would have focused more closely on things like his profession and Katie's disappearance. Once there was a second and then a third victim, however, the focus of the investigation shifted from the victims to the killer. As soon as the police became convinced the killings were the

work of a serial killer who'd made his motive obvious in the hate messages
he carved on the corpses, they stopped looking for any other motive. Certain they were dealing with a psychotic, the cops discounted the minor dissimilarities in the murders, and while I'd been aware of them, I'd drawn
the wrong conclusion—that they indicated there was more than one murderer. What they actually revealed was that the first murder, Alex's murder,
was different from the other two, because the latter murders were a horrific
cover-up, an attempt to disguise the motive in the first killing. As long as it
appeared there was a rampaging serial killer on the loose, the police would
never figure out that Alex was murdered to prevent him from blackmailing
Asuras.

It *was* the perfect crime. Only Richie and I knew the motive and
identity of the real killer, and our proof was mostly conjecture and the
most tenuous of circumstantial evidence. But wait, I thought, we weren't
the only ones who knew the truth about the murders. There were two
others. Asuras and Donati. Nick had to have known. He was my way
to Asuras, but I had to have something solid with which to approach
him.

I BEGAN AT the beginning. I had my investigator, Freeman Vidor, look into
the firebombing of Alex's car. He reported to me that the car had been leased
for Alex by a company called Samsara. When he went to the dealership to
determine who had signed the lease on behalf of Samsara, the dealer refused
to give him the information. So, instead, he followed the other line, back to
Samsara.

"Samsara had a phone number and a mail box at an answering service
in Beverly Hills," he reported back to me.

"Had," I repeated. "Past tense."

"It was canceled about six months ago. I bribed the girl at the counter
to give a copy of the contract."

"Who signed it for Samsara?"

"Josephine Walsh," he said.

"That name doesn't mean anything to me."

"No? She listed a number, and when I called it, I got Nick Donati's office
at Parnassus Studio. Walsh was his paralegal."

"Fax me the contract."

"Will do," he said.

"And, Freeman, I have another little job for you."

"Shoot."

"I want you to get Alex Amerian's phone records for the months of May and June."

"That's going to cost you."

"Spend whatever it takes," I said.

"Music to my ears," he said.

THE CONTRACT CAME over the fax and I recognized Donati's number beneath the prim signature of Josephine Walsh. That connection made, I thought about others as I searched through my Travis files and came across the name Joanne Schilling. The eleventh-hour eyewitness whom Gaitan had procured. I had obtained her number from Serena Dance but after Travis's death, an interview seemed pointless. I remembered Serena had told me that Schilling gave her a description of the cab driver that matched the one she'd given Gaitan almost verbatim. I thought he might have coached her. I dialed her number.

A woman answered. "Hello."

"Hi," I said. "May I speak to Joanne?"

There was a pause. "Who?"

"Joanne Schilling," I said.

"I'm sorry," the woman said quickly. "She doesn't live here anymore."

"It's very important that I talk to her," I said. "My name is Rios and I'm a lawyer. Ms. Schilling was a witness in a murder case. The victim's family is considering a civil suit and they've hired me to represent them. Do you know where I can reach her?"

"No, no, I don't," the woman said nervously. "Sorry, but I've got to go."

"Do you know where she works?"

"I can't help you," she said, and hung up.

I waited a half hour and then called back. I reached an answering machine.

"Hi, this is Josey, and I can't come to the phone right now but if you leave a message I'll get back to you as soon as I can."

Josey. Josephine.

"GOOD MORNING, PARNASSUS Studio. How may I direct your call?"

"Josey Walsh, please?"

"One moment."

"Hello, this is Miss Walsh's office."

"Nick Donati," I growled.

"Oh, let me get her, Mr. Donati."

"Hi, Nick? Are you returning my call from yesterday or the day before . . ."

She had the same voice as the woman I'd spoken to when I dialed Joanne Schilling's number. I hung up, phoned Richie, asked him to do me a favor and waited for his return call. It came fifteen minutes later.

"Josey Walsh is a producer at Parnassus," he said.

"Six months ago she was Donati's paralegal," I said. "Is that typical lateral movement at a studio?"

"Paralegal to producer? It's a stretch."

"But it is a promotion."

"Obviously. Henry, what is this all about?" When I hesitated, he said, "Look, honey, if you're going to play Hollywood, you'll need a guide."

"I don't exactly trust you, Richie."

"Can I buy your trust?"

"Huh."

"Do you want to know who blew up Alex's car?"

"It was Asuras."

"He didn't set the bomb himself, Henry," Richie replied impatiently.

"You know who did?"

"I looked into the bombing for the piece on Duke, but in the end I decided the article was too long and I didn't use it."

"Use what, Richie?"

"You have to remember that Duke makes movies, he thinks in movies. If he's going to blow up a car, he's going to use a special-effects guy. The Industry's got all these little specialties where you go to one guy if you want a building blown up, another for a boat, and then there are guys who spend their entire lives blowing up cars."

"You have a name?"

"You go first," he said. "What are you up to?"

"I'm looking for a woman named Joanne Schilling."

"Joanne Schilling," he laughed. "I can tell you how to find Joanne Schilling. Call the Screen Actors Guild."

"She's an actor?"

"Never much more than an extra," he said. "She worked a lot in the seventies in those big-budget disaster movies. She was the girl with tits who got killed off by the second reel, drowned, burned, dropped off skyscrapers, swallowed up by the earth, boobies jiggling like a Greek chorus."

"Trust you to remember."

"I see her on sitcoms now and then. Not the quality ones. I'm talking Fox, UPN."

I made a note. "Okay, Richie, the car bomber?"

"The best car bomber in Hollywood is a guy named Jim Harley."

"How can you be sure he was the one who blew up Alex's car?"

"Because, Henry, he's the best, and Duke would only use the best."

"He would commit a felony for Duke Asuras."

"Honey, there are people who would slaughter their firstborn for Duke Asuras. This is Hollywood, Henry. There are maybe six people in town who can greenlight a picture. Duke is one of them, and his pictures make money. If you plan to work, you stay on his good side."

"Do you have a picture of Jim Harley?"

"In my files somewhere. Why?"

"This has gone beyond amateur hour. I need official help."

"You're not going to go to the police."

"The DA's office," I said. "Serena Dance." And maybe, I thought, Odell.

"The dyke, no?"

"Lesbian, Richie."

"Henry, they like being called dykes. They call themselves dykes."

"Not with the sneer I hear in your voice."

"Sneer, schmeer, what can she do?"

"She was in charge of the task force. Maybe I can talk her into reopening the case."

"Then you'll have to quit playing Nancy Drew."

"That would be fine by me."

LATER THAT DAY, Freeman Vidor delivered copies of Alex Amerian's phone bills for May and June. There were two things of particular interest. The first was that on the day he was killed, he had made a call to a number I recognized from looking through my Travis files. It was Travis's number. Earlier that same day he'd made a call to another familiar number. Donati's office. I fully intended to turn my findings over to Serena, but I couldn't resist finding out from Donati what he and Alex had talked about for ten minutes on the morning of the last day of Alex's life.

NICK SEEMED GLAD to hear from me: "Henry, I've been meaning to call you." He was too busy to get together for dinner, but he could manage a drink. Not tomorrow, the next day. My house.

chapter 18

THE NEXT EVENING, Donati showed up at my house in black-tie. I answered the door in gray sweatpants and a button-down shirt. He followed me into the living room, discreetly taking inventory. I saw through his eyes the mismatched furniture, faded Oriental carpet, scuffed floor. There were ashes in the fireplace from the previous winter, a pair of loafers beneath the dusty glass-topped coffee table, a bundle of dry cleaning on an armchair, a scattering of used coffee cups.

"Excuse the mess," I said. "You want a drink?"

He smiled. "I thought you didn't drink, Henry?"

"My lover kept a bottle of scotch under the sink," I said. "It's probably still there."

"Scotch is great," he said, then, gesturing toward the deck. "Nice view. Mind if I go out?"

In the kitchen, I scoured beneath the sink for Josh's bottle of Glenlivet. I poured some into a tumbler over ice, remembering the once familiar routine. Ice, glass, bottle. On a typical night I was good for a fifth of Jack Daniels. I grabbed a Coke and carried the drinks out to the deck, where Donati was standing at the railing, looking at the sky. It was filled with the fantastic colors of sunset in Los Angeles, neon pinks and screeching oranges, reds that throbbed like open wounds; the palette of pollution. A dry wind crept through the thick canyon undergrowth with a sound like an old man clearing his voice. Donati took a quick shot from his drink and emitted a deep, reflexive noise halfway between a sigh and a shudder. I remembered that sound from my own drinking days; the groan of addiction with which the body gratefully received the first drink of the day.

"You must worry about fires up here," he said.

"Fires in the summer and autumn," I replied. "Mudslides in the winter, earthquakes all year long."

"Tell me about it," he said, knocking back half his remaining drink. "You couldn't have planned a worse place to put a city than LA."

"You're not native?"

"I grew up outside of Boston," he said. "I miss the East. There's history there. Out here, it's all landscape." He finished his drink "Mind if I have a refill?"

"The bottle's in the kitchen. Knock yourself out."

He looked at me strangely, but the lure of scotch was greater than any umbrage. When he returned to the deck, I noticed he'd removed the ice from his glass.

"You're all dressed up," I said.

"The gay archive's having a big fund-raiser tonight at the Century Plaza," he said. "I'm surprised you're not going."

"I'm surprised you are."

"It's business," he said. "An important producer is on the board of directors. We bought a table to show respect."

"Asuras going?"

He glanced at me sharply. "No, I'm representing him."

"That seems to be one of your jobs."

He put his drink on the railing. "Is there something I can do for you, Henry?"

"The question is whether there's something I can do for you and Duke."

"I don't understand."

"Travis told me something the day he died I thought might be of interest to you."

He sipped his drink. "What was that?"

"He said Asuras killed those boys."

Donati had been looking out over the canyon. Now he turned to face me. "Jesus Christ, Henry, you dragged me up here for this?" He set the drink down. "You've been spending too much time with Richie. I've got to go."

"He gave me a manuscript," I said, to Donati's back. "He said Alex Amerian left it in his car the night he drove him up to Asuras's house. It describes some pretty rough sexual stuff between Alex and Asuras."

Donati stopped, turned back. "You have it?"

"Come inside," I said. "Don't forget your drink."

I told him to make himself comfortable while I got the manuscript from my office. He took me at my word. When I came back to the living room, the bottle of Glenlivet was on the coffee table beside his glass.

"Here," I said, tossing him the manuscript. "A copy. I'm keeping the original at another location."

He skimmed it and announced, "This is garbage."

"Travis was convinced it was the real thing. He said Asuras is into some serious kink."

Donati gave me a long, searching look. "Why didn't you say anything about this before?"

"A hundred thou only goes so far, Nick. My lover, my late lover, he died of AIDS. He was sick for nearly two years, without health insurance. I'm sure you know what treatment costs. My house is in foreclosure. I'm facing bankruptcy."

For a moment, he looked astonished, disbelieving, but then his face hardened. "And you want to improve your financial situation with blackmail."

I shrugged. "Maybe you should go, Nick. Obviously I'm talking to the wrong person. I owe Asuras a call anyway, to thank him for the video."

"What video?"

"*Letters?* You must've seen it, since it's one of your movies," I said. "About a killer who covers his tracks by making his intended victim seem like part of a serial killer's rampage?"

"He sent you that?"

I nodded. "Yeah, out of the blue."

Donati picked up the manuscript. "You say Alex left this in the cab?"

"Cab? I didn't say cab. I said Bob's car."

Donati shrugged. "Car. Cab. Whatever. Have you ever talked to a woman named Josephine Walsh?"

"Walsh? No, I don't think so." I said.

"You're sure about that?"

"Positive."

He stood up. "What are you going to do with the manuscript?"

"I don't know. What do you think?"

"I think you should wait to hear from me."

"Okay."

"Thanks for the drink," he said. "Goodnight."

I HAD HARBORED a grain of doubt that Donati was in on the murders, but now I was certain of his involvement. He could only have known I'd called Josephine Walsh if she had told him and she wouldn't have told him without also telling him I was looking for Joanne Schilling, the mystery witness. I knew he didn't believe me when I denied making the call. It was also clear when he pretended to read Alex's manuscript that he was familiar with its contents. Most damning of all, he let slip that Bob was driving the Lucky cab when he took Alex to Asuras's house. He couldn't have known that detail without being deeply involved. It explained why he had searched and then cleaned the cab. He wasn't trying to protect Travis, he was trying to protect Asuras. And himself.

I had counted on Donati being so imbued with Hollywood cynicism that he would buy me as a blackmailer without batting an eye, but it still disappointed me a little that he hadn't even seemed surprised. I thought there was more to him than the price of his suits. I kept seeing him with his dogs the night Travis died, lost and exposed, croaking in his deepest voice like a little boy fending off the monsters that he fears lurk beneath his bed or in his closet. I rinsed his glass, certain that he would soon call with either a bribe or a threat, either of which would show, as the law so elegantly put it, "consciousness of guilt." Now that the pieces were falling together, it was time to talk to Serena Dance.

SERENA EMERGED CAUTIOUSLY from her office to the lobby, where I'd arrived without an appointment and asked to see her. She greeted me with a puzzled, doubtful grin.

"Hello, Henry. What can I do for you?"

I glanced at the marshal who guarded the eighteenth floor. "Could we talk privately?"

Reluctantly, she jutted her chin toward the door. "Come on, but I can only give you a few minutes."

In a corner of her office was a stack of cardboard boxes, all labeled *West Hollywood Inves.* Her radio was tuned to NPR, where a Chardonnay-voiced newscaster chuckled at his own mirth. There was a new picture on the wall, a child's drawing of a house with two women and a little boy standing outside of it. In the corner of the picture was a carefully written "Jesse, 5."

"So talk," she said, crisply, planting herself behind her desk.

"I have new information on the West Hollywood murders," I said.

I expected dismissal or disbelief, but instead there was a neutral, "Uh-huh."

I opened my briefcase and handed her copies of Alex's manuscript and the contract from the answering service signed by Josey Walsh. I launched into my story about Asuras and Alex, the Samsara connection to Parnassus via Josey Walsh, the possibility that the car bomb had been set by a special effects expert named Jim Harley, and the odd coincidence that Joanne Schilling and Josey Walsh had been roommates.

"Are you accusing me of suborning perjury?" she asked, when I finished.

"What?"

"You're implying that Joanne Schilling was going to give false evidence against Travis."

"I'm not implying that you knew about it."

"So I was duped?"

"Serena, if any of this is provable, we were both duped."

She pushed the papers across the desk and said, unconvincingly, "We had hard evidence on Travis."

"I'm not claiming he wasn't involved," I said.

She drummed her fingers softly on her desk. "I thought you had come here to gloat."

"What do you mean?"

"Odell told me you were right that Gaitan planted evidence in the cab," she said. "Ironic, isn't it, Henry? You were sure Gaitan was trying to frame Travis because he was gay, and now you're telling me Travis was guilty all along."

"He was an accomplice, not the principal. That was Asuras."

She tapped the papers. "This isn't evidence, it's guesswork."

"I notice you haven't thrown me out of your office," I observed.

"I should," she said, ruefully. "As far as everyone else is concerned, this case is closed."

"Everyone else but who, Serena? Me or you?"

She tugged distractedly at her hair. "I got an anonymous call after Travis died," she said, "from a woman who saw me interviewed on TV that night. She wanted to report a hate crime. She told me a male friend of hers who had worked for Duke Asuras had been sexually harassed by him and could I do something about it, because no one else would."

"You took her seriously?"

"I knew it wasn't a crank call because she was very upset and she was very specific. I told her that technically, it wasn't a hate crime, so it was really out of my jurisdiction. Then she told me Asuras had raped her friend, who was straight, and did that make it a hate crime. Before I could respond, she hung up. We all have our buttons. Rape is one of mine. I made a few calls, to try to corroborate her."

"I bet you didn't find anything," I said.

"Why do you say that?"

"Even if a guy was willing to report a rape, I doubt whether the cops would take it seriously."

"No one had any record of a criminal complaint," she said. "I figured the same way you did, that either it wasn't reported or it wasn't taken seriously.

It occurred to me if the police blew him off, the victim might have filed a civil action, so I checked the register for the last five years."

"Did you find anything on Asuras?"

She nodded. "It's amazing how often those studio guys get sued. In the last three years, Asuras has been named in over a hundred suits, most of the time as a *pro forma* defendant, but I did find three wrongful termination actions that specifically alleged sexual harassment by him."

"Was one of them your anonymous victim?"

"All three cases were dismissed well before they ever got out of the pleading stage."

"You look at the complaints?"

"Sealed," she said.

"Sealed? They're public records."

"I know, I was surprised, too. They were sealed by Judge Matermain. It turns out she was a partner at a big entertainment firm before she got put on the bench. Parnassus was one of their clients."

"You were thorough," I said.

"It smelled bad," she replied. "Really bad. I decided to track down the plaintiffs and talk to them."

"What did they have to say?"

"The first plaintiff was a woman," she said, getting up and going to her file cabinet. She pulled out a file and came back to her desk. "Elizabeth Ybarra."

"Asuras sexually harassed a woman?"

"Don't get excited, Henry, he's not polymorphous perverse. The allegation was not that he personally sexually harassed her but that by favoring men over women he created a hostile environment for women workers. A technical allegation. The case was settled, and as part of the settlement, the judge imposed a gag order."

"What about the other cases?"

"The second plaintiff was a nervous young man named Michael Moran. He said the lawsuit was a big mistake based on a misunderstanding and he actually really liked Asuras. He said if I wanted any more information I would have to call his lawyer."

"And the third case?"

"Jeff Cain," she said, reading the name from the file. "But before I could talk to him, the DA called me upstairs, told me he heard I was violating court orders on civil cases that were none of my fucking business and embarrassing a powerful supporter of his, so I should drop it."

"How did Asuras find out?"

"Moran, I think. He was either bought off or scared into silence."

"You take the DA's advice?"

"Are you kidding?" she laughed. "I left his office and drove myself straight to Jeff Cain's apartment. Bingo."

"He was your man?"

She nodded. "He got a job at the studio just out of film school as kind of a glorified gofer. Asuras took a shine to him. I could see why. This kid is gorgeous. He said the trouble began when Asuras asked him to travel with him as his assistant. As soon as Asuras got Jeff out of LA he started coming on to him, very, very strongly."

"How strong?"

"Jeff said Asuras was physically aggressive."

"Why didn't Jeff quit?"

"Not many twenty-four-year-old boys get to be personal assistant to the head of a studio."

"Jeff gay?"

"No," she said, "and after I met his girlfriend, I figured out who my anonymous caller was."

"What happened?"

"Jeff thought he could control the situation if he let Asuras have sex with him."

"That's funny logic, especially for a straight boy."

"You're wrong," she said. "He thought if he gave in, Asuras would get over it and eventually leave him alone. That's classic date-rape victim thinking."

"What happened?"

"Jeff hadn't counted on the type of sex Asuras was into."

"The S&M stuff."

"I don't know much about S&M, Henry, but as I understand it, it's mostly dressing-up and fantasy. This guy hurts his partners for real. They were in New York when Jeff finally gave in. The encounter turned into a violent rape. Jeff said it was like Asuras was punishing him for agreeing to have sex with him. After it was over, he got out of the room and took the next plane back to LA. He never went back to work. Asuras continued to call him, offering him money, threatening to hurt him. When Jeff went to the cops they called Asuras who persuaded them Jeff was trying to blackmail him. Finally, he sued."

"Why was his suit dismissed?"

"Asuras was careful that there were never any witnesses when he came on to Jeff, so it was Jeff's word against his. Plus Asuras's lawyers told Jeff's lawyers why the police had declined to press charges and threatened to have them arrest the lawyer for conspiracy to commit extortion. He quit."

"Jeff's story plus Alex's establishes a pattern of conduct," I observed.

"For rape, not murder," she said. "Which, as you know, is completely inadmissible, anyway." She closed the filed. "Unfortunately."

"You believe me about Asuras, don't you?"

"I believed Jeff Cain," she said. "I believe what's in this manuscript. Asuras is a sexual psychopath."

"Who would commit murder to protect himself," I said.

"There's not enough evidence even to file on him."

"What if he offers me a bribe to keep my mouth shut?"

"What are you talking about, Henry?"

I told her about my meeting with Donati.

"That was really stupid, Henry," she said. "Donati could turn around and have you arrested for blackmail."

"I'm gambling he won't."

"Even if Asuras offered you money for the manuscript, that doesn't imply responsibility for the murders."

"He's not going to confess, Serena," I said impatiently. "We'll have to build the case against him a brick at a time."

"We? Why should I risk what's left of my career here and go after the guy?"

"You answered that question when you decided to ignore the DA and talk to Jeff Cain," I said. "Asuras is the kind of predator that all gays and lesbians are accused of being. We can't get let him get away with those murders."

"The case is closed, Henry."

"Get the cops to reopen the car bombing investigation," I said. I slipped the picture of Jim Harley across her desk. "Have them take Harley's picture around. Maybe someone will recognize him."

"How do I explain where I got this tip?"

"You don't have to explain, you're the DA," I said. "The cops are supposed to do what you tell them."

"You saw how well that worked with Gaitan." She took the picture. "All right, I'll see what I can do."

"There's one more thing," I said. "You can help me find Joanne Schilling."

She nodded. "Yeah, I would like to talk to her."

"I'm glad we're finally working on the same side," I said.

"That remains to be seen," she replied. "As far as I'm concerned, I'm not in yet."

"What are you worried about, Serena?"

"I'm worried about working with someone who uses blackmail to obtain evidence."

"It's a setup," I said. "The cops do it all the time."

"Try to remember something, Henry," she said. "You're not the cops. You're acting as a private citizen and if you get yourself into trouble, don't count on me to bail you out."

"Asuras has you spooked, hasn't he?"

"No, you do," she said. "I'll be in touch."

THE PHONE WOKE me just after one in the morning. I listened to it ring resentfully because I knew I had to answer it even though at this hour it was likely to be a wrong number. Still, between clients with a propensity for being arrested in the middle of the night and friends with AIDS who had their own nocturnal horrors, I could never be sure. I rolled over, saw the call was coming in on the office line and picked up.

"Yeah," I barked.

An unperturbed operator said, "Will you accept a collect call to anyone from Rod?"

"Yes, I'll accept."

There was a hesitant, "Mr. Rios? It's Rod Morse. You said I could call you if I needed to talk?"

"Absolutely," I said, sitting up. "What's going on, Rod? Everything okay there?"

"My parents found out."

I was now sufficiently awake to register that he was whispering. "They found out what?"

"That I'm gay," he said.

"What happened?"

"This is kind of embarrassing," he said, after a moment.

"Did they catch you with someone?"

"What? Oh, no. I mean, I wish there was someone." He hesitated. "I buy these magazines . . ."

"Porn?"

He laughed a low, unfunny laugh. "Like I could get porn here. No,

GQ and *Details* and, you know, men's fashion magazines." Another shamed pause. "I look at the pictures of the models. I cut out the ones I like and keep them in a shoebox at the bottom of my closet. My mom found them."

"Pictures of models?"

"A lot of them were just in underwear," he said, guiltily. "Some of them were naked, but only from the back. You couldn't see anything."

"What was your mother doing rooting around in your closet?"

"I told you they've been trying to catch me."

"What did you do?"

"I tried to tell them the pictures were to remember what the clothes looked like, so I could buy them."

"They didn't believe you."

"No," he mumbled, close to tears. "My dad asked me, 'Are you a homosexual?' I said no, but they didn't believe that, either." He was silent. "I thought he was going to hit me, but he told me to go to my room and stay there. This all happened Saturday. Tonight they told me, when school starts next month, they're sending me to a Christian school in Utah."

"You think they're going to send you to that hospital that claims to cure gays?"

"I know they are," he said. "I know that's where they're going to send me." He started sobbing, softly. "You said you'd help me."

"Can you e-mail me the name of this place in Utah?"

"Yeah, as soon as I hang up," he said.

"Call me back in two days."

"I have to call late, after they go to sleep."

"Don't worry about that but give me two days."

"I will," he whispered. "Thank you."

THE NAME OF the hospital in Utah was the Foster Institute. I knew that Richie, because of his own adolescent experience, supported a gay public-interest law firm that represented gay and lesbian kids. I called him the next morning and told him about Rod. He put me touch with a lawyer in San Francisco named Phil Wise. Wise had heard of the Foster Institute.

"They're notorious," he said. "Most of these places are kind of indirect about what they do, but at the Foster Institute they pretty much claim they can cure homosexuality."

"It's a psychiatric hospital?"

"Duly accredited by the American Psychiatric Association."

"I thought the APA removed homosexuality from its list of mental illnesses twenty years ago."

"That's right," he said. "Places like the Foster Institute hospitalize kids under a diagnosis of GID, Gender Identity Disorder, an approved diagnosis in the APA's Diagnostic and Statistical Manual. You know about the DSM?"

"You bet," I said. Every criminal lawyer knew about the DSM, the handbook used by medical health professionals to diagnose psychiatric disorders. "What the hell is Gender Identity Disorder?"

"It relates to gender confusion," he said, "the desire of a male to be a female and vice versa. Adult transsexuals have to be diagnosed with GID to qualify for hormone treatment and sex change surgery. That's the legitimate use of GID."

"Rod hasn't expressed any desire to be a girl to me."

"It doesn't matter," he said. "Kids who don't conform to gender stereotypes get diagnosed with GID and off they go into places like Foster where they're treated with heavy psychiatric drugs like Thorazine and lithium. They're also subjected to behavior modification and in some cases shock treatment. Since gay and lesbian kids are the kids who are most likely to reject gender stereotyping, they're the ones who fill these places. On their parents' dime, of course. These places are raking it in."

"What do you mean by rejecting gender stereotypes? Little boys playing with their sisters' Barbies? Little girls who hate dresses?"

"Let me read you something out of the DSM," he said. "One possible symptom of GID for boys is 'aversion to rough-and-tumble play and rejection of male stereotypical toys, games and activity.'"

"These hospitals claim they can cure homosexuality by making kids conform to gender stereotypes, as if teaching your son to play baseball will prevent him from growing up gay?"

"Right, right," he laughed. "And wearing lipstick and a dress means your daughter won't be lesbian."

"This is a joke."

"I wish it was," he said. "Gay kids get packed off to these hospitals by the thousands, and by the time they come out most of them are so fucked up that a lot of them end up killing themselves."

"Can we stop Rod's parents from committing him?"

Wise was silent for a moment. "It's tough, Henry," he said. "Rod's a minor. His parents can pretty much submit him to any legitimate medical treatment they believe is in his best interests."

"The kind of treatment you're describing is medieval. How can it possibly be in his best interests?"

"Obviously, it isn't," Wise said. "I think it's a form of child abuse to send a kid to one of these hospitals. The problem is persuading a court."

"Here's your chance," I said. "Richie Florentino told me if you'll take the case, he'll finance it."

"The problem is no court anywhere has ever declared that treating a child for homosexuality is child abuse," Wise said. "Certainly not in Utah."

"That's all the more reason to act while Rod's still in California."

"Okay, let's talk to the kid. Can you arrange a conference call?"

"Phil, he calls me in the middle of night after his parents have gone to sleep."

"All right," he said. "You explain the situation and give him my number. Tell him to call me day or night, but soon. If we're going to save him, we need to get started now."

"WHAT DO YOU mean, go to court?" Rod asked when he called at two in the morning.

"Before your parents try to send you to Utah, Phil will file a petition in juvenile court to have you declared a ward of the court and remove you from your parents into foster care, while the court decides whether they have the right to try to cure your homosexuality."

"A foster home?" he asked, scared.

"Yes, temporarily."

"How long?"

"Until the court makes its decision."

"What if the court says my parents can send me to Utah?"

"Phil's ready to appeal all the way to the California Supreme Court," I said. "At the very least, he can tie your parents up in court until you're eighteen. That's the worst-case scenario, Rod."

"I'll be in foster care the whole time?"

"Yes," I said, because there was no point in lying to him. "Phil asked me to give you his phone number. He needs to hear from you now."

He didn't answer for a long time. "Okay," he said. "Give it to me."

I gave him the address. "Rod, what's bothering you? Foster care?"

"Yeah," he said. "I don't want to live with strangers."

"Your parents are trying to commit you to a mental hospital. Don't you think you'd be better off somewhere else?"

"They're still my parents," he said. "I still love them. I know they love me."

"Weren't you ready to run away to Katie?"

"Katie was family," he replied, testily.

"I don't know what to tell you, Rod. You wanted my help, this is the help I'm offering."

"Can't you just talk to them for me?"

"I will if you really think they'd listen to me. From what you've told me about them, they'll probably think I'm a child molester."

Silence. "You're right. If they knew I was talking to you, they'd put me on a plane tomorrow. We used to be a good family, when I was little. My mom and dad were great. Now it's different. It's like aliens took over their bodies."

"They might feel the same way about you."

"I want my old parents back," he said. "I don't want to have to choose between being gay and my family."

"It seems to me your parents have made that choice for you."

"Maybe," he said, distantly, and then, remembering his manners. "Thank you, Henry."

"Keep in touch," I said.

"I have to go now," he replied. "Thanks."

After a couple of days, I sent him an e-mail, but a week passed and he didn't respond. I called Phil, who hadn't heard from him either, but who counseled patience, reminding me that we'd basically told the kid his only chance was a court order out of his family.

"What I don't understand is how he could feel any loyalty to his parents when they're trying to do this to him."

"He's a child, Henry," Wise said. "Children need to believe in their parents."

"Too bad parents don't always reciprocate."

chapter 19

A FEW DAYS after our meeting, Serena Dance phoned about Asuras. It was a quarter after eight in the evening and from the sounds in the background—a TV, a child—I knew she was calling from home rather than her office.

"Bringing work home?"

"I'm working on this case on my own time," she said.

"Are you being scrupulous or paranoid?"

She paused before answering. "A little bit of both. The DA warned me off Asuras. If he knew I was investigating him in a murder case that's been officially solved, I'd be out of a job."

"Would that be so bad?" I asked. "He only keeps you around for political window-dressing."

"I prosecuted over fifty cases last year," she said, seething. "My conviction rate was ninety-two percent. That's better than the office average."

"I didn't mean you don't do your job," I said. "But you have to admit, you don't get much help."

"Joanne Schilling has disappeared," she said abruptly.

"What? Did you talk to Josey Walsh?"

"Yes, of course. She gave me the same story she gave you. Schilling lived with her, moved out and she doesn't know where she's gone."

"She's lying."

"Thanks, Henry, I couldn't have figured that out for myself. Of course, she's lying. I called her building manager. Walsh lives alone, has always lived alone. I called her back and she claimed she didn't tell the manager because having a roommate violated her lease. Then she changed her story and said they weren't exactly roommates. Schilling was a friend who needed a place to stay for a couple of weeks."

"You think if they were that close, she'd know where Schilling was."

"You'd think," Serena said. "I tracked down an address for Schilling through the Screen Actors Guild. According to the manager of that building, Schilling's lived there for the last four years. I decided to pay her a visit."

"You didn't find her in."

"Her mail hadn't been collected for at least a week," Serena said. "I bluffed the manager into letting me into her apartment. The closets were filled with clothes, there was food rotting in the refrigerator. No sign of her."

"Did you go back to Walsh?"

"Out of town until Monday, according to her answering machine," Serena replied. "She was pretty huffy the last time we talked, and I had to back off because I didn't have any leverage. Now I've got a missing person, thank God. Something to justify all this snooping."

"What about the investigation into the car bombing?"

"There's a problem. The detective who was on the case retired, so reopening it means pulling someone off an active investigation. I don't have that kind of pull with the sheriff, at least not without explaining why I'm so interested, and you can imagine how that would go over."

"It's time for a meeting with Odell."

"What makes you think he'll help us? He told me he thought Travis was guilty, even with the planted evidence."

"Because maybe he's wrong about Gaitan's motives in planting the evidence," I said.

"What are you talking about?"

"Gaitan found Schilling, right? How did he find her?"

She was silent. "Good question. I assumed she just came forward because of all the publicity about the murders."

"We can't assume anything in this case except that what looks like a coincidence probably isn't. How about lunch with Odell later on this week?"

"Away from downtown," she stipulated.

"Can I call you at your office?"

"Fine," she said, "but if I'm not there, don't leave a voice mail. Just call back later."

"You really are paranoid."

"Better safe than sorry. You might remember that."

I MET SERENA and Odell for lunch at Langer's, an old deli near McArthur Park, site of the famous and incomprehensible song. There was no cake to be seen, melting or otherwise, from the restaurant's grime-streaked windows, only the brightly dressed throngs of Mexican and Central American immigrants who inhabited the neighborhood. Sixty years earlier, this had been an opulent shopping district, the Beverly Hills of its time, where movie stars shopped at Bullock's Wilshire and I. Magnin, then lunched at the

Brown Derby or Perino's. Some of them lived in luxurious apartments in the grandiose Art Deco buildings that still dotted Wilshire Boulevard, like the Talmadge, named for the actress who had once owned it. The shells survived, but the apartments were more likely to house refugee families from Honduras than contract players from nearby Parnassus Studio. The Brown Derby had been razed, Perino's was shuttered, as was I. Magnin's, while Bullock's Wilshire, undergoing perhaps the worst fate of all, was being converted to a law school.

The neighborhood had still been vibrant the first time I came here, with Josh. After we'd moved to Los Angeles, we spent weekends driving around the city with a map and an architectural guide. One Sunday we stumbled into this district of sad, decaying wealth and cheerful, teeming poverty. We looked at five-hundred-dollar sweaters at Bullock's, then ate fish tacos at a storefront taqueria down the street. Later, I thought, the city's schizophrenic nature had never been clearer to me than in that afternoon of cashmere and salsa.

Serena was waiting at a booth at the back of the restaurant when I came in, intent on the extensive menu, as venerable a dictionary of pastramis, corned beef and smoked fish as Langer's itself, a throwback to the time when the neighborhood was Jewish.

"Odell's not here yet?" I asked, slipping into the booth.

She glanced up. "No. This menu is more complicated than the bar exam." She set it down, looked over my shoulder, and said, "There he is."

I felt a big hand squeeze my shoulder. "Counsel."

Odell pushed in beside Serena, his big stomach barely clearing the edge of the table. He was wearing his mirrored sunglasses. When he removed them, I was again struck by how much of his personality resided in his eyes.

"This lunch a social thing?" he asked me.

"Not exactly," I replied.

He smiled. "I didn't think so," he said. He looked from Serena to me. "This have something to do with—what did they call it—the Invisible Man killer?"

"That description was more accurate than any of us knew," I said.

The Latina waitress came by the table and stood over us like an impatient recording angel as we pored over the vast menu.

"We found the invisible man," I said, after she left.

"Beg pardon?" Odell said.

"Travis didn't commit those murders alone," I said. "In fact, I doubt if he was much more than a pretty unimportant accomplice. The man who murdered those boys was—"

"Mind you, this is just Henry's theory," Serena said.

"Duke Asuras," I said.

"Parnassus Studio Asuras?" Odell asked, not missing a beat.

"That's the one," I said.

Odell started laughing. "You really know how to pick 'em, Henry."

"I was right about Gaitan," I reminded him.

"I never said you weren't one smart fella," he replied.

"Gaitan may be implicated in this part, too."

"I'm listening," Odell said.

I gave him my spiel over sandwiches and drinks, Serena occasionally interjecting a caution when she thought I was making too great a leap from fact to conclusion, but at the end she contributed her own bombshell.

"Gaitan was the cop who found Joanne Schilling," she said.

"What do you mean 'found her'?" Ode asked through a mouthful of pastrami.

"I thought she'd volunteered her evidence. His report said he found her by canvassing her building."

"So what? That's just good footwork."

"I went through my files on the case," she said. "As far as I can tell, hers was the only building Gaitan personally canvassed, and he went there weeks after the murder, long after your deputies had already been through the neighborhood."

"When exactly did he find her?" I asked her.

"Two days before the lineup," she said. "And yes, he knew about the lineup. He brought in the other witnesses, remember?"

"Sorry, folks," Odell said. "You're going to have to connect the dots for me here."

"Two days before the lineup Gaitan goes to a single building in a neighborhood that's already been canvassed and finds the only eyewitness who swears she saw Bob Travis in the alley the morning Alex's body was dumped there," I said to Odell. "Is a picture beginning to emerge?"

Odell chewed thoughtfully, swallowed. "You're saying she was a plant?"

I nodded. "She had to be."

"Gaitan put her up to it?"

"No," I said, "that's too risky, even for him. It's one thing to drop drugs or a gun or plant fiber evidence, that's your word against a defendant's, but suborning perjury from a civilian witness is pretty damn unpredictable. If she breaks, it's all over for him."

"Who planted her then?" Odell asked.

"Asuras," I said. "We already connected her to him through Josey Walsh."

"We connected her to Josey Walsh," Serena said. "To be precise."

"Come on, Serena, the path to Asuras is obvious."

"Serena's right," Odell interjected. "You have to be careful the conclusions you jump to, Henry. I don't know that I want to follow you except that the woman disappeared."

"That bothers me, too," Serena said, "because it was obvious from the condition of her apartment that she wasn't planning on being gone for long."

Odell sipped a tumbler of Diet Coke, belched softly. "They found that other girl in Griffith Park."

"Katie Morse?"

He nodded. "Good place to bury your mistakes."

"Isn't that the first place the cops would look?"

"Only if they have a reason to look." He pulled his notebook out of his shirt pocket and scribbled a note. "You want me to find out about the bombing, Serena?"

She nodded. "Here's the picture of the guy Henry thinks might have been involved," she said, handing him an envelope. "Maybe your deputies could walk it around the neighborhood? I can't get any cooperation."

He took the envelope. "I'll take care of it."

"What does this mean Odell? You in?"

He shrugged. "I'm curious, that's all. This is strictly off the books."

TWO DAYS LATER, there was a message on my machine from Odell when I came home from court: "LAPD found Joanne Schilling in the park. Two shots through the back of the head from close range. From the state of decomposition, it looks like she was probably killed sometime in the last two weeks. They buried her fast. The grave wasn't much more than a couple of shovels of dirt. I'm at the station."

I called him back.

"Where was the body?" I asked him.

"Down a ravine in the gay cruising part of the park."

"Wasn't Katie Morse's body found in that area?"

"Yeah," he replied. "Not far. Must be the perp's favorite spot."

"Or a familiar one," I said. "Any way to connect her killing with the other murders?"

"She was shot with a service revolver," he said.

"What? A cop's gun?"

"Uh-huh," he said. "One of ours."

"Is there any way to trace it?"

"There's eight thousand cops in the county."

"How about narrowing it down to the one named Gaitan?"

"Is that how you figure it?" Odell asked.

"Don't you?"

He was silent for a moment. "Tell you the truth, Henry, I don't know what to think. But it sure complicates your theory that Asuras is our killer."

"Gaitan's on the take from him, so he shot the woman. What's hard about that?"

"You don't know what you're saying," he rumbled, as to an errant child.

"What? Cops don't kill people."

When he spoke again, I heard the unimaginable in his voice—doubt. "Not like this, Henry. This is first-degree murder. Say what you want about Mac, he thinks of himself as a cop, first and last. He's never done anything for strictly private gain. Why would he start with murder? It don't add up."

"Maybe Asuras made him an offer he couldn't refuse."

"There you go jumping to conclusions again. You're going to jump yourself off a cliff," he said sharply.

"Huh?"

"You still can't connect this woman to Asuras, much less that he ordered a hit on her, but you're ready to take Gaitan to a jury."

"She is connected, through Walsh, through Donati," I said, beginning my litany.

"I know the speech," he said impatiently. "Save it. I want you to think about what you're saying, son. According to you, Asuras is responsible for what, five murders? Suborning a veteran cop? Framing an innocent man? Unless you start backing this up, it's crazy talk, that's all."

"Do you believe me?"

"I'm not the people you have to convince. As far as the department is concerned, Travis killed those men, he's dead and the case is closed. The two women, they're LAPD's problem. You want the sheriff to reopen the investigation, you need more and better than what you've got."

AFTER I GOT off the phone with Odell, I surveyed my situation and discovered, to my chagrin, that he was right. The threads connecting Asuras to the murders were fragile: a history of sexual violence, gossip, the threat of blackmail, a movie plot, a hearsay document, a contract signed by an underling. In desperation, I took a legal pad and made six columns, one for Asuras and the others for his putative victims, Amerian, Baldwin, Jellicoe, Morse, Schilling. Beneath each name, I wrote down everything I knew about that person. Then I combed my files to make sure I hadn't missed anything. When I finished, I went over the columns carefully, searching for an overlooked connection, a fresh lead. The fourth time through, my eye fell upon the words *ex-agent* in the Asuras column and *'70s actress* in Schilling's column. Agent, actress. A match. I called the Screen Actors Guild.

Joanne Schilling had last been represented by an agent named Carson Kahn. He listed his address as Beverly Hills, but his office, in a building on the southeast corner of San Vicente and Wilshire, fell several blocks short of its ambition. From the outside, the building was imposingly stark, but once inside the starkness revealed itself to be nothing more than cheap and hasty construction. Everything about the place screamed 80's tax shelter. The hallway carpeting was coming apart, wires dangled from the light fixtures, the walls were apparently made of cardboard and held together with staples. The offices were occupied by enterprises like Pounds Away, Inc. and Scott Alan, Ph.D., Aesthetician and Electrolysist. There were, needless to say, many, many production companies and casting agencies. There were even more empty offices which, having never been inhabited, were not even haunted by the shades of former tenants, just lifelessly vacant.

Carson Kahn shared a suite with a half-dozen other agents. Their receptionist's perfectly rounded, gravity-defying breasts were a tribute to modern science. She smiled encouragingly as I leafed through six-month-old issues of *People* and *Variety*, while Kahn kept me waiting to impress me with how busy he was.

"Is he on the phone?" I asked her, fifteen minutes into my wait.

She glanced at her bank of blinking lights. "Gee, no. Sorry."

Thirty minutes later, I asked, "Is someone with him?"

"Don't think so," she said, tilting her head pertly. "I guess he's in there doing, whatever."

I skulked back to the couch, which was upholstered in a vaguely Southwestern plaid, to match the vaguely Southwestern lamps and carpet, and read another article about the travails of Sarah, Duchess of York. At two o'clock, exactly one hour after our appointment, he emerged from his office, a bony, middle-aged man with hair implants and bags beneath his brown, doggy eyes.

"Mr. Rios?" he said, looking me over, as if mentally casting me for the role of lawyer. He extended a soft, damp hand. It was like shaking a wad of used Kleenex. "Come on back. Honey, hold my calls will ya?"

"Yes, Mr. Kahn," she squealed, with such patent campiness I gained sudden respect for her intelligence.

Kahn's office was furnished with blonde Nordic furniture that could either have been very expensive or purchased at Ikea. His walls were covered with the obligatory framed movie posters, presumably of movies his clients had appeared in. I didn't recognize any of the titles. I sat down across the yellow expanse of his desk in a slightly elevated chair that gave me an unavoidable view of his hair plugs.

"So, Rios? That's Mexican, right? You're a lawyer? What can I do for you?" he gusted.

"Thanks for your time, Mr. Kahn. I'll be brief. I have some questions about one of your clients, Joanne Schilling. You probably know she was murdered."

"Joanne," he said. "I read her obit in the *Times*. A tragedy. But wha'cha gonna do? This city? *Meshuganah*. Am I right?"

"Yes, a tragedy. She was a great talent."

He looked at me to see if I was baiting him, and when he was satisfied I wasn't, offered a tepid, "A real star."

"How long have you been her agent?"

He shook his head. "I took her on what? Six, seven months ago, as a favor. Before that, she hadn't been represented in a long time."

"A favor to whom?"

A glint of feral menace appeared in the doggy eyes. "What's it to you?"

"I'm sorry," I said. "I represent her estate."

"Her estate? Ha!"

"There was some money," I said, confidingly.

"Yeah? How much?"

"I can't say. Attorney-client privilege and all that. I'm surprised you didn't know, since I assumed she earned it from work you got her."

"Yeah, right."

"I understand she had quite a career in the seventies."

"I know," he said. "She showed me her clippings. Lots and lots of clippings."

"This money," I said. "I've got to figure out where it came from and whether she paid taxes on it."

"Sorry. If she was getting money, it wasn't from me."

"You said you took her on as a favor for someone. Maybe that person could help me. Who was it?"

"Duke Asuras," he said with pride.

"The head of Parnassus? How did he know her?"

"He was her agent when she was working," he replied.

"Back in the seventies?"

"Yeah, like that. The lady had some problems, he wanted to help her out. He sent her to me."

"You spoke to him?"

"Well, no, not personally. The guy runs a fucking studio. I got a call from an exec who told me Duke would be grateful if I helped get her career back on track."

"Any luck?"

"I got her a couple of parts," he said. "Small parts, TV. Hey, she'd been out of the business fifteen years, dead drunk most of it. She wasn't looking her best, either. Then the bitch turned on me, dragged out the clippings, said the parts were too small and started turning them down. She was a real piece of work, that one."

"Why did you continue to represent her?"

"Because for the first time, I'm getting my calls to Parnassus returned the same day I made them."

"You have no idea how she supported herself."

He shrugged. "It had to be Asuras."

"Why would he give her money?"

"Who knows? I figure he was shtupping her back when he was her agent. He bumps into her, feels sorry for her, tries to help her clean up her act. For old-times sake."

"Who knew Asuras was such an easy touch," I said, falling into the agent's cadences.

"Asuras? A prince," Kahn said fervently. "A great man, a leader of the industry. You seen his grosses?"

The Hollywood equation: success equals character.

"Thanks," I said, getting up to go. "Listen, do you remember the name of the executive at Parnassus who asked you to represent Joanne Schilling?"

"Yeah, yeah, some stuck-up bitch. Talks like she's got a dick in her mouth." He flipped through his Rolodex. "Josey Walsh."

I MET SERENA for dinner at Galaxy Burgers, a fifties diner in Silver Lake, midway between my house and her office. The restaurant looked like two concrete pie plates stuck together and encircled by a band of round, nautical windows. To create the illusion the building was hovering, it sat on a raised platform disguised by shrubs. The metallic silver paint had long ago faded to gray and was adorned by gang graffiti. Inside, the floorboards were visible beneath a shredded electric-blue carpet. Rips in the red vinyl booths were repaired with electrician's tape and the white Formica tables were stained with forty-odd years of spilled food and drink. In a couple of old photos by the bathrooms, the waitresses were shown in their original form-fitting, high-collared Judy Jetson spacesuit uniforms, but the waitresses had been replaced by waiters as the neighborhood got tougher, and they wore grease-stained black trousers and short-sleeved white rayon shirts with clip-on black bowties. The food was only passable, but the menu boasted a "bottomless cup of coffee" and no one cared how long you occupied the booth. Galaxy Burgers was a favorite of derelicts and slackers and I liked it, too, because the spaceship that never quite got off the ground was one of my private metaphors for LA. Plus, when they said bottomless cup of coffee, they meant it. A coffee-hound's heaven.

I was already in my favorite booth when Serena came in, her fair sunburned skin, yuppie pinstripes, athletic stride and perky lesbian hair causing a commotion among the skulking regulars who clung to their booths like spiders to their webs.

"Jesus, Henry," she said, surveying the room. "Is this where you find your clients?"

"You're the one who insisted on meeting at a neutral spot." I handed her a grease-stained menu. "Have whatever you want, I'm buying."

"I'll eat at home," she sniffed. "You said you found something."

I gave her a summary of my meeting with Carson Kahn, concluding, "Josey Walsh is the key. Have you talked to her again?"

"She won't budge," Serena replied. The waiter appeared with a coffeepot and filled our cups. "She said she told me everything she knows about Joanne Schilling."

"Did she know Schilling had been murdered?"

Serena sipped the coffee, made a face, put the cup down. "I broke the news to her. It rattled her for a second, but then she went back into denial mode."

"Did you point out that while she claimed Schilling needed a place to stay, she was paying rent on an apartment in the Valley?"

"Of course, I did," Serena snapped. "Walsh said she didn't know anything about that. All she knew was the hard-luck story Schilling told her."

"Did she know Schilling was a witness in the Travis case?"

"She says not," Serena replied.

"What about the coincidence of Donati hiring me to represent Travis?"

"She said she hadn't worked for Donati for several months and didn't know anything about it."

"With that kind of memory, she ought to go into politics."

"She may start remembering when the police come around."

"What do you mean?"

"I notified the LAPD homicide detectives investigating Schilling's murder that they might want to talk to her dear, intimate friend, Josephine Walsh."

"Why would she be more forthcoming to them?"

"I could tell she wasn't taking me very seriously because I'm a woman. I get that more often than I care to admit. From other women, I mean. I assume men don't take me seriously," she said, throwing me a sharp look. "She'll pay attention if it's a man asking the questions."

"Did you tell LAPD about the connection to the Morse murder?"

"What connection, Henry?" she said, wearily.

Having just had this argument with Odell, I let it go. "What about the car bombing investigation? You heard anything from Odell?"

"He promised to get back to me by the end of the week if he had anything." She tried the coffee again. "God, I'm beat. I've got a backlog of a hundred cases with new ones coming in every week. I've got swastikas at synagogues in Fairfax, arson threats at black churches in South Central, and some asshole going around Union-Pico, pretending to be the INS and extorting illegals. Plus Donna's threatening me with couples' counseling and Jesse cries whenever I leave the house." She belched softly. "And heartburn."

I listened quietly to her speech. "Are you flaking on me, too?"

"No."

"Odell thinks I'm turning into a conspiracy junkie, seeing Asuras beneath every bed. You, too?"

"We talked," she admitted. "He told me you think Asuras hired Gaitan to kill Joanne Schilling—"

"Odell was the one who said she was killed with a service revolver."

"So naturally it's Gaitan," she said. "That's the problem, right there. You're still gunning for him."

"Fine," I said, "I'd be happy to get out of the business of doing the cops' job for them if you persuaded the sheriff to reopen the investigation."

"The sheriff's not interested in reopening the investigation," she said brusquely.

"How do you know? Did you ask him?"

"I wrote a memo suggesting there were some loose ends that needed looking into. Whether Kate Morse's murder was related to Amerian's, the murder of a key witness. The answer came back through channels this morning. Travis was the killer, the case is closed. These other two murders are completely unrelated."

"How can they know that before they investigate?"

"Think about it, Henry," she said. "The department's got its hands full investigating open cases, plus those killings in West Hollywood were a political hot potato for the sheriff, thanks to you. You made him look bad. Do you really think he's going to admit the killer is still out there somewhere? And not just any killer, Henry, but the head of a major studio. He might as well arrest the mayor."

"But we know Asuras did it."

"We don't know that," she said. "All we know is he's connected to one of the victims and to Schilling. The rest is conjecture."

I looked at her. "I'm not letting up."

"I've got to go," she said, scooting out of the booth. "Don't do anything crazy, Henry."

"What, like murder a bunch of people?"

"HENRY," DONATI GREETED me in his deepest register. "I've been meaning to call you, but, you know, there are a lot of demands on my time."

Thus put in my place, I replied, "I can only imagine."

"So what can I do for you?"

"You were going to get back to me about Alex's manuscript."

"Oh, that," he said. "I don't think we have anything else to talk about."

"Asuras doesn't care if I go to the cops?"

"I told you when you first asked for a payoff that we weren't interested in doing business with you," he said. "That hasn't changed."

"No, what you said was—" I stopped. Something in his tone alerted me that he was speaking on the record. "Are you taping this call?"

"As a matter of fact, I am, Henry. I wanted it on tape that you're trying to blackmail Duke Asuras."

"If you actually practiced law," I said, "you'd know secretly taped phone calls are inadmissible in court."

"But not at a disbarment proceeding," he reminded me. "Different rules of evidence."

I couldn't think of anything to say that wouldn't incriminate me.

"I don't know if I've offended you, or if you're just nuts," Donati said, "but this is going to stop. The other night at your house you tried to extort Duke with a phony document you obviously acquired from your friend Richie Florentino. It was the same slanderous piece of crap he tried to use in his hatchet piece about Duke. You know you're not going to the police with it, because if you do, I promise you, Henry, I'll see to it you lose your license to practice law. I promise."

He hung up.

I WAS AWAKENED at one in the morning by a call coming in on my office phone. I reached for the phone.

"Mr. Rios? It's Rod."

"Rod," I said, sleepily switching on the lamp. "What's going on?"

"School starts next week," he said. "Tonight my dad showed me the tickets for Utah. I made up my mind, I want to take them to court."

"I know it wasn't an easy decision," I said.

"I talked to Mr. Wise. He's coming down from San Francisco to meet me Saturday." He paused. "Could you come, too?"

"I'll be there," I said. "I'll call Phil in the morning and we'll coordinate."

Rod said, "I hope this is the right thing."

"I don't think they've left you any choice," I said.

"Unless I change," he said sadly. "I've got to go."

He hung up and then, a second later, I heard the click of another receiver hanging up. At first I assumed one of his parents had been listening, but then I heard the distinct sound of footsteps at the other end of my house, in the office. I hopped out of bed, threw on some clothes, grabbed the baseball bat I kept beneath the bed and burst out into the living room.

"Who the fuck is out here!" I shouted, switching on the light.

The front door slammed. Footsteps echoed off the steps to the street. A car started just outside my house. I ran to the kitchen window as it sped past: a blue-and-white cab, the logo Lucky's Taxi Service painted on the door.

chapter 20

THE NEXT MORNING I was standing outside my office window with Jim Kwan. In his capacity as our neighborhood watch captain, he was inspecting the hole that had been cut out in the corner of the window from which, presumably, the intruder had reached in and unlatched the lock.

"Yeah," Kwan said. "Looks like a professional. You didn't hear him come in?"

"No," I said. "I was asleep. If the phone hadn't rung—" I decided against pursuing that line of speculation. "I wonder if you could canvass the neighbors, see if anyone saw anything."

"Sure," he said. He looked at me, his round, open face clouded. "Listen, Henry, there's something I got to tell you."

"About what?"

"I was talking to old Mrs. Byrne down the street," he said, referring to the terror of the neighborhood, a bigoted old woman who spent her days reading a Bible and casting a censorious eye on the rest of us. "She said she saw a meter man hanging around your house a couple of days ago. Said he walked around from one side and came out the other."

"The meter is in the back."

He nodded. "I know, but Mrs. Byrne said everyone's meters were read last week. She also told me this guy didn't go anywhere but to your house. I should've said something to you, but half the time she makes things up to have a reason to talk to me."

"Sounds like someone was casing my house."

"I'm going to tell the security service to pay special attention to your place," he said. "You should take care of this window as soon as you can. Did they take anything?"

"No," I said.

"You were lucky then."

"Yeah, lucky."

ON SATURDAY MORNING I drove to the outlet mall at the edge of the central valley town where Phil Wise and I were meeting with Rod Morse. I took

Highway 99 through a landscape of field, farmland and long horizons, familiar to me from my own childhood in the valley. A dusty haze hung in the cloudless September sky. A new subdivision appeared like a weird mirage in the midst of tomato fields. A banner outside a junior high school proclaimed, YOU ARE ENTERING A DRUG-FREE AND GUN-FREE ZONE. The mall resembled a collection of barns, a tribute to the valley's agrarian culture that was being rapidly displaced by things like subdivisions and outlet malls. Soon, all of California would be a suburb either of San Francisco or Los Angeles. Small towns like this would disappear, and while there was something to be mourned by their loss, at least urban culture might moderate the rancid local bigotries that had driven me out of my hometown and which would probably drive Rod out of his. I pulled into the parking lot in front of the Mikasa outlet store and made it to the McDonald's, with five minutes to spare. A thin, goateed man in an electric-blue vintage suit waved me to his table.

"Henry? Phil Wise. Rod's not here yet."

I slipped into the booth across from him, the remains of an Egg McMuffin between us. I estimated Phil's age at twenty-eight or twenty-nine. The suit was from the sixties and he carried it off with Gen-X panache. He had long fingers but his nails were bitten to bloody stubs.

"Nice to finally meet you face to face," I said.

"You, too," he replied. "I really admire you, Henry. Not many boomer lawyers are still fighting the good fight."

Ouch, I thought, but said, "How did you get interested in this work?"

"Pentecostal parents," he replied, smiling. He had smoker's teeth.

"I thought things were better for your generation."

"In the big cities, maybe," he said. "Not in places like this or where I was raised."

"Which was?"

"Colorado Springs," he said. "I'd like to go over a couple of points with you before Rod gets here."

"Sure, but I want to make clear, this is your show. I'm just here for moral support."

We became so intent on our conversation, we didn't notice that the crowded restaurant had grown very quiet as a phalanx of deputy sheriffs surrounded our table. Then Phil looked up and nudged me. I looked around at the beefy, glowering uniformed men.

"Is there a problem?" I asked the nearest one, a black man whose name tag identified him as Deputy Collins.

A middle-aged woman suddenly burst through the circle of cops pointing at us. "That's them," she shouted. "Those are the child molesters who've come for my boy."

Collins said, "Philip Wise, Henry Rios. Get up."

"What the hell is this?" Wise demanded.

"I said, get up," Collins replied, jerking him to his feet by his shirt collar. "You're under arrest for conspiring to commit kidnapping."

"I want them in handcuffs," the woman, who I now realized was Rod's mother, screamed.

Collins complied.

FOUR HOURS LATER, we were sitting in a conference room at the DA's office with a pudgy, bespectacled assistant DA named George Holly, who was trying to talk Phil out of suing the county for false arrest and false imprisonment.

"The sheriffs had a good faith belief there was probable cause to arrest you based on what Mrs. Morse told them," Holly said defensively.

"Good faith!" Wise screamed. "Two faggots are coming to town to abduct our son? That's your idea of probable cause? Where did you go to law school, you Nazi?"

"You were planning to remove Rod from his family," Holly replied, his plump, pale face going apple red.

"I'm the kid's lawyer," Wise shouted. "Not a goddamned child molester. What I want to do and what I plan to do is get him away from those fundamentalist crazoids. By court order."

"His lawyer? Counsel," Holly huffed, "it's first-semester contracts law that a minor has no capacity to make a contract for personal services, yours or anyone else's."

"Actually, George," I said mildly, "you're only half-right. A contract with a minor is voidable, not void per se, but let's not split hairs. Phil, you sue the county if you want to, but I'd like to talk to Rod. The Morses do realize they can't prevent Rod from talking to us, don't they, George?"

He licked his lips, a bad sign. "That's kind of a moot point."

"What do you mean?"

"I want you to understand I'm not the enemy here," he said.

"Okay," I said. "Understood. Why can't we talk to Rod?"

"Mrs. Morse says Rod and his Dad flew to Utah last night."

Completely deflated, Phil uttered a low, "Shit." He looked at me. "How did they find out?"

"I don't know," I said. "Maybe they pressured it out of him."

"No," Holly said. "Mrs. Morse said she got a anonymous call yesterday. That's how she knew."

Phil scowled at me. "I didn't tell anyone I was coming here."

"I didn't, either," I said, and then remembered the second hang-up when I'd spoke to Rod about coming down. "I think I know what happened. Someone listened in on my conversation with Rod."

"Who?" Wise asked.

I shook my head. "I'll worry about that," I said. "You try to find him."

I HAD LEFT home before eight in the morning. Twelve hours later, I turned the corner to my street and saw a large black car parked in front of my house. An old Rolls-Royce. I pulled into my driveway and got out. At the same time, the driver emerged from the black car. He was in a kind of uniform, black suit, white shirt, black tie. He was tall and muscular, and when he was near enough for me to see his face, I recognized his eyes; a saint's eyes. My stomach dropped. Adrenaline pounded through my veins the primal message, *fight or fly*, but before I could make a conscious choice he was standing in front of me, blocking my path.

"Mr. Asuras would like to talk to you," he said, in the voice I remembered from the desert instructing me to get on my knees.

"You work for him," I said, "not Gaitan."

"He's waiting in the car."

"Your partner, too? Which one of you killed Joanne Schilling?"

He turned away, walked back to the limo, and opened the back door. I followed him and stood outside the car, looking in. A flood of frigid air drifted from the vehicle into the end-of-summer evening.

"Henry," I heard Asuras say from within. "Are you free for dinner?"

"With you?" I asked, peering in. "I'd rather dine with John Wayne Gacy."

From out of the darkness, he laughed. "I'm better company," he said. "Come on, Henry. You have questions, I have answers. I promise you safe passage."

"You promise, huh? That's a great comfort."

"The Asian man who lives next door to you came outside a half-hour ago and very conspicuously wrote down the license-plate number. Your security service questioned my driver. What else do you want, my fingerprints? A blood sample? Either get in or close the door."

I got in.

"You're very paranoid, Henry," he said.

"Can't imagine why," I replied.

THE CAR SOUNDLESSLY negotiated the curving streets of my hillside neighborhood and descended into Hollywood. A thick glass partition divided the front compartment from the back. The seats, upholstered in soft, burgundy calfskin, smelled like old money. Asuras was dressed in tweeds and leather. The car was freezing.

"A drink?" Asuras asked, indicating the small bar built into the seat between us.

"No, I don't drink."

"AA?"

"I don't drink."

"A man who doesn't drink is a man who doesn't trust himself," Asuras said, filling his glass from a decanter marked SCOTCH. "Ergo, not trustworthy." He raised his glass to me. "Skoal."

"Nick Donati must have your complete confidence," I replied.

He shrugged. "Nick's not untrustworthy, he's just weak. There are things he can't face without a little help."

"Which he pours out of a bottle." When Asuras didn't reply, I asked, "Have you been parked outside of my house all day?"

He set his drink down. "You left the valley at five-thirty," he said. "With traffic, I thought eight was a safe bet. How did your business go up there? Find the boy?"

There was the faintest trace of a sneer on the big, Roman emperor face.

"You know I didn't."

"For obvious reasons, I prefer not to be seen with you too publicly," he replied. "I reserved a table at a quiet place in Brentwood. Italian. That all right with you?"

"As long as it's not Mezzaluna."

AT THE RESTAURANT, the host greeted Asuras with murmured obsequiousness and led us unobtrusively through the main dining room to a private one where a waiter, the wine steward and a busboy were lined up at soldierly attention. The room, like the rest of the place, was paneled in dark wood, dimly lit, hushed; as much a bubble of luxury and privilege as Asuras's car. And just as cold.

After we were seated, the waiter approached. "Mr. Asuras, may I suggest . . ."

"No," Asuras said, "you may not suggest. This is what I want. A salad of hearts of romaine, the inner leaves only and they must be torn, not cut, into bite-sized pieces, with a vinaigrette of extra-virgin olive oil and balsamic vinegar, which you will bring to the table so I can dress the salad myself. After that, a veal chop, seared on the outside, pink on the inside, no more than a half-inch in thickness. If it's a millimeter thicker, I will throw it in your face. I also want you to bring me a plate of sautéed spinach and a plate of roasted red potatoes. When we are finished with our meals, you may offer dessert and coffee only after the tablecloth, our napkins and our settings have been completely replaced. I hope you got that, because I do not repeat myself."

The waiter's hands were trembling. "Yes, sir," he said, "and for the other gentleman?"

Asuras turned his most charming smile on me. "What will the other gentleman have?"

"I don't care," I said. "A green salad and whatever your special is tonight."

"Sir," the waiter said, gulping, "we have several specials." He rattled them off.

"The first one," I said, "the seafood pasta. Thanks."

Asuras was consulting with the wine steward. "Yes, a half-bottle of this."

"I'm sorry, sir, but we don't have half-bottles of this particular wine."

Asuras said to me, "It's too bad you don't drink, Henry. This wine is spectacularly good."

The wine steward said, softly, "Sir . . ."

Asuras gazed at him. "You're still here?"

"The wine, sir. Do you want the full bottle or . . ."

"You appalling asshole," Asuras said quietly. "Did I not say I would have a half-bottle? Didn't you hear me?"

The wine steward bristled and opened his mouth to speak.

"Don't you dare," Asuras said. "Not if you want to keep your job. Now go bring the wine and a decanter and I'll teach you how to pour a half-bottle from a full one."

"Yes, sir," the steward said, turned on his heel and marched, stiffly, out of the room.

"Do you make movies the same way you order dinner?" I asked when we were alone.

"With the same attention to detail? Yes?"

"No, I meant, are you as abusive to the people who work for you?"

"Abusive?" he repeated. "Am I abusive?" He smiled. "No, I'll admit to impatience from time to time, but I'm not abusive, because abusiveness is cruelty that serves no purpose but to degrade another person. I don't do that, ever."

"Your cruelty always serves a purpose?"

"We're not in court, Henry," he said. "Don't cross-examine me."

The wine steward returned with the wine and a decanter. Asuras excused himself and they went to a sideboard where the wine was opened and poured. Their backs were to me, and I couldn't hear what they were saying, until Asuras threw his arm around the man's shoulders, massaged his neck and murmured, "Relax, you're doing fine. Really great." The steward visibly relaxed. They returned to the table. The steward poured the wine.

"Don't forget to taste it," Asuras said.

"No, sir, I won't," the steward said. "Thank you, Mr. Asuras."

"What were you talking about?" Asuras asked, when we were alone. "Oh, yes, abuse."

"What do you want from me?"

He sipped his wine. "Astonishing," he said approvingly. "Just a sip, Henry? No, I suppose that would ruin your program, wouldn't it? You'd have to go into one of your AA meetings and raise your hand as a newcomer again just because you had a sip of the finest wine on earth. What a terrifying little life you lead, Henry." His smile was openly mocking. " 'I'll have the special. No, you don't need to tell me what it is. All food tastes the same to me.' Tell me something, Henry, are you even alive?"

"I'm more alive than Alex Amerian is."

His dark eyes gleamed. "The question isn't what I want from you, it's what do you want from me. How have I injured you, Henry? What have I done to you to explain your harassment of my associates and the terrible things you're telling people about me?"

"Five people are dead," I answered, "You're responsible."

"Six people, actually," he replied. "Since you're keeping score."

"Bob Travis."

We were interrupted by the arrival of our food. Asuras was as solicitous of the waiter now as he had been peremptory before. I remembered Alex's description of Mr. King, the initial charm followed by belligerence, and Serena's story about the boy Asuras had made into his assistant, then raped. Was Asuras simply a man to whom people had said yes for such a long time, he could no longer conceive of any other answer? Or was he something else, darker and more frightening? In our last conversation, he'd asked me if I believed in evil and taunted me with, "You think it's all the result of bad parenting?" when I denied that evil was the result of innate depravity. I watched our waiter plump himself up on Asuras's praise, almost against his will. "Since you're keeping score . . ." I was ready to reconsider my position. Asuras emanated cruelty and seduction, but they were so twisted together it was hard to say which attracted and which repelled. It was like looking down into a cavern and seeing something glitter at the bottom that could either be precious or lethal.

"I'm a warrior, Henry," he said, when the waiter departed. "I do what needs to be done, but I take nothing personally. Nothing. Vendettas are not my style, they interfere with business. Don't you agree?"

"I'm not in the rape and pillage business," I said.

"When you try a case," he said, ignoring me, "you don't hate the lawyer on the other side, or the judge who rules against you, or the jury that con-victs your client. No, you submit to the system and fight like hell within it, but if you lose, you shake it off and walk away."

"Alex was blackmailing you. You had to stop him."

"As I was saying, Henry, we submit ourselves to a system from the minute we take our first breath. In this system, there are various ways to get what you want. Say you want someone sexually. How do you go about it? You can try to charm them into bed, or you can buy the use of their bodies, or you can take what you want from them by force. As far as getting what you want, any of those methods works. Are you following me?"

"Rape and seduction are not the same thing."

"I didn't say they were," he replied, impatiently. "The means are not the same, but the end is. That's all I'm saying. There are means people and there are ends people. The means people create distinctions among means and call it morality. The ends people understand that in this world, in this system we're born into, anything that gets you what you want is a good thing."

"Is that the Buddhist perspective?"

"The Buddha taught there is no right and wrong, only action and con-sequence. There are certain esoteric teachings that go one step farther and prove that karma itself is an illusion. Once you understand that, you can do anything without fear or guilt."

He cut into his veal, the juice ran red and pooled in the white plate.

"You personally killed Amerian, didn't you? You raped him and butchered him and then you raped and butchered those other two men."

Through a mouthful of meat, he asked, "What do you want? And don't tell me money. I'm not Nick Donati. You can't take me in with childish threats of blackmail."

"You don't have anything I want."

"But you have some things you'd like to keep. Your reputation, for instance. Your friends. I can take them away from you, the same way I took that boy away from you this morning."

"What are you talking about?"

"Your friend Richie is wrong when he says the studio system is dead," Asuras replied. "It's true we don't have actors and technicians on staff the way they did in the thirties and forties, but I have access to incredible talent. Actors, detonation experts, wiretap experts, computer hacks. The bigger and more complicated the movies, the more sophisticated the talent, and all of them need me if they want to work. It's amazing what people in this town will do to stay on my good side. There's really nothing I can't do, Henry."

I got up. "The more people you bring into this, the likelier it is one of them will talk. All I have to do is find that person."

"Please, Henry, what can you offer them? The rosy glow of self-righteousness?" he said. "Sit down. Finish your meal. We'll talk afterwards. I'm promoting Nick to head of the TV division. We're launching a Parnassus channel. You want his job?"

"You're crazy."

"You disappoint me," he said, frowning. "But all right, have it your way. My driver will take you home."

"No, thanks. The last time he took me for a ride, I barely survived it."

"Then next time," he said, and resumed eating.

I CALLED SERENA from a pay phone on Sunset and asked her to come pick me up. Twenty minutes later, she pulled up in front of the 7-Eleven where I was waiting for her. I had told her a little about the day's events on the phone, but when I explained them in detail, she abruptly made a U-turn on Sunset and drove in the opposite direction of my house.

"Where are you going?"

"Home," she said. "You're sleeping on my couch tonight."

"I don't think that's necessary."

"This guy breaks into your house, listens in on your calls, has you followed and buys you dinner so he can threaten you," she said. "Humor me. Stay at my place tonight."

"Actually, he offered me a job," I said. "Legal counsel to the studio."

She glanced at me. "He really is psycho."

"If he had wanted to hurt me, he would have done it already. I've provoked him enough. I think what he wants from me is an audience."

"Why choose you?"

"Because I know what he's done, and there's nothing I can do about it."

"That's unfortunately true."

DONNA WYNN, SERENA'S partner, was a tall, slender woman, her pleasant face framed by straight, fair hair. She listened dubiously to Serena's heavily edited explanation of why I needed to crash on their couch.

"This is a first," she said to me. "She's never brought a man home before."

"I promise I'll remember to put the toilet seat down."

"Honey," she said to Serena, "Jesse wants you to tuck him in."

"Make yourself at home," Serena told me, as she ascended the stairs from the foyer where we were all standing.

They lived in a townhouse, a duplex. In the car, Serena had said they owned both units and rented out the other to two gay men. I followed Donna into the living room, where a fluffy white dog was asleep in front of the fireplace. The room was a controlled mess, the furniture comfortable but plain, a child's toys strewn on the floor. I felt something beneath me when I sat down, a chewed-up tennis ball. I rolled it toward the dog, who perked up for a second, then buried its head in its paws. Meanwhile, a black cat about the size of a bowling ball appeared in the doorway and stared at me, its whiskers twitching.

"Who's that?" I asked.

"Hekate," Donna said.

The cat leapt heavily into my lap. "What should I do?"

"Pet her," Donna said. "You're not much of an animal person are you?"

I tentatively patted the cat. She purred. "Animals make me nervous."

"Well, she seems to like you."

I stroked the black fur, looked into glittering green eyes. "She probably recognizes the scent of her master on me."

AFTER DONNA WENT up to bed, Serena and I sat up talking strategy.

"I got an idea while Asuras was bragging about his omnipotence," I said.

"I'm almost afraid to ask, but what is it?"

"He's dragged a lot of people into this. We have to find a weak link," I said. "Donati won't break. Our best hope is Josey Walsh."

"She's stonewalled us so far. Why should that change?"

"Because she doesn't know the whole story," I said. "All she knows is that Schilling was murdered. She doesn't know about Kate Morse or Bob Travis. If we tell her about them, we may raise the level of her anxiety until she decides it's in her best interests to talk."

"How do you know what she knows?"

"I don't, but Asuras is smart. He realizes the less you let your co-conspirators know about the crime they're participating in, the less they can incriminate you if they break."

"You think Walsh only knows her little piece?"

"Yes, but helping to suborn perjury in a murder case is a pretty crucial little piece. And if she has any smarts, she's drawn some inferences from Schilling's murder. Once we tell her about the others, that might push her over the edge."

"Henry, there's no proof Bob Travis was murdered."

"Asuras implied it."

She rolled her eyes. "You said the man's a megalomaniac."

"Even without proof, we can still scare Walsh with it."

"We?" Serena mumbled.

"After what happened to me tonight, do you still have any doubt about Asuras?"

"If Walsh doesn't break, and this backfires, I could be in real trouble," she said. "Abusing the authority of my office."

"I need you because you have that authority."

She nodded. "All right, but it's all or nothing. You understand? If this doesn't work, you have to count me out."

I SLEPT ON Serena's couch, with the cat at my feet, and the next day she drove me home on her way to her office. There was a message from Phil Wise on my machine. I called him back.

"Any word on Rod's whereabouts?" I asked.

"No, I've been calling up and down the chain of command at the Foster Institute, but they won't say if he's there or not. I'm going to go ahead and file the dependency petition in the superior court down there in the valley."

"Rod's not in the state," I pointed out. "How does the court have jurisdiction?"

"He was taken from the state against his will. A de facto abduction."

"Phil, he was taken by his father," I said. "Can a parent abduct his own child?"

"It happens all the time in custody cases," he replied, an edge to his voice. "But this isn't—"

"I know," he exploded. "I'm trying to figure out a way to get him back. You're not helping."

"I'm asking you the same questions the judge will be asking you. You need a better answer than getting mad."

After a long pause, he said, "I lose a lot of these kids. It works my nerves."

"What can I do to help?"

"Keep asking the tough questions, Professor Kingsfield," he said. "I'll go back and work on my answers."

WHEN SERENA PICKED me up that evening to visit Josey Walsh, she was considerably more optimistic than she'd been the night before.

"Remember I told you I'd sic'd the LAPD on Walsh?"

"Yeah?"

"I checked in with one of them this morning. They talked to Walsh about Schilling. She was sticking to her story, but he said she was very nervous."

"She wasn't nervous when she talked to you?"

"She was like ice. She's either finding it hard to keep her lies straight or she's getting worried about her own safety." She grinned. "Scaring her just might work." After a couple of minutes, she added, "If she does want to make a statement, I'll have to take over. I mean, you don't have any official position, Henry."

"I've been ready to turn this over to you from the beginning," I replied, miffed. "Once you overcame your doubts. If you want the credit, take it."

"That's not the point," she said.

"Whatever. After tonight it's your show, Serena. I do have my work to do. I'm perfectly happy to let you do yours."

We drove the rest of the way in silence.

JOSEY WALSH LIVED in a condominium not far from where Travis had lived, on another tree-lined West Hollywood street just off Santa Monica Boulevard. Serena pulled up to the curb and we got out and went to the door. She found Walsh's name on the directory and reached for the security phone. I stopped her.

"We have to surprise her," I said.

"How are we going to get in?"

"We'll wait until someone comes out."

A moment later, a muscular man holding the leash on a golden Labrador retriever came out of the building. While I patted the dog, and flirted with his owner, Serena wedged her foot in the door. The building was a rectangle built around a courtyard and swimming pool. Walsh lived on the top floor in unit 302. I rang the bell, and a moment later, the door opened a crack and I saw a sliver of a woman's face.

"Yes?"

"Miss Walsh?"

"Who are you?"

"My name is Rios, Miss Walsh. I'm a lawyer. This is Serena Dance, from the DA's office. I think you've talked to her."

"I don't have anything to say to you," she said, closing the door.

I wedged my foot in the door. "Miss Walsh, your life is in danger."

Her face again appeared in the crack. "Who writes your dialogue?"

"You know who killed Joanne Schilling," I said. "She wasn't their first victim. She won't be their last."

She didn't move for a moment, then she opened the door and sighed, "Come inside."

I got my first good look at her. In her early thirties, thin, pretty, she should have looked relaxed in her jeans and Gap tee shirt, but instead she radiated tension. Behind her, the curtains were drawn against the dusk and her carefully furnished living room was dark.

She turned a lamp on, sat down, stared at us. "What do you mean my life is danger?"

Uninvited, we sat down. "You're helping Donati cover up a series of murders committed by Duke Asuras," I said. "The last three people Donati recruited were themselves murdered. You're next on the list."

"I don't know what you're talking about."

"Three men were murdered in West Hollywood this summer," I began. "One of them was trying to blackmail Asuras. We know Asuras killed him, then killed the other two to hide his tracks and make it look like there was a serial killer on the loose. The police arrested a man named Bob Travis for the murders. Travis worked at Parnassus, he was Donati's ex-boyfriend. The police didn't have much of a case against him until Joanne Schilling turned up with a positive identification of Travis at one of the crime scenes. I think Donati made a deal with Travis. Travis agreed to take the fall—to allow himself to be arrested and maybe even tried for the murders—and Donati promised to control the evidence to make sure there wouldn't be enough to convict. Donati double-crossed him by producing Schilling. When Travis threatened to expose the deal, he was murdered. You know what happened to Joanne Schilling. She turned up in a shallow grave in Griffith Park but she wasn't the first. There was a third victim, a young girl named Katie Morse who knew about the blackmail scheme against Asuras. She was also murdered."

"You understand what's going on here, Josey," Serena said. "Everyone Asuras uses to protect himself ends up dead."

Josey Walsh said, "Nick is gay? That asshole."

"HE DIDN'T EXACTLY propose," Josey Walsh was saying, sometime later. We were sitting at her kitchen table. She was knocking back bourbon while Serena and I drank Tab, the industrial-strength diet drink. The kitchen had an unused cleanliness to it that reminded me of Donati's kitchen. She had opened the windows. It was now dark outside and the scent of honeysuckle drifted on the warm air.

"He led you on?" Serena asked.

"He talked about the future in a way that included me. You know, what a great power couple we'd make. He'd leave Parnassus and we'd start our own production company, that kind of thing."

"Was this while you were still working for him as a paralegal?" Serena asked.

She nodded. "I was a lousy paralegal, but it was a way into the studio." She belted back bourbon. "I couldn't get into a decent film school and I wanted to make movies."

"Did Nick know that?" I asked.

"Yes, I was very up-front about it," she replied. "Not that Nick noticed me at first. He supervises ten lawyers and eight other paralegals. I knew I had to get his attention."

"How?" I asked.

Her smile was a slash across her pretty face. "Feminine wiles, Mr. Rios." She glanced at Serena. "I know it's not politically correct, but Hollywood is still a boy's club. I was ready to do what I had to do."

"Did Nick respond?"

"Yes and no. Or maybe I mean, yes to a point. He seemed flattered and he would flirt back sometimes at the office, but it never went past mild innuendo. I thought he was afraid I'd scream sexual harassment if he actually asked me out. I guess that wasn't his worry."

"He was completely closeted at work?" I asked.

She nodded. "Completely. He'd show up at office parties with dates, different girl, same tits, but he was a big studio exec and you expect them to be pigs." She shrugged. "Plus, the story around the office was he'd been married once and had a bad divorce that soured him on relationships."

Serena asked incredulously, "This was your idea of a good catch?"

"No, he was my idea of an E-ticket."

"A what?" I asked.

"An E-ticket," she said. "They used to sell them at Disneyland. They were good for every ride."

"It must've worked," I said. "Don't you have some kind of producing deal with the studio?"

"They gave me an office, a phone and a half-time secretary," she said, bitterly. "Oh, and $10,000 a month for two years to develop projects. I report to some twenty-three-year-old VP, who reports to some twenty-five-year-old VP, who gets maybe ten minutes a month with Duke. I was closer to him when I was working for Nick."

"What did you give them in exchange?" Serena asked.

"After weeks of flirting back and forth, Nick asked me to dinner. We ended up at his place." She looked at me. "Yes, we had sex. All right, so it wasn't very good sex, but he seemed to enjoy it. God knows what he was thinking about while we were doing it. No, wait, I know what he was thinking about, the busboy at the restaurant. I thought I saw Nick give him the eye." She drained her glass. "Anyway, for the next month it was dinners and parties and premieres. The Hollywood high life. I was dazzled. That was when Nick started dropping hints about the future and then one night he invited me to Duke's house for dinner, just the three of us. The first words out of Duke's mouth were, 'So, Nick tells me you want to produce.' After that I would've agreed to anything."

"What exactly did you agree to?" I asked.

"It was this very odd thing," she said. "I was supposed to make it look like I was sharing this place with this Joanne Schilling woman. They wanted me to put her name on the mailbox and the answering machine and take messages for her and relay them through Nick."

"You ask why?" Serena asked.

"No," she said.

"Why not?"

"There was something in the way Duke asked me that was . . . ," she searched for a word, ". . . menacing. It was like, this conversation never happened. I can't explain why, but I knew I wasn't supposed to ask for an explanation."

"Is that why you agreed to it?" I asked. "Because you felt threatened?"

"No," she said. "I agreed because he offered me a production deal." She looked back and forth between us. "Or would I be better off if I said I felt threatened?"

"Then what happened?" Serena asked.

Walsh directed her answer to me. "I did what I was told. I put her name on the mailbox, on my machine."

"Did you ever meet her?"

"No," she said, splashing bourbon into her glass. "I had no idea who she was. For a long time, nothing happened, but then I began to get messages from the police and from her." She indicated Serena. "That worried me, but Nick told me it would all be over soon."

"You and Nick still going out?" I asked.

"Once I signed the deal memo, he dumped me," she said. "It wasn't crude, but the invitations stopped coming, the calls were all business. I got the hint. I can't say I cared much, because I got what I wanted from him, and despite his talk about the future, I knew he wasn't exactly lovestruck." She sipped, scowled. "Maybe if I'd had a dick."

"I thought you didn't care," I said.

"Maybe I did, a little." She stared at her glass, then said, fiercely, "You know he never could get it up for me. I thought it was because he was usually pretty drunk by the time we got to that part of the evening. We always ended up with him going down on me. He was good at oral sex. I guess he'd had a lot of practice."

"When did you start figuring this out?" I asked her.

"I had a lot of time on my hands, sitting in my producer's office in my little power suits, waiting for anyone to return my calls. I hadn't paid much attention to those killings around here this summer. I mean, I was busy, and from what I heard, the victims were all gay men. I felt safe, for once. But when everyone started asking me about Joanne Schilling, I got curious about her, too. Her name was familiar, but I couldn't think why, so one day I ran a search on the Internet and I came up with about thirty hits. Most of them were from twenty years ago. That's how I found out she was an actress. The last one was from July, in an article about the murders. It said she was a witness who saw the killer driving out the alley where one of the bodies was found. I did some more research and figured out that the alley was about two blocks from here."

"You put two and two together and realized that Asuras and Donati had hired her to pose as a witness living in this neighborhood?"

"Oh, no," she said. "That's too byzantine for me. All I figured out was for some reason they wanted me to say she lived here, and by a bizarre co-incidence, she was a witness in this local murder. All I wondered is what she was doing in the neighborhood."

"When did you realize it was more than a coincidence?"

"Nick had told me the calls for her would stop, and he was very upset when I told him the two of you had called. Very upset. Unhinged, almost. When I found out Schilling had been murdered, I started to think there was something very bad going on here."

"When was the last time you spoke to Nick?" I asked.

"Two days ago," she said, "after the police came and interviewed me about Schilling. I could tell they weren't buying my act. I called Nick in a panic and asked him what I should do. He told me not to do anything, that it would all blow over soon. But he sounded kind of panicked himself, so I wasn't reassured." She paused. "I haven't been to work since. I'm afraid to go back there."

"Have you been threatened?" Serena asked.

"No, but I could see the writing on the wall. Joanne was hired to play a witness, I was hired to play her roommate and she ended up dead. Nick, who never breaks a sweat, is frantic. I don't know how this movie ends, but I'm not liking where my character's going."

"It might be a good idea for you to stay somewhere else for a while," Serena said.

Walsh got up and opened a drawer, removing an envelope. "Airplane tickets," she said. "I'm flying up to Seattle tonight to spend some time with family."

"I'll need a statement from you before you leave," Serena said.

Walsh hesitated, "I don't know about that."

"If you want to be able to come back someday," Serena said, "you're going to have to help us out here."

Walsh looked at me. "Is that true?"

"I'm afraid so, Josey."

"All right, but I want something in exchange."

"What?" I asked.

"When this is all over, exclusive movie rights to your stories."

SERENA DROPPED ME at the bottom of the hill to my house, then she and Josey Walsh continued downtown to Parker Center, where she had arranged for Walsh to make a statement to the detectives investigating Schilling's murder before she flew to Seattle. Walsh had given us the first solid evidence that connected Asuras to any crime, albeit suborning perjury rather than murder. If the cops did their job, the charges could be ratcheted up. While we waited for Walsh to pack, Serena told me she thought she would try to use Walsh's statement to persuade the sheriff to reopen the investigation into Alex Amerian's murder. She was, in fact, full of plans.

"What about your boss, the DA? Won't he be pissed when he gets wind that you're going after his friend, Asuras?"

"I'm not going to tell him," she said. "And hopefully, he won't find out until it's time to indict the asshole, in which case Jack will get some very nice headlines out of it."

"You'll get some nice headlines out of it, too."

"Oh, screw you, Henry. You've patronized me from the very beginning. You really don't think much of me as a lawyer, do you?"

"I'm sure you're a perfectly competent lawyer, Serena."

"Then what's your problem?"

"You let yourself be used before in this case by the DA and the sheriff," I said. "I'm not sure it won't happen again."

"Watch me," she said.

"Don't worry," I replied. "I will."

I CAME DOWN the steps from the street to my front door. I hadn't left the porch light on and it was very dark. I wanted to change clothes, eat something and vegetate in front of CNN for a while before calling it a night. As I fumbled with my house keys, I heard rapidly approaching footsteps behind me. I jerked around and saw a man emerging from the shrubbery, holding something in one of his hands. I swung wildly, connected with his chest and knocked him to the ground.

"Who the hell are you?" I said to the figure sprawled beneath me.

"Henry?" he panted. "Mr. Rios? It's me, Rod. Rod Morse."

chapter 21

"ROD? I'M REALLY sorry."

The boy slowly got to his feet. He was tall, an even six-footer at least, but hunched his shoulders slightly, making him seem shorter. The object he'd been carrying was a backpack. He picked it up with one hand, and with the other tamped down a mass of greasy, black hair. There was a stubborn patch of acne on his chin and a faint trace of beard on his cheeks. His clothes—slacks, a white shirt, a blue blazer—were dusty and soiled. The sweaty, sour smell of fear issued from his thin body. Only his eyes were beautiful—large, dark, clear: his sister's eyes.

"That's okay," he mumbled. "I didn't mean to scare you."

"Someone broke into my house recently. I'm a little jumpy. Come inside," I said, unlocking the door. I led him into the kitchen and automatically set about making a pot of coffee. "How did you get here?"

He fell into a chair, dropping his backpack. "I ran away at the airport. We had to fly to San Francisco to catch a plane to Salt Lake. When they started calling our flight, I told my Dad I had to use the bathroom. As soon as I saw him board the plane, I ran outside and jumped on a bus that took me to San Francisco. I wandered around there for a day deciding what to do. I went to the Greyhound station to buy a bus ticket to here, but I only had enough money to get to Santa Barbara. I hitchhiked the rest of the way."

"Why didn't you call Phil Wise in San Francisco?"

"I only talked to him once. I didn't know if he would help me. I knew you would."

"You look like you've been traveling for weeks."

He grinned with shy pride. "I know. I've never done anything like this before."

"When did you get into LA?"

"Yesterday. My ride dropped me off at the beach. I slept there last night and then I started walking to your house. This is a big city. It took me all day."

"You walked here from the beach? Why didn't you call me?"

"I needed time to think," he said.

"To think about what, Rod?"

"Everything that's happened since my dad told me he knew about you and Mr. Wise. It's been like bam! bam! bam! One thing after another." His voice trembled. "And this city, it's so big, Mr. Rios. There are so many people and all of them look like they hate being here. It's totally overwhelming."

"Especially on an empty stomach. I'll order some takeout while you clean up," I said. "I'll show you the guest bathroom. You can take a shower if you want."

"I don't have any other clothes," he said.

"We're about the same size," I replied. "You can borrow a pair of jeans and a tee shirt." I glanced at his feet; they were boats. "You're on your own for shoes."

He started to laugh, then broke down, shaking and sobbing. I didn't understand why an offer of clothes should have that effect on him, but then I hadn't spent two days on the road, running away from parents who wanted to commit me to a psychiatric hospital to a stranger who might or might not take me in. And I hadn't been sixteen in nearly thirty years, but I remembered, dimly, that emotionally, sixteen was like walking over a suspension bridge in a high wind, and if you were gay on top of it, those winds could reach hurricane velocity. Whatever the trigger, he had earned his tears.

I squeezed his shoulder. "It's all right, Rod. Everything will work out."

He wrapped his arms around my waist and buried his face in my stomach.

I WATCHED HIM empty carton after carton of Chinese food, pausing only to ask, "What's this?" before he inhaled it. Cleaned and combed, in a white tee shirt and black jeans, he looked as wholesome as a Gap ad except for the incipient worry lines that bracketed his mouth and furrowed his forehead. As he drank a liter of Coke, I remembered the line from Robert Frost, "A boy's will is the wind's will, and the thoughts of youth are long, long thoughts." But it wasn't any kid stuff that had etched those hard lines in his face or caused the hurt in his eyes. He explained what had happened after an anonymous caller told his father Rod was about to abducted by two adult homosexuals.

"He said you and Mr. Wise would torture me and murder me," Rod said between bites of kung pao chicken. "Like that guy who kept people in his refrigerator . . ."

"Jeffrey Dahmer," I said. "What did you tell your father when he confronted you?"

"I told him the truth," he said. "I said you were lawyers who were going to help me stop him from sending me to a mental hospital. I told him I wasn't crazy, I was just gay, and that's how I was born and nothing was going to change it."

"How did he take that?"

"He hit me. He said he was going to beat the devil out of me. My mom had to stop him. He told me to pack." He mashed a grain of rice with his fork. "My dad never hit me before. Never."

"He panicked. People don't behave very well when they panic."

He stuffed another bite of food into his mouth and chewed anxiously. "What's going to happen to me?"

I'd been expecting the question, and dreading it. Rod was now a runaway, but that didn't change his legal status as an unemancipated minor subject to the control of his parents. Pending the outcome of the petition Phil had filed in juvenile court, I was duty-bound to notify Rod's parents of his whereabouts and return him to them. They would then ship him off to Utah and remove him from the California court's jurisdiction. If I harbored him until the court acted on the petition, I would be breaking various laws including, but not limited to, contributing to the delinquency of a minor. Moreover, I couldn't even tell Phil that Rod was in my custody without putting him in the position of either having to disclose Rod's whereabouts to the court or risk contempt by refusing.

"I don't know yet," I said. "Phil filed the petition to declare you a ward of the court. It's set for hearing next week. We'll have to show up for that."

He frowned. "What if my parents try to take me back?"

"You'll be with Phil and me."

"What if the court says I have to go with them?"

"Then you'd have to go with them," I said, "but we could ask the court to order them to keep you in the state until the case is resolved."

"You know they'll send me away," he said.

"They would be breaking the law."

"My dad says there's man's law and there's God's law, and if there's a conflict, a Christian has to follow God's law." He pushed his plate away. "If the court makes me go back to them, you'll never see me again."

"If I don't return you to your parents, then I'll be breaking the law and unlike your father, it's the only law I have. Anyway, we both know they'll come looking for you here."

He bolted from the table outside to the deck. I went after him and found him searching the red night sky.

"Rod . . ."

"This girl in my history class gave a report on the Underground Railway for Black History Month," he said. "She said there were people who would take the slaves from the South to Canada by following the Big Dipper." He pointed to the faint glimmer of the constellation above a row of palm trees. "They stayed in safe houses on the way. I was looking at the Big Dipper last night on the beach. I thought I would be safe here."

"You can't run away from being a minor, unfortunately. When you're eighteen, your parents won't be able to touch you."

He turned, leaned his thin frame against the railing, and looked at me. "What is it like to be gay?"

"What do you mean, Rod?"

"You've been gay all your life," he said. "What is it like? You live alone, don't you?"

"I haven't always lived alone," I said. "My lover died about a year ago."

"He had AIDS?"

"Yes," I said.

"Do you?"

"No, Rod, not every gay man has AIDS."

"When I was in San Francisco," he said, "I found the gay neighborhood, what's it called? Castro Street. I saw a man in a wheelchair. His face had purple scars and he was so skinny I couldn't believe he was alive. He had AIDS."

"Probably," I said.

"I guess I was staring at him because he asked if I was cruising him. I mean, he's half-dead and still thinking about sex." He crossed his arms. "There were men in leather clothes, and guys dressed up like nuns with their faces painted like clowns. I didn't see anyone my age. They were all old. They didn't look happy."

"You can't tell by looking at someone whether they're happy or not."

"Are you?"

"You mean, am I happy to be homosexual?"

He nodded. I sat down at the edge of the chaise lounge where Josh had spent his last days lying bundled up in the sun, staring at the sky. I looked at the thin, dark-haired boy and saw myself at sixteen, the age when I also realized I was gay, and tried to think what answer I would have wanted to hear to his question. I knew that answer, but it wasn't the one I could provide. I couldn't tell Rod that once he came out his troubles would be over.

"Happy and unhappy are feelings, Rod," I said. "They come and go and they don't have much to do with character. I mean, the worst person in the world may be happier than the best person in the world, but which one would you rather be?"

After a moment's hesitation, he said, "I would rather be happy. I don't know if I can find that out here, but I know what's waiting for me at home. I'm not sure I'm going to make it to eighteen if you send me back."

"All right," I said. "I'll think of something. I'll find you a safe house."

I PUT HIM to bed in the guest room and pondered my next move. Gradually, I formulated a plan. The first step involved calling Richie. I reached his answering machine, which now said, "Miss Otis regrets . . . You know the rest." When I said "urgent," he picked up.

"It had better be urgent," he sniped. "It's eleven o'clock at night. I'm getting cold cream all over the phone."

"I need a favor from you, Richie," I said. "A very big favor."

"A big favor? That calls for a cigarette." I heard him strike a match. "All right."

"Rod Morse turned up at my doorstep tonight."

"I thought his evil parents shipped him off to the snake pit in Utah."

"He ran away at the airport."

"You go, girl!" Richie said. "Good for him."

"But not so good for his case," I said, and explained why.

"You're not going to send him back to the Himmlers," Richie said.

"His parents? No, I can't bring myself to do it," I replied. "But I can't keep him here, either. They'll come looking for him, Richie. I was hoping you'd take him in."

"Me? Why me, Henry? I don't know anything about kids."

"You're paying his legal bill," I pointed out.

"Writing checks is one thing, changing diapers is another."

"He's sixteen, Richie."

"Oh, great, he probably wears black tee shirts, listens to heavy metal and sniffs hair spray out of paper bags."

"He's a nice kid, naive, scared. You were institutionalized when you were a kid, Richie. You must know how he's feeling."

After a moment, he said, "How long?"

"A week or two, max," I said.

"Well, it would be fun to have someone to watch movies with," he allowed. "That's all I'm doing these days."

"Great," I said, "you can screen the great camp classics for him. I doubt if he's seen them. Just tread gently."

"What does that mean?" he asked waspishly.

"Like I said, Richie, he's naive. His parents have been filling his head with scary ideas about gay people . . ."

"Are you calling me scary?"

"You can be a little overwhelming. It's just a matter of bringing your fabulousness down a notch or two."

"You asshole!"

"I'm trying to protect him."

"Against what? The parts of fag culture you personally despise?"

"He's been through a lot, Richie, and he's going to go through a lot more. I'd like him to feel safe for a while."

"There's no safety for us," Richie said.

"He doesn't need to know that yet. I'm sorry if I offended you, Richie. He's just a kid . . ."

"Henry, are you okay?"

"It's been a long day."

"Listen, honey, I'll take care of the rugrat. You pull yourself together."

"Will do. By the way, Richie? You'll be breaking the law by helping us out."

"I wouldn't have it any other way."

THE NEXT DAY, I called Phil Wise in San Francisco and lied to him.

"Rod's in Los Angeles," I said. "He called me yesterday and told me he managed to give his dad the slip at the airport and hitchhike down here."

"Where is he?"

"He wouldn't tell me. He's afraid I'll tell his parents. I told him you filed the petition in dependency court and he agreed to show up for the hearing, but listen, I have a better idea. Dismiss the petition up there and refile it here in LA. We stand a much better chance of winning here." I laid out my reasons, more liberal judiciary, greater familiarity with the problems of gay kids. "What do you think?"

"Brilliant, Professor K.," he said. "Are you sure he's down there?"

I looked across the room to Rod. "I'm positive."

"I need to see him," Phil said. "I can fly down tomorrow morning with the papers."

"He's calling me this afternoon," I said. "I'll arrange a meeting."

"Call me back," Phil said. "And Henry, it's better that neither of us knows where he's staying, in case the court asks."

"I understand."

I hung up. "Come on, Rod, let's go. Richie's expecting us."

"What did Phil say?"

"I'll tell you in the car."

As we drove to Richie, I explained the situation.

"Thank you for not calling my parents," he said. "I know this could get you into trouble."

"I'm trying to avoid that."

"What if they say you kidnapped me?"

"They can say whatever they like. A judge will decide what's true. In the meantime, you have your safe house, although Richie's not exactly Harriet Tubman."

"What's he like?"

"When Richie was a kid, his parents committed him to a mental hospital where he was supposed to be cured of being gay, just like your parents want to do with you. As you'll see, the cure didn't take."

JAVIER LET US into Richie's apartment. Rod was studying the pink and blue mural depicting the rape of Ganymede that was painted on the wall of the entry hall when Richie emerged from his room in parrot-green silk trousers and a bright yellow shirt. He air-kissed the sides of my face. I introduced him to Rod.

"Bubbie," he murmured maternally.

"You're Richie?" Rod said, wide-eyed.

"None other," Richie said, "but think of me as your Auntie Mame."

"My what?"

"You don't know about Auntie Mame?" Richie asked grandly.

"She's a character in a movie," I explained. "A kind of fairy godmother."

"More fairy than mother," Richie added.

"May I use the bathroom?" Rod said.

"Javier, show him the powder room," Richie commanded.

After he left, I said to Richie, "Knock it off, Richie."

"Are you sure he's gay?"

When Rod returned, I took him aside and said, "I have to go now. You've got my page number. Call me whenever you feel like talking. Don't let Richie scare you. He's really a very good guy."

He was staring at the mural on the ceiling, a sky held up by four lascivious cherubs. "His house is like a museum. I was afraid to dry my hands on the towel in his bathroom. You're sure I can't stay with you?"

"Richie's harmless," I said. "I'll call you later."

PHIL WISE CAME down from San Francisco the next day, met with Rod, and filed a new dependency petition in juvenile court in LA that included an emergency request to have Rod declared a ward of the court to prevent his return to his parents. We were lucky to draw a judge named John Fuentes who had run a child's advocacy organization before his appointment to the bench. He scheduled a hearing on the emergency request for the following Monday. In the meantime, Phil served Rod's parents.

The next day, Phil phoned. "The Morses filed their response to our petition," he said. "You won't believe the shit their lawyer let them put in their declarations."

"Bad?"

"They actually use the phrase 'agents of Satan,' " he said, gleefully.

"That's great. The crazier they sound, the better we look."

"Unfortunately, it's not all ranting and raving," he said. "They also filed a motion to dismiss the LA petition on jurisdictional grounds and haul us back into the valley."

"Rod's physically present in LA," I said. "That confers personal jurisdiction."

"He's a runaway, Professor K.," Phil replied. "That's the only reason he's in LA. His home is with his parents. Got an argument?"

"Fuentes won't dismiss our petition if we can persuade him that by sending Rod back to the valley, he'll be sealing his doom," I said. "He's the one judge in the entire county who may agree with us that trying to cure your gay kid of being gay is child abuse. All we have to do is keep his eye on the substantive issue instead of the procedural one."

"You're right," Phil said, brightening. "But you're going to have tell Rod when he shows up in court on Monday there's a chance he'll be returned to his parents. Can you guarantee he'll be there?"

"Yes," I said, though I wasn't sure at all.

"I'm counting on you," Phil said.

I TOOK ROD to lunch, where I explained the status of his case. I forced his reluctant agreement to show up for the hearing, even at the risk of being ordered home. I had no sooner dropped him off at Richie's when my car phone rang. It was Serena Dance. She was jubilant.

"Good news, Henry," she said. "Odell came through. He found a witness who identified Jim Harley at the scene of the car bombing. He arrested Harley last night, and not only did he cop to the bombing, he incriminated Asuras and your friend Donati."

I had been too preoccupied with Rod to give much thought to the Asuras case, but I was worried by Serena's overconfidence. "What exactly did he say?"

"Donati approached him about doing the job. When he balked, Asuras personally called him. They paid him a hundred thousand dollars. I'm working on arrest warrants for Donati and Asuras for conspiracy."

"Have you run this past the DA?"

She bristled. "I don't need his permission to file the case. I have hard evidence."

"A co-conspirator's statement isn't admissible against another unless it's corroborated by independent evidence," I reminded her.

"I know what the law is," she huffed. "This is enough to arrest them. Now I can go after them for the murders."

I started to object, but thought better of it. "Great. I'm here if you need me."

THAT WAS WEDNESDAY, The arrests of Asuras and Donati made national news the next morning. By that evening, the charges had been dropped and the District Attorney had issued an abject apology to the two men. In her haste to arrest them, Serena had forgotten that the car they had allegedly conspired to destroy was leased to Samsara, a company Asuras owned. His lawyer claimed the explosion was an experiment in special-effects technology for an upcoming movie in development at Parnassus. He pointed out that the leasing company had been completely compensated for the car so, in effect, Asuras was being charged with conspiring to destroy his own property. He also distributed a sworn statement from James Harley retracting his earlier confession to the police on the grounds it had been coerced.

I called Serena at home as soon as the broadcast ended. The answering machine picked up.

"Serena, it's Henry," I began.

"Hi," she said, wanly, picking up. "I'm screening."

"I just finished watching the news."

"You call to gloat?" she asked, bitterly. "You warned me."

"I'm not gloating. It was pretty nervy strategy for Asuras. I don't see how you could've anticipated it."

"I've been fired, Henry."

"What?"

"I have two weeks to get my cases in order and submit my resignation."

"You have civil-service protection."

"No," she said. "I was a special hire to run the hate-crimes unit. I serve at the DA's pleasure. He's not pleased anymore."

"What about Josey Walsh's statement? What about Harley's statement that he blew up the car because Alex wouldn't return it to Asuras?"

"You saw the news," she said. "Harley retracted his confession. Josey Walsh's statement doesn't mean anything unless you buy the whole package, and the DA's not buying. We had a meeting with Asuras and his lawyers. When I tried to raise the Walsh statement, Jack shut me up."

"He already knew about Walsh?"

"I laid everything out for him after Asuras was arrested. Everything, Henry," she emphasized, "including my belief that he's a murderer."

"And the DA said what?"

"I swear I heard him piss his pants," she replied, "but what he told me was to go slow and keep it out of the press. Later on, when he fired me, he told me he knew I was wrong about Asuras all along. He said if I indulged these fantasies publicly, he'd see I was disbarred."

"I'm really sorry."

"You thought I was grandstanding, didn't you? You thought I wanted the credit for my personal glory. That wasn't true, Henry. I needed to win a big case to keep the hate-crimes unit alive. Now Jack will probably disband it."

"The DA knows Asuras is a murderer and he's going to let him get away with it?"

"Incredible, isn't it," she said.

"What about the sheriff? Could he be interested?"

"I persuaded him to arrest Asuras and Donati. He'll be grateful if they don't sue him for false arrest."

"Did Donati do the talking at the meeting with the DA?"

"Donati wasn't there," she said.

"What?"

"He wasn't there," she repeated. "That's strange, isn't it?"

"Maybe it's more than just strange," I said.

"NICK, IT'S RIOS, please pick up. I know you're there because I tried your office and your secretary said you were working at home and she'd just got off the phone with you. Nick . . ."

"You never give up, do you?" Donati said thickly.

"I thought you might to want to talk to someone other than a bottle of scotch."

"About what?"

"I heard when Duke met with the DA yesterday morning, you weren't included. Either he's about to throw you to the wolves or you're finally sick of all the blood on your hands."

After a long silence, he said, "What do you care, Henry, you're not the cops."

"I'm a defense lawyer, Nick. I think you could use my services."

He cackled. "For what? I've just been exonerated by the District Attorney."

"I can believe that Asuras is a sociopath who doesn't feel any remorse for what he's done, but you're not. You drink like a man who's having trouble sleeping, Nick. I know. I've been there."

"What's this, a twelve-step call? I told you, I'm in the clear."

"So is Duke," I said. "The cops will never catch him. What's that going to do for his ego? He already thinks he's above right and wrong. What's his next trick? Who's his next victim? Are you helping him with that cover-up, too?"

He hung up. A few minutes later, the fax machine spit out a fax from him. *You're phones are tapped. Come to my house tonight at 10. Careful you're not followed. N.*

I'd only been to Donati's house once and when I tried to find it again, I got lost in Laurel Canyon's dark, twisting roads. When I finally reached his fortress, I was an hour late, but at least I was certain I hadn't been followed. Upstairs, the lights were on and there was a Land Rover in the driveway. The plates stopped me: PROUDJD. Where had I seen those plates before? Unable to remember, I continued to the house and rang the bell. I heard furious barking, followed by light footsteps, a muted voice quieting the dogs and then silence. A minute passed, then two, and finally the doorknob turned and he pulled the door back. I could smell the booze on him. His dogs snapped and growled behind him as if expressing the fear he had smothered with scotch.

"Quiet," he commanded them. He was in jeans, a button-down shirt and loafers without socks. His hair was disheveled, his face darkened with stubble. "I didn't think you were coming."

"I got lost in the canyon."

He smiled, displaying his supernally white teeth. "Like Dante. Come in. Watch me have a drink."

Things were subtly amiss in the expensively austere upper floor; a spill of whisky on the burnished dining table, the Doré lithograph of the wood of the suicides jammed between the cushions on the couch and the stale smell of heavy drinking in the air.

He picked up a smudged, half-filled glass. "You mind?"

"No."

He came toward me. "I can't imagine you drunk, Henry. I can't imagine you out of control."

"Drinking is a sickness. It has nothing to do with self-control. If anything, I imagine getting drunk gives you what little control you have over your thoughts. I saw pictures of what Asuras did to Alex Amerian. That's not something I'd want to see every time I closed my eyes."

"Don't be too sad for that little whore."

"I know he tried to blackmail Asuras," I replied. "He still didn't deserve that kind of death. The other victims deserved it even less."

He sprawled on the couch. "I didn't kill anyone."

I sat down across from him. "I believe you."

"That's a comfort," he said, taking a slug from his drink.

"But you did help Asuras with the cover-up," I said. "That makes you an accomplice with the same liability as his. Now's the time to make a deal with the cops, Nick."

He laughed. "The cops. The fucking cops were in on it, Henry. What's his name? Gaitan. How do you think he got to Bob?"

"What do you mean?"

He put his glass down with a drunk's precision. "The cop and I planned it," he said. "There would be enough evidence to put Bob on trial, but not enough to convict him. Things would disappear, witnesses would change their stories." He grinned. "You would give an excellent summation."

"How did you talk Bob into that?"

"I told him he could move in with me when it was all over."

"If Bob agreed, why was he killed?"

"The fucking cop did that," he said. "Duke's orders."

"Gaitan killed Bob Travis? Why?"

"When Bob realized he was actually going to be arrested and go to jail, he panicked. Duke was afraid he'd crack, so he told Gaitan to take care of him. I didn't know, I swear."

I remembered how distraught he'd been the night Travis died. "Asuras didn't tell you because he was afraid you'd object."

He nodded. "Bob didn't have to die. I could've handled him."

"Was that the only time Asuras double-crossed you?"

"I didn't know about Schilling either," he said.

"He's a megalomaniac."

"Duke? That's like saying the sky is blue. Everyone at Duke's level is a megalomaniac. Duke's crossed the line."

"What line?"

"The M'Naughten line," he said, referring to the legal standard for insanity in criminal cases. "But since this is Hollywood, no one's noticed. The Industry rewards ruthlessness and cruelty, and if you're powerful enough, you can rob, cheat and steal and people look the other way. Not just people in the Industry, the police, prosecutors, judges. I was relieved when we were arrested. I thought it would finally be over, but even I underestimated Duke."

"I need to know what your part was in the murders."

"Why?"

"To figure out what kind of deal I can make for you."

"You said it yourself, Henry, I'm as guilty as he is."

"That depends. What happened, Nick?"

"I helped with . . . disposal."

"Were you coerced?"

The drunken eyes focused. "Is that what you would tell a jury? I was afraid for my life so I followed orders because I wasn't man enough to stand up for myself?"

"All I want to know is what happened."

"I was a fifth-year associate at an entertainment firm, and I was going nowhere when I met Duke. He hired me to run the legal department at the studio because he said he saw the warrior in me. I was going to help him conquer Hollywood."

"He knew you were gay," I said.

"That's why my career had stalled at the firm. The partners thought I was a little too light in the loafers for their celebrity clients. They didn't think I'd be tough enough. They found out how tough I am when I negotiated with them for Parnassus."

"Asuras didn't care that you were gay, obviously."

"Obviously? Duke doesn't think he's gay, if that's what you mean."

"Neither did John Wayne Gacy," I replied. "But he couldn't escape who he was, either, and when you start running from yourself, you end up in some pretty dark places."

"Are you saying if Duke had come out, those men would still be alive? I don't think so, Henry. I know Duke. The one thing he's not is repressed."

"If you knew that, why did you help him?"

"I was gradually sucked in," he said. "I knew Amerian was trying to blackmail Duke, so I arranged the meeting and had Bob bring Amerian to Duke's house. Using the cab was Duke's idea. At the time, I wrote it off to paranoia. Later I realized he had planned all along to kill Alex and to incriminate Bob and me in the murder. But when he called me at three in the morning in a panic, I didn't consider the possibility he was acting, especially after I got to his house. Amerian's body was floating in the hot tub. Duke said he and Alex were doing an S&M scene that went too far. I told him to call the police."

"What did he say?"

"He said he had a better idea."

"Which was?"

"Make it look like Amerian had been murdered by gay-bashers."

"Why didn't you call the cops yourself?"

"I saw the knife wounds and I knew it wasn't an accident. He had murdered the kid. If it was obvious to me, it would be obvious to the cops. Amerian was a blackmailing little whore. I didn't owe him anything. That's how I justified going along with Duke."

"So what happened?"

"I got Bob back up to Duke's house. Together we wrapped the body up, put it in the trunk of the car and drove down to West Hollywood, where we dumped it in the alley."

"You helped dump the body?"

He nodded. "Afterwards, we went to a self-service car wash and cleaned the car from top to bottom."

"Joanne Schilling was going to testify she saw Bob coming out of the alley by himself."

"She wasn't there," he replied. "She was paid to say what we told her to say."

"What about the second murder?"

"The same thing," he said. "A call at two in the morning from Duke. I get to his house and find another body in the hot tub."

"Jackie Baldwin," I said. "Did Travis pick him up in the cab?"

He shook his head. "No, that was Duke free-lancing, but he used the cab to further incriminate Bob. We got rid of that body, too."

"You didn't say anything to Asuras? Like, stop."

"Duke said he was afraid the police would suspect him in Alex's murder unless another victim turned up to divert them. It made a certain amount of sense," he said wearily, "but by then I was in so deep there wasn't any way out. He said there would have to be a lot more victims before the police was convinced it was a serial killer. The best I could do was talk him down to one more."

"Jellicoe," I said. "Who picked him up?"

"Bob," he said. "I told him it would be the last time."

"Too bad for Bob it wasn't," I said. "Who killed Joanne Schilling?"

"Gaitan," he said. "He seems to enjoy killing people almost as much as Duke." He finished his drink, but when I looked into his eyes, I saw he was sober. "When I found out about her, I realized the killing would never stop."

"If I were you, Nick, I'd be concerned about my safety."

"You're my insurance, Henry," Donati said. He dug into his pants pocket and removed a key. "This key opens a locker in the international terminal at the airport. Inside you'll find envelopes, addressed to the District Attorney, the police chief and you. Each of them contains my sworn affidavit laying out everything I told you tonight."

"Why not just go to the police now, Nick?"

"There's something I have to do," he said. "The affidavits are my protection."

"I know I could work out a deal for you with the DA in exchange for your testimony against Duke."

"What kind of deal, Henry? Life in prison instead of death row? No, thanks."

"This affidavit's not going to be admissible if you disappear," I said.

"I've taken care of its admissibility. The airport locker's on a twenty-four-hour timer," he said, glancing at his watch. "You have about an hour to get to them."

"I'm coming back and we're going to the cops."

"You're a rescuer, Henry, aren't you? Fixer of broken lives."

"Wait for me."

He smiled. "I'll be here."

chapter 22

LA CIENEGA WAS bumper-to-bumper from Sunset to the Santa Monica freeway. The pale faces of other drivers drifted by like images in a dream, floating heads entombed in the machinery of their cars. The street flashed around me: bursts of neon alternated with darkness; knots of people waited outside the restaurants on Restaurant Row for valets to retrieve their cars; a homeless man was reflected in the window of a Jaguar dealership, pushing his shopping cart toward Beverly Hills. An enormous bronze sculpture of John Wayne presided over a desolate intersection of shuttered storefronts. Farther down, the freeway lurched above the street; a row of palm trees kept austere vigil over a neighborhood of the poor; in a vacant lot a sidewalk vendor displayed velvet paintings of Martin Luther King and Diana Ross. This was Duke Asuras's city, a place of dark dreams and wastelands and the hovering presence of the angel of death. I kept my eye on the rearview mirror, spooked by the possibility I was being followed.

I parked illegally outside the Tom Bradley International Terminal, a monument to the mayor under whom the city had erupted into civil war. I hurried through the bright corridors until I found Donati's locker near the gates for Aerolineas Argentinas. There was no timer on the locker. Inside I found three sealed envelopes. Attached to the one addressed to me was a handwritten postcard that contained Donati's suicide note:

> Dear Henry,
> You will find in this envelope an affidavit under penalty of perjury that incriminates Duke Asuras in the murders. It incriminates me, too, but I couldn't face the fall. I guess that makes me a coward, but you already knew that about me, so no surprises there. Listen, I cracked the law books for the first time in twenty years and this affidavit should be admissible either as a statement against penal interest or a dying declaration. You're smart—you'll get it in. Just remember, Henry, don't underestimate Duke.
> Later, Nick.

"Shit," I said. The Doré engraving. The wood of the suicides. He'd been studying it before I arrived. The ruse with the timer on the locker was to get me out of his house. I stuffed his letter into my pocket, grabbed the envelopes and made a dash to my car, arriving just as it was being hitched to a tow truck.

The airport cop who'd called the tow was unimpressed by my story about preventing a suicide, but the truck driver let me ride with him to the yard, where I bailed my car out. It was well after midnight before I reached Donati's street. I didn't get far. Two police cars and a paramedic unit blocked the road. Curious neighbors huddled a few feet away. I pulled over and got out of my car.

"What happened?" I asked a white-haired woman in a quilted bathrobe.

"I don't know," she said. "I was in bed reading and then all hell broke loose. Sirens, lights. I've been standing here for a half hour. So far the only thing that's come out of the house are the dogs."

"The dogs? Where are they?"

"There," she said pointing. The delicate greyhounds lay lifelessly on the sidewalk. "I guess he killed them. Isn't that strange? But I still don't understand why . . ."

She stopped mid-sentence as a couple of burly paramedics emerged from Donati's house and hoisted a stretcher into the ambulance, a sheet drawn over a small body.

I COULDN'T GO home. I couldn't face my empty house. I kept seeing the frail corpses of Donati's dogs laid out on the sidewalk. A bizarre, sad touch. Did he kill them to protect them from the pound or was he afraid, at the last minute, to meet the darkness alone? I drove around in circles for an hour before I found myself pulling up to Serena Dance's darkened townhouse in Santa Monica. I walked to the door, carrying Donati's affidavits. I hesitated, but then a dog yapped from within, startling me out of my uncertainty. I pressed the bell. The dog yapped even more frantically. Lights, footsteps. I felt a presence on the other side of the door peering at me from the peephole. Slowly, the door opened. Serena was wearing a pink chenille bathrobe over sky-blue flannel pajamas. She was stuffing a handgun into her pocket.

"Henry? What the hell are you doing here?"

"Donati confessed," I said. "He left an affidavit describing the murders and implicating Asuras."

"Left?" she repeated, groggily. "Did he run?"

"No," I said. "He killed himself."

"Get in here," she said, yanking me across the threshold. She looked up and down the street, closed the door and dead-bolted it. "Come into the kitchen. I'll make some coffee. When did Donati . . . ?"

"A couple of hours ago. He sent me off on a wild-goose chase to get these and while I was gone, he killed himself."

She gave me a long, assessing look. "You're not going to blame yourself for this," she announced.

"I could've stopped him."

She sat me down at the kitchen table and said, "Start at the beginning."

AFTER I RELATED the events of the evening, we opened the envelope addressed to me and found the original of Donati's affidavit. It contained a complete confession, filled with details he could only have known about by having been present when they occurred. The last page was signed under penalty of perjury, and notarized.

"This is powerful stuff," she said.

"Enough to get the DA off his ass?"

She poured the last of the coffee into her cup. "Didn't you remind me that the uncorroborated testimony of an accomplice to a felony isn't admissible against the principal if that's the only evidence?"

"Donati's affidavit is a roadmap to corroborating evidence."

"I'm not talking law now," she said, "but politics. The DA's been burned once before. He's not going to jump back into the fire."

"What more does he need? Asuras's confession?"

"Works for me," she said.

"Are you seriously telling me that, even with Donati's confession, the DA won't reopen the murder investigations?"

"Not without giving Asuras a chance to respond," she said. "And you know what he's going to say. He'll lay it on Donati and Travis. Both conveniently dead."

"That's not plausible."

"Isn't it, Henry? Two crazy gays go on a murder spree and then one of them knocks the other one off before he kills himself."

"Why would they blame Asuras?"

"Revenge? Insanity? It doesn't matter. The fact that Donati killed himself reflects badly on his credibility."

"Nick also left a copy of the affidavit for the chief of police," I said. "We can go to LAPD and bypass your boss."

"LAPD doesn't indict, the DA does," she said. "The first thing the chief's going to do is call Jack. Look, if I've learned anything from this, it's that LA's a company town and the name of the company is Hollywood. No politician wants to antagonize the movie people and the chief's as much a politician as the DA."

"What are we supposed to do, Serena? Burn the affidavits and walk away from this?"

"Of course not," she said impatiently. She stared out the window where the darkness had begun to lighten. There was a shuffle of footsteps and then a discreet cough at the door. We both looked up.

"Honey," Donna said, her face knotted with worry. "What's going on? Is everything all right?"

"Excuse me, Henry," Serena said. She and Donna went into the living room, had a whispered conversation, and then Serena returned alone.

"Donna must think I'm the houseguest from hell."

"No, it's not you," she said. "We've been getting some strange calls."

"Hate calls?"

"Threats," she said, "but not exactly threats. A stranger calls and tells us he followed Jesse home from school."

"Is that why you're toting a gun?"

"I wouldn't think twice about using it."

"Who's making the calls?"

"They started after I had Asuras arrested."

I nodded. "He tapped my phone, he's had me followed."

"Donna's taking Jesse out of school. They're going to Denver for a few days, to stay with her sister."

"They have to come back, eventually. The only way to protect them is to stop Asuras." I tapped the affidavit. "What are we going to do with this?"

"There's only one other prosecutor who might be interested and has concurrent jurisdiction over LA," she said. "The state Attorney General."

"Lundlin? He's a fascist. He owes his political existence to the Christian right."

"That's why he'll go after Asuras," she argued. "He has no constituency in Hollywood and nothing to lose by alienating the Industry. His supporters will love it. Plus, he won't have to rely on LAPD because he has his own investigators."

" 'Merchants of cultural rot,' " I said, quoting one of the AG's recent characterizations of the leaders of Hollywood. "He wants to be Governor. The publicity from this case will win him the primary."

"The only other possibility is going to the feds, and there's been no violation of federal law. Besides, Asuras was co-chairman of Clinton's California campaign."

"And a regular guest in the Lincoln Bedroom."

"It's the AG or nothing."

"But Serena," I said, "he's the Devil."

"I'm sure he says the same thing about gays and lesbians."

"That presents another problem. How do we get access to him?"

"He's a politician, Henry. There are limits to his principles."

WE AGREED SHE would fly to Sacramento on Monday morning and present the AG with the copy of the affidavit intended for the DA, while I kept the original and the second copy locked up in my safe deposit box at the bank. I drove home at dawn and fell asleep in my clothes on the couch. I was awakened by a call from Phil Wise, who was flying in the next day, Sunday, for a last-minute strategy session. He gave me his flight information. I showered, changed clothes and went out to get the paper. Jim Kwan was coming down the steps to my front door.

"Hey, Henry," he said. "I saw your car in the driveway."

"Hey, Jim." I stooped to collect the paper. "What's up?"

"Were you home last night?" he asked.

"Why, did I break curfew?"

He smiled mechanically. "There was a car parked outside your house at around midnight," he said. "Looked like someone was waiting for you."

"An old Rolls?"

"That's the one," he said. He handed me a scrap of paper from his back pocket. "I wrote down the license plate."

"Thanks," I said.

"How long did he wait for me?"

"The car was still there when Letterman was over. You in some trouble, Henry?"

"Come in for a second," I said.

Inside, I gave him the second sealed copy of Donati's affidavit.

"What's this, Henry?"

"If something should happen to me, I want you to get this to Sergeant Odell at the West Hollywood sheriff's station," I said. "I'll write his name down."

"I'll remember," Kwan said. "Odell, West Hollywood sheriff's station."

"Tell him the original is in my safe-deposit box at the Great Western on Sunset and Crescent Heights."

"Yeah, okay." He grinned nervously. "You got me worried, man."

"I'm a little worried myself, Kwan."

I DEAD-BOLTED THE door after Kwan left and glanced through the *Times*. On the front page of the Metro section, beneath the fold, was a picture of Donati in black-tie beside a story captioned: *Studio Exec Apparent Suicide*. I was reading the story when the phone rang.

"Hello," I said, my eyes falling on the words "overdose," "barbiturates." The Marilyn Monroe exit. That surprised me. I would've figured Nick for a gun or a noose.

"It's Richie, Henry. We have a problem."

I folded the paper. "What kind of problem?"

"Rod's disappeared."

"Disappeared?" I repeated. "What are you talking about?"

I'm trying to keep the line open in case he calls," Richie said. "Can you come over?"

"I'll be right there."

RICHIE WAS FRIGHTENED and defensive, so I tried to tread gently. "What happened, Richie?"

"He'd been cooped up in the apartment since you brought him over," he replied. We were in the bedroom. Every few seconds he'd glance at the phone, as if willing Rod to call. "He's a sweetheart, Henry, but we had a little bit of a generation gap. I mean, he didn't know Susan Hayward from Rita Hayworth, and I can only watch *My Own Private Idaho* so many times before Keanu Reeves's bad acting begins to torture me. He was really antsy this morning. I asked him what he wanted to do most and he said he wanted to have his ear pierced. So I dropped him off at the Gauntlet . . ."

"The Gauntlet?" I said. "That's on Santa Monica?"

"Yeah, the purple building across from Twenty-Four Hour Fitness."

"Okay, so you dropped him off. Then what?"

"I had to run down to Fred Segal's. I told him I would be back in a half hour and I'd take him to lunch. He was supposed to wait for me out front if he finished before I returned."

"He wasn't there when you came back?"

"I ran a little late," Richie said.

"How late?"

"I don't know," he whined. "Twenty, forty minutes."

"Richie! You were supposed to watch him."

"It's hard to take care of someone who doesn't want to be around you."

"Were you and he having a conflict?"

"How do I know, he wouldn't talk to me."

"Okay, let's get back to what happened this morning. What did you do when he wasn't there?"

"I went into the Gauntlet. The girl at the counter said he'd left a long time ago."

"Alone?"

"Yeah," he said. "Alone."

"Okay, then what?"

"I thought he might've walked down the street into Boystown," Richie said. "I searched the bars, the coffeehouses, the bookstores. I didn't find him."

"How much money did he have on him?"

"I gave him a fifty."

"Did you have a fight with him?"

"I told you, I talked, he watched cable."

"So he would have no reason to run away?"

"He was bored. He wanted an adventure."

"He may be getting more than he bargained for."

"What do you mean, Henry?"

I told him about Donati. He left the room, then returned with the paper folded to the Metro story. "Unbelievable."

"Have you noticed anything out of the ordinary lately?" I asked him. "Strangers around the building, funny noises on your phone?"

He looked up from the paper. "There are people in and out of here all the time. Why?"

"Asuras has had me followed. Serena's son, too. Nick said my phone was tapped. Someone broke in the other night. Am I being totally paranoid?"

"Duke had Alex's car blown up," he reminded me. "How hard would it be to have you watched?"

"Or you," I said.

"You think he took Rod?"

"Unless he ran away, it's a good possibility."

Richie paced to the window. "Maybe he did take off."

"What happened?"

"I told him I had AIDS," he replied. "I had to. He caught me taking my meds. After that, he kept his distance, like he was afraid he could catch it from me by being in the same room. He's not just naive, Henry. He's still halfway in the closet."

"I know he's struggling with being gay, but he's come this far."

"He probably thought once he got this far, the struggle would be over. Instead, he ends up with a scary old queen." Unconsciously, he touched his bruised neck. "A fag Norma Desmond. I didn't mean to become a stereotype, Henry."

"There's no time for this, now," I said, gently. "Not with Rod out there."

He nodded. "You should go home. If he's going to call anyone, he'll call you."

"I have my pager. I can wait here."

Richie struck a pose. "I vant to be alone." He touched my hand. "I'll be all right. Go home. If he calls you, tell him . . ."

"Tell him what, Richie?"

"Tell him not to feel so much contempt for what he doesn't understand."

I WENT HOME to wait, though I wasn't sure for what. There were no messages on my answering machine and, when I asked Jim Kwan about it, no reports of large, black cars idling in my driveway while I was gone. Nick's note was on the dining table, warning me not to underestimate Asuras. I had been convinced Asuras had abducted Rod, but after talking to Richie I wasn't so sure. Whatever Rod thought of Richie, it was unimaginable to me that he would return to his parents. But where else would he have gone? He knew Phil Wise was flying in tomorrow for the hearing on Monday. My best hope was that he'd run off to clear his head. I didn't want to consider the alternative. Asuras. When I remembered what he was capable of, it made me frantic for the boy's safety.

At half-past nine, the phone rang. I grabbed for it.

"Henry?"

My heart sank. "Asuras."

"I have something of yours. Would you like it back?"

"In one piece."

He chuckled. "It's in perfectly good condition. Untouched."

"Keep it that way."

There was a long pause. "We'll see. You have something to trade? A document?"

"How did you know that?"

"Nick was not a computer whiz. He never really got the hang of delete. There were bits and pieces of a document left in his hard drive that was of particular interest to me. The document wasn't in his office or at his house. He sent you off to the airport last night, so I have to assume it was there."

"I want to talk to Rod."

"There's a bathhouse out in the Valley called the Bull Dog Baths," he said. "Be there at twelve-thirty, with the document. Don't try to copy it, because I'll be watching you. Your friend will pay for your mistakes."

He hung up. I put the phone down. He wasn't omniscient after all. He didn't know that Nick had already made copies or that I had left one with Serena. A copy would be easier to challenge in court, harder to authenticate, and that might affect the AG's willingness to jump into the case. Serena and I could deal with that later. The important thing was getting Rod back. Untouched. I remembered Asuras's "We'll see," and it sent a chill through me. There was nothing to do now but wait. So I waited.

THE BULL DOG Baths was located in a business park deep in the Valley. It looked like a warehouse from the outside and the owners had thoughtfully provided a wheelchair-access ramp up to the door of mirrored glass. Inside was a small anteroom, where an attendant sat behind a window at a booth, like a ticket-seller at a movie theater. I paid my twelve dollars, checked my wallet, but not the envelope I was carrying, and was given in exchange, the key to a locker and a towel. The attendant buzzed me through a door into the locker room. My one excursion to a bathhouse had been twenty years ago. In memory, at least, far from being a den of debauchery, it was about as alluring as a bowling alley with its bright lights and loud music, and as erotic as a Boy Scout circle jerk.

The Bull Dog was pretty much as I expected: a big, brightly lit room with rows of lockers on one side and communal showers on the other. A muscular black man was slowly soaping himself in the shower for the benefit of passersby. A Latino boy emerged from the lockers wearing a thin gold chain around his neck and nothing else. A slow sexy smile spread across his face. I looked at my key. I found my locker. This was as far as

Asuras's instructions had gone, and while I assumed someone would turn up to give me further instructions, I had no idea who or when. A slow parade of men passed between the lockers and the showers, some glancing my way, most not. By the time some of them had passed a second, then third time, it was obvious I couldn't just stand there. I inspected the towel I'd been given. It seemed about the size of a postage stamp. I quickly undressed and tied the towel around my waist. Taking the envelope, I set off.

Adjacent to the locker room was a room with a sauna and a hot tub. From there, a ramp led upstairs to two rows of cubicles facing each other across a narrow hall. The doors of the cubicles were numbered. An open door to number 10 revealed a mattress on a platform where a large bearded man lay on his stomach. Loud dance music filled the space. The hallway was dark, but not so dark as to prevent the dozen or so men who paced the hall from peering into each other's faces as they passed. Some smiled cheerfully while others scowled, lust being a barometer of temperament. I searched their faces, looking not for assent but recognition. I passed the Latino boy again, now decently clad in his towel, and he whispered, "Oh, papi." I didn't think this was the sign from Asuras, so regretfully I moved on.

On the third floor was a TV room, a snack bar, a weight room and a pool table. I bought a Coke and wandered into the TV room, where a gay porno was running on a big-screen TV. The only other occupant of the room was holding a cigarette with one hand and idly masturbating with the other. I sat down, sipped my Coke, and wondered whether this wasn't simply a joke Asuras was playing on me.

"Are you Henry?" I turned around. A spectacularly handsome man, also attired in a towel, repeated, "Henry?"

"Yeah, I'm Henry."

He gestured to the envelope. "Is that for Duke?"

"Where's the boy?"

"You give me the envelope and wait here."

"I want to see the boy."

"The envelope first," he said, menacingly.

"No."

He got up and left. A few minutes later, he dropped into the seat beside me. "Here," he said, slipping me a key.

"What is it?"

"It opens a room downstairs," he said. He glanced at the watch he was incongruously wearing. "Duke said to wait ten minutes. The envelope. Please."

"How do I know . . . ?"

"Look, give me the fucking envelope or you'll get the kid back one piece at a time."

I handed him the envelope.

"Great," he said. "Pleasure doing business with you."

He got up and left. I waited ten minutes then went down to the second floor and found the cubicle that matched the key. I unlocked the door. Rod Morse sat up on the bed, huddled against the wall, naked, his arms around his knees.

"Rod?"

His eyes were dead.

"Rod," I said, shaking his shoulders. "Rod. It's Henry. Are you all right?"

"Henry," he grunted. "I'm going to be sick."

Vomit sprayed from his mouth. When I helped him off the bed, I saw a fresh blood stain on the sheet where he'd been sitting.

I CALLED A friend, a doctor named Iris Wong, who directed me to the emergency room of a hospital in the Valley, where she met me. She took him into an examining room and emerged a few minutes later, pale and angry.

"What the hell happened to that boy?"

"He was abducted from the street yesterday," I said. "He called me from the bathhouse."

"Who is he, Henry?"

"His name is Rod. He's a runaway. He was staying with me while I tried to straighten things out with his family."

"A minor?"

"Sixteen. What's wrong with him?"

"He was injected with an opiate," Iris said, "probably heroin, and penetrated."

"Penetrated?"

"He was raped," she said. "With some kind of foreign object, and whoever did it went out of his way to hurt the boy. I stitched him, up but it's going to be very painful down there for a long time and there's a danger of infection. You better get him to a specialist as soon as possible. Have you called the police?"

"I'd like to get him home tonight," I said. "He can talk to the cops tomorrow."

"You make sure he does," she said. "The man who did this to him was a monster."

"I know," I said.

A COUPLE OF hours later, I was sitting beside the bed in the guest room when Rod woke up. With a dazed look, he said, "You said I would be safe."

"I'm sorry, Rod, but it's over now."

"I want to go home," he mumbled, then fell asleep again.

chapter 23

"WHAT HAPPENED YESTERDAY?" I asked.

Rod wrote his initials in the dust on the dining room table, the plate of food in front of him untouched. It was nearly four, but he had only been awake for a little while. He raised his shaggy head and said, "I don't want to talk about it."

"He raped you," I said. "You need to talk about it."

"Not with you."

"What does that mean?"

"Everything happened because of you," he said, looking away. "You made me stay with Richie. I could've caught AIDS from him."

"You don't get AIDS from breathing the same air as someone who has it," I said. "You know that."

"He said he knows you."

"Who said that?"

"The man . . . Duke." He rubbed the dust from his fingers. "Don't you ever clean your house? You have some nasty mold in the bathroom."

"What else did he tell you?"

"He said you knew I was with him. He said you told him it was okay."

"You know that's not true."

"He made me crawl on the floor and beg him not to hurt me," he said. "But he hurt me, anyway."

"There's a cop I want you to talk to," I said, thinking of Odell.

"No," he said. "I'm not telling anyone what happened."

"This man needs to be in prison."

"For what?" Rod demanded. "Being gay?"

"Duke Asuras is a sexual sadist," I said. "That's a different category altogether."

"How do you know him?"

"He killed Alex Amerian," I said. "And your sister."

"He's Mr. King," Rod said. "From the disc."

I nodded. "Alex was trying to blackmail him."

"Katie, too?"

"I don't know. She had the disc, so she knew something. Too much for her own good. That's why Asuras killed her."

"Was he going to kill me, too?"

"No, he kidnapped you to get something from me. A document. A confession from a man who helped him commit the murders."

He looked at me. "Did you give it to him?"

"Yes."

"How are the police going to catch him?"

"There is other evidence," I said, "and if you talk to Odell, my cop friend—"

He shook his head. "No, I just want to forget about it. I never had sex before yesterday."

"Rape isn't exactly sex," I said.

Not looking at me, he said, "It's not sex when you come?"

"Orgasms are involuntary, physical reactions," I said, conscious of how pedantic I sounded. "The fact that you have one doesn't mean you consent to what's being done to you."

"He put things in my head," Rod said.

"What things? Did he threaten you?"

He bit his lip. "No, sex things. Maybe they were always there." He looked at me. "I don't think I like being gay."

"You've been traumatized, Rod. You need time, you need to talk to someone. I won't make you talk to the cops, but I have a friend, a therapist who specializes in counseling rape victims. She can help you through this."

"Yeah," he muttered. "Maybe. Maybe so."

"Phil gets here in about an hour," I said, glancing at my watch. "Do you want to come to the airport with me?"

He shook his head.

"Are you going to be all right for the hearing tomorrow?"

"I'll be fine," he said.

ON THE DRIVE to my house to the airport, I explained to Phil as concisely as I could what had happened. He was incredulous, then angry.

"We have to go to the cops."

"He doesn't want to do that right now," I said. "He needs time."

"No, not for him, Henry," he said. "For you. What do you think his parents are going to be alleging if they find out about any of this?"

It took a moment for his implication to sink it. "That I hurt Rod? That's crazy."

"You have no idea how ugly cases like this can get," he replied.

"Rod knows what happened."

"They'll say he's lying to protect you or you threatened him."

A wave of panic surged through me. "You're serious, aren't you?"

"Haven't you heard?" he said, bitterly. "All gay men are child molesters."

Rod, however, refused to talk to the police, even after Phil explained the necessity for it. When Phil continued to press him, he transformed himself into a sullen, taciturn adolescent. Phil finally gave up and I drove him to his hotel.

"I smell trouble," he said, getting out of the car.

"He's been through a lot," I reminded him. "He'll come through it all right."

"I hope you're right."

ROD SAID VERY little to me the next morning as we drove downtown to the courthouse, but I sensed he was thinking and from his bedraggled look it seemed obvious he'd been up most of the night. Phil met us on the steps of the courthouse, beneath the frieze of justice and her minions. It was a hot, smoggy September morning. As we climbed the steps to the entrance, Phil coached Rod on what to say should he be called to the stand. Rod nodded, but his eyes were far away. We went into the courthouse and took the escalator to the fifth floor, where Judge Fuentes had his chambers. At the end of the polished hall were Rod's parents and their lawyer.

Phil wrapped an arm around Rod's shoulders. "Are you ready?"

Rod shrugged him off. "I'm not doing it."

Phil yelped, "What?"

"I want to go home with my parents."

"Do you mean that, Rod?" I asked.

"You know they'll commit you to the Foster Institute," Phil warned.

"Maybe that's where I belong," Rod said. "I don't want to be a homosexual. Can't you understand that?"

"This is because of Asuras," I said.

"No, it's not," Rod replied. "I don't want to be like Richie. I don't want be like you, either, Henry, some lonely, old man living in a dirty house."

Phil said, "We've gone through a lot of trouble for you."

"I changed my mind," he replied, with adolescent finality. "You can't make me go through with it." He dashed down the corridor toward his parents.

"Let him go," I said.

"That little shit," Wise said. "That little shit."

"It's his life, Phil."

"He can fucking have it," Wise muttered, as we watched the Morses embrace their son. "I'm outta here."

The Morses' lawyer came toward us, with a delighted but confused expression.

"What's going on?" he said.

"My client's changed his mind about the petition," Phil said formally. "He wants to go home. Is that acceptable to your God-fearing clients?"

"Yes, yes, I'm sure it is," he replied.

"Great," Phil said. "Let's go inside and I'll make a motion to dismiss."

I watched Rod cling to his parents like a drowning man to a raft.

THE MOTION WAS granted. Afterward, I drove Phil to the airport. I pulled up in front of the Southwestern terminal. He started to get out, stopped and looked at me.

"That case was a winner," he sighed. "We could have made new law."

"There will be other cases," I said. "Some other parents trying to commit their kid for being gay or lesbian."

"You got that right. Take care of yourself, Professor K.," he said. "And for the record, I don't think you're a dirty old man, or whatever the hell the kid said. I think you're pretty hot."

"You comfort me in my old age," I said.

"Give me a call next time you come up to the city," he said.

I CALLED RICHIE from the car phone to tell him the outcome of the hearing.

"It's all my fault," he said.

"Don't be ridiculous, Richie. You didn't rape the boy."

"Now he's going to spend the rest of his life either hating himself or hating other gays," he said. "Or both. Asuras. I'm sorry Alex didn't shoot that fuck when he had the chance. Maybe I should. I have nothing to lose."

"I'll take care of Asuras," I said.

ODELL GAPED AT me when I finished my story. We were in his office at the sheriff's station, the door closed. He rubbed his temples.

"Where's the affidavit?"

I handed him the sealed envelope I had retrieved from Kwan before coming over. "This is the copy Donati intended for the chief of police."

He took a penknife from his desk, slit open the top of the envelope and removed the affidavit. He read it slowly, shaking his head. When he got to the last page, he looked up at me, puzzled.

"You said this was a copy."

"Yeah?"

He held up the document. "This is his signature. This is an original."

I studied Nick's signature and the signature of the notary public. "He must have executed three originals."

"Are you giving this to me?"

"Yeah."

"I'm going down to pay a call on the sheriff," he said, raising his bulk from behind his desk. "Good work, man."

THE PHONE COMPANY had sent someone to check my line for taps and he was waiting for me when I returned from the sheriff's office.

"I didn't find anything," he said.

"You're sure?"

"I'm not saying your line wasn't tapped," he explained. "I'm just saying it's okay now. If you have any other trouble, you give me a call."

I took his card and went in, picked up the phone and listened to the innocent buzz of the dial tone. When I put the receiver down, it started ringing. I jumped, then cautiously picked it up.

"Hello," I said, half-expecting Asuras.

"Henry?" It was Serena, calling from Sacramento. "You've got to take the next plane up here."

"The affidavit was an original, wasn't it?"

"How did you know?"

"I gave the other copy to Odell. We opened it in his office."

She hesitated. "I thought your phone . . ."

"The phone guy was just out here. He says it wasn't tapped. Asuras isn't as powerful as he likes people to think. That's how bullies are."

"We have a meeting with the Attorney General first thing tomorrow," she said.

"Is he going to prosecute?"

"He took the affidavit with him. He'll let us know in the morning."

AFTER A FOUR-HOUR meeting the following morning, the Attorney General, a trim, telegenic man with reptilian eyes, said yes.

Two weeks later, at a packed press conference, with the LA County sheriff at his side, the Attorney General announced the indictment of

Duke Asuras on six counts of first-degree murder and Montezuma Gaitan on two. He concluded with a swipe at the LA District Attorney, whom the AG accused of having been corrupted by Hollywood money. That night, Gaitan drove out into the Mojave and shot himself. His decomposing body was found ten days later. The day after the AG's press conference, Johnnie Cochran was in court on Asuras's behalf with motions to dismiss the indict-ment and postpone arraignment. The court continued arraignment for thirty days in order to study the motions to dismiss.

The media went crazy. Not since the Simpson trial had there been a murder indictment against so high profile a member of the entertainment industry. Asuras's lawyers and Parnassus's public-relations department im-mediately took the offensive. They claimed Donati was the actual murderer who had posthumously attempted to incriminate Asuras in his crime. The Industry's "creative community" also rushed to Asuras's defense. Full-page ads began to appear, first in the trade papers, then the Los Angeles and New York *Times* and the *Wall Street Journal* signed by some of Hollywood's elite, in which phrases like "witch hunt" were bruited about. The Los Angeles DA also joined the fray, asserting that his office had found insufficient evidence to prosecute Asuras, and suggesting that the Attorney General's indictment was pure politics. Even the President got in on the act, piously reminding his fellow citizens of the presumption of innocence when questioned about the case at a press conference. Later, after the evidence began to pile up against Asuras, his press secretary asserted that the President scarcely knew Asuras but then he was forced to admit Asuras had spent several nights in the Lin-coln Bedroom, and Republicans in Congress demanded a special prosecutor. Asuras added a half-dozen of the country's best lawyers to his defense, but, as often happens, new evidence emerged as witnesses stepped forward and the sheriff's department pursued the investigation with all the vigor of a po-litical campaign. The ads stopped running, Hollywood fell silent, and then it was announced that Asuras would be taking a leave from his position in order to defend himself. The Democratic National Committee returned his contribution.

The day before his arraignment, Duke Asuras borrowed the private jet of a movie-star friend and flew to Brazil, a country that, conveniently, had no extradition treaty with the United States. By week's end, an arrest warrant had been issued for him. This was followed by a report that, between the time the indictment was announced and his departure, he had transferred most of his wealth outside the country. A state bar committee was convened to investigate whether his lawyers had knowledge of his plan to flee. The results were inconclusive. Equally inconclusive was the Attorney General's attempt to indict the movie star for aiding Asuras's flight. The movie star later made a substantial contribution to the AG's gubernatorial campaign.

From somewhere in Brazil, Asuras issued a press release in which he said that he was the victim of a homophobic, right-wing, religious zealot—the Attorney General—in a country "where gay people, such as myself, are routinely persecuted by the same legal system that is supposed to protect us. In the current climate of hatred and discrimination against gays, I have no confidence that my innocence, and I am completely innocent of these ridiculous charges, could be proven. Therefore, rather than risk conviction for a crime of which I am innocent, I have chosen to exile myself from my country until such time that I can be sure, as a gay man, of receiving a fair trial. God bless America."

"CAN YOU BELIEVE it?" Serena said to me. I was sitting in her living room, Hekate purring on my lap, having just watched Asuras's statement being read on TV.

"He's trying to turn his case into a discussion of homophobia the same way Simpson turned his case into a referendum on race. I guess it's not surprising. They have the same lawyers."

Serena switched the TV off. "Why not go the whole nine yards, then, and stick around for the trial?"

"Because, unlike Simpson, Duke couldn't count on any sympathetic jurors. I mean, he *is* right about how hard it is for gay people to get a fair hearing from the cops and the courts. You know that better than anyone."

She picked up her beer. "Yeah," she said, "and I also happen to know that there are death squads in Brazil that routinely murder gay men. Quite an improvement over the old US of A."

"He can't be extradited," I reminded her. "I think that was the attraction."

"So we're going to have to listen for the rest of our lives about how Duke Asuras, who murdered four gay men, was driven into exile by homophobia."

"Chalk it up to life's little ironies."

SIX MONTHS AFTER he fled California, Asuras was appointed special assistant to the minister of culture in Brazil for the express purpose of encouraging movies to be filmed in that country. His old friend, the director Cheryl

Cordet, immediately announced that she would make her next movie in São Paulo as a gesture of solidarity with Asuras.

DUKE ASURAS WAS beaten to death in a Rio de Janeiro hotel by a hustler whom he'd picked up at the beach. The hustler was ultimately convicted of Asuras's murder but, owing to Brazil's extremely lenient sentencing laws, served a total of eight months. In handing down the sentence, the judge observed that the deceased was a homosexual and therefore at least as culpable for his own death as his killer.

Asuras's body was eventually returned to Hollywood and interred at the Westwood cemetery, where his neighbors included Marilyn Monroe and Truman Capote. His memorial service was canceled when it became clear that no one of any prominence in the Industry intended to show up for it.

ONE MORNING A few days after New Year's, my phone rang as I was working in my office. I picked it up.

"Hello, Henry?"

The voice was familiar, but it took me a moment to place it, because I had not expected to hear it again. "Rod?"

"Yeah, it's me. Rod Morse." He sounded older, almost adult.

"Where are you? How are you?"

"I'm fine," he said. "Really good." He paused. "I'm calling to Christian witness you, Henry."

"To what?"

"I'm calling to tell you that homosexuality is not part of God's plan and to beg you to turn from your sinful ways and receive Jesus in your life."

"Is this a joke, Rod?"

"I'm deadly serious," he replied. "You could be a good man if you would open your heart to Jesus."

"What happened to you, Rod? Did your parents send you to the Foster Institute?"

"What happened to me is that I surrendered myself to Jesus," he said. "You can, too. Henry, in 1 Corinthians 6, Paul tells us that no homosexual will possess the kingdom of God."

"Don't be ridiculous, Rod. The word 'homosexual' didn't even exist until the nineteenth century."

"And in Leviticus," he continued, gathering steam.

"Stop, Rod. I know all the passages, I know what they say, I know how they're used and I'm not impressed. Did you hear Asuras was killed in Brazil?"

There was a pause. "I read about it," he said, grudgingly, then added, "The wages of sin are death."

"I'll admit he did a lot of evil and there was a certain poetic justice to his death," I said.

"You do believe in evil," Rod said, triumphantly.

"Not the kind you're thinking about," I said. "Not Christian evil. That's more of a political category than a moral one, but yes, after Duke Asuras, I definitely believe in evil."

"Homosexuality is evil," he said. "It's an abomination condemned by God. He sent the plague of AIDS as a judgment on your lifestyle."

In my appointment book was a plane ticket to San Francisco where, on Sunday, I would be attending a memorial service for Grant Hancock.

"Someday, when you realize what you've just said, you won't be able to forgive yourself."

"I meant it."

"You can't run away from yourself forever," I said. "You can't hide in someone's Bible for the rest of your life."

"It's not someone's Bible," he corrected me. "It's the word of God."

"It's a book written by human beings about a God they imagined and any God that any human can imagine is imperfect. Don't look for God in the sky, Rod. Look at what's inside of you."

"I feel sorry for you, Henry, because you're going to hell."

"Hell's not a place, Rod, it's something people do to each other."

"I'll pray for you."

"All right," I said, "but hang on to my number because someday you may want to call me again. When you stop running."

He hung up.

THAT AFTERNOON, I made my weekly visit to Josh's grave. I walked up the steps of the Court of Remembrance, past the tomb of Bette Davis to the Columbarium of Radiant Destiny. As I approached the grave, I saw a woman in late middle age, her back to me, running her fingers across the raised surface of the lettering on the marker.

"Selma?"

She turned. It was Josh's mother.

"Hello, Henry," she said. Her heart-shaped face was careworn and showed signs of recent tears, though it was dry now.

"Is this your first time here?"

"I've been coming since we got your letter telling us where to find Josh," she said. "I thought we would probably run into each other." She turned back to the plaque and read, " 'Little friend.' What is that?"

"An endearment."

"I see," she said. "Did you have to put it here?"

"I'll leave you," I said. I gave her the rose I'd brought. "Will you put this in the vase?"

She took it, looked at me, seemed to thaw a little. "I don't mean to run you off, Henry."

"I'll come back later," I said. "I'm usually here on Tuesdays, around this time."

She nodded. "I'll try to remember."

"Goodbye, Selma."

But she had already turned away from me again and was replacing the wilted rose in the vase by Josh's marker with the fresh one.

I GOT INTO the car and started down the long, winding drive out of the cemetery. A fleet of trailers and trucks turned into the front gate. I pulled over and let them pass, equipment trucks, caterers, performers' trailers, a caravan that could mean only one thing: someone was making a movie.